Large Print Sma
Small, Bertrice.
Rosamund

Rosamund

This Large Print Book carries the
Seal of Approval of N.A.V.H.

Rosamund

BERTRICE SMALL

Thorndike Press • Waterville, Maine

Published in 2003 by arrangement with NAL Signet, a member of Penguin Putnam Inc.

Thorndike Press Large Print Romance Series.

The tree indicium is a trademark of Thorndike Press.

The text of this Large Print edition is unabridged. Other aspects of the book may vary from the original edition.

Set in 16 pt. Plantin.

Printed in the United States on permanent paper.

Library of Congress Cataloging-in-Publication Data

Small, Bertrice.
    Rosamund / Bertrice Small.
      p. cm.
    ISBN 0-7862-4987-0 (lg. print : hc : alk. paper)
    1. Great Britain — History — Henry VIII, 1509–1547 — Fiction. 2. Catharine, of Aragon, Queen, consort of Henry VIII, King of England, 1485–1536 — Fiction. 3. Women landowners — Fiction. 4. Land tenure — Fiction. 5. Large type books. I. Title.
PS3569.M28 R67 2003
813'.54—dc21   2002075026

For One of My Favorite Readers,
Barbara Morizzo, of
The Seashell Restaurant, Southold, NY

Prologue

The Friarsgate Inheritance

Cumbria 1492–1495

Prologue

The first time Rosamund Bolton was widowed she was six years old. The second time she was not quite thirteen, and still a virgin. She was beginning to wish she wasn't a virgin, but the idea of being free of a husband for a year's term of mourning was very enticing. She had been married for all but three years of her short life.

Perhaps if her parents had lived it would have been different. If her brother, Edward, had not died in the same epidemic of plague that took their parents it certainly would have been otherwise. But they had all perished in that rainy summer of fourteen ninety-two, and when they had, Rosamund Bolton had suddenly found herself the heiress of Friarsgate, a vast tract of land with its great open flocks of sheep and herds of cattle. She was barely three years old. Her paternal uncle Henry Bolton had come to Friarsgate with his wife, Agnes, and their son. Had Rosamund succumbed when her family had, it would have been Henry Bolton who inherited Friarsgate, for he was now his sire's sole legitimate heir. But Rosamund had not died. Indeed, she appeared to be an inordinately healthy child. Henry was a practical man. He did not need to be the lord of Friarsgate in order to control it, but control it he would nonetheless. Without waiting for a dispensation from the church, he married off his five-year-old son, John, to Rosamund. The dispensation would come eventually, and at the right price.

But two years later, the newly arrived dispensation finally locked away in the strongbox beneath his bed, Henry Bolton stood in danger of losing Friarsgate once again. A spotting sickness had infected both children. While Rosamund easily survived, seven-year-old John did not. His wife had given him no other living children. Henry now berated her fiercely for it. Were they to lose Friarsgate to strangers because of her inability to give him another son? Desperately Henry Bolton cast about for a way to protect his interests in the estate. To his relief he found the perfect solution in the person of his wife's much older cousin, Hugh Cabot.

For a good deal of his adult life Hugh

Cabot had served as the steward in the household of Agnes Bolton's brother, Robert Lindsay. But now Lindsay needed to provide a place in life for his own second son, so Hugh was to lose his position. Agnes had become privy to this information, as her sister-in-law was a gossip. In an effort to cool her husband's anger, she offered Henry her knowledge, thus regaining her husband's favor once more as Henry Bolton saw the simple solution that his wife had so neatly provided to his problem.

Hugh Cabot was sent for, and when he had come and had spoken with Henry Bolton, an arrangement was made. Hugh would wed the six-year-old Rosamund, and oversee Friarsgate. In exchange he would have a home and would be comfortable for the remainder of his days. Hugh saw what Henry Bolton was about, but having little choice, he agreed. He did not like his reluctant benefactor at all, but neither was he a doddering fool, as Henry obviously thought him to be. If he lived long enough, Hugh decided, he just might be able to influence his child-wife to protect her own interests against her grasping uncle.

Agnes Bolton found herself miraculously with child again. Unlike her many previous pregnancies it appeared she would carry this baby to term as she had John. Henry made immediate arrangements to return home to Otterly Court, which was his wife's dower portion. Elated, he was certain the child his wife now carried was the longed-for son. When Hugh Cabot finally died, Henry decided, he planned on wedding this son with Rosamund. The Friarsgate inheritance would once again be in his firm grasp.

Henry and his wife were at last packed and ready to depart. The wedding day arrived. The bridegroom was a tall, painfully thin man, his slender stature and a shock of snow-white hair giving the impression of frailty. But Hugh was not frail, as anyone looking carefully into the bright blue eyes beneath his sandy-gray bushy eyebrows could see. He signed the marriage papers, his elegant hand quivering slightly for effect, his broad shoulders stooped, never quite meeting Henry Bolton's eyes. Henry did not notice. All that mattered to him was that Rosamund could not be snatched up in marriage by strangers. He was confident that Friarsgate was still firmly within his control.

The bride wore a simple, tight-fitting gown of grass-green jersey with a long waist. Her long auburn hair was loose about her narrow shoulders. The amber eyes in her small face were curious, but cautious. She was dainty, like a fairy child, Hugh thought as he took the tiny hand in his to repeat his vows before the elderly priest. The girl piped her vows in singsong fashion, having obviously learned them by heart.

Henry Bolton stood smiling broadly, and perhaps a trifle smugly, as he and Agnes witnessed Rosamund's second marriage. Afterward he said to Hugh, "You are not to tamper with the wench even if she is now your wife. I'll want her a virgin for her next marriage."

For a brief moment Hugh felt a black anger filling his soul, but he hid his distaste of this crude and greedy man, saying quietly, "She is a child, Henry Bolton. Besides, I am past such emotions as passion."

"I am glad to hear it," Henry said, now jovial. "She's usually a meek girl, but you can beat her if she isn't. That right is yours, and I will not take it from you."

Then Henry Bolton took his leave of Friarsgate, riding over the hills that separated Otterly Court from his niece's rich holding.

Part 1

THE HEIRESS OF FRIARSGATE

ENGLAND 1495–1503

Chapter 1

On the day she had married Hugh Cabot, the child, Rosamund Bolton, watched silently as her uncle and his wife had ridden away. Finally she turned to her new husband and asked, "Are they gone for good, sir? My uncle always behaved as if this were his house, *but it is mine.*"

"So you understand that, do you?" Hugh replied, amused. What else did she understand? He wondered to himself. Poor lambkin. Her life to date had surely not been easy.

"I am the heiress to Friarsgate," she answered him simply yet proudly. "Edmund says I am a rich prize. That is why my uncle Henry seeks to control me. Will my uncle return?"

"He is gone for now," Hugh answered the child. "I am certain he will return to see how you fare."

"He will return to cast his eye on my lands and see how they prosper," Rosamund responded astutely.

He took her hand in his. "Let us go inside, Rosamund. The wind is chill and hints of the winter to come, lass."

Together they reentered the house, settling themselves in the little hall by the warm fire.

Sitting opposite him, her child's face grave, she said, "So, now you are my husband." Her slippered feet did not touch the floor.

"I am," he agreed, his blue eyes twinkling as he considered where this conversation could possibly be going.

"How many wives have you had before me, sir?" she asked him, curious.

"None," he answered, a small smile touching his angular features.

"Why?" she demanded of him. Reaching out she stroked a large gray hound that had come to sit by her side.

"I had not the means to support a wife," he explained. "I was my father's youngest son. He died just before I was born. He, too, was a younger son, dependent upon his family for everything. Long ago I did my cousin a great favor, or so I thought. By convincing her brother to give her the small

18

manor of Otterly, I made her a desirable bride for your uncle Henry. Agnes was a plain girl, but had no calling for the church. She needed something to set her apart from the other marriageable young girls of modest means. By convincing Robert Lindsay that a woman with her own property was more apt to receive an offer, I made Agnes an attractive marriage prospect."

"Like me," Rosamund remarked.

"Yes, like you," Hugh agreed with a chuckle. "You understand a great deal for one so young."

"The priest says that women are the weaker vessel, but I think he is wrong. Women can be strong, and they can be intelligent," Rosamund told him frankly.

"Are those your own thoughts, Rosamund?" he asked her. What a fascinating little girl she was, this child who was now his responsibility.

She looked suddenly fearful at his question, sitting back in her chair, whereas before she had been leaning forward enthusiastically. "Will you beat me for my thoughts, sir?" she queried him nervously.

The question disturbed him deeply. "Why would you think that, lass?" he inquired of her quietly.

"I have been very forward," she told him.

"My aunt says a female must not be forward or bold. That it is displeasing to their menfolk and they must be beaten for it."

"Did your uncle ever beat you?" he demanded.

She nodded silently.

"Well, lass, I will not beat you," Hugh said, his kind blue eyes meeting her fearful amber ones. "I will always expect that you be open and honest in your thoughts with me, Rosamund. When people dissemble with one another foolish misunderstandings arise. There is much I can teach you if you are to be truly the mistress of Friarsgate. I do not know how long I will be with you, for I am an old man. But if you are to control your own destiny, free of interference, then you will learn what I have to impart lest Henry Bolton come again to rule over you."

He saw a flicker of interest leap into her face at his words, but she quickly masked it, saying thoughtfully, "If my uncle knew that you planned to turn me against him, I do not think you would be my husband this day, Hugh Cabot."

He chuckled. "You misunderstand me, Rosamund," he replied smoothly. "I do not wish to turn you against your family, but if I were your father, I would want you to be independent of them. Friarsgate belongs to you, lass, not to them. Do you know your family motto?"

She shook her head in the negative.

"*Tracez Votre Chemin*. It means, *Make Your Own Path*," he explained to her.

Rosamund nodded. "Please live long, Hugh, that I may be able to choose my next husband all by myself," she replied, her eyes dancing with merriment.

He laughed aloud. It was, she decided, a good sound. Rich and deep, with no malice in it at all.

"I will try, Rosamund," he promised her.

"How old are you?" she inquired of him.

"Today is the twentieth day of October," he replied. "On the ninth day of November I will be sixty years of age." The blue eyes twinkled at her. "I am *very* old, Rosamund."

"Aye, you are," she agreed soberly, nodding her auburn head. He chuckled again, unable to help himself. "We shall be friends, Rosamund," he told her. Then he fell on his knees before her, and taking her hand in his said, "I vow to you on this, our wedding day, Rosamund Bolton, that I will always put you, and the interests of Friarsgate, before all else, as long as I may live." Then he kissed the little hand in his.

"Mayhap I will trust you," Rosamund decided out loud. "You have kind eyes." She withdrew her hand from his grasp. Then she smiled a mischievous smile. "I am glad that you were chosen for me, Hugh Cabot, although I think if my uncle Henry knew your true worth, he would not have picked you, no matter my aunt's debt."

"My child-wife," he addressed her, "I suspect you have a taste for intrigue, which I find interesting in one so young." He pulled himself to his feet and sat again.

"I do not know what *intrigue* means. Is it a good thing?" she asked him.

"It can be. I shall teach you, Rosamund," he assured her. "You will need all your wits about you when I am gone and can no longer protect you. Your uncle will not be the only man who desires to gain Friarsgate through you. There may be one day a man who is even stronger and more dangerous than Henry Bolton. Your instincts are sound, lass. You but need my tutelage that you may survive and become stronger."

So had their marriage begun. Hugh quickly came to love and cherish his child-wife as he might have loved a daughter had he had one. As for Rosamund, she, too, loved her elderly mate as she might have loved a father or grandfather. The two were easily companionable. The morning after their wedding day they rode out. Hugh upon a sturdy nut-brown gelding, and Rosamund upon her white pony, which had a black mane and tail. Hugh found himself surprised again, for Rosamund knew a great deal about her holding. More, he considered, than he would have thought any child could know. She was very proud of Friarsgatc, showing him the lush meadows where her flocks grazed and the verdant pastures where her herds of cattle browsed in the autumn sunlight.

"Did your uncle share his knowledge of the land with you?" Hugh asked her.

Rosamund shook her head. "Nay. I am naught to Henry Bolton but a possession to be controlled so he in his turn may control Friarsgate."

"Then how is it you are so well informed?" he wondered.

"My grandfather had four sons," she began. "My father was the third born, but the first two were born on the wrong side of the blanket — before my grandfather wed. That is why my father was the heir. Uncle Henry is the youngest of my grandfather's sons. The eldest is my uncle Edmund. My father loved all his brothers, but he loved Edmund the best. Uncle Henry was not born until my father was five. The other two were closer in age, and grandfather, I am told, made no distinction between his lads, but that my father was the heir. My uncles Edmund and Richard were given permission to take the family name. Uncle Henry hates them, but especially he hates Edmund, for my father loved him best.

"My grandfather gave Richard to the church to expiate his sins. He is at the abbey of St. Cuthbert's nearby. Edmund he made his steward when he was grown and the old steward died. Uncle Henry dared not dispossess his elder brother, for Edmund knows too much about Friarsgate and Henry does not. Edmund has kept out of his way, of course, but both he and Maybel have explained everything to me."

"Maybel?" Here was another new name.

"My nursemaid," Rosamund replied. "She is my uncle Edmund's wife, and more mother to me than my own. Mama was never strong after I was born, they tell me, but she was, I remember, a sweet lady."

"I should like to meet Maybel and Edmund," Hugh said.

"We will ride to their cottage, then," Rosamund responded. "You will like them!"

Now Hugh Cabot realized another reason Henry Bolton had chosen him to be Rosamund's husband. Certainly it would irritate Edmund Bolton, an obviously good steward, to be so subtly replaced. He would have to mend that fence quickly else it cause a breach. Nothing must detract from keeping Rosamund — and Friarsgate — safe. If Edmund Bolton was as his niece had said he was in character, they should all get along together.

They reached their destination, a stone cottage located on an isolated hillside overlooking a small lake surrounded by the hills. It was well kept, its roof thatched tightly, its whitewash clean. There was a single well-worn bench beneath a front window. A narrow ribbon of pale gray smoke arose from the chimney. A few late roses bloomed by the door. After dismounting from his horse, Hugh lifted Rosamund from her pony.

She hurried into the cottage, calling as she went. "Edmund! Maybel! I have brought my bridegroom to meet you!"

Hugh ducked beneath the lintel of the door. He found himself in a cheerful room, a bright fire burning in the stone fireplace. A man of medium height, his face brown with the outdoors, his amber eyes curious, came forward, bowing.

"Welcome, my lord," he said. "Maybel, come and meet the new lord." He drew his plump wife forward.

She was a tiny woman of indeterminate

age, her gray eyes sharp. She looked Hugh Cabot over carefully. Finally, obviously satisfied, she curtsied to him. "Sir," she said.

"May we offer you a cup of cider, my lord?" Edmund queried politely.

"It would be appreciated," Hugh agreed. "We have been out riding my wife's lands all the day long."

"And my child has not had a bite to eat since early morning?" Maybel demanded. "Shame!"

Rosamund giggled. "I have not been hungry," she assured her nurse. "This is the first time I have been out of the house in weeks, Maybel. You know it to be true. Uncle Henry never let me out of his sight but to pee and sleep. It was glorious riding the hills!"

"Yet Maybel is correct, wife," Hugh said in his quiet voice. "Like you, I enjoyed the day, but you are a growing lass, and need to be fed in a timely manner." He turned to his host and hostess. "I am plain Hugh Cabot, and would be pleased to have you address me by my Christian name, Edmund and Maybel Bolton."

"When we are together, by ourselves," Edmund agreed, "but before the servants you must take the mantle of lord, Hugh Cabot. Your wife is, after all, the lady of

26

Friarsgate." Edmund found himself pleasantly surprised by Hugh's tone and his gentle manners.

"Sit down!" Maybel ordered them. "I will feed you." She bustled about the room, taking bread from a basket by the fire, cutting it open, and hollowing out the trenchers. She set them upon the table and filled them with a delicious-smelling pottage of rabbit, onions, carrots, and gravy. The trencher before Rosamund and Hugh was twice the size of the other two. They would be expected to share it. Maybel supplied them with polished wooden spoons with which to eat. Then she sat down to join them. Edmund plunked down upon the table pewter goblets of cider that had been pressed just that morning.

Rosamund found to her surprise that she was indeed very hungry. She ate enthusiastically, her spoon dipping swiftly into the trencher again and again, shoving the pieces from the insides of the cottage loaf that Maybel had put in a dish before them into her mouth.

Maybel watched them surreptitiously, noting that Hugh Cabot deferred to the child, letting her eat her fill while he pretended to do the same. Only when Rosamund was obviously satisfied did he seriously eat himself. Well, well, Maybel considered, this is an interesting turn of events. But she was not yet ready to believe that Henry Bolton had done his niece a good turn in choosing this ancient bridegroom. Still, it appeared that Rosamund liked the man. She was usually cautious of strangers, especially those connected with her greedy uncle.

"That, Maybel, was the best rabbit stew I have ever eaten!" Hugh Cabot pronounced when he had finished. He pushed himself away from the table with a satisfied sigh.

Edmund Bolton smiled. "She's a good cook, my Maybel," he said. "A bit more cider, Hugh?"

"Nay, I think not, Edmund. We must leave you shortly if we are to find our way home before dark."

"Aye, the winter's coming soon enough with its dark days," Edmund answered him.

"Before we go, however," Hugh rejoined, "I would put matters straight, for Henry Bolton has sought to make trouble between us, and I will not have it. For many years I have served as steward to Agnes Bolton's brother. I was asked to train his son to fill my position, and I did. When Agnes learned I had lost my place she suggested that I become Rosamund's husband to protect her husband's interests in Friarsgate."

"Henry Bolton has no interest in Friarsgate!" Edmund said angrily.

"I agree," Hugh quickly replied. "Friarsgate belongs to Rosamund, and her heirs after her, but Henry Bolton has cleverly attempted to replace you by marrying me to Rosamund. Friarsgate does not need two stewards. As far as I am concerned I was asked to marry my wife. Nothing more — though Henry has assumed I will take over and thus push you from the place your own father assigned you. I will not."

"What will you do instead, then?" Edmund queried the older man cautiously.

"Teach Rosamund to read and to write and to keep her accounts, so that when the day comes that neither of us are here for her, she will know what to do. The priest, I assume, has not attempted to teach her. He seems a rather ignorant and dull fellow."

"Henry Bolton does not believe it necessary that a woman know anything other than her housewifery. He thinks it best our niece learn only womanly pursuits, like making soap and conserves, or salting fish," Edmund said.

"And how do you feel about that?" Hugh wondered.

"I think she should learn both," Edmund

responded, "but old Father Bernard can't teach her. He learned the mass by rote, and cannot be counted as an educated man. Hell, he's older than you surely are, Hugh Cabot, and not just a wee bit queer in the head these days."

Hugh laughed heartily. "Then it is agreed between us, Edmund. You will continue to administer the estate, and I will educate my wife."

"We will meet regularly," Edmund said. "You must know all so that Henry Bolton may be convinced that it is you who now manages Friarsgate. And it is best that you sit in judgment at the manor court, which is held every three months. To all appearances you are now lord of Friarsgate."

"I hope to play my part well," Hugh replied graciously.

"This child is falling asleep while you two men plot," Maybel said sharply. "Get you gone home with your wife, Hugh Cabot, before night falls and you cannot find your way. There are yet robbers about, for we are close to the Scots border as you must know."

"I have lived farther south," he answered her. "Are you subject to raids often?"

"Usually we are safe here at Friarsgate, unless," Maybel said dryly, "the kings and the great lords wish to fight. Then it is the poor and the helpless who suffer the most. The Scots sometimes come for sheep, or cattle, but they generally leave us in peace."

"Why is that? I wonder," Hugh mused aloud.

" 'Tis our hills," Edmund explained. "They are very steep about Friarsgate, and to drive a flock, or a herd, or even a few animals quickly away, the terrain must be flatter. It would take a serious quarrel with the Scots to make us vulnerable to them," Edmund concluded.

"Who is the nearest border lord to Friarsgate?" Hugh asked.

"The Hepburn of Claven's Carn," Edmund replied. "I met him once when he came to a cattle market with his sons. He's probably dead by now, and one of the sons in charge, though which, who knows. The Scots are an argumentative people, and the sons undoubtedly fought over their father's lands."

"Aye," Hugh nodded. "The Scots are like that. They are yet more wild than civilized." He arose from his place at the table and looked to Rosamund, who was nodding sleepily in her place. "Edmund, take her up. I'll carry her on my horse and lead the pony."

"Nay, I'll ride the beast," Maybel said. "I should go back with you to watch over my lass, Hugh Cabot."

"Come along, then," Hugh replied, and he strode toward the door, opening it and stepping outside into the late afternoon. He unhitched his horse and mounted it, and then reached down to take the sleeping child from Edmund Bolton, settling her gently in the crook of one arm, his other hand gathering the reins up firmly.

Maybel hurried out, pulling her hooded cloak about her. With her husband's aid she mounted the white pony, saying, "I'm ready. Be sure you leave the cottage clean when you come tomorrow, Edmund Bolton."

"Aye, my dearie," he answered her with a small smile. Then he smacked the pony gently on its rump. It moved off alongside of the new lord of Friarsgate. Watching them go Edmund thought that at last his niece had a weapon with which to fight Henry Bolton. If, indeed, Hugh Cabot was all that he appeared to be. But Edmund had a good feeling about the new lord. He chuckled to himself. His greedy and mean-spirited half-brother believed he had chosen a feeble old man to husband their niece. Edmund chuckled again.

Henry had always been a smug fellow.

Edmund knew just what he was about, for he was as transparent as a piece of glass. Henry had made this marriage for Rosamund because the child was yet too young to be mated and bred. Hugh Cabot was surely past such things. Yet the heiress to Friarsgate was still a married woman, safe from the predators who would marry her and disregard Henry's wishes. Henry wanted Friarsgate for his own heirs. If the child Agnes carried was a son, Edmund had no doubt that Henry would have married that son to Rosamund as soon as it was possible. Even if the child was still at his mama's breast. No matter that the bride would be older than the groom. Such things were common in marriages where land was the paramount issue. But if Hugh Cabot was the honest man Edmund believed him to be, then Rosamund would be safe from her uncle Henry, who had probably outfoxed himself in this matter at long last.

Edmund watched as the two riders disappeared over the hill. Turning, he went back into his house to neaten it up. He would return to his duties as Friarsgate's steward in the morning. Together he and Hugh would teach Rosamund all she needed to know to husband her lands when they were no longer there to do it for her.

Friarsgate had chafed beneath Henry Bolton's rule. Now with its new lord it once again became the happy place it had been in the time of Rosamund's parents and grandparents. On All Hallows' Eve, which was also the feast of St. Wolfgang, bonfires were lit on all the hillsides at sunset. In the hall at Friarsgate, a tall, large candelabra was placed at the center of the room. Garlands of greens hung with apples were suspended about the chamber, decorating it. The highlight of the meal was the crowdie, a sweet apple-cream dessert shared among those at the high board. Within the crowdie had been placed two rings, two coins, and two marbles.

"I've a coin!" Rosamund shouted excitedly, laughing, as she pulled the penny from her spoon.

"So do I!" Hugh chortled. "So, wife, if the legend is correct, we shall be rich, but then I already am with you."

"What did you get, Edmund?" the child asked her uncle.

"Naught," he said with a laugh.

"But that means your life will be fraught with uncertainty," Rosamund said. She dug her spoon into their common dish of crowdie. "I will find you the ring!"

"He's already wed wi me," Maybel reminded her charge. "Leave the rings for the lasses in the kitchen who will enjoy what is left, my little lady."

"Did you get a prize?" Rosamund queried her nursemaid.

"The marble," Maybel admitted.

"No! No!" the little girl cried. "That means your life will be lonely, Maybel!"

"Well, it ain't been lonely yet," Maybel replied with a chortle. "I got you to look after, and I got my Edmund. It's all a bunch of tomfoolery anyway."

Escorted by her husband, Rosamund went from the hall out into the early evening to pass out crisp apples from a woven willow basket to her tenants who were gathered about the All Hallows' Eve fire on the hillside. Apples at this time of year were considered good fortune. Rosamund's fruit was accepted with curtsies and bows and thanks from the people of Friarsgate.

The following day was All Saints', and a feast was held to honor all of the saints, known and unknown. On November second, All Souls' Day was celebrated. The Friarsgate children went singing — a-souling — from door to door, and were rewarded with "soul cakes," a small sweet oatcake with bits of apple in it. On the ninth

35

day of the month Rosamund surprised her husband with a small feast to celebrate his natal day. She also presented him with a silver broach decorated with a black agate that had belonged to her father and her grandfather.

Hugh looked down at the broach nestled in its wrapping of delicate blue wool cloth. He had never in all his life — not once in his sixty years — been gifted with anything. He looked down at the girl who was now his wife, and his eyes shone with tears. "Why, Rosamund," he said, his voice tight in his throat, "I have never received anything as fine as this." Bending, he kissed her rosy cheek. "Thank you, wife."

"Oh, I am so glad that you liked it," she responded. "Maybel said you would. 'Tis for your cloak, Hugh. 'Twill look so fine!"

Two days later they celebrated Martinmas with roast goose. On the twenty-fifth of November St. Catherine's Day was observed with cathern cakes, which were shaped like wheels, and lamb's wool, a frothy drink that was served from a cathern bowl. Afterward circle dances were danced in the hall. The harvest was long gathered in, and many of the ewes and she-cattle were ripening with young to be born in the next few months.

The Christmas season came beginning with the first day of the twelve to follow on the eve of Christ's Mass. It was the happiest time Rosamund could ever remember in all her life. There was no word from her uncle Henry. In the hall a huge Yule log burned night and day. Mistletoe and greens were hung along with branches of holly. There were twelve candelabrums all burning by Twelfth Night. Twelve dishes were served at each meal. There was a wassailing for each day, and sweet foods were especially popular. There was frumenty, humble pie, mince pie, and pudding, but Rosamund's favorites were Yule dolls, which were made of gingerbread.

Rosamund's gift to each tenant family was that they might hunt rabbits each Saturday for the winter months. Since it had been a good harvest, her stone granaries were full, and she would also be able to feed the Friarsgate folk during the cold weather. Grain was distributed once monthly to be taken to the miller and ground into flour. In her own cellars were baskets of onions, apples, and pears, and carrots and beets were hung from the cellar rafters.

January fifth was the last day of the Christmas feast, known as Twelfth Night. Rosamund and Hugh were entertained in the hall that night by six dancers from the village dressed up as oxen complete with horns and bells. When they had finished their amusement, Rosamund chose one among them as the "best beast." Giggling, she placed upon its horn a hard oat cake in the shape of a doughnut. The best beast then tried to shake off his reward while Rosamund and Hugh debated heatedly over whether the cake would fall before or behind the dancer. Finally the cake flew up off the beast's horn and onto the table before the young mistress of Friarsgate. Rosamund burst out laughing, and clapped.

"Bravo!" she cried as the oxen danced from the hall.

The meal finished, the lord and lady of Friarsgate arose with their goblets and went outside into the clear cold night. Above them in the black sky the stars twinkled silver, blue, and red. Before the house stood a great gnarled oak with branches that spread themselves out in all directions. It was said to have been there before the building was constructed over two hundred years ago. Their cups contained cider, and they had with them three small pieces of seedcake. Rosamund and Hugh toasted the ancient tree, and then they each ate a single piece of cake, offering the other two bits to the tree.

Then they circled the tree, singing an ancient tune and pouring the remainder of the cider onto the tree's knobby roots that lay upon the surface of the hard earth.

"This is the best Twelfth Night I have ever had!" Rosamund declared happily.

"Yes," Hugh agreed as he walked with his young wife back into the hall, "it has been for me also, lass."

Now the winter months were here. Rosamund set about to learn how to read and write. With infinite patience, Hugh, himself, taught her, making the letters with a piece of charcoal upon a scrap of parchment. She was, to his surprise, left-handed, which was, of course, very unusual. Following his lead she carefully copied the letters over and over again, speaking aloud their names. She was very serious in her endeavors, and quickly became a good student. Within a month she knew her alphabet by heart and could write each letter neatly. Next he taught her to write her name. She was fascinated when she first saw it, the letters spread out upon the worn parchment. She swiftly began to learn how to write other words, and by late winter she was beginning to read.

"I fear she will outstrip me," Hugh told Edmund. "She is very intelligent. By summer she will read better than you or I."

"Then teach her — we shall do it together — how to do her sums, so she may know how we keep her accounts," Edmund said. Then he chuckled. "Henry will not be happy when he learns this."

"He can do nothing," Hugh replied. "I am Rosamund's husband. Under the law I am responsible for her behavior and her lands. We both know he chose me because he wanted to keep the child safe from other families' offers of marriage until he can wed her to his own son after I am gone."

"The older she gets the more difficult she will be to manage," Edmund remarked. "She is much like her father. I see it even now."

The hillsides began to grow green with the spring. The lambing had yielded a goodly crop of new sheep. Rosamund's herds had also increased with several young heifers and two young bulls. One would be kept for breeding purposes, and the other sold. Over the winter months the houses of Friarsgate's tenants had been repaired by their occupants. Roofs had been patched, and chimneys had been resealed. Now it was time for the fields to be plowed so that grain and vegetables might be planted.

On the last day of April, Rosamund's seventh birthday was celebrated by her husband, her uncle Edmund, and Maybel. She delighted them all by her enthusiasm over her gifts. From Maybel an embroidered girdle of green silk decorated with gold thread. Her uncle Edmund presented Rosamund with a leather-bound ledger of blank pages to do her sums, along with a small sharpened goose quill with which to write. Hugh, however, gave his wife a pair of doeskin gloves trimmed with rabbit fur that he had made himself, and a sheer lawn veil for her head that he had bought from the first peddler of the spring.

The crops were planted, and the fields were already green when Henry Bolton arrived at Friarsgate for the first time since he had left the previous autumn. He came with a long face to tell them that his good wife, the lady Agnes, had been delivered of a puny daughter on the feast of St. Julia. The child was with a wet nurse, for Agnes Bolton had died of childbed fever shortly after her daughter's birth. He and Hugh sat together in the hall that evening.

"Rosamund appears in good health," Henry Bolton said. His niece had greeted him dutifully, and then after the meal politely requested permission from her husband to retire.

"She is a sturdy child," Hugh replied.

"She seems to favor you," Henry noted.

"I am like a grandfather to her," Hugh murmured.

"You do not spoil her, I hope. You used the rod on her?" Henry peered closely at the older man.

"It has not been necessary . . . to date," Hugh said. "She is a good child, and obedient. If she should prove otherwise, I will remedy the situation, I assure you, Henry Bolton."

"Good! Good!" Henry responded. Then he sighed. "And you, Hugh? You are in good health, too?" Damn Agnes, he thought, as he asked it. If this old man who was Rosamund's husband should die before he had another son, he would surely lose Friarsgate.

"My health would appear to be excellent, Henry," Hugh said blandly, knowing exactly what was on his companion's mind and struggling not to laugh aloud.

"I must marry again," Henry burst out.

"Aye," Hugh agreed. " 'Twould be wise."

"Agnes' brother says Otterly must be returned to him," Henry told Hugh.

"Nay, it is yours. It was a gift to Agnes when she wed you. It was hers to do with as she pleased. Tell Robert that I have said so, for I was the one who drew up the papers

42

transferring the manor to her. Look among her things, Henry. You will find those papers. Robert Lindsay has the same papers. He knows Otterly belongs to you. He only seeks to see if he can steal it back. I will testify for you before any manor court. If you tell your brother-in-law that, he will not pursue the issue further."

"Thank you," Henry Bolton said, grateful.

"So after your year's mourning is completed you will seek another wife," Hugh said cheerfully. "She was a good woman, my cousin Agnes. It will be difficult to find another as fine."

"I've the new one already picked. I cannot mourn Agnes for a year's time. You will not live forever, Hugh. You know I mean for my next son to marry with my niece. The lad should at least be out of leading reins when it is done," Henry Bolton said bluntly.

"Indeed," Hugh replied, not knowing whether to be angry at his companion's callousness or amused by it. So poor Agnes would not be mourned decently.

"She's the daughter of a freedman with a small holding that borders Otterly. There are two siblings and little chance of Mavis finding a husband as good as me, so her father has given her a third of his lands, the ones matching mine, for a dowry. We'll marry after Lamastide. She's young and should prove a good breeder."

"Yet she is only one of three," Hugh noted astutely.

"Her brother has fathered half a dozen sons already, and their father has several more on his mistress. Mavis' mam was a cold woman, but she is not," Henry said, chuckling. "I've already been up her skirts, and she was more than eager for it."

"She was a virgin, of course," Hugh said. "You would be certain, Henry, that your firstborn is indeed your blood."

"Aye, she was a virgin," Henry responded. "I put my finger inside her to make certain before I first used her. Her father encouraged it."

"You will bring your bride to meet Rosamund, I hope, before you get her with child," Hugh remarked.

"Aye, I will," Henry agreed. Then he said, "Friarsgate thrives?"

Hugh nodded. "It does. We had a goodly lambing in late winter, and many cattle born, too. The fields are doing well, and the orchards are heavy with fruit. It will be a good year, Henry. A prosperous year."

"And the Scots?"

"They keep to their side of the border," Hugh replied.

"Good! Good! I have been told that they avoid Friarsgate because the land about us is steep and difficult to run stolen animals over, but with the Scots one cannot be too certain, Hugh. Keep a sharp eye out," Henry advised pompously.

"I will, Henry. I certainly will," Hugh agreed.

The following morning Henry Bolton departed. Rosamund came to bid her uncle farewell. He looked her over carefully a final time. Aye, she was a healthy little bitch, he thought. She had surely grown taller since he had last seen her. Her auburn hair shone with golden lights. The amber eyes looked him in the face briefly before lowering modestly as she curtsied to him.

"Well, girl, I do not know when I shall come again," Henry said to her. "Next time I shall bring your new aunt, eh?"

"You are always welcome at Friarsgate, uncle," Rosamund replied. Then she handed him a small wrapped bit of wool tied with a thread.

"What's this?" he demanded of her.

"It is a cake of soap, scented with heather, that I have made for your bride, uncle," Rosamund told him.

Henry Bolton was surprised. He was not so insensitive that he did not realize he was not his niece's favorite person. A gift for Mavis was a surprising gesture on the child's part. "I shall take it to her, and you have my thanks, Rosamund. I cannot fault your manners, and it pleases me that you learn womanly skills."

"The mistress of Friarsgate should know many things, uncle. I am young, but I am capable of learning them," Rosamund responded. Then she curtsied to him again, and moved to stand by her husband.

"Rosamund made soap to keep us clean the winter long," Hugh quickly said before Henry Bolton could consider his niece's words. Discretion, he thought. We must teach Rosamund not to display her tactics so openly. Then he smiled at Henry. "Godspeed," he said.

"Aye, uncle, God speed you and protect you," Rosamund echoed. Then she stood watching as he rode away from Friarsgate, slipping her hand into Hugh's as she did. "If he but knew," she said softly.

"But he will not, until it is too late," Hugh answered her.

Rosamund nodded in agreement. "Nay, he will not," she replied.

Chapter 2

During the few years that followed, Rosamund grew from a charming little girl into a gangling young girl, who sometimes seemed to be all legs and flying hair. They saw Henry Bolton but once in all that time. He brought his new wife, Mavis, a buxom girl of sixteen with careful eyes, to meet his niece. Mavis thanked the heiress to Friarsgate for the soap as she openly admired Rosamund's house and lands.

"Henry says our son will be your husband one day," she boldly told the younger girl. "This is a fine inheritance for him."

"Are you with child?" Rosamund inquired with apparent innocence.

Mavis giggled. "I ought to be, considering how active a bed partner your uncle is, but you would not know of such things being a child yet."

"Perhaps you will have a daughter,"

Rosamund said. "My poor aunt Agnes did, you know." She smiled sweetly.

"God and his Blessed Mother forbid it!" Mavis cried, crossing herself. "Your uncle wants sons. I will light as many candles as I must to gain my husband's wishes. You are a wicked girl to suggest I have daughters. Perhaps you put the evil eye on your uncle's first wife and caused her death."

"Do not be silly," Rosamund responded. "I never saw my aunt again from the day she departed Friarsgate. Besides, I liked her." This Mavis had fewer brains than a milk cow, Rosamund decided. "Tell me, if you know, what has happened to my cousin, Julia?"

"When she is weaned from the farmer's wife's teat, she will go to St. Margaret's Convent, where she will be raised to become a nun," Mavis said. "I don't want to raise another woman's daughter. Besides, the convent will take a smaller dower portion than any man would. Your aunt Agnes was no great beauty. Henry says the bairn favors her."

"It is comforting to know my cousin is safe," Rosamund remarked dryly. How sad that her poor little cousin should be disposed of so easily and so callously. She knew that Henry Bolton would have done the same to her had it not been for Friarsgate.

Rosamund was relieved when Mavis and her uncle departed. In the next three years the news came with monotonous regularity that Mavis delivered first one son, then a second, and finally a third. Her fourth child was a daughter, and after that they heard no more of Mavis Bolton's fecundity. Her uncle did not visit. She was left to wonder about her cousins. They were probably, she decided, blond, blue-eyed blobs very much like their mother. The eldest of them, called Henry after his father, was supposed to be her future husband. *As if I could wed with a four-year-old*, Rosamund thought. *Why, I am practically twelve!*

She could now read anything they put before her. She wrote with a beautiful hand as she transcribed the figures into her account books. She knew how to purchase supplies, the few they did not grow or make themselves at Friarsgate. She had learned exactly what they needed to survive comfortably. She was beginning to bargain for her holding when she, Hugh, and Edmund went to the cattle and sheep markets in the nearby town. She had a keen eye for horseflesh, and had even begun to breed animals for later sale.

Rosamund also took an interest in her great flocks of sheep. Unlike many farms that sold their raw wool to brokers, Friarsgate kept theirs. After the animals were sheared, the wool was washed, dried, combed, and carded twice in order to make the wool extra fine, and hence more valuable in the marketplaces of York and London. Next the wool was dyed. There was a lovely golden brown, a fine red, and a green, but Friarsgate wool was known for an exquisite blue color that no one else seemed capable of duplicating. It was unique to Rosamund's estate, and highly prized. As mistress of Friarsgate the formula for Friarsgate Blue was entrusted to Rosamund by her uncle Edmund. It was his gift to her upon her tenth birthday, when he told her that she was old enough to know. But it was important that the secret remain with her alone, until she felt it could be passed on to the next heir, or heiress, to Friarsgate.

Rosamund nodded somberly, understanding the importance of what Edmund was imparting to her. "I may share my knowledge with no one?" she asked quietly.

"No one," Edmund repeated.

"How do we get our colors so clear and bright, uncle?" she asked him. "I have seen other wools, and they are not at all as fine as ours are. How is it done? Is it the formula for the dyes?"

Edmund chuckled. "We set the colors with sheep urine, lass," he told her, grinning. "That is the secret of the blue color, too. It is darker in the dye vat, but once we move it into the pee, it turns that fabled color so highly prized."

Rosamund laughed, too. It was so simple, and an absolutely delicious secret. She wished briefly that she might share the secret with Hugh, but she knew she would not.

Once the wool was dyed it was distributed among the cottages to be spun on the looms kept in a separate room in each weaver's home. This kept the wool from being impregnated by smoke, or food odors, or heat, which might turn the delicate colors. The long strands of the wool were woven into an extra-fine cloth that was highly prized and greatly sought after. The shorter bits were turned to a fine felt.

Rosamund learned all of the processes, and she was very proud of her knowledge. Hugh and Edmund were proud of her, too. The child who they both treasured was growing into a young woman whose passion for knowledge could not be quenched. It disturbed them that they had nothing more to teach her.

The winter before her thirteenth birthday

Hugh Cabot fell ill with an ague. He was slow to recover. It was that spring that Henry Bolton chose to pay a visit to Friarsgate. It was the first he had made in several years. He was accompanied by his eldest son, five-year-old Henry. The oddly coincidental timing of his visit made Rosamund suspicious that she had a spy among her servants.

"Find out," she curtly instructed her uncle Edmund.

Henry Bolton eyed his niece critically. She was tall, and no longer had a childish look about her. "How old are you now, girl?" he demanded, noting how her blue wool gown with its long tight sleeves clung to newly budding breasts. She was ripening, he considered nervously.

"You are most welcome to Friarsgate, *uncle*," Rosamund swept him a rather elegant curtsy. "I shall be thirteen in a few weeks." She waved her hand gracefully. "Come into the hall for some refreshment." Then, turning, she led the way, her blue skirts swinging behind her as she walked. "And how is my aunt?" she inquired politely. "Doll, bring wine for my uncle and cider for his little lad," she ordered a serving woman.

"I am to be your husband, girl!" the little

boy announced loudly. He was small, Rosamund thought, for a child of five. He had his mother's blond hair and bovine look. There was nothing, she thought, that was Bolton about him, but perhaps the set of his jaw, reminded her strongly of her uncle Henry.

"My name is Rosamund. I am your cousin, and I already have a husband," she told him, looking down at him.

"Who lies dying," the boy said boldly. "You and Friarsgate are to be mine, *girl*." He stood, legs apart, glaring at her.

"He has no manners, uncle," Rosamund remarked, ignoring the boy now. "Do you not beat him? Obviously not." She sat down by the hall fire, indicating that her uncle should do the same.

Taken aback by his niece's attitude, Henry Bolton sat heavily. "He is high-spirited, that is all," he excused his son. "He will grow into a fine man one day. You shall see."

"Perhaps I shall," Rosamund replied. "Now, uncle, what brings you to Friarsgate? It has been many years since we have seen you."

"Can I not pay you a visit, Rosamund, after all this time, and bring young Henry to meet his future wife?" the older man protested.

"You do nothing, uncle, without a reason. That I learned quite young. You have not been here in several years because you trusted Hugh to manage everything for you. Now you have learned that my husband is ill, and so you have come, posthaste, bringing this ill-mannered brat of yours with you, to see for yourself the truth of the situation," she said harshly.

"I think it is you who needs a beating, Rosamund," Henry Bolton snarled. "How do you dare to speak to me like that? I am your guardian!"

"You relinquished your guardianship when you gave me to my husband, *uncle*," she snapped back.

"And when he is dead you will be in my keeping once again," Henry Bolton threatened. "You had best mend your ways, niece. Now, I have brought the betrothal papers with me, and you will sign them. They shall be dated at the appropriate time, *but you will sign them today.* I will have no one stealing you and Friarsgate out from beneath my nose after I have been so patient."

"I shall sign nothing without my husband's permission," Rosamund said. "If you try to force me I shall complain to the church. They will not approve of your high-handed tactics, uncle. I am no longer a frightened and malleable child who can be coerced by threats. Ah, here is our wine. Drink up, uncle. You are looking positively apoplectic." She tilted her own goblet to her lips and drank delicately.

For a moment all was red before Henry Bolton's eyes. Taking his niece's advice he gulped down his wine, trying to calm his thoughts and the pounding pulses in his temples. The girl who sat so self-assuredly before him was more than pretty. And had not the old Countess of Richmond given birth to King Henry VII at thirteen? His niece was no longer a child. She was practically a woman, and a strong-willed woman at that. How in the hell had this all happened in just six years? Henry Bolton's chest felt suddenly tight. He struggled to master himself. The amber-eyed bitch sitting across from him viewed him gravely.

"Are you all right, uncle?" she asked him solicitously.

"I want to see Hugh," he demanded of her.

"Of course, but you will have to wait until he is awake. While his mind is perfectly clear, my husband is no longer strong. He sleeps much. I will have him told of your arrival when he awakens, uncle." Rosamund arose. "Remain here, and warm yourself by the fire," she advised. "I will have more wine brought." She smoothed her blue skirts down with her long fingers. "I must leave you."

"Where are you going?" Henry Bolton almost croaked.

"I have my work, uncle." She turned away.

"What work?" he demanded of her.

"It is spring, uncle, and there is much to be done in the spring. I must tot up the monthly accounts and arrange a schedule for the plowing, and see how much seed I will need to distribute for the planting. We have had more lambs born this winter than we could have possibly anticipated. A new meadow must be cleared and planted to contain the increased flock. I am not some fine lady who can remain by the fire to entertain you."

"Why are you doing these things?" he challenged her.

"Because I am mistress of Friarsgate, uncle," she answered him. "Surely you didn't expect I should grow up only to weave at my loom, or make conserves and soap."

"Those are women's pursuits, dammit!" Henry Bolton shouted. "Of course those are the very things that you should be doing. You should leave the stewarding of

Friarsgate to the men!" His face was growing very crimson once again.

"Fiddlesticks!" Rosamund answered him pertly. "But if it will soothe your mind, uncle, I can also do all those things as well. Friarsgate, however, is mine. It is my responsibility to care for its welfare, and the welfare of my people, as any good chatelaine would do. I dislike being useless and idle."

"I want to speak with Hugh!" Henry Bolton practically yelled.

"And so you shall, uncle, *in due time.*" Then she turned about and left the hall. Behind her she could hear Henry Bolton sputtering his protests, and then she heard his son.

"I don't like her, father. I want another wife."

"*Shut your mouth!*" Henry Bolton shouted savagely at his heir.

Rosamund grinned as she hurried off to seek her husband, who was indeed resting in his chamber. Catching hold of a passing serving wench she instructed the girl, "Find Edmund Bolton, but send him to the lord's chamber and not to the hall where my uncle waits."

The servant nodded her understanding and dashed away.

Hugh Cabot was sitting up in his bed

when she entered his room. He had grown thinner and was very frail, but his bright blue eyes still danced with an interest in everyone and everything. "I hear we have a visitor," he said with a small smile.

Rosamund laughed. "I vow, my lord, that you know everything before I do." She went and sat on the edge of her husband's bed. "What we have, Hugh, is a spy among our people. I have told Edmund to find out who it is. Aye, we have not one visitor, but two. He has brought me my *next husband*."

"And do you favor the lad, Rosamund?" Hugh teased her, a wicked smile lighting his narrow lips.

"He's an arrogant, snot-nosed little brat from what I have observed. And I will wager he's wearing his first pair of breeches, Hugh. He struts like a small barnyard cock, and 'tis not much bigger," she told him.

He laughed. Then he coughed, waving the cup she offered him away. "Nay, lass, I don't need it."

"What you mean is you don't like it," she scolded him gently, "but the herbs do soothe your cough, Hugh."

"And taste like swamp water," he grumbled good-naturedly, but he drank down several swallows of the brew to please her.

"My uncle wants to see you. Are you up to

it? I will not let him near you if you wish it, Hugh," she said earnestly. "I don't want to lose you, my dear old man."

Hugh smiled at her. Reaching out he patted Rosamund's hand. "You are going to lose me, my dearie. Sooner than later I fear. Now, do not shake your head at me, Rosamund. I have taught you to be more pragmatic than to allow your emotions to overrule your common sense."

"*Hugh!*" She softly chided him.

"Rosamund, I am dying, but you need not fear my going. I have made preparations to keep you safe from Henry Bolton." He lay back against the pillows and closed his eyes.

"What preparations?" she queried him. "What have you done, my dear Hugh? Don't you think I should know what fate you have planned for me?" What had he done? she wondered. Over the winter months there had been much whispering between her husband and Edmund.

"It is better that you not know until you need to know," Hugh advised his young wife. "That way your uncle cannot accuse you of any collusion with me in order to cheat him out of Friarsgate."

"Friarsgate isn't his. It never was," Rosamund said irritably.

Hugh opened his eyes and fixed her with

his blue gaze. "I know that, and you know it, dearie, but Henry Bolton will never be convinced of that fact even when he is dead. I truly believe he would commit murder in order to possess these lands, if he believed he could get away with it. That is why you must be protected in such a way that he dare not render you any harm. It was different when you were a child. You are no longer a child. You cannot easily be controlled anymore, and when your uncle Henry sees it, you will be in danger."

"Will you tell him what you have done?" she asked.

Hugh Cabot smiled a wickedly mischievous smile. Then he chuckled. "Nay, I shall keep my secret. But when he attempts to gain a hold of your person and your lands, you will have the supreme pleasure of seeing his dismay to discover they have been put out of his greedy hands for good and for all."

"But how will my uncle know what you have done?" she questioned him. He was so pale, Rosamund thought. And the tiny blue veins on his eyelids were almost black now.

"I am owed a favor from a powerful man. I have sent for someone to come from him. He will, even now, be on his way. And, too, Edmund knows what I have planned," Hugh said mysteriously.

"Surely you have not contracted another marriage for me," Rosamund said nervously.

" 'Tis not my place to do such a thing," Hugh exclaimed, "and I should not, Rosamund. You must choose next time."

"Oh, Hugh, I wish you would not leave me! I do love you, you know. Not as a woman loves a man. I know naught of such love, but I love you nonetheless. I have not been as happy in my whole life since my parents died than I have been with you," Rosamund told him.

"And I love you, my dearie," he said quietly. "You are the child I never had. Because of you my last years have been happy and comfortable. I know you will bury me with honor, and the place will be marked. It is more than I could have hoped for, Rosamund."

"It is so little," she said, "especially when you have given me so much, my dear husband." Her slender fingers closed about his gnarled and cold hand, offering her youthful warmth to his chilled frame.

Hugh closed his eyes again, a small smile upon his lips. "I will see him after the meal. Hopefully with a full belly Henry Bolton will be less choleric. Bring me some broth, my dearie. 'Tis all I can stomach. I will sleep now for a bit."

She released the delicate grip she had on his hand, and arose. Then, drawing the coverlet up over his chest, she bent and kissed his brow. "I'll bring the soup myself, and feed you," Rosamund said. Then she turned and left the chamber. Aye, he was dying, she reluctantly admitted to herself for the first time. She felt the tears pricking at her eyelids again and blinked them back. Hugh was right. She could not allow her emotions to overcome her practical nature. Not now. She had to keep her wits about her for his sake, for her sake, for all of their sakes.

Reentering the hall she said to her uncle, "My husband will see you after he has supped. He is very weak. You must not remain with him for too long, sir."

"Why can he not see me now?" Henry demanded irritably. "This is outrageous! Hugh Cabot behaves as if he were to the manor born when the truth is I am responsible for putting him in this place. He owes me obedience, and respect, yet he renders me neither."

"He is a dying old man, uncle, *and* if the truth be known, you married him to me in order to protect what you perceive as your interest in my lands. I must remind you that Friarsgate is mine. *Not yours.* You have never cared what happened to me as long as I could not be used by another. But God has a way of protecting the helpless and the innocent. Hugh Cabot is a good man, not that that ever mattered to you, uncle."

"You think him a good man because the old fool allowed you to run wild, niece. Your bold stance and your words tell me he did not beat you enough, if indeed he beat you at all," Henry Bolton snapped. "I can see I shall have to begin again with you, but when I am through, you will be a meek and subservient wife for my son."

"That brat you spawned on your bovine bride will never be my husband, uncle! Put it from your mind *now*. I will choose my own husband this time, but certainly not until I have mourned my Hugh for at least a full year, as is proper and expected. Try and foist your bantam cock on me and you shall regret it!"

"You will damned well do what I tell you, Rosamund! I am your uncle! I have dominion over you!" Henry shouted, red-faced.

"Mistress! Come to the table," Maybel interjected, coming into the hall. "The food is ready."

"Uncle, you are certainly hungry, and my cousin, too. Maybel is correct. Come and eat before the food goes cold. Then you will speak with my husband." Rosamund was once again the good hostess, the well-mannered chatelaine. She brought her angry relation and his son to the high board. Then she filled their pewter plates herself, heaping them high with beef and goose, and ladling rabbit stew into hollowed-out trencher loaves. Maybel poured the matching pewter goblets full with the last of the October ale for Henry Bolton and apple cider for his young son. Rosamund pushed the bread, a crock of sweet butter, and a wedge of hard cheese down the table in front of her uncle.

He began to eat, and the worst of his anger slowly drained away. He was pleased to note that his niece kept an excellent table. The food was hot, and it was fresh. It was not overcooked, nor was it filled with spices to disguise rot or decay. He speared a piece of beef with his knife and chewed. Tearing a piece of bread from the loaf, he smeared butter across it with his big thumb and crammed it into his mouth. Maybel kept his goblet filled, and he drank generously. The ale was clean and sharp, stripping away at his tongue so that the food tasted even better.

Rosamund ate sparingly, and then she arose. "You will excuse me, uncle. I must bring broth to my husband." She then turned her gaze to her young cousin. "There is a sweet for you when you have finished your supper, *boy*." Then she noted, "Uncle, he has no manners. Does your wife not teach him?" And she was gone from the hall before Henry Bolton the elder might protest her observation.

"Use your spoon," he snapped at his son. "Why do you eat with your hands like a peasant?"

"I don't have a spoon," the boy whined.

"You have one!" his father said, and he shook his fist at his namesake. "Use it, dammit! The little bitch is right. You have no manners. I shall have words with your mother over this, boy!"

Behind the hall, connected to the house by a stone colonnade, was the kitchen house. Between the columns on either side a kitchen garden grew. Above was an arbor made up of flowering vines just now show-ing the first signs of green. Rosamund hur-ried to the kitchen. After complimenting the cook on a fine meal, she obtained a bowl of soup for her husband, and a piece of bread. She carried the small burden back into the house and up the flight of stone stairs to Hugh's chamber. He was awake again, and he smiled at her as she entered. She smiled back, and setting the bowl down, drew a napkin from the folds of her skirts to tuck beneath his chin. Then she took the piece of bread from her pocket and broke it into small bits that she dropped into the soup. Sitting finally, she began to feed him.

Hugh ate slowly and with difficulty, for swallowing was painful for him now. After a time he held up his hand to signal that he had had enough, yet the bowl was still practically full. "I can eat no more, my dearie," he told her.

"A spoonful or two more," she coaxed, but he shook his head in the negative. "Oh, Hugh, how can you get well if you do not eat?" Her amber eyes were filled with concern for him.

"*Rosamund,*" he chided her gently.

"I know," she half-whispered, "but I don't want you to go."

He smiled a slight smile again. "I wish I could stay with you, Rosamund. In another year or two you will flower into true womanhood. It will be glorious. I should like to be here for that, but I shall watch for you from the other side. Never doubt that while my body may lie rotting in the good earth of Friarsgate, my spirit will watch over you, my dear young wife and friend."

Rosamund put down the bowl. Unable to help herself, she began to weep. "What shall I do without you, Hugh?" she sobbed.

Reaching out, he comforted her, patting her hand, saying, "You can trust Edmund, and I promise that you will have a far greater protector than I, my dearie. Now, my strength is quickly ebbing. Send Henry Bolton to me."

She half-stumbled to her feet, wiping her eyes with her sleeve. "I'll sit with you after he is gone," she promised him.

"I should like that," he agreed with a weak smile.

She gave him a half-smile back and went from the room. In the hall her uncle was just finishing his meal, wiping his plate clean with a chunk of bread. Her cousin was shoveling the apple tart and cream into his mouth as fast as he might use his spoon. "Hugh will see you now, uncle. Try not to tire him, please." Her voice trembled.

Henry Bolton looked at his niece sharply. "Do you actually care for him?" he demanded of her. Then his eyes narrowed. "He has not tampered with you, has he?"

She knew precisely what he meant, and she gave him a scornful look. "He is like my father, uncle. How vile your thoughts are, but I shall lose my virginity long ere you can try to wed me to your little brat." And she laughed at his outraged gape of shock.

"You need a good beating, girl," he told her fiercely.

"Raise a hand to me, if you dare, uncle, and I shall cut it off, I promise you," Rosamund answered him calmly. "Now, go and speak with my husband while you still can."

Henry Bolton almost ran from the hall. He did not like the way his niece was behaving or the way in which she spoke to him. What had happened to the frightened and obedient little girl she had once been? He had not had Hugh Cabot wed her in order for Rosamund to turn into an independent and obviously literate female. All the man was supposed to have done was protect Henry Bolton's interests in Friarsgate until his death, at which time Rosamund would have been married to his son. But Rosamund was suddenly outspoken and damned self-possessed.

"I do not like it," Henry muttered to himself. "I do not like it at all." But then he considered if Hugh Cabot were indeed dying, Rosamund would shortly be back in his power. He would correct the problem she now presented him. Especially after Hugh signed the betrothal agreement between Rosamund and young Henry Bolton. He opened the door to the bedchamber and stepped over the threshold.

"Good evening, Hugh," he said, frankly shocked by what he saw. Hugh Cabot was certainly dying, by the looks of him. He was gaunt and pale, but his blue eyes were yet lively, indicating his strong spirit.

"Come in, Henry Bolton, and sit by my side," Hugh invited. "We have not seen you in some time. Your good wife is well?"

"Aye," Henry answered curtly. "Rosamund says I must not tire you so I will come directly to the point."

"Of course," Hugh responded.

"I had heard that you were dying, and I can see that it is so," Henry began bluntly. "Legally you are my niece's lord and master, by virtue of your marriage. It is therefore up to you to provide for your widow's future before you depart this life."

"Aye, it is," Hugh agreed.

"I have brought the betrothal agreement for Rosamund's next marriage, to my son Henry the younger. Rosamund will, of course, mourn you for a full year's time, but the agreement must be in place so that the marriage can be celebrated when her bereavement is concluded."

"You are most solicitous of Rosamund, Henry," came the amused response. "However, I have already provided for my wife's future when I am no longer here to guide her." Hugh watched the look of utter and complete astonishment explode across Henry Bolton's face.

"You have no right!" he cried.

"Actually, I am the only one who does have the right under the laws of England, Henry." Hugh was enjoying himself immensely.

"I am her nearest blood relation!" Henry's voice rose.

"But I am her husband, thanks to you," Hugh replied with a small smile. "A husband's rights take precedence over that of her nearest male relation, Henry. You will have neither my wife nor Friarsgate for your heir."

"You will sign this agreement!" Henry growled at his companion.

Hugh could not help himself. He had never thought to see desperation in Henry Bolton's eyes, or hear it in his voice, but it was there. He burst out laughing, shaking his head as he did so. His laughter, however, dissolved into a fit of great coughing. He struggled to reach the goblet of medicine that his wife had brewed earlier for him. He could not reach it, and seeing what he sought, Henry moved it farther out of the dying man's reach. As he actually felt his heart slowing to a stop, a look of under-

70

standing filled Hugh Cabot's blue eyes, to be followed by one of vast amusement. He struggled to form the last words that he needed, and finally he managed to croak them out. *"You have lost!"* he gasped, falling back against his pillows, the light fading swiftly from his blue eyes.

Henry Bolton cursed softly beneath his breath as he pushed the medicinal goblet back near his victim so no one would know what he had done. He had failed to get Hugh's signature. He dared not attempt to forge it. Still, with Hugh dead he was now his niece's master once again. She would do what he wanted her to do, or he would kill her with his own bare hands. Reaching out with a hand he closed Hugh's blue eyes. Then, rising, he departed the chamber, returning to the hall and saying, "Your husband has fallen asleep again, Rosamund. He wanted me to tell you that he would speak with you on the morrow."

"You will remain the night, uncle?" she replied. "I will take you and my cousin to your chamber now."

"Show young Henry the way, girl. I know where the guest chamber is in this house now, don't I? I would remain here for a time. Bring me some wine before you go," he instructed her.

She did his bidding and then led her cousin to the guest quarters, bidding him good night as she closed the door quickly behind the boy. Then she hurried off to see that Hugh was comfortable for the night. To her great shock she discovered her husband dead. Stifling her cry of distress Rosamund summoned a servant and said, "Go quietly and fetch Master Edmund. Be certain that my uncle Henry does not see him. And send Maybel to me." She had earlier sent for Edmund yet he had not come. Obviously he had not been nearby. Pray God he was now!

"Yes, mistress," the servant said, and left her alone again.

Maybel came, and seeing Hugh Cabot realized immediately what had happened. Her hand flew to her mouth. *"How?"* she asked.

"We must wait for Edmund," Rosamund replied stonily. Then she sat down next to her dead husband and took up his cold and stiffening hand in hers, as if she might restore the life to him.

Edmund Bolton came into the chamber finally and posed the same question his wife had. *"How?"* he asked.

"I suspect my uncle Henry of some treachery," Rosamund replied. "I am going to kill him with my own hands!" Tears began to pour down her pale face.

"Tell me," Edmund said. "If you can convince me, I will kill him myself, and we will make it appear to be an accident." His gray eyes were very serious.

"He came in to see Hugh. When he returned to the hall he said Hugh had gone to sleep, that he would speak with me in the morning. I left my uncle in the hall while I took his brat to his chamber. I then came here and discovered my husband dead."

Edmund bent down and carefully inspected the stiffening body of his old friend. There were absolutely no marks of violence on Hugh. There was even a faint smile upon his thin blue lips. Looking up at his niece Edmund said, "Rosamund, he has died a natural death. We were expecting it." He put his arm about his distraught niece. "You are in shock, my child. It came quicker than we anticipated."

"Henry Bolton is involved," Rosamund said stonily. "I do not know how, but in my heart I sense it, Edmund. Hugh was fine when I left him. Now he is dead. What else am I to think?"

"Even if your intuition is correct, Rosamund, there is no proof. Hugh was ill unto death. Everyone knew it. However, since Henry does not know he has died, or wants us to believe he does not know that Hugh has died, we will say naught until morning. Where is my half-brother now?"

"In the hall, swilling wine. I doubt he has changed, which means he will drink himself to sleep," Rosamund said bitterly. Then she sighed deeply and straightened her shoulders. "Maybel and I will prepare my husband's body for burial." She looked up at Edmund. "Have you discovered our informant?"

Edmund shook his head in the negative. "It may have been just a careless word on someone's part," he suggested. "And that gossip was picked up and traveled on the wind as gossip is wont to do."

"My husband is to be laid out in the hall so he may be honored," Rosamund answered. "I will pray by his bier tonight. It is unlikely that my uncle will even notice in his drunken stupor." She looked at Edmund Bolton. "Hugh said he had made provision to protect me from Uncle Henry. He said you would know what he had done."

"I do," Edmund admitted; then he chuckled softly. "My half-brother could not have known the day he married you to Hugh Cabot that it would be a fatal misstep in his plan to gain Friarsgate for himself. Rest assured, niece, that I will not let Henry override your husband's last wishes for your safety and well-being. Someone is coming, Rosamund. Hugh had hoped it would be before he died, but that someone will be here shortly, and then all will be revealed. We need the authority of our expected guest. Will you trust me?"

"Always, uncle!" she replied, her amber eyes meeting his.

Maybel swiftly crossed herself reverently. Then she enfolded Rosamund to her ample bosom, clucking with sympathy.

To her great surprise the girl began to cry, the sorrow pent up within her pouring forth. Neither Maybel nor Edmund uttered a word as Rosamund vented her anguish. Then finally she ceased, wiping her face with her sleeve, feeling relief and peace overwhelming her very soul. She had never been a girl to weep. Her amber gaze met those of her companions. She drew herself up straight, saying as she did so, "Let us begin. My husband's body must be washed preparatory to being sewn into his shroud. Edmund, see that the coffin is brought here to his chamber."

"At once, my lady," Edmund Bolton said, and hurried off.

"Henry Bolton has had a hand in this

death tonight," Rosamund insisted to Maybel. "Edmund says he can find no sign of such a thing, but I know it to be so. One day I shall have my revenge on him for it."

"If Edmund could find no sign, then there is none," Maybel responded thoughtfully, "which is not to say you're not correct. A pillow held to the head of a weak man could kill him."

Rosamund nodded slowly. "Whatever he did he will regret," she said. "I will not let Hugh die unavenged. He was a good friend to me. As his wife I owe him that duty."

Rosamund and her nursemaid set about preparing the corpse for his coffin. They stripped the nightshirt from the body and gently washed the stiffening limbs with warm water from a pitcher in the fireplace coals. Maybel went to the chest at the bed's foot and drew out a piece of linen. She tore it into a long strip and carefully wrapped it about Hugh Cabot's head and beneath his chin so that his mouth would not hang open. She fixed the linen strip with a small pin, even as Rosamund was pulling her husband's shroud from the same chest where it had been waiting for this moment.

The girl and the woman struggled to wrap the baglike shroud about the body, drawing it up and around him so that he was finally fully enclosed within it. Only his head showed, and it, too, would be covered once it was time for the burial. His long arms had been folded across his chest beneath the cloth. A simple wooden crucifix was laid upon the body. Rosamund reached out to smooth her husband's silvery white hair with a gentle hand. She felt the tears pricking beneath her eyelids once again, and forced them back.

Edmund returned. "Henry is indeed drunk with your wine, niece. I have had him carried to his bed. The men are here with the coffin to carry Hugh to the hall. The bier has already been set up with candles at each corner. The prie-dieu awaits you."

Rosamund nodded, and with a final look at her husband departed his chamber to await his arrival in the hall. When the coffin had been placed upon the bier, she lit the candles herself and then knelt in prayer. "I will pray until he is interred in the ground," she told her servants. "Make certain his grave is dug deep."

"It will be done," Edmund assured her. He looked to his wife questioningly, but she waved him away, and he departed.

"I'll watch with you a while," Maybel said.

"Nay," Rosamund said. "I prefer being alone."

"But child . . . ," Maybel protested.

"I am no longer a child," Rosamund replied softly. "Now go, but come back to me in the hour of the dawn." She knelt down, her knees sinking into the little cushion of the prie-dieu, her hands clasped in prayer. Her back was straight, her head bowed.

Maybel looked at the young girl and sighed softly. Nay, Rosamund was no longer a child, but neither was she a woman grown. What was to happen to her now? She walked slowly from the hall. She knew what was going to happen. Henry Bolton would marry off his niece yet a third time, and a second time to one of his sons. The sniveling little boy he had brought with him would be the new master of Friarsgate, while Rosamund would remain a pawn for Henry Bolton to use. She sighed again. And yet, Maybel thought to herself, had not Edmund said something about Hugh making arrangements for Rosamund's safety? But if she knew Henry Bolton, and she certainly did, he would probably ignore Hugh Cabot's last will and testament. They would be able to do nothing about it.

Troubled, she entered her own bedchamber to find her husband waiting. "You left her alone?" he asked.

"She wanted it that way," Maybel replied. She pulled her veil from her head and sat down heavily. "Lord bless me, husband, but I am weary. And surely my young mistress is even wearier, yet she will pray through the night for her husband's good soul." She paused, and then she said, "Do you think there is anything to what Rosamund says about Henry Bolton being responsible for Hugh's death?"

"He was weak, and he was dying," Edmund said softly, "but I did not think him ready yet to give up the ghost. I saw no marks of violence or physical force that would have caused his death, though. There was even a small smile upon his lips, as if he were amused by something that had been said. Yet his eyelids had been drawn down and closed. I have never, however, known Henry Bolton to be a man of wit." He shrugged. "Perhaps it was just Hugh's time. We will never know for certain, Maybel. So we must be guarded in what we say, and we must make certain our young mistress is also discreet. We can prove naught. What we may think, or even suspect, is another matter."

"What will happen now?" Maybel asked him. "Did you not say that Hugh had made provision for our Rosamund? What did he do that your half-brother will now undo?"

Edmund chuckled. "Be patient, wife," he said with a smile. "I can say nothing until the appropriate moment. Henry will be foiled, I promise you. There will be nothing he can do. Both Rosamund, and Friarsgate, are now safe from him and from his sons."

"If I must wait to learn this miracle, then I shall wait," Maybel said, standing up once again and beginning to unlace her gown. "It is late. The morning will come early. Let us go to bed, husband."

"Agreed," he replied, rising slowly. "Tomorrow will be a long and difficult day for us all."

Chapter 3

"Your husband is dead?" Henry Bolton feigned surprise. "Well, then, niece, I shall not need his signature to marry you to my son, shall I? You are now once again in my charge, *and* you shall do as I tell you to do." He smiled toothily at her. "Let us get him in the ground and be done with it, Rosamund. I think, perhaps, I shall take you home with me so you may be guided in your behavior by my good wife. Hugh has given you ideas unsuited your station. I shall, against my better judgment, put Friarsgate back into the keeping of my father's bastard, Edmund Bolton."

"My husband will be buried before sunset," Rosamund told him. "His tenants wish to do him honor and have been coming into the hall since the dawn." Her voice was measured and controlled although her heart was racing nervously. She would run away before she would allow Henry Bolton to remove her from Friarsgate, but she trusted Edmund, and she had trusted Hugh, God rest his good soul, to save her.

"If you wait to bury him late in the day, Rosamund, then I must remain here another night," Henry complained.

"Hugh Cabot was a good husband to me, and a good master over the people of Friarsgate, *uncle*. He will be allowed an honorable burial, not hustled off havey-cavey into his grave because it is inconvenient for you and your brat," she answered him sharply. Her face was pale, and there were dark circles about her eyes.

"Oh, very well," Henry replied surlily. "Another day away from Mavis' carping is to the good, I suppose, but we depart on the morrow, Rosamund."

"I cannot possibly be ready to leave Friarsgate with only a day's notice," she protested. "Besides, Hugh's will is to be read by the priest on the morrow."

"His will can make no difference to you, niece!" Henry was getting a belligerent look upon his beefy face.

"He was my husband, and had charge over me. I must obey his last wishes, uncle, whatever they may be," she answered him sweetly.

"His wishes are of no account. I am your nearest male relation. You are in my charge now, as you have in reality always been since your parents' deaths. The law, both man's and God's, says you must do what I command you to do, Rosamund. I will hear no more about it!" Henry Bolton reached for his cup of wine, swallowing down a great gulp of it. Then he slammed the cup upon the high board. "Do you understand me, niece? I am your master. None other."

"My husband's last wishes will be honored," Rosamund said firmly. Then she turned and left the hall.

"Little bitch," Henry grumbled. "I think I shall whip her every day until her overproud spirit yields to me. And then she shall be whipped twice weekly just to remind her that I control her fate. Yes," he said smiling. "The wench needs firm and frequent discipline. She shall get it in my house." Besides, he thought, he had noticed upon his arrival that his niece was truly growing breasts. That meant her juices must be flowing. Best to keep a tight rein over her lest she disgrace the family. She would be a virgin when his Henry mounted her for the first time, or he would know the reason why! He intended to put his son to his niece when the boy reached the age of twelve. Seven more years.

Rosamund would be twenty then. He would obtain a chastity belt and lock his niece up in it to assure her virtue. It was his grandson who would inherit Friarsgate, and none other. He glared at the servant by his elbow, and the man quickly poured more wine into his cup. Henry Bolton drank it down. Then, with a belch, he arose and stared down at the body of Hugh Cabot.

The Friarsgate folk were moving in an orderly line past his coffin. All wore solemn faces, but some were weeping openly. What had they to cry about? he wondered sourly. Hugh Cabot hadn't been family. He had been married to Rosamund to protect the Friarsgate inheritance. He had probably been soft with them, Henry considered. They mourned him because they feared a harsh new taskmaster, and that was all.

To Henry Bolton's surprise his half-brother Richard was the priest saying the service over Hugh Cabot. "Why did they send for you?" he demanded rudely of his elder sibling. "Where's Father Bernard?"

"Good day to you also, Henry," Richard Bolton said, amused. "Poor old Bernard died three years back. There has been no priest in residence since his passing. Edmund called me for Hugh." The priest looked the youngest of his brothers over with a sharp eye. "You are getting fat, Henry," he said. "Too much food and wine is not good for a body." Richard Bolton was a tall, slender man with an elegant aesthetic face. The black robes of his order, belted with its white silk rope, hung on him as beautifully as court dress.

"Let us get Cabot buried without further ado," Henry snapped. "I must leave tomorrow. I am taking Rosamund with me."

"You cannot depart until I have read Hugh's will," Richard said calmly. Then his eye lit on his nephew. "Is this your son, Henry?"

Henry Bolton the younger had been standing with his thumb in his mouth. Now his father snatched it from between his lips and pushed him forward, saying, "This is Brother Richard, the priest."

"This is my holding," Henry the younger announced by way of greeting the cleric. "The old man died, and now it is mine, but I don't like the wife they have chosen for me. She is bold and speaks meanly to me. You must tell her she will go to hell if she does not respect me. My father says I am to be her lord and master."

Richard Bolton swallowed back the shout of laughter that threatened to erupt from between his lips. His gray-blue eyes danced wickedly, and he very much enjoyed his youngest brother's chagrin at the boy's pronouncement. "Indeed," he said, and nothing more, struggling further with his mirth as Henry the elder cuffed Henry the younger, and the lad set up a great howl and cry.

"You have the will?" Henry demanded. "What does it say? Not that it matters, for Rosamund belongs to me to do with as I please."

"The will shall be read after the feast, as is customary, Henry," the priest answered.

"Oh, very well, make a great mystery out of it if it pleases you, Richard, but it will change nothing," Henry snapped irritably. He turned to his son. "Will you cease that sniveling, boy?" he snarled.

Hugh Cabot was buried on a hillside overlooking the valley. Rosamund kissed his cold lips before they nailed his coffin shut, and she wept for the good man who had been more father to her than any in her brief memory. She stood for a time afterward as the sun set behind the green hills. Then she returned to the hall to oversee the funeral feast for her husband. She stopped a moment to look at her three uncles seated at the high board. Edmund and Richard with their gray-blue eyes, both with almost noble faces, she thought. And then there was

Henry. Plump and dyspeptic, a dissatisfied look upon his fat face, his blue eyes darting to and fro over the hall as if he were taking an inventory of everything there. She took her place between him and his young son.

The meal was gracious, as Hugh would have liked it. There was salmon, its pink flesh studded with rare green peppercorns. There was venison, roasted and in a pie. There was rabbit, goose, and duck, each with a different sauce. There was braised lettuce and tiny boiled onions, fresh bread, butter, and cheese. And afterward the last of the winter apples appeared baked with cinnamon and served with heavy cream. Wine and ale was plentiful, and the entire hall was served the generous meal, much to the delight of those below the salt who had expected little else but pottage and rabbit stew.

When the meal had finally been consumed Henry Bolton said, "Well, priest, what of the will? Not that it will matter, but the formalities should certainly be observed for the law's sake." He leaned back in his chair. "Remember I wish to depart with the morning."

"And so you shall, *brother Henry*," Richard Bolton replied, reaching into his robes, drawing forth a rolled parchment. "Hugh Cabot made this will in his own hand and gave me a copy." He held the cylinder up for the entire hall to see. Then he broke the seal that fastened it together, unrolling it slowly with a great show. " 'I, Hugh Cabot,' " the priest began, " 'do hereby make my last will and testament. I have but one possession on this earth, my beloved wife, Rosamund Bolton. I therefore give my wife into the keeping of my friend and liege lord, Henry Tudor, King of England. This is my last wish, and God have mercy on my soul, Amen. Signed this first day of March, in the year of our Lord fifteen hundred and two.' "

There was a deep silence in the hall, and then Henry Bolton spoke. "What the hell does it mean?" he demanded. "I am Rosamund's guardian as her nearest male relation."

"Nay, *brother Henry*, you are not her guardian," Richard Bolton said. "Not any longer. Hugh Cabot, as Rosamund's husband and legal guardian at the time this will was written, has placed his young widow into the keeping of the king himself. You can do nothing about it. A copy of the will was sent to the king. A brief message was returned that the king was sending someone to take charge of Rosamund. You no longer have any authority over her," the priest concluded.

"You have all plotted against me!" Henry shouted. "You cannot do this! I shall go to the king myself and protest. Hugh Cabot was Rosamund's husband because I made him so in order to protect Friarsgate."

Rosamund suddenly spoke up. "*Protect it for whom?* You have wanted this holding your entire life, uncle, *but it is mine.* I did not die when my parents and my brother died. I did not die when your eldest son, my first husband died. I am, praise God, strong and healthy. It is God's will that Friarsgate belong to me and not to you. I am glad Hugh has done this for me. I dreaded with every fiber of my being the thought I should have to be in your *tender* charge again."

"Be careful, girl, how you speak to me," Henry Bolton warned her. "When I tell the king the truth of this matter he will give you back to me, and then, Rosamund, you will learn the things your late husband never taught you. *Obedience. Your place in life. Modesty. The virtue of silence in the presence of your betters.*" His face was almost purple with his outrage. His weak blue eyes bulged from his head. "This will cannot stand! I will not allow it!"

"You have no choice," Richard said quietly.

"Why would the king give such favor to

Hugh Cabot?" Henry wanted to know. "A younger son of no importance, a soldier, a wanderer, and finally thanks to my late wife, Agnes, may God assoil her soul" — he crossed himself piously — "a place in her brother's house as little more than a servant. The king does not give his friendship to such a man as this."

"Ah, good sirs, but he does," came a voice from the far end of the hall, and there upon the steps they saw a tall stranger, still in his traveling cloak and gloves. "I am Sir Owein Meredith," the gentleman said, stripping off his gloves as he walked into the hall and toward the high board. "I have been sent by his majesty, Henry Tudor, to investigate this matter of Rosamund Bolton and the Friarsgate inheritance." He strode between the tables, handing off his cape to a servant while another servant hurried up with a goblet of wine for the visitor. "Which among you is Hugh Cabot?" he asked authoritatively.

"My husband died a day ago, sir," Rosamund responded. "This is his funeral feast. We have finished, but let me have my servants bring you some food. You are surely famished after your time on the road."

"Many thanks, lady," he told her, thinking she was a very pretty young girl, just barely out of her childhood, but she had dignity and was well-mannered. "I have not eaten since morning, and should indeed appreciate a meal." He bowed to her.

She liked him immediately, Rosamund considered. He had the same sort of elegant features that Hugh and her two elder uncles had. His face was long, as was his nose. His lips were narrow, but his mouth wide. He was obviously not a man who sat idle, for his skin was bronzed, and there were small wrinkles at the corners of his eyes. But he was not close enough for her to tell their color. His hair, however, was a dark blond, and cropped short. His face with its square chin was clean-shaven, and there was just the faintest of dimples in the center of that chin. He was, Rosamund decided, rather handsome.

"Come, sir, and sit with us," she invited graciously, and as he moved to join them she shoved her cousin Henry the younger from his seat, hissing at him, "Get up, you little toad, and give your place to the king's man!"

The boy opened his mouth in protest, but then he looked at Rosamund, and his mouth snapped shut as he scrambled from his seat.

"Thank you, cousin," Rosamund murmured sweetly.

If Sir Owein had noticed the byplay between the two he was far too polite to mention it. A plate of hot food was brought to him, and he began to eat while his hosts waited politely for him to finish. His goblet was filled and refilled, and when he had mopped the last of the gravy from his pewter plate, he finally felt warm for the first time in almost two weeks.

"Well, sir, why have you come?" Henry Bolton demanded rudely.

To their surprise Sir Owein spoke directly to Rosamund. "My lady," he began, "your late husband, Sir Hugh Cabot —"

"*Sir Hugh?*" Henry Bolton began to laugh. "The man was no lordling, sir. Is it possible you have come to the wrong house?"

"Sir Hugh Cabot was knighted on the battlefield many years ago. He saved the life of Edmund Tudor, the king's father, when he was eighteen," Sir Owein said quietly. He did not like the man with the fat face. He was rude, and had he been worth the trouble, which Owein Meredith concluded he was not, he would have thrashed him soundly.

"It is true," Edmund Bolton said.

"*You know?*" Henry Bolton was incredulous.

"Hugh was a modest man. While he was

grateful to his friend for knighting him and the honor it entailed, he was landless. He thought it presumptuous for a man without property to use a title, and so he did not. But he had the right to do so, and our niece is Lady Rosamund, Henry," Edmund Bolton concluded, staring hard at his youngest sibling.

Sir Owein turned back to Rosamund, whose face was a mixture of surprise and shock. "Your husband knew he faced his death, my lady. He wished you to be safe from those who might attempt to steal your rightful inheritance. So it was that he sent to the king and asked him to accept you as his ward with all the responsibilities it entailed. King Henry has graciously agreed, and has sent me to bring you to his court. I have been told that your uncle Edmund Bolton will have the stewardship over Friarsgate in your absence. Is this satisfactory to you?"

Rosamund nodded slowly. "Aye, sir, it is. But why must I leave Friarsgate? It is my home, and I love it here."

"Do you not wish to meet the king, my lady?" Sir Owein asked.

"*Meet the king?*" she repeated. "I am to meet the king?"

"The king is placing you in the queen's household for now, my lady. Eventually, when your period of mourning is over, a suitable husband will be chosen for you. It is then you will return home, my lady," Sir Owein explained to the girl. "The queen is a gentle and good lady with daughters of her own. Princess Margaret is about your age, I would think. Princess Katherine, Prince Arthur's wife, is now a widow, as are you, and then there is the Princess Mary, a most charming imp."

"I have never been farther from Friarsgate than a few miles," Rosamund said. "This place is all I know, sir. Could the king not leave me here to be as I have always been?"

"Your late husband, Sir Hugh, believed it better that you leave Friarsgate for a time," Sir Owein replied. "You need not come alone, my lady. You may bring a servant with you."

"There has been a mistake," Henry Bolton finally spoke up. "My niece is in my charge, and so she has been since the deaths of her parents, my elder brother Guy and his wife. Hugh Cabot had no authority to give her wardship to the king. You must return to him and tell him this, Sir Owein. Rosamund is to wed with my son Henry."

"I would never marry that snot-nosed brat," Rosamund cried.

"Was not Sir Hugh Cabot Rosamund's

legal and lawful husband?" Owein Meredith asked them.

"He was," Richard Bolton said. "I have in my possession the betrothal papers he gave to me when they were wed."

The king's man turned to Rosamund. "Do you remember a ceremony being performed, my lady? Before a priest?"

"We were wed on the twentieth day of October, by Father Bernard. I wore a gown of grass-green jersey. It was just before Hugh's sixtieth birthday. Aye, I remember my wedding day to Hugh Cabot. It was a happy day for me," Rosamund said quietly.

"This being so, you have no authority, legal or otherwise, over your niece, Henry Bolton," Owein Meredith said. "Her husband held the authority, and he has passed it to the king. The Lady Rosamund will return with me to Richmond and take her place in the queen's household."

"I . . . I . . . I shall go to the courts!" Henry Bolton sputtered angrily.

Owein Meredith was forced to laugh. "The king, sir, is the highest authority in the land, but if you wish to pursue the matter, you must do so," he told him.

"When must I leave?" Rosamund asked the king's man.

"Not until you are ready, my lady," the

knight assured her. "I realize that a lady decamping her household for another place needs time to gather her belongings, arrange her affairs, and pack. I am in no hurry to return south. Cumbrian springs are fair as long as the Scots don't come over the border to pillage, but there is little danger of that now. The king has arranged a marriage between his eldest daughter, the Lady Margaret, and the Scots king, James IV. You must take your time so you will be comfortable in your new life. And, of course, you will need horses as well as your servant. There is a great deal to be done, my lady. It will surely take several months before you are ready to depart. Perhaps we will leave in late summer or early autumn, eh? In the meantime I will send to the king to tell him of the death of his old friend and that his young widow is grateful to be in his royal charge." Sir Owein smiled at Rosamund, and she saw that his teeth were even and white.

"You must bide a while with us, sir," Rosamund said to him. "You have traveled a long distance, and have yet again a long distance to return. Rest yourself and your beastie for a bit before you go."

"I shall, my lady, and you have my thanks for your hospitality."

"Prepare a room for our guest," Rosamund ordered a servant. Then she signaled that more wine be served. She could see her uncle Henry was already well in his cups while Henry the younger had fallen asleep by her chair beneath the table. She looked at Sir Owein and asked in a soft voice, "Am I really safe from him?" nodding to Henry Bolton. "He cannot force me to wed his odious little son?"

"Nay, lady, he cannot," the king's man said softly. "It is my understanding that your late husband wished otherwise. Normally I should not be privy to a communiqué between the king and a correspondent, but his majesty wanted me to have a clear understanding of the situation here at Friarsgate so I would not unwittingly or unknowingly circumvent your husband's wishes."

Tears sprang to Rosamund's amber eyes. "He was such a good man, my Hugh," she said. "My uncle never considered that when he married me to him. His only interest was to protect Friarsgate until he had a son he might foist on me. My first husband was also his son, you know. I hardly remember John. Do you think there are many widows of thirteen, for I shall be thirteen in a few weeks, who have outlived two husbands and are still virgins?"

Owein Meredith choked upon his wine at this revelation. He struggled to regain his breath as a fit of coughing overtook him. Then he burst out laughing, and he laughed until the tears rolled down his cheeks. About him those seated at the high board stared, surprised. When he finally regained control over himself he managed to say, "The wine went down the wrong way."

"But your laughter?" Richard Bolton inquired, curious.

"Something the Lady Rosamund said. I doubt anyone else should be amused, but her words struck me humorously," he explained, not wanting to repeat what his young and ingenuous hostess had just said. Her uncles might not find it amusing at all. He looked closely at Rosamund. She was hardly a woman, but then neither was she a child. Her skin was like cream, smooth and fair, with no blemish, the faintest touch of rose in her cheeks. Her amber eyes were fringed with dark lashes. Her hair was a rich auburn in color, parted in the center, a rather flat coiffure with a braid down the back. She had a straight little nose within her oval face, and a mouth that was inclined to be generous, the lower lip fuller than the upper.

"Why do you stare at me so?" Rosamund asked him.

"Because I find you very pretty, my lady," he answered her frankly.

Rosamund colored. She had never received a compliment from a handsome man. Oh, Hugh had always told her she would be a beauty one day, but Hugh loved her. She was like his child. "Thank you," she replied shyly. "Should a lady at court express gratitude for a compliment, sir?" she next inquired of him, curious.

"A lady at court would acknowledge such acclaim with a gracious nod of her head, but say naught," he told her with a small smile. She was a very charming girl, he thought, and quite unaffected. Then he continued, "But if the praise were from someone the lady did not favor she would ignore it and turn away."

"Will they understand me at court, Sir Owein?"

"I understand you," he said.

"But certainly my Cumbrian accent will not be comprehended by some," Rosamund fretted.

"While I am with you," he said, "I will help you to smooth the north from your speech, lady."

"And you will correct my manners if I do what would not be done at court?" She eyed him anxiously. "I do not want to disgrace myself or my family's good name."

"I will gladly tutor you, lady, in all you need to know," he promised her. "And will you trust me when I tell you we must leave Friarsgate and go south? I will give you time, lady, but I realize it will be difficult for you to leave. Will you trust me to know the right time?" He gave her an encouraging smile.

"We will not go too soon?" she queried him nervously.

"I think September is a good month in which to travel south," he replied, again smiling. She was afraid. Of course she was, having never been more than a few miles from her home. It would be an adventure, but Rosamund Bolton didn't look like a girl who would welcome adventure easily. She was a solid girl. A practical girl, as he had already observed.

"Then I will put my trust in you, sir knight," Rosamund answered him finally. "But will the king not expect you back sooner than the autumn?"

Owein Meredith laughed. "Nay, lass, he will not. I am just one of the king's many servants. I am known to be loyal and reliable with any task given me. They know at court that I will return when I have completed my duties. I am hardly important in the scheme of things, my lady."

"A knight is not important?" She was puzzled.

Around the table her uncles listened as carefully as did the girl, except for Henry Bolton, who was already in his usual evening drunken stupor. Both Edmund and Richard Bolton, while relieved that Rosamund had been rendered safe from Henry, wondered if Hugh had indeed made the right decision for Rosamund by putting her in the wardship of virtual strangers. They leaned forward to catch Sir Owein's every word.

"Like your late husband, lady, I am only a younger son. The youngest, in fact. My mother died giving me life. My father died when I was thirteen. My family is Welsh mostly. I served as a page to Jasper Tudor, the king's uncle, from the time I was six years old, then as his squire. I was knighted after the battle of Stoke."

"How old were you then?" Edmund asked.

"I was past fifteen," came the answer.

Edmund caught Richard's eye at this revelation. They silently agreed that they were impressed by this quiet, seemingly gentle man who had been sent to escort Rosamund to court.

"You will certainly be tired by now, sir," Rosamund said, remembering her duties as chatelaine. "One of the servants will escort you to your chamber. You are most welcome at Friarsgate." She turned from him and spoke to a large serving man. "Take my uncle to his chamber now, Peter. Then come back and put my young cousin to bed." She arose from the table. "Sirs, I will leave you to your wine. My day has been a long and sad one." Curtsying, Rosamund quietly departed the hall.

"She prayed the night by her husband's bier," Edmund noted to Sir Owein.

"She is a good Christian girl," Richard chimed up.

"She is very young to know her duty so well," the king's man observed. "She is thirteen?"

"On the last day of this month," Edmund replied.

"The king's mother was six months gone with child and widowed at thirteen," Sir Owein remarked. "The Lady Margaret is an amazing woman. I imagine she was very much like your niece at that age."

"She has no experience of the world," Edmund said.

"Has she been educated at all?" the knight asked him. "Those who do the best at court are those who are well-schooled."

"Hugh taught her to read and to write.

Father Bernard taught her church Latin. Her knowledge of mathematics is excellent. She keeps all the accounts for Friarsgate, and has done so for the past two years," Edmund explained. "She is probably more educated than most country lasses, sir. What does she lack?"

"I will teach her French and proper Latin," Sir Owein said. "Can she play a musical instrument? The court loves music. Young Prince Henry is most adept at composing both music and words. He is an amazing young boy. His father meant for him to be the Archbishop of Canterbury one day. Now with Prince Arthur's passing, he will be king. Not that the king teaches the lad how to rule. He has, perhaps, too tight a hold over his throne and his son." Then Sir Owein flushed. "I become garrulous with your excellent wine, sirs. I should find my bed." He rose and followed the servant assigned him from the hall.

The two brothers refilled their own cups from the pitcher on the table and sat in silence for a time. Then Richard said, "How much of what Hugh plotted did you know, Edmund?"

"Not a great deal," Edmund admitted. "He told me he had a highly placed friend, and he would make a will placing

Rosamund into the care of his friend. He said with her beauty and the Friarsgate inheritance, his friend would probably make an excellent marriage for our niece. That such a marriage would add luster to our name. I had no idea that his *friend* was the king. When he realized that he would probably not recover, he sent a message south. I think he meant to tell me, but he died so unexpectedly."

"You did not expect him to die?" Richard was puzzled.

"Yes! Yes! But not quite when he died," Edmund answered. "Rosamund believes there was foul play, but I could find no real evidence of it. Still, the coincidence of Henry's arrival and Hugh's death is to be considered. Henry came to get Hugh to place Rosamund back into his *tender* care. I do not think he was pleased to find Rosamund so outspoken. He would have blamed Hugh."

"Do you think our half-brother had a hand in Hugh Cabot's death, Edmund?" the priest asked his eldest brother.

Edmund sighed. "I do not like to believe it, but I cannot say I believe him entirely innocent. Nothing can be proved of him, however, no matter what I think, or what Rosamund thinks."

Richard nodded, understanding. "Should we be content to allow our niece to go to court?" he wondered aloud.

"Hugh wanted what was right and good for his wife. She is becoming a woman, Richard. Maybel tells me the lass' courses are now upon her. She is a virgin. Her next marriage will be consummated, and she will birth heirs for Friarsgate. Henry's son is just a bairn. Our niece would be into her twenties and the boy barely old enough, if she were forced to wait for him. Better she go south to court, and when she returns with a husband, she will bring new blood to strengthen the Boltons of Friarsgate. Besides, it is past time that our half-brother ceased to lust after these lands. They belong to Rosamund."

"Once she leaves, once she sees the world beyond Friarsgate, she may not be satisfied to remain here," the priest said thoughtfully.

"Nay, Rosamund will return, and she will remain. She gains her strength from Friarsgate, brother," Edmund told him.

"I will depart for St. Cuthbert's tomorrow," Richard said. *"After I have seen Henry off."* He chuckled. "Henry will awake on the morrow with a sore head, I predict. He drank more tonight than he usually does. He will wake hoping it was all a dream and that Rosamund were still in his clutches. I should not get such enjoyment out of his discomfort. It is hardly Christian of me, yet I do get enjoyment from his discomfort," Richard admitted. "You will let me know when Rosamund is leaving so I may come and bid my niece a proper farewell."

"I will," Edmund said.

"Then I will bid you good night, brother Edmund," the priest said, and he stood up. "Sleep well and dream of angels." He walked from the hall, his black robes showing no indication of motion so smooth was Richard Bolton's gait. The white robe belt about his midsection stood out in stark contrast to the dark fabric of his robe.

Maybel came from her place by the fire and joined her husband. "You should have told me," she said, rebuking him.

"You were not sitting so far from the table that you did not hear me tell Richard that I knew little. Hugh kept his plan close, and he was right to do so. Henry may cry to the heavens, but he cannot claim any collusion between Hugh Cabot and me."

"He will claim it, but if you are being candid with me, husband, then he cannot prove collusion just as we cannot prove he had a hand in Hugh's death," Maybel returned.

"You must go with her to court," Edmund said.

"I know," Maybel returned, "though it does not please me to leave you, Edmund. Still, it will not be forever, and you are a man more concerned with his duties than a well-turned ankle," she said, chuckling. "I can trust you, Edmund Bolton, for there are those only too willing to tell me should you stray from the straight-and-narrow path."

He chortled and put an arm about her. "And you, wife? Will you be tempted by the excitement of the court?"

"*I?*" Maybel looked offended by the question.

"Well," he said with a grin, "you are a fine figure of a woman, lass, and when you smile, ah, it cheers a man, it does."

"Flatterer!" She swatted at him affectionately and colored becomingly. "My only concern will be in seeing to Rosamund's safety and happiness. I must make certain there are no more marriages arranged for anyone's good but our lass'."

Edmund Bolton nodded. "Aye," he said, "we don't want her married off to someone like my brother Henry."

"God forbid!" Maybel cried. "I will see that she isn't. Naught will happen too quickly, I am certain. Rosamund is not important enough to be bothered with by the high and mighty. She will join the queen's household and do what she is told to do. She will not be considered until they need an heiress to marry off," Maybel concluded wisely.

"And you, my good wife, will be there to guide her," Edmund noted with a smile.

"Aye, I will, Edmund," Maybel responded.

In the morning Henry Bolton came slowly into the hall of the manor house as his half-brother had predicted. His head hurt him dreadfully and he had almost forgotten the arrival of Sir Owein, the king's man.

"Where is Rosamund?" he asked. "She is to go with me today, is she not?" He sat down at the high board and shuddered as a trencher of bread filled with hot oat stirabout was placed before him.

"Do you not remember?" Richard Bolton said quietly. "Our niece was put into the king's care, and will go to court in the late summer with the knight sent to fetch her."

"I thought I had dreamed it," Henry Bolton said sourly. "Richard, you know the law. Is what Hugh did legal? Do you want our niece leaving Friarsgate and being wed to some stranger?"

"There is no talk of marriage," the priest replied.

"But eventually they will use her, for her inheritance is a goodly one," Henry almost moaned. He pushed away the trencher.

"You have used her," Richard noted quietly. "Ever since Guy and Phillipa died you have employed every means at your disposal to retain control over Rosamund's inheritance. You married her to your eldest son first. Then to Hugh Cabot. Now you would force her to wed with your second son, a child of five. You care nothing for Rosamund. Only what she possesses. Hugh was right to see her sent from here for a while. Let her see a little bit of the world. Let her meet the rich and mighty. Our niece is a winsome girl, Henry. Perhaps she will have the good fortune to fall in love with the man chosen for her. Perhaps she will make powerful friends, which cannot hurt this family. When she returns home to us, and she will, I hope she will be happy. But whoever becomes Rosamund's new husband, she will be happier than if she were yet in your clutches. Now go back to Otterly Court and mind its business. You have three sons and three daughters to provide for, as well as Sister Julia, who you may be pleased to learn, thrives at her convent."

Henry Bolton's stomach rolled with his nausea. "Julia," he muttered, "was provided for when she went to St. Margaret's."

"Your oldest daughter will take her final vows in another few years, brother. I will expect you to deliver a goodly sum to the convent at that time in thanksgiving. The sum you settled on the child when you placed her there has hardly been enough for her maintenance. St. Margaret's is not a wealthy house. She is a godly young girl."

"She was an ugly baby," Henry said gloomily. "Mavis' girls are beauties, every one of them, but they will still need good dowries."

"Which you, undoubtedly, planned to siphon from Friarsgate's resources," Richard observed dryly. "Otterly has good lands, Henry. Small, but fertile. You've helped yourself liberally to the livestock here over the years. Your flocks and herds should be good and they should be thriving. Make them even more prosperous. Your girls will have the dowries they deserve one day. They are yet bairns and you have time if you are industrious. You are a Bolton, Henry! Where is your pride? It seems to have disappeared in your quest for what is not yours."

"Has becoming a priest made you forget from whence you sprang, *bastard?*" Henry snarled at his oldest brother.

"Our father gave me life on the loins of his mistress, it is true, Henry, but it is our father in heaven who has made me equal to any. I would also remind you that both our father and your mother treated *all* of his sons with love," the priest replied.

"You will want to begin your journey back to Otterly shortly," Edmund Bolton interrupted quietly. "Shall I have cook pack some bread and meat for you to eat as you ride? Ah, here is your son."

"I'm hungry," Henry the younger announced loudly as he climbed up to the high board. "My mother always feeds me oat stirabout and cream in the morning."

"Your mother isn't here!" his father snapped. "We're leaving!"

"But I'm hungry," the little boy repeated.

"Then sit down and eat what I cannot," his father shouted, grabbing up his son and slamming him into a chair.

Henry the younger dipped the spoon into the trencher that had been set before his father. *"It's cold,"* he whined.

"Then don't eat it!" Henry the elder roared back.

"But I'm hungry!"

"Fetch Master Henry some hot oat stirabout," Rosamund said, coming into the

111

hall and hearing the commotion. "Uncle, take some wine. It will help your head. Father Richard, I thank you for the mass this morning. It was lovely to hear mass in our wee church again."

"Would you like me to send you a young priest, niece?" came the question. "There is a lad at St. Cuthbert's who I believe would suit admirably. A manor such as Friarsgate should not be without a priest. A small remuneration and his keep will suit Father Mata."

"*Mata?*" Henry Bolton looked suspicious. " 'Tis a Scots name."

"Aye," Richard answered.

"You would bring a Scot into Friarsgate? Are you mad?" Henry said loudly. "You know the Scots are not to be trusted."

"He is a priest, Henry," came the calm reply.

"Priest, or no priest, he will have clansmen eager to steal our sheep and our cattle! I will not have it, Richard!" Henry declared.

"Mata is the son of a Scot's lass, the bastard of the Hepburn of Claven's Cairn, and an English man-at-arms," Richard said. "He has been raised at St. Cuthbert's and knows naught of clan. His mam died giving birth to him, Henry. He is as English as you are. Before she died his mother asked that he be called by the Scots for Matthew, so he would know his whole heritage. He is a gentle young man and will serve Friarsgate well."

"And the decision is not yours to make, *uncle*," Rosamund spoke up. "Edmund? What do you think?"

"I would welcome a priest again," Edmund said. "There are several marriages that need to be celebrated, and quite a number of bairns in need of baptizing."

"But a Scot?" Henry said again.

Edmund pierced his youngest brother with a fierce look. "Richard says that this priest is a good man for Friarsgate. When was our brother ever disloyal to the Boltons, Henry?"

"I will welcome Father Mata," Rosamund interjected quietly.

"He shall be sent, niece," Richard told her with a small smile.

Rosamund now turned to her uncle Henry. "I have my work to do, uncle. There is seed to be distributed this morning, and I must supervise. I wish you a safe journey home. You will remember me to your good wife and my little cousins." Then she looked directly at Henry the younger. "Good-bye, boy," she said, and hurried from the hall.

"I'm glad I don't have to marry *her*," Henry the younger said. Then he continued shoveling hot oat stirabout into his mouth.

"Shut up, you lackwit!" his father shouted savagely, and his fingers closing about the cup that had been placed before him, he gulped down the wine in it, but he did not, as Rosamund had promised, feel any better.

Chapter 4

Owein Meredith was surprised to learn that while his young hostess was hardly educated to court standards, she was learned in many other ways. She would never, he thought to himself, be truly happy anywhere but at Friarsgate. Rosamund Bolton had become an integral part of the manor. Despite her youth she was looked up to by her tenants and her workers. In this, her uncle Edmund and her late husband Hugh Cabot had been successful. Once Henry Bolton had gone, everything done on the manor was done in Rosamund's name only, thus reinforcing her position as Friarsgate's heiress.

From the spring on, Owein had watched, fascinated, as she oversaw every facet of the manor's varied life. Friarsgate was practically entirely self-supporting. Several varieties of grain, vegetables, and fruits were grown. It was Rosamund who determined which fields would be tilled and which would lie fallow. It was she who set the schedule for pruning the orchards. Cattle were raised for milk and meat, for sale or for barter. At Hugh's suggestion Rosamund grew interested in raising horses. But it was the sheep that gave Friarsgate its greatest source of wealth, for Friarsgate wool was highly prized.

The manor possessed a small mill with a resident miller. There was a small church and a priest's house that was now swept out, to be prepared in anticipation of Father Mata's arrival. There were meadows and pastures for the cattle, the horses, and the sheep. There were woodlands, common pastureland, and common woodlands where Rosamund's people might hunt and fish or graze their own livestock. Most of Friarsgate's people had once been serfs, but Rosamund's grandfather had freed them. While a few families had departed Friarsgate to seek their fortunes, most had remained to be treated as free men and women.

Friarsgate was not the holding of a great family, but it was considered a very large manor and its young mistress an heiress of value. Its land was well-watered and always lush. Rosamund learned to move her flocks and herds so her acreage did not become overgrazed and barren. It had never been a poor place. Over the past few years they had become very prosperous. Not one family among its peasants was without a cow, or some pigs, or poultry. And while free to make most of their own decisions, the men and women of Friarsgate were fiercely loyal to the Boltons, going even so far as to give them three days a week of labor, as they had in days of old. The free men and women of Friarsgate also had their own strips of field as their serf ancestors once had. Here they raised their own produce to feed their families and sold what was excess. And it was in the manor court that Rosamund, with Hugh and Edmund's guidance, had learned to settle disputes among her people.

Owein Meredith, raised among the powerful, had forgotten that such manors as Friarsgate still existed. His childhood, prior to entering the household of Jasper Tudor, was a memory mostly forgotten, if he indeed remembered it at all. And so as the summer progressed he watched in fascination as Rosamund went about her duties as mistress of this prosperous manor with such seeming ease that she almost made it appear simple. But that he knew it wasn't. Early each afternoon after the main meal of the day had been served and eaten, he schooled the king's new ward, teaching her French and proper Latin, the kind spoken and written in the court.

It was difficult for her, he saw, as foreign tongues were not easy for Rosamund, but she struggled to learn with such a fierce determination that he was forced to admire her. The only women he had admired prior were the king's mother, Margaret Beaufort, the Countess of Richmond, who was known as *the Venerable Margaret;* and the king's wife, Elizabeth of York. These were women of a certain age and vast experience, yet this young girl put him in mind of them both. Like the queen, she was dutiful and gentle. Like the Venerable Margaret, she was determined and loyal. Owein Meredith found himself worrying how a country girl like Rosamund, born without a great name or powerful relations, was going to fit in at the court of King Henry VII. And then it dawned upon him that other than delivering her to her guardian, he was not responsible for Rosamund Bolton.

The summer was drawing to an end. Lammas came and with it the harvest. Lammas was a holiday in which bread played the chief role. At sunrise Rosamund exited the house with a dish of crumbs she had made by breaking up one quarter of a year-old loaf. She scattered it for the birds. Her tenants were all invited into the hall for a meal, most of the dishes consisting of bread or flour. There was a piggling stuffed with bread, nuts, cheese, eggs, and spices; entrails — a sheep's stomach stuffed with bread, vegetables, eggs, cheese, and pork; mortrews — a meat dish made with beef, eggs, and bread crumbs; barley bannocks — a bread made from barley, flour, salt, and buttermilk; a large wheel of cheese; and frumenty pudding made from wheat and milk, spiced with cinnamon. Lamb's wool, a spicy cider with floating apples, was also served.

And when everyone had eaten their fill the games began. Outside the men played a game in a meadow that involved kicking a stuffed sheep's bladder about from one end of the field to the other. There was an archery contest. Then men shot long bows at straw butts that had been set up in front of the house. The winner was presented with a large mug of ale. And as the afternoon wore on they returned to the hall where the married women played a game called Bringing Home the Bacon. Each in her turn was given a negative and hypothetical situation that involved her husband. It was up to each woman to negate this unfavorable state and turn it into something positive. The wife who could accomplish this while amusing her listeners was declared the winner and rewarded with a blue silk ribbon. At day's end everyone was presented with a small baked loaf made from the newly harvested grain. They departed to their homes with the loaves, each of which had a lit candle embedded in it.

The day after Lammastide Owein spoke with Rosamund about their departure. "You must consider a date for our leaving, my lady," he said. They had been sitting in the hall practicing her French, and he spoke to her in that language.

She looked up startled, and so he knew that she had comprehended his words, but she said, "I am not certain of what you said, Owein Meredith. Please speak to me in our own good English tongue."

"You are a little fraud," he gently teased her, still in French. "You understand me quite well, Rosamund."

"I don't!" she cried, and then clapped her hand over her mouth, realizing that her answer had confirmed his suspicions. "The day after Michaelmas," she said in English.

"That is almost two full months, Rosamund," he told her.

"You said the king did not need you back,

sir. That you were not important. Neither am I. The king but fulfills a debt to Hugh Cabot. Why should we have to go at all?"

"Because if we do not your uncle may petition the king to regain custody of you, Rosamund," he explained quietly. "Such a petition might not even be seen by the king, but rather one of his secretaries, who would squeeze monies from your uncle in exchange for his cooperation. Voila! Your wardship would once again be in the hands of Henry Bolton, and Henry the younger would be your spouse. If this is what you truly want, then I shall return south, tell the king, and it shall be done. But if you choose to honor your husband's wishes for your future, you will cease being afraid of the unknown, and come with me." The hazel-green eyes looked directly at her, questioningly.

"But Michaelmas is when I rehire my servants for the coming year and pay them," she half-whispered.

"Edmund will do it," he said. "September first, Rosamund."

"It is too soon!" Her amber eyes began to fill with tears.

Owein Meredith gritted his teeth and hardened his heart against her female wiles. Women, he had learned, always wept when they wanted their own way. "Nay, it is not. It gives you almost a full month to pack your belongings and delegate your authority to Edmund and the others. You have known this day was coming. I have been here almost four months, Rosamund. I have been gone from court for almost five. It is time. Think of Maybel. She, too, must prepare. She leaves her husband in your service."

"I have rarely been off my own lands in all my life," Rosamund told him, and he nodded, understanding. "I am not really afraid, but I am not a girl who welcomes adventure, sir."

He chuckled. "There is little adventure in a journey between Friarsgate and the king's court, Rosamund. And for you there will be little, if any adventure, in the queen's household. You will be assigned certain duties, and your days will be filled with them. It will not, I fear, be very exciting for you. The only difference is that you will not be the mistress there."

"But when will I come home again?" Rosamund wondered plaintively.

"After a term of service the queen may release you to visit Friarsgate. Or you may return with a husband, chosen for you by the king. You do understand that eventually you will be wed again and probably to a man that the king wishes to do honor."

"In other words my husband shall once again be chosen for me," she responded, feeling not just a little irritated by the fact.

"That is the way of the world, Rosamund," he answered her.

"I had hoped this time to marry a man I loved," she said to him.

"Perhaps you will," he replied. "Or perhaps you will learn to love the husband chosen for you, but no matter, you will do your duty, Rosamund. I have come to see that you are that kind of girl."

"Aye," she said, nodding, "I am. Still, it would be fun if I could follow my family's motto," Rosamund told him. *"Tracez Votre Chemin."*

"Make Your Own Path." He nodded, too. " 'Tis a good motto, and who knows, my pretty lass? Perhaps one day you shall make your own path. None of us knows what the morrow will bring, Rosamund. Despite our desire for sameness, life is always filled with surprises. I shall tell Edmund Bolton that we are leaving on the first day of September. Eh?"

She nodded, but he could see the reluctance in her agreement. "How many carts may I have for my things?" she asked him.

"We will take one packhorse," he told her, and then he explained, "You will have no privacy, or very little of it at court, Rosamund. You and Maybel will sleep in a large room with the rest of the queen's women and their servants. Your small trunk will be all the space you will have for your possessions. Everything must be portable so that it can be moved quickly from place to place. The king and queen never remain in one house for long. They travel from their palaces in London to Greenwich to Richmond to Windsor and back. And come the summer the court will go on the annual royal progress, which involves visiting the great and small noble houses. You will have even less accommodation then for yourself or for your things, if you are invited to go. With luck you will be left behind. At least then you will have a bed."

"It doesn't sound very comfortable," Rosamund noted dryly.

"It isn't." He grinned. "Bachelor knights have it the worst, I can assure you. If we are lucky we end up sleeping in the hall by the fire. If not, 'tis the stables or a dog kennel for us."

"At least you're warm," she replied. "You are not married? No," she answered her own question, "you would not be. You are like my Hugh and cannot afford a wife."

"Aye," he agreed. "My eldest brother inherited from our father. My next brother serves the church. I have three sisters. One is wed and two are nuns. I was fortunate to have obtained my place in Jasper Tudor's household. My father knew his high steward. He was my mother's kinsman, and he felt sorry for me."

"Did you not miss your family?" Rosamund asked Owein.

"Nay. My father was angry that my birth took my mother's life. I don't think he spoke more than a dozen words to me before I left his care. My sister Enit was his eldest child. She was twelve when I was born. It was she who saw to my welfare until she wed when I was four. How I missed her!

"My eldest brother had no use for me, for he desired above all things to please our father. As our sire ignored me, so did he. And no sooner had Enit wed, than my eldest brother was married. By the time I was six, his wife had already birthed the next heir, much to father's delight; my middle brother was in his monastery and my two other sisters in their convent. Only I remained. The loose end, my brother called me. Then Jasper Tudor's high steward came to pay his respects to my mother's grave. He saw the problem I presented to my family. When he left, I went with him. There was a place for a page in his master's household, he told my father. Of course my sire was only too glad to see me go."

"How fortunate that was for you," Rosamund noted. Why, his childhood had been even worse than hers. When she had children she would make certain they were loved and cherished.

Owein Meredith laughed. "There was no place, but my kinsman made one for me. Then he taught me my duties. He was more father to me than my own was. Without him I don't know what would have happened to me. Because of his kindness I strove to advance myself."

"You became a knight, of course," Rosamund said.

"I served in Jasper Tudor's household until his death. I was a page until I was thirteen. Then I became a squire to my master," Owein explained to Rosamund.

"When did you become a knight?" she asked him. It was the first time he had spoken so openly and in depth about himself. She was absolutely fascinated. He was like Hugh, and yet he wasn't. And he was handsome. Hugh, she remembered, had had a yellow streak in his white hair, which he had told her had been fair in his youth. Owein Meredith was a darker blond, but there were golden streaks in his hair, which she very much liked.

"As I told your uncles," he responded, "I was knighted at the age of fifteen. It was after the battle of Stoke when we defeated the pretender, Lambert Simmel."

"What was he pretending, and why was it necessary to fight him?" Rosamund inquired curiously.

Owein chuckled. "It was before you were born, Rosamund. The previous king, Edward IV, had had two sons. Their uncle took his brother's throne upon the death of King Edward. It was said England did not need a child king. But there were two young boys. They disappeared, never to be seen again. It is said their uncle, King Richard III, murdered them, secreting their bodies in the Tower of London."

"*Did he?*" Rosamund's amber eyes were wide. What a terrible thing to have done!

"I do not know," Owein said. "No one does. But it was after that that the heir to the other royal house, Henry Tudor, returned to England to fight King Richard, overthrow him, and take his place upon the throne. He married the Princess Elizabeth, elder sister to those two unfortunate princes, and heiress to the royal house of York. Their union ended a hundred years of warfare here in England, Rosamund, but then in 1487 a young man claimed to be son of the Duke of Clarence, who had a stronger claim on the throne than our own King Henry. He was not, of course. The real Edward Plantagenet was imprisoned in London. To prove this the king paraded him through the streets. But it was still necessary to meet and vanquish this Lambert Simmel at Stoke."

"You fought well if you were knighted, sir," she said.

"I did fight well," Owein admitted modestly. "I would give my life for the House of Tudor, for they took me in and raised me, and gave me everything that I have in life," he declared passionately.

"And what is it you do have, sir knight?" she wondered aloud.

"I have a home wherever the king goes, but more important I have a purpose in life in their service," he told her.

"I understand," she replied, "and yet it seems so little in return for your loyalty. You have no home or land of your own. What will become of you one day when you are too old to fight or to serve? What happens to good knights like you, Owein Meredith?"

"I will either die in some battle, or perhaps my brother will give me a home in my last years because it is the honorable thing to do. At that point I would bring honor to him for my years of service to the House of Tudor," he said.

"When did you last see your brother or his family?" she asked.

"I have not seen them since I left my birthplace in Wales," he responded. "But when our father died, my brother sent word. He has not forgotten me, Rosamund."

No, he had probably not, she considered. It could not hurt Owein Meredith's brother to have a friend at court, no matter that his brother was not a man of wealth or real influence. He would know men of wealth and influence, and could even petition the king for his family, should it become necessary to do so. It would be what she would do, Rosamund thought. It was the practical way.

Now the days seemed to speed by in a manner that was almost disconcerting. Rosamund cherished each moment she had remaining at Friarsgate. She did not look forward to leaving. If only Hugh had consulted her, but Owein Meredith was correct when he said if she remained her uncle would find some way to regain her person and his hold on her manor. Leaving was the price she must pay for being the heiress of Friarsgate. She was a little frightened, although she would never allow anyone to know it. *Tracez Votre Chemin.* She would make her own path.

Maybel wondered and fretted over what to take, cramming as much into the small trunk as she could. Sir Owein suggested to Edmund Bolton that it would be advisable to put a certain amount of gold with a London goldsmith for Rosamund to draw upon, for she would quickly learn that her wardrobe was too countrified and it would need to be remedied. He would direct Maybel to an honest and reliable mercer for fabric, but she would need coin for her purchases. Better they not carry too much currency with them to be robbed. The monies could be taken to Carlisle, and from there it would be credited in London with a reputable goldsmith.

The route was carefully mapped out and a rider sent ahead to arrange accommodations in convent and monastery guesthouses along their way. The trip would take a fortnight or more, depending upon the weather. While Sir Owein was used to traveling great distances, he knew his young charge was not. She had, he knew, never been off her own lands but a couple times to purchase cattle or horses in the company of her husband and uncle. She had never even seen a real town.

Rosamund spent her last few days at Friarsgate riding from one tenant to another, bidding them farewell and reminding them that while she might be gone, Edmund would be in charge in her absence. It was he who would speak for Rosamund Bolton. They were to obey him without question. Some of her people offered her small gifts made with their own hands: a comb of sweet applewood carved with two doves amid the apple blossoms, a needle case that had been made from a piece of leather and lined with a scrap of Friarsgate red wool felt. The woman who had won the blue ribbon at Lammastide had embroidered it with a bit of gold thread she had obtained from heaven only knew where. She now returned it to her mistress saying, "It's beautiful, my little lady, but 'tis more suited to yerself than to an old shepherd's wife. See, I've made it with stars so you will remember the night sky over Friarsgate when you are among the high and mighty. You will come back to us, lady?" Her worn face was anxious.

"As quickly as they will let me, Mary, I swear it!" Rosamund said with fervor. "I would as soon not go, but I fear my uncle would attempt to gain my custody and my lands again. This would seem to be the only way that I will be safe."

Mary nodded. " 'Twould seem the gentry has their problems, too, my lady," she observed.

Rosamund laughed. "Aye," she agreed. "Nothing, it seems, is simple in this life."

Several days before she was to go her uncle Richard came from St. Cuthbert's, bringing with him the young priest, Father Mata. Rosamund liked the young man immediately, as did Edmund. He was of medium height and a bit plump. His blue eyes danced below his bushy eyebrows. He had rosy cheeks in a baby face. The hair around his tonsure was a bright red, and his skin was very pale.

He bowed to her, saying, "I am grateful, my lady, for the living that you have offered me."

"It is not great," Rosamund told him, "and you will always be busy. But you will be well-fed, and the roof of your house does not leak, nor is the chimney drafty."

"I shall say the mass daily," he promised her, "and celebrate All Saints' Day, but first the unchurched must be properly wed and the bairns baptized."

"Aye," Rosamund agreed. "We are all glad you are here."

"And when will you return, my lady?" the

young priest inquired.

"When I am permitted," Rosamund replied.

"Come," Edmund said, seeing his niece beginning to lose heart again, "let us take the good father to his house, Rosamund. I have an old woman, Nona, who will keep it swept. You will take your meals in the hall with me, Father Mata. I will welcome the company." He moved off in the direction of the priest's cottage next to the little church.

The morning of September first dawned cloudy and windy with the rain obviously imminent before the noon hour. Nonetheless Sir Owein insisted that they keep to their schedule. He knew that another day would make it no easier for Rosamund, whose fears were now threatening to overwhelm her despite their best efforts. Father Mata said an early mass even before the sunrise, had they even been able to see the sun. The fast was broken in the hall, fresh trenchers of bread, still warm from the ovens and hollowed out for the oat stirabout, were set at each place. Rosamund could not eat. Her stomach rolled nervously.

"You cannot go the day without a good meal," the king's man told her firmly. "This will be the best meal you have for many a day, my lady. The guesthouses of the church are hardly noted for their food or the quality of their drink. You will be sick the day long if you do not eat now."

Rosamund dutifully shoveled the hot cereal into her unwilling mouth. It lay in her stomach like a stone. She sipped her goblet of watered wine. It lay sour atop the oat stirabout. She nibbled at some cheese, but it tasted salty and was dry. Finally she arose, reluctantly. "We had best start," she said.

Her house servants lined up to wish her Godspeed. She bid them good-bye with tears in her eyes, and the women among them began to weep. She walked through the door of the manor house. There outside her mare awaited. Rosamund turned suddenly. "I have forgotten to say farewell to my dogs!" She ran back inside.

They waited patiently for her return, but when she did she said, "I wonder if Pusskin has had her litter yet. I must look in the stable before we go." And again she disappeared.

"Put her on the horse, Edmund, when she returns," Maybel said irritably. "My bottom is already hurting from this beast, and we have not gone a step yet."

Edmund and Owein laughed.

Rosamund reappeared. "Did you pack the embroidered ribbon, Maybel? I am certain I saw it on the floor of my bedchamber. I had best go back and see to it."

Edmund Bolton took his niece by the hand, quickly leading her to her mount. His fingers closed about her waist as he lifted her up into her saddle. "Everything is packed, Rosamund," he said sternly. He handed the lead from his niece's mare to Sir Owein. "Go now, lass, and Godspeed! We will all look forward to your return, which will come all the sooner if you will go now." Then he smacked the horse upon its rump and watched as it moved off.

"I want to hear no gossip when I return," Maybel told her husband. "Take care of yourself, old man. Wear that flannel I sewed for you on your chest this winter or you'll catch an ague for certain."

"And you, woman, don't go flirting with all those handsome gentlemen at the court. Remember you are my dear wife," he responded with a warm smile. "You're a bit bossy, lass, but I'll miss you."

"Humph!" she snorted, and then turned her horse away from him, following after Sir Owein and Rosamund.

Rosamund had been off her lands but twice in her life, and both times no farther than a few miles from her home. Her husband and her uncle Edmund had taken her to a horse and cattle fair. Once she had gone to a wool market. She had never spent a night away from Friarsgate, nor from her own bed. Had Hugh known what he was doing when he had put her into the custody of a virtual stranger? She almost wished her uncle Henry had prevailed and she was still at Friarsgate. *Almost.*

As her initial fears wore off, Rosamund actually began to enjoy the ride. And mindful of the fact his charge had never spent an entire day on horseback, Sir Owein stopped in midmorning so they might stand and stretch, and eat the food that the Friarsgate cook had prepared and packed. And Rosamund found that her appetite had returned as she ate roasted capon and rabbit pastries still warm from the oven, bread and cheese and crisp pears from her own orchards. They rode on to stop again at a small convent in midafternoon. The rain had finally caught up with them. As they were expected they were welcomed, but Sir Owein was sent to the guesthouse for men, while Rosamund and Maybel remained with the nuns. They were, however, the only visitors that night.

It was that first evening that Rosamund

realized the truth in her guardian's words. Their meal consisted of a thick pottage of root vegetables served them in a small trencher of brown bread and a narrow wedge of hard cheese. The ale was bitter, and they drank little. Their bedding was not much better. Two pallets, their straw mattresses flattened down with much use and somewhat bug ridden. In the morning they were served oat stirabout, which they ate with wooden spoons from a common pot. A single slice of bread was given them to share. When Sir Owein had offered the donation, they departed.

The walled town of Carlisle was the first real town that Rosamund had ever seen. Her eyes grew wide as they passed through the Rickard's Gate. Her heart beat faster as they traversed the narrow streets, its houses side by side with no gardens to be seen. They moved down the High Street, crossing south to the church of St. Cuthbert's, which was allied with Richard Bolton's monastery, and in whose guesthouses they would spend the night.

"I don't think I like towns," Rosamund said. "Why does it stink so much, Owein?"

"If you look carefully in the streets, lady, you will see the contents of the town's night jars as they make their way in the gutters to the sewers," he explained.

"My cow byres smell better," she responded.

"Come, lady," he teased her, "a country girl such as yourself shouldn't mind a few odors."

Rosamund shook her head. "Do town folk like being so closed in?" she wondered aloud. "I do not like it at all."

"The town is walled to prevent invaders from breaking into it," he said. "There is much to steal here, and the Scots are still quite near. Carlisle is a place of safety for many in the countryside hereabouts. And from here a defense can be mounted effectively."

They departed Carlisle the next morning, much to Rosamund's relief, traveling south once again through a corner of Westmorland with its bleak moorlands, hills, and lakes into Lancastershire with its forests and deer parks. They rode, Sir Owein told them, along a road that had been constructed by a people called Romans over a thousand years ago. They moved through Cheshire, a flat county despite the hills that bordered it, and on into Shropshire, where the weather became distinctly autumnal. She was glad for her blue wool cape with its hood.

Rosamund liked the black-faced sheep

she saw grazing in the fields of Shropshire. Their wool, she told Sir Owein knowledgeably, was even better than Friarsgate wool. She hoped, she said, to eventually purchase a flock, although such sheep were difficult to come by, as their owners were reluctant to part with them. Still, if she could find a breeding ram and just two fertile ewes it would be a start.

"Here I am taking you to court, and you are thinking about breeding sheep," he laughed.

"I know Hugh meant to protect me and expose me to more of the world," Rosamund replied, "but I am a country girl at heart. I hope I shall be allowed to return home quickly. From what you have told me I doubt I can be of any importance to the king or any use to his family. When I meet the king I shall suggest to him that he let me go home immediately. When I wish to wed, should I ever find a man to suit me, I shall not do it without his royal permission."

"I do not know when you shall meet the king," Owein told her. "At least not right away. You are wise to understand that you have no real place among the mighty, Rosamund." Had she grown prettier since he first met her last spring? he wondered to himself. Having spent time at Friarsgate he

139

understood her desire to remain there. He suddenly realized that he would have liked to remain there. It was not easy being in service all of your life.

"Will I like being at court?" Rosamund asked him. He had been staring at her so hard that it made her uncomfortable. She sought to gain his full attention once again.

His greenish eyes met hers. "I hope so, Rosamund," he told her. "I should not like to see you unhappy." Having met Henry Bolton he fully understood Hugh Cabot's desire to protect Rosamund from him; whether removing her from her home was the solution, he was unsure.

The roads in Staffordshire were dreadful and poorly maintained, especially considering one must use them to travel south. It began to rain once again and the road they were on flooded badly. There were not enough river crossings. It took them almost a full hour to traverse a small bridge one afternoon, so heavy was the local traffic. The wooden span creaked and groaned beneath the heavily ladened carts, the horse traffic, and a small herd of cattle. The countryside was heavily forested with ancient woodlands, but the meadows, where they found them, were particularly lush. However, ugly open pits where coal and iron were mined spoiled some of the countryside. They had now been on the road over two weeks, but Sir Owein was pleased that they were making excellent time, considering his two female companions were not used to such travel.

Warwickshire was beautiful to Rosamund's eye with its fine pastures and meadows. The market towns, of which they learned there were eighteen, were prosperous and busy. Rosamund was now used to the towns, but she still opined to Maybel, who was quick to agree, that she would rather live in the countryside than in a town. They moved on across Northamptonshire, which seemed strangely isolated and rural in comparison to the other counties through which they had passed. Herds of cattle and sheep grazed in meadows that were still verdant and green at September's close. As was Buckinghamshire, where, Sir Owein told her, cattle and sheep on the last stage of their journey from Wales to London were stopped and fattened.

They came to the town of St. Albans in Hertfordshire, and knowing she would have little time for pleasures soon, Owein took both Rosamund and Maybel to see the saint's shrine at the great abbey. He was England's first saint and had been a Roman soldier. Rosamund had never been in a church like the abbey. The great stone edifice soared above their heads. The stained-glass windows cast multicolored dappled shadows upon the stone floors. Neither Rosamund nor Maybel had ever before seen colored glass.

"How Father Mata would marvel at such beauty," Rosamund said. "One day I shall put such windows in our wee church, though not as fine or large, of course."

"They would be even lovelier unencumbered by other buildings, and with the pure light of Cumberland shining through them," Owein noted quietly. "I think I shall miss your Friarsgate."

"Perhaps you will be assigned to escort me home," Rosamund said hopefully. "Mayhap I shall return in the spring."

"Then you are resigned to spending your autumn and your winter at the court," he remarked.

"It would seem I have not been given the choice, have I?" she said with a half laugh. "When will we get to London?"

"We will go to Richmond first," he answered her. "I suspect, as it is the king's favorite place, he will be there to hunt. If he is not there they will know where he is. Another day on the road, Rosamund."

The king, however, was at Richmond. As they approached the palace through the park they could see his standard and the red Pendragon banner flying from the towers in the brisk afternoon breeze. Beyond they could see the Thames River sparkling in the sunlight.

"Stop! Please stop!" Rosamund begged her escort. She brought her horse to a halt and stared with eyes wide. Finally, after a few moments, she said, "It is so very big. I cannot live in a place that is so very big. How will I find my way about?" She was, he could tell, close to tears.

Owein dismounted and lifted Rosamund from her mare. "Let us walk a ways together," he said. "Maybel, you come, too." And he lifted the older woman from the back of her beast, setting her upon her feet gently.

Maybel shook her skirts and rubbed her bottom. "Ah, sir, that is much better," she declared.

Her companions laughed, and then Owein took Rosamund by the hand, and they walked together, leading their horses with Maybel following.

"We have been traveling almost a month," he began. "I realize that never having been far from your beloved Friarsgate all you have seen has been very new and perhaps just a bit frightening for you. Towns, abbey churches, and now a palace. It is a big place, but in a short while you will know your way about easily."

"Are all the king's houses so very big?" Rosamund asked him.

"Some are bigger and some are smaller," he told her. "Richmond is built on the ruins of a palace called Sheen. It burned to the ground on St. Thomas night three years ago. The king and his family were in residence for Christmas, but everyone escaped the flames. The king, however, loved this place so much that he rebuilt a fine new palace here. It has all the most modern conveniences and is quite frankly one of the nicest royal residences, although I do have a fondness for Greenwich and Windsor, too. Here you will actually have your own bed, Rosamund. When the queen comes to Richmond, there is room for all of her ladies. You will never be left behind when she comes here, as happens more often than not when the royal household travels about from one residence to another."

"But what will I do here? I do not enjoy being idle," Rosamund responded. She eyed the great palace nervously. *Oh, Hugh!* she thought silently, *why did you do this to me?*

Couldn't I have remained at home and still been protected from Uncle Henry?

"You will do whatever task the queen assigns you, Rosamund. A queen has many needs. That is why she has so many ladies."

Rosamund grew silent now as they walked along, her amber eyes taking in the great cluster of buildings ahead of her. The palace faced the river to the south. They now approached it across the greensward from the north. Richmond spread out to the east as far as Friar's Lane; beyond that one could see the convent of the Observant Fathers that the king had founded two years previously. The palace was built of brick with towers at each corner and more towers set at various angles about the structure and in the midst of the buildings. The gates were made from heart of ash, studded with iron nails and held closed each night by means of heavy iron bars. The left-hand gate, Owein told Rosamund, led into the Wine Cellar Court with its open tennis courts beyond which stretched the privy garden. The garden was surrounded by a twelve-foot-high brick wall and filled with fruit trees, roses, and other flowering vines. There was a menagerie of carved stone beasts, lions, dragons, and the like. Behind the privy garden was a fairly good-size orchard that con-

145

tained a dovecote and a gallery that led to the privy lodgings.

The main gate to Richmond, which was on the right, led into the Great Court. They remounted their horses now and rode through into this court. Above the gateway was a great stone plaque into which was carved the king's arms, the Red Pendragon of the Tudors and the Greyhound of the queen's Yorkist family. They dismounted, the two women following Sir Owein across the paved courtyard. A liveried servant had magically appeared and now carried their belongings as he trotted along behind them.

"The buildings about this court are for the king's gentlemen and the wardrobe," Owein said as he led them through a turreted gateway into another courtyard. "This is the Middle Court," he explained.

The two women stared. In the court's center was a great fountain carved around with lions and dragons and griffins and other magical beasts. There were red and white roses planted about the fountains, which ran with crystal water. The bushes, in their sheltered location, were still in goodly bloom.

"There the Lord Chamberlain lodges," Owein said, pointing to the left, "and the prince's closet as well. Behind them is the chapel royal. And here to the right is the queen's closet," he told them, pointing to a two-story brick building.

Rosamund and Maybel followed Sir Owein into the building. A servant in the queen's livery immediately came up to them.

"This is the Lady Rosamund of Friarsgate in Cumbria. She has been made a ward of the king," the knight said. "I was instructed to fetch her from her home and bring her to the queen's house. I am Sir Owein Meredith, in the king's service."

"Come with me," the servant said, and hurried off without so much as a backward glance.

They followed after him as he led them up a flight of stairs and down a hallway, flinging open a door at its end. The chamber was filled with women of various ages. In a large upholstered chair, her feet upon a velvet stool, sat a sweet-faced lady who, seeing her visitors, beckoned them forward.

"Sir Owein, isn't it?" she said in a gentle voice.

The king's man knelt and kissed the queen's hand, "It is good of you to remember me, your highness." Then, at her nod, he arose and stood before Elizabeth of York.

"And who is this pretty child you have

with you?" the queen asked. Her blue eyes were curious.

"This is the Lady Rosamund Bolton, widow of Sir Hugh Cabot and heiress of Friarsgate in Cumbria. Her late husband put her into the king's care, you may recall. I was sent to fetch her several months ago and was told she was to be put into your charge. We have only now arrived, your highness."

"Thank you, Sir Owein," the queen said. "You may tell my husband you have returned and that you have properly discharged your duty. He will be happy to see you back. No one challenges him at chess quite like you do." She smiled, and immediately her face was transformed into a thing of beauty. She extended her hand to the knight again.

He kissed it and was thus dismissed. He turned briefly to Rosamund. "I will leave you now, lady. Perhaps we will meet again." He bowed to her, and with a friendly wink at Maybel, left them.

Don't go! She wanted to scream it aloud. She and Maybel stood seemingly alone amid the queen and the other women in the chamber. Then suddenly the queen fixed her gaze upon the girl and spoke.

"It was a long trip, I expect," she said.

"Yes, madame, it was," Rosamund replied, curtsying.

"And you are terrified by all of this, I expect," the queen noted in her gentle voice.

"Yes, madame." Rosamund felt close to tears.

"I remember how frightening it was the first time I was sent away from home," the queen remarked. "Yet in a short time you will feel right at home among us, my child. At least you speak the language. My late son's widow is not particularly conversant in our tongue or any tongue but her own. She is a Spanish princess. There she is across the chamber, surrounded by those black crows she brought with her from Spain. She is a good girl though. Now, what shall we do with you, Rosamund Bolton of Friarsgate?"

"I don't know, your highness," Rosamund said, her voice quavering.

"Well, first you must tell me why your husband put you into our care," the queen gently pressed the girl standing before her. "And who is your companion?"

"This is Maybel, your highness. She is my nursemaid and raised me. She left her husband to come with me," Rosamund explained. "And I did not know that Hugh, may God assoil his good soul, was placing me into your care until after his death. He

149

did it to prevent my uncle Henry from marrying me to his five-year-old son and stealing Friarsgate from me. Uncle Henry has wanted Friarsgate ever since my parents and my brother died when I was three. He married me to his eldest son, but John died of a spotting sickness. Then he arranged my marriage with Hugh Cabot because I was yet a child and Hugh an old man. He thought to keep me safe for his next son, who wasn't even born then. But Hugh was a good man. He saw what my uncle was about. As my husband it was his right to decide my future before he died. He sent me to the king to protect me," Rosamund finished in a great rush.

The queen laughed softly. "But you wish he hadn't, don't you, my child? Still, we will indeed protect you from such a man as your good husband wished. Eventually we will find another good man worthy of you, Rosamund Bolton. Now, what shall I do with you?"

"I don't know, your highness," Rosamund said forlornly.

"You are too big to go into the nursery with Mary. You look to me to be about my daughter Margaret's age. How old are you, Rosamund Bolton?" the queen asked.

"I was thirteen years this past April

thirtieth, madame," came the answer.

"You are six months older than my daughter Margaret. She is the Queen of the Scots, having been betrothed to King James several months ago. I could put you with her for a short time. She is to wed her king next summer. Perhaps then these wars between us will cease," the queen considered. "Yes, I shall put you with Margaret and with Katherine, my son's widow. You are all of an age. You will be a companion to them both for the time being. Princess Katherine." The queen beckoned to the girl across the room.

The princess arose from her seat and hurried to her mother-in-law. She curtsied deeply. *"Sí, madame?"*

"Katherine, this is Lady Rosamund. She will be a companion to you and to Queen Margaret. Do you understand?"

"Sí, madame. I understand," the seventeen-year-old Katherine of Aragon answered.

"Take her to Margaret and explain my wishes," the queen said.

"Sí, madame," came the reply.

"The word is *yes,* Katherine," the queen said wearily, "You must speak English, my child. You are to be Queen of England one day."

"I thought that her husband was —"

Rosamund stopped at the stricken look upon the queen's face.

"It is hoped," the queen finally said, "that Katherine will wed with our second son, the new heir, Prince Henry."

A serving woman placed a goblet of wine in the queen's hand and said, "Run away, lasses. The queen is tired with the new life she will soon bear. She needs her rest."

"Yes," Elizabeth of York said. "You are dismissed, Rosamund Bolton. I welcome you to our household and hope that you will be happy with us." Then she closed her eyes.

"Come!" There was a tug on her skirts.

Rosamund turned and followed the Spanish princess, who led her from the queen's chamber. They were suddenly surrounded by four ladies in black who jabbered at the princess in their foreign tongue.

"Your language is difficult for me," the older girl said slowly, "but I speak better than they suspect. One learns more by feigning ignorance, but you will say nothing, Rosamund Bolton, eh?"

Rosamund giggled and replied, "Nay, your highness, I will not tell on you. Who are these ladies with you?"

"My duennas," was the answer. "They are each from good families, but act as serving woman, companion, and conscience for me, especially Dona Elvira. They make no effort to speak English and can sometimes be very tiresome. Is your nursie like that?"

Rosamund nodded. "Sometimes," she said, "but I would honestly be lost without Maybel. Where are we going?"

"To my sister-in-law's apartments. When Arthur died and they brought me back to court, they put me in there with her. What will happen when she is sent to marry the King of the Scots next summer I do not know, but I doubt that either you or I will remain in such fine accommodations then. We will let this young queen decide where you are to sleep, as it is her lodgings to which we have been assigned." Katherine of Aragon stopped before a double door and opened it, stepping through.

Rosamund followed and found herself in an exquisite chamber with pale paneled wooden walls. The windows were hung with heavy velvet drapes of deep blue. The fireplace was flanked by pink marble angels. It burned with a fragrant applewood fire.

"Margaret," Katherine called, "I have brought us a new companion."

The door to an inner room swung open, and a beautiful girl, her look proud, her hair a glorious golden red, her deep sapphire eyes sharp with curiosity, stepped forth. "We are crowded enough as it is," she said pettishly.

"This is Lady Rosamund, and she is a ward of your father's, the king. Your mama has sent her."

"Your gown is very dusty and quite old-fashioned," Margaret of England said as she walked slowly around Rosamund. "But I expect we can do something about that. What do you think, Kate? Turning her into a lady of fashion will keep us amused while everyone goes hunting."

"You are most rude!" Rosamund burst out angrily. "I have been traveling close to a month to reach here. And we have no need for fashion in Cumbria among the sheep. Clothing is for warmth and modesty. I wish I were anywhere but here right now!"

Margaret burst out laughing. "Oh, thank the gods you are not some milk-and-water lass like our good Kate. She bores me to death sometimes with her goodness. You won't bore me. You come from the north? Do you know any Scots? I was betrothed to James Stuart last summer and am now their queen. I am to marry the king next summer. He's very old, but they say he is a tireless lover. I certainly hope he is. You will sleep with me, Lady Rosamund of Cumbria. Now, say thank you, and we will get you out of that dusty old gown as quickly as possible. We cannot go to dinner with you looking like *that*."

Chapter 5

For the first time in her life Rosamund had friends of her own generation. Although Katherine of Aragon was almost four years older than she was, Margaret of England was just half a year younger than Rosamund. Katherine was shy and reserved. Margaret was haughty, bold, and outspoken. She had not, of course, been crowned yet, but her betrothal had made her a queen, and she was every inch a royal. Still the girl from Cumbria managed to get along with the two princesses, treating them with a mixture of awe and respect. In return the two princesses treated their new companion as one of them, educating her and guiding her through the intricacies of court life.

Margaret Tudor, whose intimates called her Meg, was oddly kind despite her pride and her volatile nature. She was far more so-phisticated than Rosamund. But Rosamund had a greater knowledge of the average man's world and was more practical. They complemented each other. The queen was pleasantly surprised, for the princess, her second child, had always been a headstrong creature, quite prone to finding trouble. In Rosamund's company she seemed to settle herself. Her rebellious spirit grew calmer.

"My mother thinks you are an angel," Meg said, laughing as they sat in the privy garden a month after Rosamund's arrival. "She says you have been a good influence on my behavior."

"You do as you please, Meg; there is no secret to that," Rosamund replied with a small smile, "but if you have been encouraged to follow my behavior then I am honored."

"You are not a prig like Kate," came the reply.

"Kate, I have learned, is but a product of her upbringing. The Spanish seem to be terribly strict with their daughters. She is the way she is because of it, as I am the way I am because of my late husband."

"What was he like? Was he a good lover?" Meg demanded, curiously.

"I was six when we wed, and too young when he died for us to have had a physical relationship," Rosamund explained, blushing. "Hugh was a father to me more than he was a husband."

"My grandmother bore my father when she was our age," Meg said. "You have not met her yet, but you will. They call her the *Venerable Margaret*. I am named after her, of course. I do not know if I like her. Sometimes she frightens me. She seems to love me though. She is very wise and very powerful. The most powerful person in the kingdom next to my father."

"Where does she live?" Rosamund wondered.

"She has a house in London called Cold Harbour, and several other houses scattered about the countryside as well. There are apartments here at Richmond for her, but she will not come until Christmas. We're going to Windsor soon, but we'll be back at Richmond for Christmas. When I was little it was Sheen, the old place, but it burned down one winter. Our father rebuilt Richmond in its place. After, we shall probably winter in London, as mother's child is due in February," Meg informed her companion.

"Why do you not remain in one palace?" Rosamund asked. "It seems more trouble than it is worth going from place to place."

Margaret nodded. "I don't disagree with

you, but it is our way to show ourselves to the people in this manner. And too, wherever we are, it is the responsibility of the neighborhood surrounding us to provision us. One area could not be expected to do that year-round. So we go from place to place. Wait until you see Windsor," she said, giggling.

"Poor Maybel," Rosamund replied with a grin. "She is just recovering from our trek from Cumbria. Now we are going to move again? I know she is faithful to me, else she would go directly home to her husband." Then Rosamund sighed. "Do you think they will find a husband for me by the time you must go north to Scotland next summer?"

"You are a prize to be given as a small reward to someone the king wishes to honor," Meg said bluntly. "That is what royal princesses and girls of property are. We are sugarplums, spoils to be doled out. I have known this since I was old enough to understand who I was. Now that is what you are. You are not from a great family, it is true, Rosamund, but your lands are great and from what you have told me, fertile. You have large flocks of sheep, herds of cattle, and horses. It is serious enough wealth that your minor lineage can be overlooked. My father, who is a clever man, will give you to a husband sooner rather than later. It will be a man he trusts, and one who can be of further use to him and to the crown along the Scottish border, you may be sure."

"It seems so cold," Rosamund noted.

" 'Tis no more calculating than your uncle seeking to control you and your lands by marrying you to a little boy," Meg responded. Then she said, "Have you ever been kissed? I haven't. If you have, tell me what it is like."

"You mean a passionate kiss such as from a lover?" Rosamund said. "Nay, I have not been kissed."

"You mean that Sir Owein did not attempt to seduce you?" The princess was most disbelieving. "He is very handsome. Did you not notice? Of course you did! Why, you are blushing!"

"He never kissed me," Rosamund denied, "but, aye, I thought him very handsome, *and* he said I was pretty."

"They say the ladies all like him. Were he not so poor he would be an excellent husband for any wife," Meg confided.

"Why do the ladies like him?" Rosamund wondered.

"He is very kind and gallant," Meg said. "He knows how to laugh at a good jest. He is very loyal, and he is in my family's favor.

But as a man wants a woman of property, so too, a wise woman wants a man with property. Poor Sir Owein. It is not likely that he will ever wed."

They decamped Richmond, first for London where the king liked to celebrate All Hallows' Eve, All Saints' Day, and All Souls' Day. They came by barge, cruising the river to Westminster Palace in the city of London. The king's barge came first. Both he and the queen, in open view of the crowds lined up on either side of the riverbanks to cheer them, were dressed in full regalia including their crowns. Prince Henry was with them as he was now the heir. They cheered him, for he was handsome and personable and obviously enjoyed their adulation. Rosamund had yet to meet young Henry Tudor, who was two years her junior.

The spectators nodded their approval as the queen was quite visibly with child. They spoke among themselves about the robust appearance of the new heir, relieved. A second equally beautiful barge carrying the Venerable Margaret followed the king's vessel. The family matriarch, beautifully garbed, waved regally.

After Prince Arthur's death there had been a rumor that Princess Katherine was with child. The rumor was quickly proved false. Now she, Margaret, and their companions rode in the third barge. Rosamund sat with them. Awed, she stared at the city about her. Her fingers nervously fingered her new black silk skirt, and she wondered if her black-on-black-striped bodice with its gold beading and threadwork was perhaps a trifle too elegant for a country girl. Margaret Tudor, however, had assured her it was not, as she helped her new friend into the garment that she had just given to Rosamund.

"If you are going to be my companion, you must look the part," she said. "I've outgrown this bodice and skirt, but they are perfect for you, Rosamund. Hopefully by Christmas we can come out of our mourning for my brother and wear color again. I think so much black makes our skin sallow."

"She's hoity-toity, but has a kind heart," remarked Maybel to her mistress. "Imagine my baby being friends with a princess!"

Poor Katherine with her olive skin looked more sallow even than usual in her black mourning, Rosamund thought, as their barge glided on the waters of the river. She leaned over and murmured softly to Katherine, "I think I look like a crow in all this black, though I mean no disrespect to your late husband."

The princess of Aragon nodded ever so slightly, saying low in her stilted and accented English, "Black is not a color for youth." Meg, however, looked wonderful in her black velvet gown with its gold embroidery and beading. She didn't look unattractive at all, for her milky complexion, like Rosamund's, had rosy cheeks. She waved gaily to the onlookers and was cheered for it. They knew she would soon wed formally with the King of the Scots, which they hoped would mean peace between England and Scotland. The barges began to make for the bank.

Rosamund could scarcely contain herself. "I thought Richmond was big," she murmured, but Meg heard her and laughed.

"Westminster isn't so bad," she said. "We stay in the south wing. Most of the rest of Westminster is the abbey itself and the parliament buildings. Mama prefers Baynard's Castle when we come to London. It is nicer. Being in the city, of course, makes everything seem a bit close. Wait until you see Windsor."

"Who are all those people gathering by the landing quay?" Rosamund asked nervously.

"Oh, probably the lord mayor of the city, his aldermen, and various members of the court," Meg said ofthandedly, "You will meet my grandmother today. There is no one like her, Rosamund, but do not let her frighten you. She expects good manners and respect, but do not grovel. Grandmama hates groveling. She has no patience with it. Everyone defers to her, even the king himself," the princess said admiringly. "I hope I can be like her one day."

They debarked their barge. The king, the queen, the Venerable Margaret, and Prince Henry were ahead of them. Rosamund dutifully followed her companions, almost lost among their attendants. In a smaller family hall the king was embracing his mother, a queenly lady with an elegant carriage and sharp dark eyes. She was dressed all in black, her hair covered by an architectural headdress with a white veil.

"You look pale, Elizabeth," she greeted her daughter-in-law, kissing her on both cheeks. "Are your women seeing you take that tonic I prescribed for you? Young Henry is robust now, but one never knows. We could certainly use another healthy prince."

"I am doing my best, madame," the queen replied with a smile. "Why is it that the responsibility for a child's sex is always placed upon the mother? You are learned, madame. Can you tell me why?"

The king's mother chuckled. "When, my dear Elizabeth, have you ever known a man to accept the responsibility for anything so important? If pressed I should say it is God's will. Still, you must continue to pray for a fair prince, my dear."

"Am I not prince enough, madame?"

All eyes turned to the young boy, standing feet apart, his hands upon his hips. He had red-gold hair and bright blue eyes.

"If you fell off your horse and cracked your pate, Henry, what would we do?" his grandmother demanded. "There must always be at least two princes, in case of an accident."

"I will have no accidents, madame," young Henry Tudor said, *and I will be king one day.*"

"What think you, my son, of this bantam cock you have sired?" his mother chuckled. "He is, I suspect, very much like me though he looks like York."

"He is nothing like you," the king replied, "but I will agree with you that he looks like York, does he not, Bess?"

"He reminds me of my father, aye, but I see you in him also, my lord," the queen answered quietly.

The Venerable Margaret cast a quick look at her daughter-in-law. Bess knew well how to dissemble *and* how to manage her husband. But she was devoted to Henry Tudor. For that her mother-in-law was grateful. "Where is my namesake?" she demanded.

"Here, madame," said young Margaret Tudor, stepping forward and curtsying to her grandmother.

"You look well," Margaret Beaufort noted. "I am glad to see it. And Kate, our Spanish Kate, come and let me see you as well. Ahhh, you all look like wee black crows in your mourning. The young should not have to wear black. Well, there is nothing to be done about it, I fear." Her sharp eyes swept the group of young women with Margaret and Katherine. "And who," she said, pointing a slender finger at Rosamund, "is that pretty child? I do not recognize her."

"She is papa's new ward," Margaret answered her grandmother.

"What is your name, child?" the Countess of Richmond inquired, peering sharply at the subject of her query.

"I am Rosamund Bolton of Friarsgate, madame," Rosamund answered, curtsying nicely. What a regal figure the old lady made, she thought. She was more royal than the queen!

"You are from the north judging by your accent," was the reply.

"Oh, dear," Rosamund said, and then she blushed. She was truly trying to speak properly.

"We have several from the north, child," the Venerable Margaret replied, "There is no shame in it. Do you know the Nevilles?"

"Nay, madame. Until I was brought to court I had never been more than a few miles from my home," Rosamund answered politely.

"Ah," came the understanding murmur. "And who put you in my son's care, Rosamund Bolton? Was it your parents?"

"Nay, madame, 'twas my late husband. My parents died when I was but three. My husband was Sir Hugh Cabot, may God assoil his good soul," Rosamund responded as she crossed herself.

"Indeed! Indeed!" the Venerable Margaret said, crossing herself as well. "Henry! Sir Hugh Cabot once saved your father's life. Did you know that? We must take especially good care of his young widow."

"Yes, mama," the king said dutifully. "While I knew this lass had been put into our care, until today I had not laid eyes on her. She has been with the queen and the princesses."

"Who brought you to court, my child?"

the Venerable Margaret now inquired of Rosamund.

"Sir Owein Meredith," Rosamund said.

"Ah, a lovely man," the Countess of Richmond murmured, a small smile touching her lips. Then she said, "My granddaughter's bodice looks well on you, child." Her sharp eyes had recognized the garment she had given to her grandchild some months back.

"I have outgrown it," Meg quickly replied. "My bosom is too full now, but Rosamund is still quite flat-chested."

Rosamund blushed furiously. She did have breasts! They were just smaller than Meg's ample proportions. It was most infuriating, especially as the princess was several months younger than she was.

"The bodice suits you," the Countess of Richmond noted in kindly tones. Then she turned to her granddaughter. "The Queen of the Scots has a good heart but a thoughtless tongue. No woman wishes to have her attributes compared unfavorably or otherwise, particularly by another woman, Margaret Tudor. I hope that you will recall that when you have come into your own. Scots women, I am told, are extremely proud."

"I will indeed remember your words,

madame," Meg replied, a faint flush just touching her cheeks, although she looked her grandmother directly in the eye.

"It is time to relieve you from a part of your mourning," the Venerable Margaret decreed. And the very next morning Meg found a pair of tawny orange sarcenet sleeves on her bed when she and Rosamund awoke.

"Oh," Meg squealed, picking up the bright silk sleeves. "Tillie!" she called to her tiring woman. "Affix them to my bodice. I shall wear them to mass. They are from grandmama, I am certain!"

"They are, your highness," the serving woman replied, "and she left a nice white pair for Lady Rosamund as well. Shall I give them to her Maybel?"

"Yes!" came the immediate decision. Then Meg turned to Rosamund. "If grandmama says we are coming out of mourning for Arthur, then we will! Mama and Katherine won't, of course, but I am glad to be done with all this black."

"Everything is still black," Rosamund reminded her in practical tones. "Our bodices, our skirts, our headdresses."

"But the sleeves will set us apart from the others," Meg said mischievously. "The gentlemen will notice us and not the others."

"But you are already wed, to all intents and purposes," Rosamund replied, confused.

"But I am not *officially* wed," Meg responded. "Besides, the King of the Scots kept a mistress, Maggie Drummond, who was, I have been told, quite dear to his heart. She was poisoned recently, and her two sisters with her. They all died. 'Tis said King James could not bear to be parted from her. Someone near to him, though who is not known, took matters into their own hands. My marriage is very important to both England and Scotland. My father will not send me north until the matter with the Drummond woman is settled."

"Then why do you wish other men to notice you?" Rosamund asked.

"Because it is fun." Meg laughed, and then with a wicked smile she said, "Perhaps we will see Sir Owein at the mass. He will surely notice you if you are wearing your beautiful white sarcenet sleeves."

Rosamund giggled. "Why should I care if he notices me or not?" She climbed from their bed and padded barefooted across the chamber to wash her face and hands in a silver basin that had been set out for her. Her companion's basin was gold.

"Because you are going to be given a husband sooner than later," Meg replied, "It might be better if you had one who came to live at Friarsgate and didn't have his own lands. Besides, your manor is in the borders, and while I do not expect the Scots to invade England once I am officially their queen, it could not hurt if my father had a man like Sir Owein in the borders. He knows that his knight is loyal and faithful. The northern lords blow with the winds. They can often be feckless and unfaithful."

"But they are English," Rosamund said, puzzled.

Margaret Tudor climbed from her bed and walked across the chamber to where her new friend stood. Reaching out, she patted Rosamund's soft cheek. "You are such an innocent," she said. "I pray that your simple honesty is never tried harshly, Rosamund Bolton."

They did not see Sir Owein at the mass, but several days later when they had been settled at Windsor he actually came to the queen's apartments to inquire politely after Rosamund. Seated near Elizabeth of York, sewing on gowns for the new baby, they saw him enter and heard his words. Meg poked Rosamund, who was blushing furiously as the queen's gentle voice called her to lay her needlework aside and come forward.

"Rosamund Bolton, here is Sir Owein Meredith come to pay his respects to you," the queen said.

Rosamund curtsied to the queen, but knew not what to say at first.

"You are well, lady, and your good Maybel?" he said politely.

"Yes, sir, and I thank you for your concern," Rosamund replied, having finally found her voice. Bravely she met his greenish gaze, and he smiled, which to her surprise set her heart to racing.

"And do you still miss Friarsgate, or has the lure of the court caught you up in its spell?" he questioned.

"The court is very grand, sir, and everyone has been kind, but aye, I miss my home," Rosamund admitted to him.

"Perhaps we will meet again," Sir Owein said, ending their conversation. Then he turned to the queen. "Thank you, your highness, for allowing me to speak with the Lady Rosamund. What reply shall I bring to your good lord?"

"Tell the king I shall eat in my chambers this evening. It is surely a son I carry, for the burden is heavy this time," the queen answered him. "Tell my lord husband that I thank him and will welcome him in my chambers should he care to come."

Sir Owein bowed and departed the chamber.

"He likes you!" Meg said gleefully.

"He was only being polite," Rosamund answered.

"*He likes you!*" the princess repeated, a knowing twinkle in her blue eyes.

"What difference does it make?" Katherine of Aragon whispered. "They will choose whom they please when it is time to marry her off. Best she not set her sights on one man when they will surely choose another."

"Rosamund is not important like we are, Kate," Meg said.

"There is where you are wrong," the Spanish princess replied. "Rosamund's lands are in a strategic location. The man they choose for her will surely be the man they best feel can defend that piece of England. And, too, Rosamund is rich in sheep and cattle. Her person with its lands and goods will not be given lightly, nor will it be given to an unimportant knight with no significant connections. You are wrong to encourage Rosamund to look to Sir Owein. If her heart is engaged there, what agony for her, and misery for the man who is finally chosen to be her husband."

"I cannot help but be a romantic,"

Margaret Tudor responded.

"You are wedding with the King of the Scots in order to keep peace between your two lands," Kate said. "There is nothing more to marriage than one's duty, as you should know better than most."

"Wed first, love afterward, is what my grandmama says," Meg said pertly. "I shall make James Stuart fall in love with me! Just wait and see if I do not, Kate!"

"For your sake, I hope it is so," the Princess of Aragon said.

"Did you love my brother Arthur?" Meg demanded to know.

"He had charm," Kate said slowly, "and he was very intelligent, but he was young yet, Meg. I am not certain he would not have made a better priest than a husband, but we shall never know now. Poor Arthur lies in his grave." She piously crossed herself.

"They say that my father will wed you to my brother Henry," Meg murmured low. "Henry looks at pretty women like a cat contemplating the finch. Papa meant him for a priest, but Henry was never suited for it. And while he stands well over six feet tall now, I believe he is still too young to bed a woman, though I should not doubt if he has begun to try."

"*Meg!*" Kate blushed.

"He is very bold and very proud," Rosamund noted, "but he is also very handsome, I think."

"God's blood!" Meg swore softly so her mother could not hear her. "Do not ever tell Hal he is handsome. He is peacock enough as it is, Rosamund. And his arrogance is boundless! You should have been raised in a nursery with him. Praise God I am no longer there! And Mary is safe from him now, too, as papa keeps him so close."

"Why does he do that?" Rosamund wondered.

"Henry must now learn to be a king," Kate said.

"Nay, papa will not teach him to be king," Meg said. "He keeps him close because he is afraid he will die, and then papa will have no son to follow him. Papa does not like Henry. He adored Arthur and invested all the love he had with our eldest brother. That love died with Arthur. I think papa almost hates Henry for being alive and being so healthy when Arthur is dead and was never very strong," Meg concluded.

"You are too harsh in your judgment of your father," Kate protested. "He is a good and devout man, and has always been good to me."

"You have not grown up with him," Meg countered. "Aye, he can be kind, and he surely loves our mother, but he can also be cruel. I hope you will never see that side of him, Kate. Remember, your papa has not paid all of your dower monies yet. For now my father considers the alliance he made with your parents through your marriage to Arthur still viable. He thinks to wed you to Henry when my brother is older. But if your father does not send the monies owed, my father will cast you aside and look to France for my brother's wife."

"Then I will go home," Kate said pragmatically.

"My father will never let you go until he is absolutely certain you can be of no further use to him," Meg said. "And, too, my father is noted for being tightfisted. He would never return the dower portion that has already been sent. I expect he seeks the rest of it in order to pay my dower portion to King James so he does not have to dip into his own personal funds," she said with a laugh.

They remained at Windsor, that great stone edifice, for almost a month. The king and the court hunted daily, but Rosamund remained by the queen's side for most of her days. Elizabeth was pleased to learn that the young royal ward could read. So Rosamund read to her mistress from a Book of Hours with small poems and prayers written in Latin. Maybel spent her time turning her mistress' few gowns into more fashionable garments with the help of Tillie, who having been with the royal house for all of her life, was very knowledgeable about the etiquette of dressing for court and knew the most current fashions.

They departed Windsor in early December to return to Richmond for the Christmas season, which was known to be the king and queen's favorite holiday. The Twelve Days of Christmas did not begin until the eve of Christmas mass. The customs were much like those at Friarsgate, except on a far greater scale. The number twelve played an important role. There was twelve of everything. Great footed iron candelabra covered in gold gilt, twelve in number — with twelve graceful arms, each burning twelve beeswax candles — were set about the Great Hall. Twelve enormous marble urns, each filled with twelve bunches of green holly, each bunch numbering twelve sprigs of the plant, tied with silver and gold ribbons and full of bright red berries, had been placed about the chamber strategically. The four great fireplaces held enormous Yule logs.

In the king's hall a green line called the *Christmas Threshold* had been drawn. The feast, Meg explained, would not begin until the Lucky Bird stepped over the threshold and into the hall to dance. They waited, almost sick with excitement. The Venerable Margaret had told her son and his wife in her firm but quiet tones that if they wished to continue to mourn Prince Arthur that was their decision, but it was Christmas, and she wanted the young people to enjoy themselves. Particularly as her favorite, Margaret, would not be with them for another Christmas.

So the princess was garbed in an elegant gown of medium blue velvet and cloth of gold. Her beautiful red-gold hair was loose and held only by a crespinette of gold and pearls. Kate had chosen to wear a fine purple velvet trimmed in marten, her thick auburn hair modestly plaited beneath a sheer gold veil. Although hardly as richly garbed, Rosamund felt very grand in her black velvet skirt, the black silk gold-beaded bodice that Meg had given her, and her new white sarcenet sleeves. Her own auburn hair was neatly plaited into a single braid, and she, like Meg, wore a crespinette of gold wire, and small freshwater pearls that the queen had given her.

Suddenly the trumpets in the minstrel's gallery blared, and into the hall leapt a tall gentleman. He was all dressed in green, his costume sewn with small gold and silver bells that jingled and twinkled as he danced. He wore a marvelous feathered masque of blue and green gold gilt that covered his eyes and his nose. Upon entering the hall he danced immediately up to the high board where the king, the queen, the princesses, the Countess of Richmond, and the Archbishop of Canterbury sat. He tipped his hat to the king, and then, whirling about, began to cavort all through the hall, gaily dancing here and there, as the reeds, the pipes, and the nakers, a double-drum, played. At each table the dancer stopped and tipped his hat. The revelers tossed coins into the Lucky Bird's hat and he danced on.

Rosamund took a penny from her pocket. When the dancer reached her table she reached out to drop the penny into the bird's hat. The coin had no sooner left her fingers than the gentleman's fingers closed about her, and pulling her up, he placed a quick kiss upon her lips before dancing off to the laughter of all present. Her cheeks burning with embarrassment, and her shyness, Rosamund quickly sat down again. She wondered if Meg and Kate had seen the dancer's outrageous behavior.

"It's all right, Rosamund," a familiar voice said, and Sir Owein Meredith pushed in next to her on the bench. "Sometimes the Lucky Bird kisses a lady. 'Tis all part of the fun. Ah, I see he left you one of his feathers. That is an honor usually reserved for those at the high board. Here, lass, put it in your pocket. Would you mind if I sat with you?" He smiled at her.

"No, sir, I should like it. I am so used to being with Meg and with Kate that I hardly know anybody else. I am not, of course, invited to the high board."

"No," he answered her. Then, "Ah, look! The bird is about to finish his dance. See, he is going a final time to the high board to importune the king for alms. The coins he collects go to the poor."

The resplendent Lucky Bird gamboled nimbly before the royal family. With a flourish he tipped his hat, first to the Venerable Margaret, feigning amazement at her donation of gold coins. Then to the queen, whom he thanked prettily, and finally to each princess. The king, he saved for the very last. Prancing gaily, he bowed to King Henry VII, and with a flourish presented his beribboned and feathered hat. The king's slender hand passed over the hat. The Lucky Bird cocked his head to one side and then shook it, disappointed. He furiously waved his cap beneath the king's long nose. A wave of laughter rippled through the hall. With a mock sigh of resignation the king reached into his robes and drew out a velvet bag. Reluctantly, he opened it, drawing forth two additional coins. There was more laughter, for the king was known to be tight with his coin. The Venerable Margaret reached out and poked the king, who with another audible sigh dropped the entire velvet bag of coins into the bird's hat.

The Lucky Bird crowed triumphantly. The crowd in the hall roared their approval of the king's actions. Henry VII favored them with one of his very rare smiles. The dancer pranced elegantly up before the Archbishop of Canterbury to present the hat filled with alms to the cleric. The bird bowed. Then he ripped off his feathered masque to reveal young Prince Henry. His appearance was met with cheering. He bowed to his audience a last time, and then took his place at the high board with his family.

"Oh my!" Rosamund said, realizing who had kissed her.

"So now," Sir Owein teased her gently, "you can return home to say you were kissed by England's next king."

"I forget he is a boy, for he is so very big," Rosamund said.

"His grandfather of York, whom he favors, was a big man as well," the knight told her.

"Was his grandfather of York so bold?" she asked.

Owein Meredith laughed. "Aye, he was. May I be allowed to say how pretty you look tonight, my lady Rosamund."

"The bodice is Meg's hand-me-down, and the Countess of Richmond gave me the sarcenet sleeves," Rosamund told him. "Maybel altered my skirt so it would be more fashionable. Meg's Tillie showed her how."

"So you are getting on better now," he remarked. "I am glad for it, Rosamund. I know how much you miss your Friarsgate."

"I hope that when the Queen of the Scots goes north to Scotland in the summer I shall be allowed to go home. I do miss it, sir," Rosamund admitted. "The court is very exciting, but I do not like moving from place to place all the time. I am a stay-by-the-fire, and not ashamed to say it. Besides, other than the princesses, I have no friends. The other girls my age think themselves too high and mighty to be bothered with me. They envy my friendship with Meg. And Kate is little better off than I am, I fear."

"Then make — and keep — her friendship as well, Rosamund. Then when the king's daughter leaves you, you will not, perhaps, be lonely. Besides, it is very likely that one day Katherine of Aragon will be England's queen. It cannot hurt to have such a lady in your debt."

"You give me good advice, sir. And will you remain my friend as well? I should like to believe that you will be my friend forever."

"I should like to be your friend forever," Owein answered her, and his look warmed her, "but someday, Rosamund, you will have a husband again. He may not approve of our friendship. You must be prepared for such a possibility."

"I should never wed a man who would not accept my friendships," she replied. "Hugh taught me that I must think for myself and decide what is best for me and for Friarsgate."

"Mayhap he should not have," Owein said sadly. "Most men are not as modern in their thought as your late husband was. Think of your uncle Henry, Rosamund. Most men are like him."

"Then I shall not marry again," Rosamund told him firmly.

He didn't know whether or not to laugh. He quickly realized that she was in deadly earnest. So he said, "I am certain that you will be able to charm any husband to your way of thinking, Rosamund." She was still so young and so damned innocent. He wondered what would happen to her here at court once her protectress, the king's daughter, departed for Scotland. Rosamund would certainly not be included in her retinue of ladies. She was neither important enough nor well enough bred. She had no significant family connections. She was just another of the royal wards, although she had been fortunate enough to catch the eye of young Margaret Tudor. Owein Meredith didn't know why he cared what happened to this girl, but he did. He certainly was not beginning to harbor feelings for her. He had no right to such feelings — but he realized that he did care.

He did not see Rosamund again until Twelfth Night, the last of the Twelve Days of Christmas. The day began with the choosing of the King and the Queen of the Bean. Twin cakes were brought into the hall. One for the men, the other for the women. Everyone received a slice of their respective cake in the search for the elusive bean. To her great surprise, it was Rosamund who found the bean in the women's cake. At first she was afraid to speak out among so many important females, but Meg, realizing her friend's good fortune, cried out for all to hear.

" 'Tis Lady Rosamund Bolton who has found the bean! Now, who will be her king?"

"I am her king," young Henry Tudor cried out, grinning from ear to ear. "I am the King of the Bean! Bring me my queen!"

Rosamund was brought up to the high board and seated next to Prince Henry. A paper gilt crown, decorated with paste jewels, was placed on her head. A matching crown was put upon the prince's head.

"All hail the King and Queen of the Bean!" the assembled in the Great Hall of Richmond Palace cried enthusiastically.

"Thank heavens 'tis a pretty girl who is my queen," the prince said as the servers began to bring the morning meal into the hall. "I feared when I found the bean that I should be shackled to some crone among the women. 'Tis why I held back admitting my good fortune."

"And had it been some *crone*," Rosamund said boldly, "would you have put your prize back amid the crumbs, my lord?"

"Aye," he admitted with a mischievous grin. "Now, who are you, mistress? I know I have seen you before." He picked up his jeweled goblet and drank down a draught of rich sweet wine.

"I am Rosamund Bolton, your highness, the lady of Friarsgate. My late husband, Sir Hugh Cabot, made me a ward of your father's upon his untimely death last spring. I have been at court just a short time."

"You are friends with my sister Margaret?" the prince asked.

"It is my great privilege to have found favor with the Queen of the Scots," Rosamund modestly responded, realizing as the words flowed easily from her mouth that she was learning, really learning, how to conduct herself at court. She must tell Sir Owein when she next saw him.

"How old are you?" the prince demanded.

"I am a few months older than your sister, the Queen of the Scots, your highness," Rosamund said.

"You are widowed?"

"Yes, your highness."

His look was assessing. "Are you a virgin?" he asked her boldly.

Rosamund blushed to the roots of her hair. "Of course I am!" she gasped, shocked by his question. "My husband was an elderly

186

man, and we were wed when I was but six. He was like a father to me."

Young Henry Tudor reached out and caressed Rosamund's hot cheek, which but increased her embarrassment. However, she could hardly slap him for his insolence, at least not here in public.

"I have discomfited you," Henry Tudor noted, but he did not look in the slightest bit sorry. "I will be king one day, my lady. A real king, and not a Twelfth Night fool. If I do not ask questions, I cannot learn." He smiled winningly at her. "Your cheek is very soft as well as being very warm." His fingers stroked her face, while his other hand offered her his own cup. "Drink a bit of wine, and your little heart will stop racing so quickly. I can quite see your agitation in the pulse at the base of your throat, Rosamund Bolton, lady of Friarsgate."

Rosamund gulped some wine. Then she courageously removed his hand from her face. "You are far too impudent, your highness. I am new to the court, and my education has been lacking in the niceties of polite behavior, but I am certain your manner is far too saucy."

"But I am your king," Henry Tudor said.

"And as your queen I am deserving of your respect," Rosamund swiftly answered him.

He laughed. "You are quick," he told her. "I like that!"

"If I have pleased your highness then I am glad," Rosamund murmured smoothly.

He laughed again. "I kissed you on the first day of Christmas," he admitted. "I think before this last day of Christmas is over I shall kiss you again, lady of Friarsgate. Your lips were sweet as untried lips are wont to be, I have found."

"You are two years my junior, your highness, and you admit to much kissing and the knowledge of tried and untried mouths?" she teased him, a smile on her own lips.

"I do!" young Henry Tudor said enthusiastically. "I have not many years, lady, but look at me. I am bigger already than most men, and I am beginning to sense I have a man's appetite as well."

"Then sir, eat your eggs, for you have more to grow," she told him, laughing, for she was unable to help herself. He was really quite a wicked boy. "Our eggs have been poached in a delicious sauce of cream and marsala wines. I have never tasted anything so good!"

"You may be older than I am," he said with a smile as he dove into the plate before him that had been filled with eggs, "and you may be new to my father's court, but I do believe, my lady of Friarsgate, that you learn easily and will do well here." He began to eat.

"I want nothing more than to return home," Rosamund admitted to him. "The court is very grand, but I miss my home."

"I have many homes," he said, pulling a piece of bread from the loaf before him. He buttered it lavishly and ate it.

"I know," she replied. "I have been to Richmond, Westminster, and Windsor so far. They are very beautiful and very grand."

"We also live at Baynard's in London. My mother far prefers it to Westminster, which is really cramped for us; and we have apartments at the Tower, another castle at Eltham, and one at Greenwich," the prince boasted as he ate the second helping of eggs served him and two large slices of pink ham. He banged his goblet upon the table for more wine. It was immediately served him, and he drank thirstily.

"One home is more than enough for me," Rosamund responded. "This moving about is quite tiresome, sir."

"Do you know why we do it?" he asked.

"Of course, sir. Your sister explained it to me, but I still do not have to like it. I hope your father will send me home when he sends your sister to her husband in Scotland," Rosamund said.

"What do you have at Friarsgate that you do not have here?" the prince said as he popped several sugarplums, one after another, into his greedy young mouth.

"Sheep," Rosamund told him drolly, "They cause me far less difficulty than trying to recall all the whys and wherefores of court etiquette, my lord prince."

"Aha! Ha! Ha! Ha! Ha!" laughed England's heir. "What an amusing girl you are, my lady of Friarsgate. Do you speak French?"

"Badly, but *oui, monseigneur*," she answered him.

"Latin?"

"*Ave Maria, gratia plena*," Rosamund parroted wickedly.

He chuckled. "I won't inquire about your Greek," he said with a wide grin.

"That is fortunate, my lord King of the Bean, as I don't have any knowledge of such a tongue. It is a tongue, isn't it?" Her amber eyes were twinkling at him.

"Aye," he said.

"I play the lute, and I can sing, or so I have been told," Rosamund volunteered. "I can keep accounts, and I will one day, with my lord's gracious permissions, tell you all about wool, of which I am very, *very* knowledgeable."

"You are learned in other ways than I would have imagined," the prince noted, "and you have enough education of a more traditional kind, which combined with your quick wit, my lady of Friarsgate, makes you a most amusing and delightful companion. Do you dance?"

"Not nearly as well as the Queen of the Scots," Rosamund said.

"Aye, Meg is light of foot, but I am even better," he boasted.

"So even she has said, your highness," Rosamund flattered him with a smile.

"We will dance this evening," he promised her. "Ah, look! Here are some mummers coming into the hall for our entertainment." He took her hand in his, and lifting it to his lips, kissed it, his bright blue gaze meeting her startled look, "I am a hundred years older than you, my lovely lady of Friarsgate. I think we are going to become very good friends eventually." Then, still holding her hand in his, he turned to watch the mummers as they danced.

Her heart was beating wildly. This boy had deliberately set her senses reeling, Rosamund thought. While she would never show it, she was not just a little afraid. She had not enough experience in such matters, but she sensed this bold prince was planning her seduction. How did one refuse England's future king? She must find Sir Owein and obtain his advice. He would know how to advise her in such a delicate matter.

Chapter 6

She did not see the prince after the Twelfth Night festivities over which they had reigned as king and queen. He had, as promised, kissed her once again, but it had been a chaste kiss. They had danced that evening, and she had, according to Meg, acquitted herself well. They left Richmond, and the queen's household settled itself into the royal apartments at the Tower to await the birth of the hoped-for prince. The Tower apartments were a warm and comfortable place, almost like her own home, Rosamund thought as she gazed out on the river Thames. Their life settled into a familiar monotony of lessons in French and etiquette. They kept regular hours, eating twice daily. The queen enjoyed music, and when it was discovered that Rosamund could sing well she found herself called upon often in the following weeks. The queen found her simple country melodies soothing.

The queen went into labor in the early morning of February second. The king was sent for, and there was much to-ing and fro-ing back and forth of serving women and physicians. The royal midwife arrived, as did the Venerable Margaret, who began to argue with her son over a name for the expected prince.

"We have had an Arthur and an Edmund, and we have a Henry," the Countess of Richmond said.

"He shall be named after my uncle of Pembroke," the king replied.

"Nonsense!" came the quick retort. "We cannot have a prince named Jasper. It is not English enough. Will you remind England that your blood is more Welsh? What about John?"

" 'Tis a bad-luck name, mother," the king said.

"Edward! You and Bess both descend from Edward III, and John is not bad fortune. My father was John. Now, Richard is another matter," the Countess of Richmond said, frowning.

"No," the king agreed. "Richard would not be appropriate, particularly in light of the slant our family took with regard to the former king. We made him the villain for the disappearance of Bess' two young brothers, although I never really thought he was responsible. 'Twas probably some damned sycophant who thought to make Richard's position more secure and gain his favor. He could not have known Richard of York well to have done what he did. Of course, when Richard learned what had happened he could hardly admit to it, now, could he? Poor man. I can almost feel sorry for him, for I know from Bess that he loved his nephews."

"It didn't stop him from attempting to prevent you from your rightful place as England's king," the Countess of Richmond snapped.

Henry Tudor smiled one of his rare wintry smiles, "No," he agreed, "it did not, mother. I was born to be England's king. Did you not always tell me that?"

She laughed. "I did," she said.

"Your highness!" A serving woman hurried from the queen's chamber. "My mistress has been delivered of her child!"

Both the king and the Countess of Richmond hurried to the queen's side. She lay pale and fragile, a small swaddled bundle in the crook of one arm. She gave them a wan smile.

"Edward?" the Countess of Richmond said hopefully.

"*Katherine*," the queen replied softly.

The king nodded. "We have a strong and healthy heir, praise God! Another daughter will bind us to another royal house, Bess, my dear. Henry will have Spain, Margaret, Scotland, Mary, well, I have yet to decide upon Mary. Perhaps France. Perhaps the Holy Roman Empire, and whoever she does not have, this fair new princess will have, eh?" The king bent and kissed his wife's brow.

The Countess of Richmond said nothing. She did not like the look of her daughter-in-law. Bess was not young, and this had obviously been a hard birth for her. There would be no more children from this queen, Margaret Beaufort thought to herself.

Prince Henry and his two sisters were brought to see their new sibling.

"What does she look like?" Rosamund asked Meg.

"Like all of mama's babies. Pale with reddish blond hair and light eyes," the young Queen of the Scots replied. "She is very quiet, too. I think she will not survive long. What a pity that mama should go through all of that for a puny girl child."

"I shall have only sons," Prince Henry boasted.

"You shall have what God deigns, Hal," Meg said.

Princess Mary was returned to Eltham to her nursery with her new sister. The prince remained with his father, but Meg and Rosamund stayed at the Tower with the queen and her women. The Venerable Margaret had gone to her London house of Cold Harbour. The queen was not recovering from her childbirth. The Tower was very quiet. Then, on the morning of February eleventh, the queen's thirty-seventh birthday, Elizabeth of York died suddenly, with barely time for the priest to come and hear her final confession.

The king was devastated. He wept openly for the second time in the last year. The first time being when he had been told his heir, Prince Arthur, had died. The court was in shock. It had not been a difficult confinement, and the birth had been relatively swift. The queen had always been healthy and so confidently strong. But now she was dead of a childbed fever as if she had been any ordinary woman. It was difficult to believe. Elizabeth of York had been well loved. The court would miss her.

The king's mother took over immediately, bringing Meg and Rosamund into her household. While a funeral needed to be planned, it was decided then and there that the princess' formal wedding to the King of the Scots would take place in August as had been scheduled. As for Rosamund, while the king remained her guardian, the Venerable Margaret took charge of her, "for sweet Bess' sake," Then, having said it, she began to decide the funeral preparations, for the king was too broken with his grief and barely left his chambers.

A funeral effigy had to be carved. It would show the queen garbed in her finest robes and furs, smiling. The court and the country would mourn on the exact replica of Elizabeth of York at her best. It would always remain a good memory for them. The effigy would sit atop the queen's coffin. She would be buried in Westminster Abbey in a tomb that would one day contain the mortal remains of her husband. The famed sculptor, Torrigiano, was summoned to take a death mask of the queen so that he might do a bronze monument to go atop her tomb. Henry Tudor had been his patron for several years, and the sculptor lived in London.

The day of the state funeral dawned gray and cold. The city was practically shrouded in a thick, wet fog. The state funeral procession departed the Tower of London where Elizabeth of York had breathed her last and wound through the streets of the dim city so that the populace might have a last glimpse of their good queen. Over fifty drummers, their instruments muffled to give the appropriate solemnity to the tragic occasion, led the mourners. They were followed by a vast number of Yeomen of the Guard, behind which came the black silk and velvet draped hearse, the carved effigy in its bright-colored robes atop it an almost startling sight. The hearse was drawn by eight coal-black horses bedecked with black silk robes and black plumes.

There were thirty-seven young virgins following the funeral cart, one for each year of the queen's life, all garbed in the whitest of white velvet robes and carrying tall white beeswax tapers. The tall candles flickered eerily in the chill air. Rosamund was among them, having been given this honor by the king's mother. The virgins, however, wore no cloaks, and Rosamund shivered with the cold, as did all of her companions. The white kid slippers upon their feet did little to keep out the damp and the wet chill. It would be a wonder, Rosamund thought to herself, if we don't all join the queen, dead of a winter ague.

They entered the great abbey where a requiem mass was then celebrated by the archbishop, followed by a eulogy, which Rosamund learned later had been written and delivered by a young lawyer of the city, one Thomas More. His deep yet smooth voice rang out with his words of tribute, filling the great church:

> *Adieu! Mine own dear spouse, my worthy*
> *   lord!*
> *The faithful love, that did us both continue*
> *In marriage and peaceable concord,*
> *Into your hands here I do resign,*
> *To be bestowed on your children and mine;*
> *Erst were ye father, now must ye supply*
> *The mother's part also, for lo! here I lie.*

As Thomas More's voice died, the soft sounds of weeping could be heard throughout Westminster Abbey. Looking toward the king, Rosamund saw him wipe his eyes. His shoulders sagged. Henry Tudor had suddenly grown very old, but beside him his mother stood straight and his children were bravely comforting each other in their sorrow. Now the queen's coffin was taken down from its place on the hearse at the end of the nave and set into its tomb. Elizabeth of York was blessed a final time by the clerics in attendance, and the funeral was over at long last.

Meg came and took Rosamund by the hand. Her eyes were red with her weeping as she and her mother had been very close, particularly in this last year. "Grandmother says you are to come home now with me. She says you played your part well, and my mother would have been pleased."

They climbed into a covered cart that the Venerable Margaret had provided for her granddaughters and the other women of her household. The gray winter's day was already growing dark as the vehicle made its way back through the misty London streets to the Countess of Richmond's London residence.

The following morning the Princess Mary, who was not quite seven, was returned to her nursery at Eltham.

"Sometimes I think I have spent my entire life wearing black mourning," Meg complained to Rosamund.

"You will be free to shed it again in a few months' time," Rosamund comforted the young Queen of the Scots, "You are fortunate, Meg, that you remember the mother you mourn. I do not recall mine at all."

"Are there no portraits of her?" Meg asked.

"Country people usually don't have portraits painted," Rosamund replied with a smile. "Maybel knew her. She says I resemble her, but I resemble my father more. It's not like really knowing though, is it? Your mother was so kind to me. I shall never forget her, and I shall name a daughter after her one day, Meg. I promise you that!"

The winter drew to a close, and at Easter the king asked that his family gather at Richmond again. They hardly saw him though, for the rumor had it that Henry Tudor's heart was broken by his loss. His counselors advised him to remarry, and small overtures were made in that direction, but in the end it came to naught. The king had married Elizabeth of York to unite their houses, to end a long and bloody war, and because her claim to the throne was actually stronger than his. But he had loved her once he had come to know her, and he had been faithful to her in life. Now that she was gone it appeared his fidelity would not waver.

"He is like me," the Venerable Margaret noted.

"But you have wed three times, grandmama," Meg said.

"Listen to me, my child," Margaret Beaufort said. "A woman may have wealth and dignity and prestige, but it matters not if she does not have a husband. That is the way of our world. We cannot escape it.

However, your father's father, my first husband, Jasper Tudor, was the love of my life, and I am not ashamed to admit it. For women of our class it is our first marriages that are arranged. Perhaps even a second. After that I believe a woman has a right to choose her own husband. Whether she will love all of them, or none of them, that is up to fate. But marry a woman must, and that is the end of it."

"Will I love James Stuart, grandmama?" Meg wondered aloud.

" 'Tis said he is a most loving man," the countess noted dryly, "and of course he will want to please you because by making you happy he makes England happy. He is said to be handsome, child. Handsome and kind. Aye, I believe you will love him."

"Will he love me?" the girl queried.

The Venerable Margaret laughed. "James Stuart will certainly love you, my child." For there is scarcely a woman he cannot love, she thought to herself.

"You must find a husband for Rosamund now, grandmother," Meg said mischievously, "I know she wants to return home to her beloved Friarsgate when I go north in late summer."

"We will find your companion a mate in time," the Countess of Richmond said.

"There is time, and he must be chosen carefully."

"You see," Meg said later when they were abed. "You are a prize to be awarded even as I am. But, Rosamund, when the time comes, make them allow you the choice. Remember what my grandmother said. That after first marriages, and even second ones, a woman has the right to choose her next husband. Remind them of that when your time comes."

They remained at Richmond for a month, but then the countess and her granddaughters decamped for Greenwich. It was the first time Rosamund had been to this palace. Like Richmond it was on the river Thames, but here she could spy the masts of the tall ships that sailed about the world as they moved downriver to the sea. Prince Henry joined them for a short while, for his grandmother had requested that he come. The king was keeping his surviving heir close. It was almost as if he believed by retaining personal custody of the boy he could protect him from anything. The prince even slept in a small chamber that could only be entered through his father's bedchamber. His friends found young Henry's predicament quite amusing, but the prince did not.

Hence a respite with his formidable grand-mother and his sisters was most welcome.

Princess Mary, brought from Eltham, admired her brother's older companion, Charles Brandon. "I shall marry him one day," the seven-year-old announced boldly. Her remark was met with much humor among her family.

"Princesses do not wed with plain gentlemen, Mary," her grandmother said tartly. "They marry kings, or dukes, or other princes of the blood. Young Brandon has charm, I will give you that, but he is an adventurer. He has no lands of his own or real wealth. Why, I should not even give him to Rosamund for a husband. He is not worthy."

"He will be someone one day, grandmama," Mary replied pertly. "And I shall marry him!"

"Do you play tennis?" Prince Henry asked Rosamund as she sat one afternoon admiring the river.

Rosamund looked up. She was wearing a green bodice and skirt with her white sarcenet sleeves. The countess had declared their deep mourning over with and had gifted her two granddaughters and Rosamund with new gowns. "Nay, your highness,

I do not play tennis."

"Come then, and I shall teach you!" Henry said, reaching down to pull her up by the hand. "How can you just sit and stare at the water? I find it boring."

"I find it peaceful, your highness," Rosamund replied.

"You will enjoy tennis," he insisted, pulling her along.

But she did not enjoy the rough game, and she tripped over her new skirt and twisted her ankle almost immediately while chasing after the ball he had lobbed at her. "Oh, if I have torn my skirt I shall not forgive you!" she cried. "*Ouch!* I cannot get up!" She winced with pain as she attempted to struggle to her feet.

At once the prince leapt over the net. Coming to her side, he bent down and picked her up. "I will carry you back to my grandmother's apartments," he said. "And your gown has not been torn, Rosamund. If it were I should buy you another," he assured her gallantly.

"You have not the coin," she answered him boldly.

"How do you know that?" he demanded. "Nay, 'tis my sister, Meg, who tittle-tattles."

"My ankle hurts," Rosamund complained.

"Put your head against my shoulder and close your eyes," Prince Henry instructed her. "You have probably sprained it. Did you hear or feel a snap?"

"Nay," Rosamund told him.

"Then nothing is broken," he responded. Then he stopped. "You are as light as a feather, my lady of Friarsgate. I am enjoying the sensation of you in my arms."

Rosamund's amber eyes flew open. "You are much too bold, my lord prince," she scolded. "Remember you are a boy, and I two years your senior. I have just had a birthday."

"I have said it before, Rosamund of Friarsgate. I am young in years, but I have a man's body. Of late I think I have a man's needs. Now, you must kiss me or I shall not proceed another step."

"Unfair! Unfair!" Rosamund cried, struggling within his arms. His shoulders beneath his doublet were very broad, and the chest she now pounded with her small fists was wide and hard. His cheek was no longer smooth, but had just the faintest hint of shadow.

"One little kiss," he wheedled, grinning at her wickedly, his blue eyes dancing.

She sighed. It was really very exciting, Rosamund considered, to be so pursued by a handsome young prince. "Just one," she finally said. "Do you give me your word, just one, your highness?"

"You may call me Hal when we are alone," he murmured.

"You have not given me your promise, *Hal,*" Rosamund said, attempting to sound stern. He was very handsome, she thought. Even more handsome than Sir Owein.

He saw the dreaminess in her amber eyes. "One sweet, sweet kiss, my lady of Friarsgate," he whispered in her ear, and then he kissed her lips, their mouths fusing together eagerly.

Rosamund's heart raced. She could feel the sudden heat from both of their bodies. Her mouth softened beneath his. She sighed, relaxing against him, feeling safe within the cradle of his strong arms, "Oh, how lovely," she told him softly as the kiss ended.

"Again?" he tempted her in a low, seductive voice.

"Aye," she agreed with another sigh of pleasure as his mouth touched hers once more. This time his demands on her were greater. She felt him sitting down on the stone bench that had been nearby. More comfortable in his embrace, Rosamund put an arm about his shoulders, her fingers caressing the nape of his thick neck. The kiss deepened. His finger brushed against her bodice, and receiving no rebuke he boldly fondled her breast. *"Oh!"* Rosamund gasped, very surprised.

"It's all right, darling," the prince assured her. "Lovers are wont to touch." He deliberately pinched her nipple as his hand moved swiftly into her bodice and beneath her chemise.

It was as if he had doused her with a bucket of cold water. Rosamund's eyes flew open. *"We are not lovers!"* she cried, "And how would you know such a thing, Hal?" She struggled to gain a more defensive position as she yanked his hand from beneath her gown.

"Do you think I am a virgin like yourself, my adorable lady of Friarsgate?" the prince asked her. "Lord, I mounted my first woman on my eleventh birthday. She was a gift from Brandon and Neville." He grinned at her. "I enjoy a good fucking with a contented partner."

"How did you know what to do?" Rosamund asked him, fascinated in spite of herself. If it hadn't been for her ankle she would have gotten up from his lap and left him, she assured herself.

"My friends found me a clean and

disease-free whore, no easy task either, who was both skilled and sympathetic. She said she was honored to be my first lover, and gaily led me down Eros' path. And I learned quickly. I was happy to try my new skills out upon any who were willing to join me in my quest for pleasure," the prince said.

"Men are fortunate," Rosamund said.

"How is that?" he asked, curious.

"You may practice your lover's skills before you are wed. No respectable girl may do so. And once she is wed she is stuck to remain virtuous while her husband may keep other women for his pleasure as well. I think that rather unfair, do you not?"

"But a good woman, especially a man's wife and his daughters, should be virtuous at all times," the prince replied primly. "Only whores and courtesans may amuse themselves with lovers."

"Do you not think me a good lass, Hal?" Rosamund inquired of him innocently.

"Of course you are good," he quickly answered.

"Then why are you attempting to seduce me — to ruin my reputation, Hal? Someday I must wed. Who will want a lass with a tarnished character? A girl considered the open road for lads? For if you have your way with me, then you will brag on it, and your friends will want my favors as well," Rosamund finished.

He flushed guiltily. "You were willing," he said sulkily.

"You demanded a kiss," she said softly. "One kiss."

"Your lips are sweet, lady of Friarsgate," he excused himself.

Before Rosamund might answer him, another voice intruded upon them. A very familiar voice, "Ah, your highness, here you are. Your father has arrived from London and wishes to see you," Sir Owein Meredith said. His look was curious, although his tone was that of a good retainer.

"The lady has twisted her ankle," the prince explained hastily. He stood up, Rosamund still in his embrace. Then he handed her off to Sir Owein. "Please take her to my grandmother with my apologies." He turned to go, but then he turned back to them. "My father is in his privy closet?"

"Yes, your highness," Sir Owein replied.

The prince hurried off without another word.

"You are unable to walk?" Sir Owein said quietly.

Rosamund nodded, her cheek warm with her embarrassment. To have been discovered in so compromising a position with Prince Henry!

"How did it happen?" Sir Owein inquired as he walked toward the palace with his pretty burden.

"On the tennis court," Rosamund managed to say. "I fell, trying to hit a ball."

"Tennis is too rough a game for a lady," Sir Owein said.

"I am inclined to agree," Rosamund told him. "You have come with the king?"

He nodded. "He has reassigned me to the Countess of Richmond's household," Sir Owein said. "He says with the queen gone from him he has not the need for so large a staff any longer. He is most melancholy and seems to miss her more every day. I am retained merely because of my long service to the House of Tudor, because I am Welsh. Were it not so I should be returned to my family like several others already have been."

"Would they be glad to see you?" she asked him.

He laughed, and the sound was almost bitter. "I think not, unless I came bearing riches. It has been so long since I have seen any of them, I doubt if I should recognize them."

"That is sad," Rosamund said. "I should

be truly unhappy if I had no one to welcome me home."

"My birthplace has not been home to me since I was six," the knight responded. "I do not remember it at all. I think more of Caernavon Castle, which was Sir Jasper's seat, as home. Now, my lady Rosamund, you should not be kissing and cuddling with Prince Henry."

"Sir!" She tried to sound outraged.

"You cannot deny it," he said with a chuckle. "My sweet Rosamund of Friarsgate, I speak for your own good. If you expect to be given a husband, you cannot allow your good name to be stained."

"All he wanted was a single kiss," Rosamund muttered. "There is no crime in a single kiss."

"Now listen to me, my lass," Sir Owein said in a stern voice. "Prince Henry has been fondling servant girls since he was barely into breeks. When he turned eleven his friends gave him a whore. It was an unspoken secret throughout the court. The prince has never looked back since. He likes women. A single kiss? His hand was in your bodice, Rosamund! You'd have shortly been on your back, I guarantee you. 'Tis the conquest that fascinates the prince. He is heedless of consequences, because there would be none for him, except a possible dose of the clap."

"*Sir!*" Her cheeks were blazing again.

"You are a virgin of good repute and family, Rosamund, but the prince would seduce you without any care for your future. What if you became with child, lass? You should be sent home in disgrace, and I have not a doubt you would be given into your uncle Henry's care. Is that what you desire, Rosamund?"

"No," she said softly. "You misjudge me, sir. I am not such a lackwit that for all my inexperience I am not aware when I am being trifled with by a young man. I had already scolded the prince, and he had ceased his bad behavior. I did not need rescuing."

"It was only by chance that I came upon you," Sir Owein answered her. "So you divined his intentions, eh?"

"A lass may be pure but still recognize the impure. I have a great care for my reputation, but I had not been kissed before by a lover. I wanted to know what it was like," she explained.

"And did you like being kissed by a *lover?*" he demanded.

"Aye, it was very nice, sir. My heart beat faster, and I even thought I might swoon with the pleasure that filled me. There was no harm in it, was there? Surely other girls have done the same and not been ruined."

They had reached the door to the Countess of Richmond's privy apartments. A servant stood outside in the afternoon air by the door. He opened it immediately, his face impassive as Sir Owein passed through with Rosamund still in his arms.

"Gracious! What has happened to Rosamund?" the Venerable Margaret cried as they entered her dayroom.

"I fell, madame, and twisted my ankle. Sir Owein was kind enough to bring me inside," Rosamund explained.

"Set her down, Sir Owein, and let us look to that ankle," the countess instructed. "Ladies, Sir Owein has rejoined my staff. I know you will all be glad for it."

He set the girl down. Rosamund gingerly raised her skirt up to reveal her ankle, quite swollen and turned purple and yellow-brown with her injury. She winced when he touched the skin.

"Oh, my," the countess said, and she shook her head. "You will have to remain inside for a few days, my child, until the swelling goes down. Ah, here is your Maybel. She will poultice it for you. Sir Owein, carry the Lady Rosamund to her bed now, and let her servant tend to her."

Maybel led the way and instructed Sir Owein to put Rosamund down into a chair in the bedchamber she shared with the Tudor princess. "Will you fetch me some hot water, sir?" Maybel asked the knight. "I will need it to make the poultice for my mistress."

He nodded and hurried off.

"You was with that wicked young prince, wasn't you?" Maybel said. "Don't deny it! The young princess saw you go off with him."

"We went to play tennis," Rosamund replied.

"You don't play this . . . tennis thing," Maybel said angrily.

"It's played with a ball," Rosamund explained. "I fell and twisted my ankle trying to send the ball back to the prince."

"It don't sound like anything a lady should be involved in, especially if it has you running all over like a hoyden," Maybel decided. She bustled about the small room, rooting around in the trunk for the herbs she needed to make the poultice for Rosamund's ankle.

A servant appeared with the hot water. "Sir Owein sent me," the servant said. "Will you need anything else?"

"Nay, this will do," Maybel replied. Then

she set to work to make the dressing for her mistress' ankle. While the herbs were drawing in the hot water, Maybel helped Rosamund from her gown and into bed. She, soaked a small length of linen in the water, affixing the poultice on the swollen limb and wrapping it. She tucked a small hard pillow beneath Rosamund's ankle. "I'll bring you some soup," she said.

"But I'm hungry!" Rosamund wailed. "I want meat, Maybel!"

"I'll see what I can do," Maybel said with a small smile as she hurried out. If Rosamund hadn't lost her appetite then she was certainly not badly injured.

Meg slipped into the bedchamber. "You were with Hal. Did he kiss you? Tell me everything, Rosamund!"

"There is nothing to tell," she feigned, and then she yawned.

"Liar!" Meg cried. "He did kiss you! What else?" she demanded.

"Why do you believe there is anything else other than a simple kiss?" Rosamund asked her friend.

"Because I know my brother, Henry," Meg laughed. "Now, tell me absolutely everything that happened! I will perish if you do not!" Her blue eyes were dancing and alight with curiosity. Her cheeks were flushed pink with her excitement.

"There is little to tell, I'm warning you," Rosamund began.

Meg leaned forward in anticipation.

"Hal, he says I may call him that in private, insisted that I learn to play tennis. I fell and twisted my ankle. He carried me from the tennis court up through the garden. Halfway to your grandmother's privy apartments he stopped and said I must kiss him. He sat down upon a bench and kissed me. I quite liked it, Meg. I did!"

"I let Richard Neville kiss me yesterday eve," Meg admitted. "I liked it, too, but of course I have not kissed him since. Especially as I am to go north in a few weeks to wed with the King of the Scots. I must guard my good name. Now, what else?"

By now Rosamund knew better than to prevaricate with the princess. "He fondled my breast," she admitted.

"*Ohhhh!*" Meg whispered, her blue eyes wide.

"I stopped him, of course," Rosamund said quickly. "I, too, must have a care of my good name."

"What did it feel like?" Meg persisted.

"I can't put words to it," Rosamund replied, "but I thought I might swoon with the pleasure it gave me." Her eyes grew dreamy with the remembrance of that big hand cupping her little breast.

"I had heard that men do things like that," Meg whispered. "And other things as well," she added, her voice dropping even lower.

"What things?" Now it was Rosamund who was fascinated.

"I don't know," Meg responded, "but most of the women I know seem to enjoy their husband's attentions. I suppose we'll both find out soon enough," she concluded with a laugh.

"You'll know long before I will," Rosamund said. "I won't be married before you, Meg, and besides, no one has said anything to me about a husband."

"And now Sir Owein is back in your world," Meg teased. "Was it nice to be carried in his arms, or did you like my brother's arms better? Of course, Henry is not for you, and never could be, but don't you like Sir Owein? All the ladies do."

"He is nice," Rosamund said slowly.

"He carried you most gently. When he thinks that no one is observing him, he looks at you so tenderly. I think that Sir Owein may have a tendresse for you, Rosamund. I think he would make a good husband for you. He is handsome and mature, and yet he is young enough to be a vigorous lover who can get children on you."

"*Meg!*" Rosamund protested, but she had to admit that she had toyed with similar thoughts. Owein Meredith with his dark blond hair and his hazel-green eyes, his straight nose, and strong jaw was most attractive. She considered what it would be like to kiss him. His mouth was narrow-tipped, but big. And his large square hands — what would they feel like on her breasts? Would they elicit the same thrill that Prince Henry had aroused in her virgin heart? And he had ever been kind to her. He had always reminded her of a younger version of Hugh Cabot.

"What are you thinking?" Meg demanded.

"Do you really believe Sir Owein likes me?" Rosamund said.

"Aye," Meg answered her, "I do. And he deserves a wife, a good wife, Rosamund. I have known Sir Owein my whole life. My mother always said that of all the family's retainers he had truly earned the appellation of *the good knight*. Mama always said that Sir Owein was the most honorable man she had ever known. And he is kind as well, which you certainly know. It is true that he has nothing but his sword, his horse, his armor, and his good name, but you cannot seek an important name for your mate anyway. Would you rather not have a man like Sir Owein as opposed to a man like your uncle? A man with a little estate who would wed you for your lands and mistreat you. I recall what you have told me about your uncle's first wife, the lady Agnes. How sad for her that she never knew real love."

"My uncle had her for her bit of land, for he had none himself," Rosamund reminded Meg. "I am certain Sir Owein would willingly have me for the same reason. But I think I want love this time."

"Love is a luxury that women of property cannot afford," Margaret Tudor told her companion. "Wed first, and with luck the love will come later. All women are sought in marriage for one reason or another, Rosamund. Love is usually not the primary concern of the matchmakers. A princess of England weds with the King of the Scots so there might be peace between their two lands, so the generation of children that they produce may have a bond with England and hopefully keep the peace.

"The daughters of the great noble houses are wed for their wealth and their family connections. You will be wed for your lands and flocks. A farmer's daughter because her mother has birthed mostly sons, and it is hoped she will too so there will be more hands to work the land. We are all taken for one reason or another, but love rarely enters into it. For the next few months my departure will be what is concentrated upon by the court and by my family. You have time to observe Sir Owein as a prospective husband. Use your time wisely, and do not dally with my brother again.

"He will be wed to Kate after our father has wheedled all he can out of the King of Aragon and Castile. That alliance is meant to be. Must be! We need to play Spain's might against France for our own safety. And, too, such a match adds to the legitimacy of my family claim on England's throne. My father has always wanted it as he has wanted the union between me and James Stuart.

"For you it is almost as if you have a choice. If you decide that you want Sir Owein, I will ask for you. They will give me what I ask. I am leaving my family, and I do it with a good heart. Whatever I want, within reason, before I go will be given me. It costs my father naught to reward his faithful retainer."

"I will think on it," Rosamund answered, thinking it would almost be like choosing.

When Meg departed she would be lost at the court. Kate was a sweet girl, but she was so very royally proper. Meg was right. Kate was going to be England's queen one day. One thing about being unimportant, Rosamund quickly learned, was that important people were unafraid to speak around you. They spoke as if you were not there because you were of no consequence to them. She had gained much knowledge just listening. The Spanish alliance was of paramount significance to King Henry. He would have it no matter what.

And Prince Henry? He was charming, but he was an unruly boy who might have a man's body but was yet thoughtless and selfish. He was not in the least concerned for Rosamund's reputation. He simply wanted to seduce a royal ward so he might brag upon it to his friends. And whatever happened to his victim afterward would be of no concern to him. He was to be England's king one day. The precepts and codes of morality followed by ordinary people did not apply to him. Rosamund understood this from her few months with the court. Princes were laws unto themselves, and always would be.

And young Henry Tudor was indeed a law unto himself. If Sir Owein had not interrupted them he was certain he would have gained the fair Rosamund's passion. He was determined to try again to breach her innocent defenses. She was not as stupid as he had anticipated. Her awareness that he meant to seduce her had surprised him, but her cleverness only made the game more interesting.

"I will have her," he told his friends.

"Let it go, Hal," advised Charles Brandon, who was several years the prince's senior. "Now that she has injured her ankle your grandmother will be watching her closely. You may be certain she knows how Rosamund was sore wounded. And Sir Owein saw you, or so you believe. He is an honorable knight, and if he believes the girl is in danger, he will make certain she is protected. You do not need to have her, Hal. Not when there are those who would be willing to entertain your randy and strong young cock. Ladies with elderly husbands who thirst for a lustful encounter with a vigorous lover. Think on it, Hal," he grinned knowledgeably.

"The fact that she is less accessible makes the game even more fascinating — and dangerous," said young Lord Richard Neville. "*A virgin!* I don't believe I've ever had a virgin, although I will certainly expect my bride to be one. To seduce the lass in her own bed, beneath your grandmother's nose would be quite a coup, Hal. If anyone can do it, I will wager it is you!" His black eyes danced wickedly.

"You're on, Neville!" said Lord Percy. "I will wager a gold rose noble that he cannot do it!"

"I thoroughly disapprove," Charles Brandon murmured, "but I will hold your wagers for you."

Prince Henry laughed. "You are foolish to bet against me, Percy. You have but whetted my appetite for virgin flesh. The girl's cherry shall be mine before week's end," he boasted.

One of the prince's serving men kept company with the countess' tiring women. He learned that the countess and her ladies would be taking a small pleasure cruise on the river several afternoons later. Rosamund would be left behind as her ankle had yet to heal. She would be alone but for a few serving women who would think the naughty prince was simply using his grandmother's absence to play kiss and cuddle with a pretty lass. A few coins, and their silence and their absence would be guaranteed.

Rosamund had developed a slight fever, and slept restlessly. She awoke suddenly, feeling the rope springs of the bed give way with the weight of another person. Turning, she looked into the laughing face of Prince Henry Tudor.

"Hal!" she gasped, startled. "What are you doing here? You must go at once! 'Tis most improper."

In reply he pulled her into his arms, murmuring, "Darling Rosamund, my sweet lady of Friarsgate, I adore you! You must let me kiss you, sweeting. Just a kiss and a brief cuddle. Then I will leave you, I swear! I have done nothing but think of our afternoon in the privy garden."

"No!" Rosamund said firmly. "You will not wheedle me this time, Hal. Even now if you were found here in my bed I should be ruined! How cruel you are that you think only of your own pleasure. You care not for me at all!"

"But I do think of *your* pleasure, sweeting." His quick hands began to fondle her breasts. "Such ripe little fruits, and surely they need to be appreciated as only I can. I can see how fair your flesh is through the linen of your perfumed chemise, Rosamund." His red-gold head dipped to kiss the twin mounds.

Rosamund gasped with the shock of his lips on her bosom. Her head reeled with a mixture of fear and pleasure. *"No!"* she cried as his other hand began to creep beneath her chemise. *"No!"* And when he would not cease she screamed. She would be ruined, of course, but she could not let him steal her most precious possession, her virtue. Whoever finally wed her would know her honesty on their wedding night. She screamed again, and his hand covered her mouth.

"Don't, sweeting," the prince murmured softly. "I only want to make us happy. You'll see, Rosamund."

She opened her mouth once again, but this time her teeth fastened on the side of his hand, and she bit him with all her might. Henry Tudor howled with both pain and outrage, as at that moment the door to the bedchamber was flung open to reveal Sir Owein Meredith, his face dark with his anger. The prince leapt from the bed, and pushing past the older man, dashed from the bedchamber without another word.

To her own astonishment Rosamund burst into tears. "Thank God you came," she sobbed. "I truly believe he meant to do me harm."

"He meant to have your virtue from you, Rosamund," was the blunt reply.

"How did you know?" she wept nervously,

clutching the coverlet to her breasts.

"Maybel found out from one of the other women that the prince s man had been asking questions. Then Maybel saw the prince enter these apartments. When she followed after him discreetly, she saw that there were no other servants in evidence. She knew at once what our fine young prince was about. She ran for me immediately."

"Oh, what am I to do?" Rosamund sobbed. "If this powerful boy is determined to have me, what am I to do?"

"I shall speak with the countess herself and explain what has happened. I believe it is past time, Rosamund, that a husband was chosen for you. If you are given a husband, Prince Henry will leave you in peace. You will have lost your allure. There can be no scandal, my lady of Friarsgate, over the prince, for his prospective in-laws of Spain are most strict in their moral code. The Spanish ambassador is most watchful and careful for the Princess of Aragon's happiness."

"Will I go home if I am given a husband?" Her voice quavered.

"It depends upon the man they choose for you," he said. "But after what has almost happened here, my lady, it is obvious that you must have a husband to protect you."

Part 2

THE LADY OF FRIARSGATE

ENGLAND 1503–1510

Chapter 7

It was after the mass the following morning that Sir Owein Meredith came to the Countess of Richmond as she was departing the chapel and said in a low voice, "I would speak privily with you, madame, on a matter most urgent."

"I will see you after I have broken my fast," the Venerable Margaret replied, never breaking stride as she returned to her apartments.

Their eyes met for a moment, and then he moved off, seeking Maybel. Finding her, he asked, "Did your mistress explain what happened yesterday afternoon? Your quick actions prevented a travesty."

"He should be whipped," Maybel replied indignantly. "I don't care if he is to be England's king one day; he should be beaten. What kind of a man, young or not, deliberately sets about to despoil an innocent young girl, sir? I know Sir Hugh, God assoil his good soul, meant well by entrusting my sweet bairn to the king, but I wished to God that we were safe at home again at Friarsgate!"

"I will protect her as best I can," Owein assured Maybel, "I have been granted a private audience with the countess after she has eaten her meal. She will not be happy to learn of her grandson's misbehavior. She will want to blame Rosamund. I will not allow it. But she will understand the difficulties of the situation. I am going to suggest that she choose a husband for Rosamund immediately and marry her off before the young prince manages to seduce the lady of Friarsgate, thereby ruining her reputation. Rosamund is intelligent, but she is also naive. She is drawn, I fear, to Prince Henry, despite her better judgment. It is exciting for a young country lass to be pursued by a prince."

Maybel nodded. " 'Tis the truth you speak, sir, but there is something else that could lead to her downfall. Her juices are flowing now. She is indeed ripe for a husband, and if not a husband, then a lover. She is too inexperienced to understand that she cannot help herself. She needs a good man in her bed, and better it be a husband."

Sir Owein nodded. "Aye," he agreed, a small hint of a smile touching his lips. "Do not fear, Maybel, I will speak with the countess, and you will stay with your mistress as much as you can. Do not leave her alone."

"I won't, sir," Maybel promised.

Just after nine o'clock of the morning, one of the countess' women came to fetch Owein Meredith. She led him to a small paneled room with a corner fireplace that blazed brightly. There were two high-backed tapestried chairs before the little hearth and a round table set between them. Margaret Beaufort was ensconced in one of the chairs, garbed in her usual black, an arched head-dress covering most of her snow-white hair. She motioned him to seat himself in the other chair as the departing serving woman closed the door behind herself.

"Sit down," the king's mother said, "and tell me what it is that you would have a private audience with me, Owein Meredith."

The knight sighed. "I beg your highness' indulgence, and your forgiveness also, for what I am about to relate, but I cannot keep silent lest an innocent girl be wronged, and one you hold dearly be guilty of a terrible crime. Will you give me leave to speak frankly, knowing that I make no judgments in this matter? I simply wish to prevent a tragedy, dear madame."

"You have never been a man to put himself forward and involve himself in what does not concern him, Owein Meredith, so I certainly must accept that what you have to say is indeed serious. You have leave to speak. I shall not hold you responsible for your words, whatever they may be," she told him. "Say on, sir."

"Your grandson, the prince, has been tempted into an act that would dishonor him, madame. Wagers have been placed on the outcome of this act. Charles Brandon advised against it but holds the wagers nonetheless. Richard Neville has been the chief instigator in this mischief."

"Indeed," the Countess of Richmond remarked dryly. "Why am I not surprised to find Charles Brandon being politic and the Nevilles being troublemakers? Go on."

"The prince, being young and filled with the juices that young men his age are filled with, thinks himself enamored with Lady Rosamund Bolton of Friarsgate. There have been shy kisses exchanged between them on one occasion. The prince would have more of the girl, but she is careful for her reputation and will not give it. Neville and the others have wagered that Prince Henry can, or cannot, seduce the lady of Friarsgate. Yesterday when you took the princesses and your ladies to the river, the prince bribed your remaining women to leave your quarters where young Rosamund lay sleeping. The prince entered the girl's chamber and attempted to force her. Only the timely intervention of her servant, who ran for me, saved the Lady Rosamund and her good name."

"God's nightshirt!" the Countess of Richmond swore. "I will have him whipped!"

"Good madame, I beg you, hear me out. Prince Henry cannot help being filled with the joy of life and a bit of lust. He is young, and God only knows he is as big as any man, in many cases bigger. He is beginning to have a man's desires. But it is his pride that is at stake here more than anything else. The situation can be easily and quickly diffused, for the prince is honorable at heart, and having been chased off yesterday probably prays for a solution that will leave his pride intact as well as Lady Rosamund's virtue."

"What do you suggest, Owein Meredith?"

"Rosamund Bolton was sent here because her uncle has mistreated her and attempted to steal what is hers. Sir Hugh Cabot sought to protect his wife. He knew that Rosamund must wed again, but he did not want her forced into a marriage with her five-year-old cousin so that Henry Bolton could hold on to Friarsgate. I have met the man, madame. He is not an honorable fellow. Choose a husband for Rosamund, and the prince will step back; I guarantee it. Rosamund will be safe, her reputation intact, and the prince can retain his pride. Even Richard Neville would not dare suggest that the prince seduce another man's betrothed wife, madame." Sir Owein sat back in his chair and waited for the countess to speak.

"It is my granddaughter's wedding that has taken up all of my time now that her mother is dead and cannot attend to it. In just a few weeks the Queen of the Scots must go to her husband, and her marriage must be celebrated. And there is poor Spanish Katherine to place as well. The king is very unhappy that King Ferdinand has not completed the payments on the girl's dowry. Especially as he intends to eventually marry her off to Henry. I have heard rumors, Sir Owein, that my grandson enjoys the ladies. Is he not overyoung for it?"

"In the prince's case I would say not, madame," the knight replied, wondering just how much the old woman knew about her randy grandson and his sexual adventures.

"I had intended to find a husband for the

Bolton girl after Margaret was sent off, but I suppose something else would interfere and the girl would be twenty before I remembered her. You brought her down from Cumbria last year, did you not?" The Venerable Margaret leaned toward the fire to warm her hands.

"I did, madame."

"My granddaughter likes her. Do you? What kind of a girl is she, Owein Meredith?"

"Sensible," he said, "and reliable. She loves Friarsgate, and was taught to manage it herself. She does it well, and her people love her. The place is prosperous. It seems to be safe from the Scots because of an unusual feature of the land about it. The hills are too steep, and consequently cattle and sheep cannot be driven away fast enough. So Friarsgate has been left in peace but for her uncle."

"How long was she orphaned?" the countess asked.

"She was three," he answered. "The uncle came posthaste and married her to his five-year-old son. The boy died. It was then she was wed to Hugh Cabot. Henry Bolton thought Sir Hugh would be content to have a place in his old age. Instead Hugh Cabot taught Rosamund how to run her own affairs. He loved her as he might have loved a daughter, and she adored him. She was most devastated when he died."

"And Sir Hugh foiled the uncle by placing his wife in the king's care," the countess said slowly. "A clever man, I would say."

"I arrived as they sat at the funeral feast. The uncle was already insisting that Rosamund wed his next son, a child, newly breeked just for the occasion. She was resisting, and only my timely arrival saved her, I believe," Owein Meredith explained.

The Venerable Margaret smiled and said in an amused tone, "You seem to have a habit of saving this damsel, Owein Meredith. Well, I thank you for bringing this little matter to my attention. I shall see that Rosamund Bolton is carefully watched and not allowed to be alone with Henry, the naughty scamp. And I shall think on a husband for the girl. She is Margaret's age, even a bit older. It is time she was wed again, and this time for good and all." She held out her hand to her companion.

Sir Owein arose from his chair, and taking her hand, he bowed as he kissed it, "I thank your highness for her kindness," he said, and then he departed the little room.

When the door had closed behind him the countess said quietly, "You may come out now, child, and join me. Tell me what you think of what you have heard."

Young Margaret Tudor stepped from behind the tapestry on the far wall where she had been hidden. She seated herself with her grandmother. "Rosamund was subdued when we returned from the river, madame, but I did not think to ask why," she said. "How like Hal to allow his pride to direct his cock. If he does not learn better it will one day lead to his downfall." She smoothed out her skirts, her long fingers brushing over the tawny orange silk.

The countess laughed. "Thank God you are a clever and wise girl, Margaret, my namesake. As Scotland's queen you may one day be called upon to make hard decisions. And, child, you will want to have your husband turn to you as well as his counselors. Now, if the decision were yours to make, who would you choose to be Rosamund Bolton's husband?"

"Sir Owein Meredith, of course, grandmama," the princess answered without any hesitation at all.

"Not the son of some good northern family? One of the troublesome Nevilles, perhaps?" the countess asked. "An heiress would put them in our debt."

"Nay, grandmama. The Nevilles are indeed troublesome. We can never be certain of them, for they blow like the wind in whichever direction they consider is best for them alone. Even while I am wed to Scotland, we can never be certain that war will never break out between our countries again. 'Twould be best to marry Rosamund to a man in whom the Tudors could have complete confidence. Sir Owein is Welsh. He has been in service to our family since before I was born. He was even younger than Mary when he entered our household. There is absolutely no question as to his loyalty to the Tudors, and to England, grandmama. We could trust him to guard our flank," the princess said.

"But he is not a great lord," the countess countered.

"He is not," Meg agreed, "and so to give this loyal servant of the Tudors an attractive young heiress, certainly something he has never expected, will put him far more into our debt than a Neville, *and* we can be sure of his loyalty. The important sons of a great name would not want, or accept, Rosamund. You would have to choose a lesser light among the unmarried men. In fact, you would have to inquire among the great lords as to which of their young men would be suitable. The lord would pick a relation who would be in the lord's debt *first*, and not in ours. It is to us, the Tudors, that the debt must be owed if we are to profit from this match. Sir Owein is our man, and no one else."

"I wonder if a man so used to being in our service would be content as a husband, not that it matters," the Venerable Margaret said. "If we say he must marry her, then he will do so."

"I believe he cares for her," Meg said. "You, yourself, noted that he is always saving her from one peril or another. And I think that she likes him very much, although she is careful not to admit it. In fact, I am certain of it, grandmama. 'Twould be a good match for them both. Sir Owein is not yet old. He will probably outlive you and my father. There will be no place for him at my brother's court. What will become of this loyal servant of the House of Tudor? Owein Meredith deserves to be treated in a kindly manner by us. Do you not think so, grandmama?"

"They would be well-matched," the Countess of Richmond agreed. "The girl is old enough to bear children now, and Sir Owein is young enough to get them on her. If they are both comfortable with each other, then, aye, 'twould be a good mating. The girl will be safe from her greedy uncle and grateful to us. Sir Owein, with his long service to us, would also be content and would remain loyal. A loyal man in the borders would be to our advantage, especially one who was not particularly made visible due to his own great wealth or a greater name." She leaned forward and patted her granddaughter's rosy cheek. "You have made a wise and thoughtful decision, my young Queen of the Scots. It shall be as you have suggested. We shall give Rosamund Bolton of Friarsgate to our good and loyal servant, Sir Owein Meredith."

"Thank you, grandmama," the princess said. She could scarcely wait to tell Rosamund of her good fortune, but then the Countess of Richmond held up a ringed hand.

"You can say nothing yet, child. I must gain your father's permission, for he is the girl's guardian," she told Meg.

"If you want it, papa will approve it," the princess said candidly. "When has my father ever refused you anything, grandmama?"

The older woman laughed. "Until your father came into his own, he and I had a rough life with the Yorkists always seeking to destroy him. All those years spent at the court of Brittany while your grandsire of York, and afterward Duke Richard, sought to kill him so that the House of Lancaster would die, I gave my youth for your father's safety, and he has always known it, though I never complained. He is a wonderful son, my darling Henry. May the son you give James Stuart be as loving to you, my child."

"I will keep our secret, grandmama," Meg responded. "But gain papa's permission quickly, for it will not be easy knowing what I know."

"Your father is to return to Richmond tomorrow with your brother. I shall ask him this evening. It must be done before you leave to go north to Scotland. Rosamund and Sir Owein can ride with your train as far as Friarsgate. That will cement our ties even more. It is a great honor to be allowed to be included in your wedding train."

"Thank you, grandmama," the princess said. Then she curtsied and left the old woman to her thoughts.

The countess' favorite tiring woman entered the small chamber, "It is almost time for the midday meal, madame," she said.

"Go to my son, the king, and tell him that I would speak with him as soon as possible," the Countess of Richmond told the woman.

The servant bowed. "At once, madame," she said, and turning about, hurried from the room. When she returned she brought the king with her, to his mother's surprise, for Margaret Beaufort had only meant to meet with her son at his convenience. Still, she was grateful for his dutiful kindness in coming to her at once.

"Henry," she said, smiling as he bent to kiss her cheek, "I could have come to you, my darling son."

"I have read and signed all the papers that my secretaries brought to me this morning," he answered, sitting himself in the chair so recently vacated by his daughter. "A visit with you, mama, is a welcome change." Then he sighed, and his look grew melancholy.

The countess' tiring woman put a goblet of mulled wine in his hand and bowed herself from the room.

The king sipped at the cup and briefly closed his eyes.

"You were supposed to come to Greenwich for a pleasant summer respite and to be with your family before Margaret leaves for Scotland," the countess said to her son. "You cannot escape the fact that Bess is dead by working yourself into an early grave, Henry," she gently chided him. "I cannot replace your wife, but I am here for you as I have ever been. The children need you. Soon your eldest daughter will be gone, and poor

Mary left alone, 'Twas sad that wee Katherine died but two months after her birth. She was the most beautiful of all of Bess' babies. She was like a small angel. Perhaps she was. And surely young Henry needs you. I know you are angry that he is not Arthur, but you cannot change what is, my son. Young Henry will be king after you, but you do not show him the ways of governance. You keep him close, but you ignore him. Arthur, may God assoil his soul, was a lovely boy, but in my opinion 'twas he who would have made the better churchman, and Henry the better king, my son."

"Do not say it!" the king cried low.

" 'Tis true, and you know it," she persisted. "But that is not what I wanted to speak with you about. With your permission I have chosen a husband for Sir Hugh Cabot's widow, who is your ward. She has been Margaret's companion since her arrival here at court, but now Margaret is to go, and the Lady Rosamund Bolton will have no place in the Queen of the Scots' train. It is time for her to return home to her beloved Friarsgate, but she must have a husband, and that husband must be a man in whom we have complete trust, for Friarsgate is in the borders, my son. While we hope that Margaret's marriage will bring a permanent peace between our two countries, you and I are more practical than most. We know that despite this union between our royal houses war can break out again. And the borders are always restless even in the best of times. We must have a man in place there who is in our trust and whose loyalty is beyond question, Henry, my son. Sir Owein Meredith has served the House of Tudor for almost twenty-five years. Because he is not a great lord he will learn more of what is happening in the region than an important person would. People will not be shy to speak around him. He is our man, and his fealty is beyond question."

"You would not have a member of one of the northern families?" the king asked his mother. He was surprised, and sought to know her reasoning before he gave his permission. An heiress was a valuable commodity to have in one's power.

" 'Tis Margaret who has made this suggestion. She has said, and wisely so, that the northern families blow with the winds. They are proud beyond reason. Even if you would do them such a favor as giving them this young heiress, they would not believe themselves in your debt, though they certainly would be. Sir Owein Meredith is our own man. Whatever happens he will not waver from our side."

"And my daughter has reasoned this out for herself?" the king said. "She has learned her lessons well. I can only hope James Stuart realizes what a treasure we have sent him. Her suggestion meets with your approval, mother?" The king drained his goblet of wine.

"Aye," the Venerable Margaret said. "My granddaughter has fashioned a good solution. The Lady Rosamund Bolton will not be unhappy with Sir Owein Meredith for a husband, not that it would matter. This betrothal and your marriage will serve our purposes as well as that of the parties involved, my son."

"Then you have my permission to betroth this girl to Sir Owein, mother. I shall have the papers drawn up."

"Do it so that Sir Owein and his betrothed may travel north in the Queen of the Scots' train as far as Friarsgate," the countess suggested. "Let Sir Owein's and Rosamund's last memories of us be filled with gratitude for the honor we give them."

"Age has not made you any less clever, mother," the king said with a small smile. "Now, what am I to do with Spanish Kate? King Ferdinand is as slippery as an eel and sly as a fox. He avoids our requests for the balance of the girl's dowry. I cannot, under the circumstances, pay for her upkeep."

"Put her in Durham House. She should not be at court, especially as her father has not finished paying her dower portion. And we will send back to her father as many of her Spanish retainers as we can. Let him understand we will not support his daughter lavishly under the circumstances. If you intend to wed her to Henry, she must be served by the English anyway, and learn our language, which she is slow to do. She is discouraged by that old dragon of a duenna, Dona Elvira. We cannot, I am sad to say, get rid of *her*, but I think her a bad influence on young Katherine. If we surround the girl with our own people, hopefully we can eventually lessen Dona Elvira's influence. And get her an English priest! Those Spanish are too harsh in their faith."

"I will get rid of her Spanish servers, at least as many as I dare, but I do not wish to pay for more servants, even English ones, mother. Let the Princess of Aragon live simply for the time being and mourn her husband as is proper."

The king arose, and taking his mother's hand in his, kissed it tenderly. "I get more done in a few minutes with you than with all of my counselors of a morning," he said, and then he left her.

The countess' tiring woman reappeared.

"Find Sir Owein Meredith. I would speak with him before the meal," the countess instructed the serving woman. "There is yet time."

"Yes, madame," the serving woman said, and turning, hurried out.

The Venerable Margaret sighed. Her granddaughter was right. It would be a good match. If Rosamund Bolton was not grateful, Sir Owein Meredith certainly would be. Not to mention surprised. The old woman chuckled. He would hardly expect such a boon, which was probably why he was worth it.

Owein Meredith looked down at the tug on his doublet. There stood a page, wearing the Countess of Richmond's badge. "What is it, lad?" he asked, a kindly smile touching his lips. It seemed so long ago that he had been in this boy's place. He wondered who the lad was and what his fate would hold.

"My mistress would speak with you immediately, sir," the page said, and he gave a small bow.

"I will come at once," the knight said, and followed the child back through the corridors of the palace to the little privy chamber where he had earlier been. He was curious to have been recalled by the king's mother at all, let alone in the same morning. Without breaking stride he entered through the door the page held open.

"Thank you, William," the countess said to her page as he backed from the room. "Sit down, Sir Owein. You are undoubtedly wondering why I have brought you back into my presence. With the princess to leave soon for Scotland, time is of the essence in the matter of Rosamund Bolton. The king has agreed that she must be wed, although I did not tell him of young Henry's untoward behavior in the matter. You are aware of how deeply he mourns Prince Arthur, who was always his favorite. Even the slightest blemish on my grandson's behavior will but depress my son further. The boy is young and filled with life. He cannot help himself, so we must. His attempts at seduction must not be allowed to continue. The Lady Rosamund will be betrothed with the king's approval to the gentleman of my choice. She and her betrothed husband will accompany my granddaughter, the Queen of the Scots, as far as Friarsgate. It is there they will be formally wed by the lady's own priest, before her own people, in order that her husband may be accepted by the Friarsgate folk, as he will be their new lord. Does that please you, Sir Owein?" The Countess of Richmond's eyes were filled with mirth. Her narrow lips twitched with silent laughter.

"It is not my place to be pleased, madame, but I am, and I thank you for the asking," he answered her. So she would be wed. It was better that she was, and safe at home. Not prey to the prince or his group of young lordlings who loved the chase but cared not for the consequences that followed their victims.

"Are you not in the least curious as to whom I have chosen, Owein Meredith? My instinct tells me that you are," the king's mother said.

"I am certain you have chosen a suitable gentleman for the Lady Rosamund," he replied, and he prayed the fellow would treat her kindly and respect her knowledge of her manor and lands. He prayed swiftly and silently that she might even find love.

The king's mother had ever been a skillful player in the game of life. It had been rumored that she was much like her great-grandfather, John of Gaunt, a son of King Edward III. She saw the emotions upon Owein Meredith's face as he attempted to conceal them. He cared for the girl. He was worried as to who her husband would be and whether the man would treat her well. Margaret Beaufort was tempted to tease the poor fellow further, but the dinner hour was near. "I have chosen you, Sir Owein Meredith, to husband Rosamund Bolton of Friarsgate," she said quietly. "You are, I hope, pleased."

"*Me?* You have chosen me?" Had he heard aright, or was he going mad?

Margaret Beaufort saw the genuine astonishment on the knight's face. Reaching out, she lay a calming hand upon his arm. "I have chosen you, Sir Owein Meredith," she responded, "and the king is pleased with my decision."

"I am to marry Rosamund Bolton?" he said, dizzy with the surprise.

"The marriage contract is being drawn up as quickly as it can be. Your Rosamund must be protected," the Venerable Margaret said.

"*But why me?*" he burst out.

Now the Countess of Richmond laughed aloud, pleased by his attitude and genuinely amused. "Do not be so modest, Owein Meredith. You have served the House of Tudor for close to twenty-five years. You have served it well. I remember when you first were brought to Jasper Tudor by your kinsman. You were so eager to please, and sang for us in your sweet Welsh voice. I am an old woman, Owein Meredith. My son is not well. The old ways are dying, and may indeed be gone with my grandson's reign. The children now serving at court will grow up in a different manner than you and I did. They will have other opportunities. You are not a young man any longer, Owein Meredith. You need a wife. It is time for you to settle down. Why you, you ask, and not another? Perhaps in my grandson's time it will be different than it is now, but my son is still considered an interloper, especially by the northern families whose loyalties today, beneath the surface, are to York. Giving the heiress of Friarsgate to them would not bring them any closer to our side. They serve themselves first, and always have. They are fair-weather allies at best.

"Friarsgate is in the borders. My granddaughter's marriage, it is hoped, will bring peace for a time. But the Scots and the English have too long a history of enmity between them to remain at peace for long. There have been English queens before Margaret. My own ancestress, Lady Joan Beaufort, was James the first's queen. We cannot trust northern families. We need a man in whom we have complete faith to watch for us in the borders. You are that man, Owein Meredith. You are not well-known outside of the court, nor do you draw needless attention to yourself. Yet those who know you like you. Your marriage should not offend any, for Rosamund is not important. It is the location of her lands that is of interest to us."

"The Scots do not harry her people, for the hills about her lands are too steep for driving cattle up and over," he said honestly. "Friarsgate is quite isolated, madame. It is unlikely I should know anything before it happened. Before your own royal warden of the northern marches knew."

"Shepherds guarding their flocks on those hills can be taught to be vigilant, Owein Meredith," the king's mother said quietly.

"In other words, madame, you want us to spy," he said.

"In a sense, aye, we do. Watching from your own lands should not put Friarsgate or its people in any danger, but it cannot hurt to be a bit more vigilant than in the past. It would please us if you were, Owein Meredith," the Venerable Margaret said.

He nodded. "It can be arranged once I am lord of Friarsgate," the knight told the king's mother. Then he said, "Have you told Rosamund that she is to be wed, and that I am to be her husband, madame?"

"Not yet," came the reply. "I wanted to speak with you first. I will speak with the girl after the meal. Then I will send her to the privy garden by the river. Watch for her. You may speak with her then. My grandson and his friends will be informed as well. By you, I think," she said with a chuckle, "after the meal and before you see Rosamund. You may tell Prince Henry that it was I who instructed you to give him this news."

"I may make an enemy of him, madame, and I should rather not do that," Owein said candidly. "Remember that it was I who found him with Rosamund. I believe it would be best not to link these two incidents."

"You are right," the king's mother quickly concurred. "I grow careless with my age. I shall have the king announce your betrothal this evening in the hall." She chuckled again. "My grandson will not need to be told to behave himself after such a royal declaration. You might, however, suggest to Charles Brandon that he return all the wagers to the young gentlemen. He will keep his peace, for he is a most politic fellow."

Owein Meredith bowed. "I thank your highness for her benevolence to me. I shall ever be a loyal servant of the House of Tudor."

"*I know*," the countess said with emphasis. "Now, I am hungry, and it is past the dinner hour. You may escort me into the hall, Owein Meredith. They will have waited for me, and my son becomes cranky when he is hungry."

Owein Meredith arose and drew the king's mother gently from her chair. "I am honored to escort you, madame," he told her.

In the hall Prince Henry attempted to attract Rosamund's eye, but while she did see him, she ignored him pointedly. His boyish companions sniggered at the prince's discomfort.

"You'll never have her," Richard Neville taunted smugly.

"You have no patience, Dick. One day I shall labor mightily between her milky white thighs," came the cool reply. "Ah, here is my grandmother. We can eat at last!"

Sir Owein Meredith found his place below the salt at a trestle full of his knightly companions. He suddenly found he had no appetite. He was to marry. It was not a dream. He had pinched himself several times when he was with the king's mother. He was really to be wed. Wed to Rosamund Bolton. He had never considered he would have a wife. He had never believed that he had anything to offer a woman, but now his loyalty and service to the Tudors had won him a bride. A bride with a goodly holding. His firstborn son would inherit Friarsgate. It was a far larger estate than his father's lands in Wales. He would have a bigger holding than his brother. He would have a home of his own at last. A home and a wife.

But what would Rosamund think of all of this? Not that it mattered in the general scheme of things. They were both bound to the king and would obey his command. But still, once more her fate had been snatched from her hands and decided by another. Would she be content to have him as her husband, or had some young man of the court caught her eye? He didn't want Rosamund discontent. He wanted her happy to be his bride because . . . *because he cared for her.* From the moment he had met her he had cared, and until this very moment he had not dared to admit his feelings to himself. How could he, and then see her given to another? But she had not been given to another. She had been given to him. Now he dared to think the thoughts he had been suppressing all these months. A grin split his face.

"Jesu!" the man next to him said. "Look, boys! Owein is smiling. I don't think I've seen him smile like that in the past two years. You've been with the Venerable Margaret twice today. What news, Owein? It must be good news to bring such a look onto your face."

"Maybe his brother died and he's to go home to his Welsh hillside and be the heir now," another man teased.

"I cannot speak on it, lads," Owein Meredith said, "but this evening I shall share my news with you. I swear it!"

They laughed and returned to their ale, satisfied, for Owein Meredith was the most honorable among them. Finally the meal ended and the hall began to empty. Owein looked for Rosamund, who had been sitting with some of the countess' women. She was already gone. He rose from his place and sought out Maybel. Maybel would know how her mistress was feeling and if she was still anxious to return home.

Rosamund returned with the countess' women to her apartments. To her surprise Margaret was not in evidence. Then one of the countess' tiring women came and said, "Our mistress would speak with you, lady of Friarsgate." Rosamund arose from her place and put down her embroidery frame. She dutifully followed the servant to the small privy chamber where the king's mother conducted her business each day.

"Come in, child," the Countess of Richmond said.

Rosamund stood before Margaret Beaufort and curtsied prettily.

"There will be no place for you among my women when my granddaughter has gone north to wed with the King of the Scots," the Venerable Margaret began bluntly. "It is time for you to return to your beloved Friarsgate, Rosamund Bolton, but you cannot go without what you came for. A husband to watch over you and keep you safe from your uncle. We have chosen that husband for you this very day. I think you will be pleased."

Rosamund's heart began to pound with both fright and anticipation. She was to go home! *With a husband.* And this time the man chosen for her would be her husband in every way. She was no longer a child. She was older than the king's mother had been when she bore Henry Tudor.

"Well, child, have you nothing to say?" the Countess of Richmond asked the girl standing before her. "Are you not in the least curious as to who this man is?"

"Does it matter, madame, if I am or not? The affair has been settled, my future decided, and I will accept the king's will," Rosamund replied, finding her voice and discovering that while she knew that this would be the result of her stay at court, she was still just a bit irritated that she had not even been consulted in the matter.

The king's mother laughed softly. "You have spirit, my child, and that is good."

"Madame, I beg your pardon if I have offended," Rosamund said, kneeling before Margaret Beaufort and placing her hands in those of the older woman. "It is just . . . just . . ." Her voice faded away.

"It is just that you hoped to have some part in this decision, Rosamund Bolton," the Countess of Richmond said. "I understand. However, when I tell you that it was my granddaughter who chose your husband for you, perhaps that knowledge will render your heart a bit lighter."

"Meg chose?" Rosamund was astounded.

"The Queen of the Scots realized that once she had gone you would be very much alone. You have no real place here at court, and the core of your very being lies at Friarsgate, does it not?"

"It does, madame," Rosamund answered softly.

"That being the case, it is time for you to return, but we cannot send you back without what Sir Hugh Cabot wished for you. A good man to husband you, to father your children, to keep Friarsgate safe and prosperous. There are many young men here at court who would willingly have a fair young heiress such as yourself to wife. Men from powerful northern families whose loyalty we wish to ensure. But my granddaughter does not believe we can buy such careless loyalties. She felt that we must put a man at Friarsgate whose loyalty to the House of Tudor is absolute and unquestioned. You know him. It is Sir Owein Meredith."

Her heart felt as if it were soaring in her chest. She smiled, and her relief was very apparent. "You said I should be pleased, madame, and indeed I am. Sir Owein is a good man, and we are friends."

"Friends," the king's mother observed, "make the best husbands, my child. I have had three husbands, and I should know. Now, Rosamund Bolton, get up and go into the privy garden where you will find Sir Owein awaiting you now. The betrothal papers are being drawn up and will be signed before my granddaughter departs for Scotland. You may wed at Friarsgate among

261

your own people, but you will travel with the Queen of the Scots as far as your home."

Rosamund took the countess' hands up and kissed them. "Thank you, madame," she said. She stood up, shaking her skirts as she did. "May I speak of this to my Maybel? May I thank Meg?"

"You may tell anyone you like, my child. The king will formally announce your betrothal tonight in the hall. You are, after all, his ward. I believe that the court should know of this happy event between one of our longtime servants and the lady of Friarsgate."

"Thank you, madame," Rosamund said once again. Then she curtsied and hurried from the countess' privy chamber. In the dayroom she found Maybel mending one of her chemises. "I am to be married!" she said softly, bending so that only Maybel might hear her. "It is Sir Owein! We are to go home soon, dearest Maybel!"

"Praise be to God on both accounts!" Maybel said, a smile wreathing her face. "I will be right glad to see my Edmund."

"I am to meet him in the privy garden now," Rosamund said. "Is my face clean? My hair neat?" she wondered anxiously.

"The man would have you barefooted in

your shift, lass," Maybel said, "but aye, you are neat as a pin. Go along now, and tell Sir Owein that I am content that you will call him husband."

Rosamund's heart was racing as she went from the dayroom and down the corridor. She had almost reached the door to the garden when Prince Henry appeared from the shadows.

"Wither goest thou, fair Rosamund?" he demanded, blocking her route. "Come, love, and give me a kiss to show me you are not angry for the impetuousness of my youth the other day."

"I am to be married, your highness," Rosamund said stiffly. "Please allow me to pass. Your grandmother has sent me to meet my betrothed in her garden, and he is awaiting me."

"One kiss, my pretty maid," the prince persisted. She was to be married? How the hell could he seduce her now? It would hardly be honorable to seduce another man's betrothed wife.

"If your highness does not step aside," Rosamund said angrily, "I shall scream for the guard."

"You would not!" he said, now nervous.

Rosamund opened her mouth and shrieked at the top of her lungs. Immediately the corridor was filled with men-at-arms.

"What is it, my lady?" the one to reach her first asked.

"Oh," Rosamund said innocently, "I thought I saw a rat. It was a very big rat, I fear. I am sorry to have caused difficulty." She smiled sweetly at the nearest man-at-arms, and brushing by him, opened the door to step out into the garden.

"Girls," the man-at-arms sniffed. Then he turned to the prince. "Did you see a rat, your highness?"

Henry Tudor nodded. "Aye, and 'twas as large as a cat, I'll vow. I should have killed it, but that the lady screamed." He watched as the door closed slowly behind Rosamund.

Outside in the privy garden Rosamund smelled the sweet air of the greenery and the faintly pungent odor coming off the river as the tide went out. The air was warm, and there was just the faintest hint of a breeze. Rosamund walked slowly down one of the neatly raked gravel paths. The king's mother had said he would be here. And then she saw him. He was standing with his back to her, facing the river, but obviously hearing her footfall, he turned.

"Rosamund!"

She swept him a curtsy. "My lord," she said softly.

He came forward, catching her hands in his, looking down into her face. "You have spoken with the king's mother and you are satisfied?" His hazel-green eyes searched her visage for any sign of discontent.

She gave him a shy smile. "I think it is a good solution to both our problems, sir. I need a husband, and you will be able, by marrying me, to continue in your loyal service to the House of Tudor," she told him gravely, "And you, sir. Are you content to be my husband?"

"I am," he answered her. "And you understand, Rosamund, that this marriage you undertake with me will not be in name only, as it was with your two previous mates? You will be a wife to me in every way that a woman may be to her wedded lord."

She blushed, but she responded, "I am old enough now, sir. I am older than the Queen of the Scots."

Still holding her by one hand, he reached up with his other hand and gently grazed her cheek with his knuckles. His look was warm. "You are so very fair," he said to her. Then he brushed her lips with his. "I will be a good husband to you, Rosamund."

"I know," she replied, and she did. In that

single moment that his mouth met hers so briefly, Rosamund Bolton knew that she had waited her whole young life for just this moment. "I know you will, Owein," she said, and she meant it.

Chapter 8

"Tonight," the king said as he stood at the high board, "I have a happy announcement to make. You all know Sir Owein Meredith. He has served the House of Tudor since his childhood. He has served it faithfully. The Queen of the Scots has requested a boon from me. She has asked that in honor of her marriage I reward this good knight. I am pleased to do so. So I give my ward, the Lady Rosamund Bolton of Friarsgate, in marriage to Sir Owein, and I grant them permission to travel as far as their home in the company of my daughter's wedding train. May their life together be a happy and fruitful one." He raised his goblet to the couple who were seated at the trestle just below the high board tonight.

At once the entire hall arose, raising their drinking vessels, and shouted with one voice, "Long life and many children!"

Rosamund clutched Owein's hand, blushing with her excitement.

"I fear Hal has lost his wager," murmured Richard Neville, who was seated at the far end of the table.

"But neither have you won it," Owein Meredith said softly, for he had heard young Neville's remark. "Master Brandon, you will bring the stakes you have been holding to the Countess of Richmond. You will tell her 'tis a donation from Prince Henry's friends for the poor. In future have more care with your gaming, gentlemen."

"It will be exactly as you have dictated, Sir Owein," Charles Brandon said, bowing from his seated position.

But Richard Neville was incensed. "Be careful, Meredith," he snarled, "My family is very powerful where you are going!"

"You acted dishonorably, sir. Be grateful I do not tell your father, who I have not a doubt would send you home immediately," Sir Owein replied sternly to the younger man. "Only that I would not have Rosamund's good name damaged, I should give you the thrashing that you so richly deserve. Do not dare to threaten me. *And* how dare you encourage England's future king to less than honorable behavior?"

Richard Neville opened his mouth to

reply, but Charles Brandon hissed sharply at him, "Be silent, Dickon! There is no excuse for what we attempted, and I knew it when I agreed to hold the wagers. We have only gotten what we deserved in this matter." He turned to the king's knight. "You have my apologies, Sir Owein," he said.

"They are accepted, Master Brandon," Sir Owein responded.

"What is this all about?" Rosamund asked the man who was to be her new husband.

"It is of no import, lovey," he answered her.

"Sir, if you persist in treating me like a witless and frail flower we shall not get on at all, I fear. Now, what is this quarrel about?" Rosamund demanded.

"We wagered on whether or not Prince Hal could seduce you," Richard Neville said meanly. "You are such a little innocent bumpkin, lady."

To their surprise Rosamund laughed aloud, "And you, sir, are a fool if you thought that Prince Henry's charm was all that was required to steal my virtue. We country lasses are clever in our own way. Perhaps we are not wise to your sophistication, but an attempted seduction be it by a prince or a cowherd, is very much the same. Although I will agree a prince's language is more flowery." She laughed again, and then as if an afterthought said, "*Oh*, and when your father wonders why I will not put my stallion to his mares any longer, tell him of this conversation we have just had. I know he was hoping to breed up several good warhorses by my King Valiant. What a pity." Then Rosamund smiled up into her betrothed husband's face and murmured, "Will you take me from the hall, sir. I find the air here has become rather fetid."

Without another word Owein arose and escorted her out, smiling and nodding at the congratulations they received along the way. When they had exited the great hall he turned to Rosamund saying with a grin, "I had forgotten how clever *and* how fierce you can be, lovey."

"I know I have been a quiet little ninny these months I have been at court," she admitted. "I have never been sure of myself in these surroundings, but now I am to go home. I can be myself once again. I hope you like who I am, sir, for you would, it seems, have no choice in the matter any longer."

He stopped, and looking down at her, took her face into his two hands. "I have liked you since the moment we met, Rosamund Bolton. I just never expected to be any more to you than a friend." The hazel-green eyes engaged her amber ones most directly.

"But now you are to be my husband," she answered him softly.

"Tomorrow we sign the papers," he told her.

"I am not unhappy about the matter," she told him. Her heart was racing madly, for he was looking at her so intensely.

"Are you flirting with me, madame?" he asked, and unable to help himself, he brushed her full ripe lips with his.

His look, his lips, made her suddenly breathless, but she yet managed to say boldly, "What, sir, is it not obvious? Then I must not be doing it very well, I fear."

"Oh, Rosamund," he said low, "you are doing it *very* well." Then he kissed her, his lips taking possession of hers and making demands that, innocent though she was, she recognized with some primal instinct.

Her arms wrapped about his neck, and she kissed him back, her mouth becoming more experienced with each passing moment that they embraced and her own passion waking and blazing up to engulf them both. She felt the hardness of his well-disciplined man's body against her, and sighed.

It was that delicious little sound that pulled him back to exactly where they were. The softness of her young breasts against his chest had rendered him weak, but they stood in a public place and could not remain there for long without being discovered. He didn't think he was up to a teasing by his friends, and they *would* tease him. Dependable, reliable Owein Meredith was obviously besotted by a lass. At least he had learned one thing. This girl who was to be his wife was filled with warmth and not afraid of pleasure. "Lovey," he whispered against her auburn hair, "we must move on. I must return you to the princess' apartments. In the morning I will come to escort you to mass. Afterward the papers should be ready for us to sign."

"But I like this kissing and cuddling with you," she told him candidly. "Can we not go someplace privily and continue it?"

He took her hand in his, and kissing it, began to walk with her. "Lovey. I am frankly astounded to have been given you to wife. I pray it is not a dream from which I will awaken. I find with you in my arms that my desires are beginning to awaken in such a manner as I have never experienced them. I admit to you that I have had women in my bed and felt lust enough to know that this is

272

very different. I do not want to share what I feel for you with anyone but you, Rosamund. Do you understand?"

"Yes and no," she admitted, "but I will be led by you in this matter, Owein Meredith, for you are wiser than I. But does this mean we shall not kiss again until we are wed?"

He laughed weakly. "I do not think I can wait that long, lovey. We will find little hidey-holes where we may be private, I promise you. But for now you must behave yourself."

They had reached the princess' apartments, where Rosamund slept. He kissed her hand and quickly left her. Rosamund entered the dayroom humming dreamily, to be met by a smiling Maybel who embraced her immediately and then sniffled.

"Ah, child, I am so relieved that they have found you a good man. Are you happy, my bairn? Sir Owein is so like Sir Hugh, but younger, and you are older now. Ah, soon my lady will be a mother herself!"

"Aye, 'tis time. I am grown enough to be a wife in all ways, Maybel. I am content with Sir Owein. He is kind, and Maybel, I think he may actually care for me," Rosamund noted.

"Well pray our Blessed Mother Mary that you have recognized that," Maybel said. "Aye, lass, he does indeed care for you. I would venture to say he is *in love* with you, although he may not recognize it as such yet. You must love him back, child. Not simply with your body but with your whole heart, if you can. You are surely the most fortunate girl I have ever known in your husbands!"

"And for all my complaining I have yet to choose one myself," Rosamund laughed. "I am happy, aye! It was Meg who did this for me, Maybel. I owe her a great debt, for had she not suggested Sir Owein as my mate, who knows whom they would have chosen for me when they wished to *honor* someone.

"Well," said Maybel, "whoever is responsible for this turn of events, I am right grateful to them. We are going home. I will be with my Edmund once more. I don't think I am of a mind to travel ever again, my child. These last months have surely been adventure enough for both of us!"

In the morning after the mass Sir Owein Meredith and Rosamund Bolton were called into the presence of the king, his mother, Princess Margaret, Prince Henry, and the king's chaplain. Upon the table were spread the parchments that they would sign.

"You are content in this, lady?" the king's chaplain asked.

"I am, Reverend Father," Rosamund replied with a smile.

"And you, Sir Owein, are also content to take this lady to be your wife?" the chaplain inquired.

"I am," Owein Meredith responded, struggling to keep the grin off his face. This was a serious occasion after all, but the lilt that had long ago been in his voice, that hinted of his Welsh origins, was again very much in evidence.

The king caught his mother's eye, and small smiles touched their faces. It was rare that their actions actually made someone so happy. They placed their signatures in witness of the marriage betrothal between Rosamund Bolton and Owein Meredith.

And when it was done, the parchments sanded and rolled back up, a copy was given to the king's knight. The second copy would be kept by the king's chaplain in the royal archives. The priest then instructed the couple to kneel before him. He blessed them, thus making official and irrevocable their betrothal. They were now, but for the marriage ceremony, man and wife.

"One day," Prince Henry boasted, "you will show this document to your children and tell them your betrothal was witnessed by a king and a queen."

"You are not yet England's king," his father said dryly. Then the king addressed Owein Meredith. "I will miss you, my faithful knight, but you are deserving of this pretty girl and a home of your own. And you, my lady Rosamund, do you think Sir Hugh Cabot would approve of the husband I have given you?"

"He would, your highness. He would very much approve, and I thank you for your kindness to me. I have received nothing but goodness in your house. First from your gracious queen, may God assoil her blessed soul. Then from your daughter and from your mother. And finally from yourself, my lord." Rosamund knelt before the king, and taking his hand, kissed it reverently. "Thank you, sire," she said. "I will always be yours to command."

The king raised the young girl up, and looking directly at her, said, "Aye. I can see in your lovely face that you are worthy, Rosamund Bolton of Friarsgate. God bless you, my child, and your good husband, Sir Owein."

"Come," said the Venerable Margaret, "we will drink a small toast to the happy couple." She nodded at a waiting servant who passed about some goblets of wine. A health was raised to Rosamund and to Owein. The wine quickly consumed, they were dismissed.

"I am informed that we will leave in less than a week's time," Owein said to Rosamund as they walked from the king's privy chamber.

"What is the date today?" she asked him. "How odd that I should not know, but I will remember it if you will but tell me."

"It is the twenty-second of June," he said.

"We are prepared to depart on the twenty-seventh," she told him. "We are going to Collyweston, which I am told belongs to the king's mother. Is it very big, Owein?"

He chuckled, understanding Rosamund's distress at the rather large royal residences she kept encountering. "Well, lovey," he began, "once it was a simple manor much like Friarsgate, but it has been renovated several times since its beginnings. A rather large guesthouse has been established there just this spring, I fear. It has a large park where the king hunts whenever he visits his mother there. We should not bide too long before we must continue on our way."

They departed Richmond precisely on schedule, arriving at Collyweston, which was just a few miles west of Stamford, on July fifth. They remained three days, entertained by the countess' choir, along with choirs from Cambridge and Westminster.

There were contests of archery and dancing and a hunt. Rosamund, however, was far more interested in the architecture of the house, particularly four great bay windows that had been specially built for this visit. They were decorated in stained glass, the first Rosamund had seen outside of a church window.

While the rest of the court pursued deer in the park at Collyweston, Rosamund questioned the countess' domestic butler on any number of household matters, for she much admired the king's mother's sense of organization. Mr. Parker was flattered that a member of the court, even one so unimportant as this girl, would be interested in how the house was run. He was most forthcoming with Rosamund.

Rosamund also spent her idle hours in the Venerable Margaret's rose gardens with the Princess of Aragon. Poor Kate had no horse of her own now, so while she enjoyed hunting she was forced to remain behind. Most of her servants had been sent away, and she was struggling to support those who remained on her meager income. It was very embarrassing for the princess who had a great sense of pride. Two years ago she had been the bride of England's next king. Now she knew not what she was to be. Her father and King Henry argued over monies while completely forgetting about her. She was grateful for Rosamund's company. While the girl seemed to favor the young Queen of the Scots, she had ever been kind, respectful, and generous.

"How fortunate you are to be going home," Kate said to her companion. "Sometimes I wish I could go home again."

"Do not despair, your highness," Rosamund said softly. "You are meant to be England's queen one day, and you will be."

"Your faith shames me," Kate replied, "I must be strong, I know, but sometimes I am so afraid."

"If you are, dear Kate, no one would know it," Rosamund responded, "and I shall certainly never tell on you," she finished with a smile.

The Princess of Aragon laughed. "You are unlike anyone I have ever known, Rosamund. You are open, and honest, and your heart is so very good. I am sorry you are going. I have few friends here."

"It matters not if I am here, or at Friarsgate, dear Kate," Rosamund answered the princess, "I am your true friend, and I shall be your liege woman always." She knelt, and kissed the princess' hand.

Young Katherine of Aragon felt tears

pricking sharply at the back of her eyelids. She fiercely blinked them back, saying as she did so, "I will remember you, Rosamund Bolton of Friarsgate. Your kind words, and your promise will help me to keep my spirits strong. I offer you my thanks for your friendship for I have nothing else to offer you now. *Vaya con Dios, mi amiga.*"

On the eighth of July, Margaret Tudor bid farewell to her father and her grandmother, as well as to many in the court. She would be under the protection of the Earl of Surrey, a soldier well-known for his suppression of border raids. The Countess of Surrey would act as Margaret's chaperon and mentor. The current Scots ambassador, the Bishop of Moray, accompanied the bridal progress, and the Somerset herald John Yonge was chosen to chronicle the entire journey for posterity.

As the royal progress began, the Earl of Surrey rode with a troupe of his armed men. He was followed in their proper order by lords, knights, squires, and yeomen soldiery. The man chosen to be Margaret Tudor's standard bearer, Sir Davey Owen, always preceded his young mistress. Mounted upon a snow-white mare, the young Queen of the Scots followed, magnificently arrayed, bejeweled, and gowned each day. Her master of the horse followed her, leading a spare mount. On the chance that Margaret should grow tired of riding, a litter was affixed between two beautiful horses.

Behind Margaret, her ladies and their squires followed along. They were all beautifully mounted upon superb horseflesh. The older women rode in unsprung carriages drawn by six fine chestnut horses each. Behind the horses came the rest of the gentlewomen, Rosamund among them. Owein, of course, rode with the knights at the beginning of the procession. It was a lonely time for Rosamund, for she really didn't know most of these women who accompanied Margaret Tudor. Some, of course, were with the court, but others had come just to be part of this historic occasion, and others joined them along the way. There was little chance for idle chatter amid the spectacle of the bridal progress. In a sense, they were an entertainment for the populace.

As they entered each town and village, drummers, trumpeters, and minstrels went ahead of the procession announcing with song and music the arrival of the young Queen of the Scots. Everyone dressed in their finest, with the badges and arms of their own houses or masters displayed. Sometimes Margaret rode upon her palfrey, wearing the crimson velvet gown trimmed in ebony black pampilyon, a fur resembling Persian lamb. It had been one of the last gifts her mother had given her before Elizabeth of York's death. The snow-white palfrey was magnificently caparisoned with a cloth of gold covering sporting the red roses of Lancaster. But in other towns Margaret entered seated within her litter, which was hung with cloth of gold edged with black velvet and jewels.

All along the route, for the journey would take a total of thirty-three days, the people came out to see the Tudor princess, to cheer the young Queen of the Scots. As they passed through the various districts the local lords and their ladies joined them. Some to go the full distance to Scotland, some simply to ride with the great progress for only a day or two.

At Grantham the bride was greeted by the Sheriff of Lincoln. A group of friars came out from the town singing anthems to her. The young queen dismounted to kneel and kiss the cross presented to her. The sheriff of each county would ride with her into the next county but for the Sheriff of Northampton, who went as far as Yorkshire. The bridal party passed through Doncaster, to Pontefract, and on to Tadcaster. The roads were lined with cheering people, calling out their good wishes to Margaret Tudor.

The Earl of Northumberland, the famed Harry Percy, joined the procession. His magnificence of dress was spectacular. He wore crimson velvet with jeweled sleeves and black velvet boots with gilt spurs when he met Margaret. The bridal progress began to swell in greater numbers as many sought to join in this historic occasion. As they headed toward York, a rider was sent on ahead to warn the lord mayor that the Queen of the Scots' procession had grown so large that it would be impossible to get it through the city's gates. In response the lord mayor removed a section of the city's ancient walls. Bells rang out joyously, and trumpeters sounded a fanfare as Margaret Tudor entered the ancient city through the wide opening created just for her. From every window people hung, curious and welcoming. It took two hours for the young queen to reach York Minster, where the archbishop awaited, so thick were the streets with revelers.

The following morning, a Sunday, Margaret attended the mass gowned in cloth of gold, her collar sparkling with precious gemstones. It was one of the few times that

Rosamund was able to join her betrothed husband and Maybel. They stood, garbed in their finest, shoulder to shoulder within the crowded cathedral. Because there were so many people attempting to crowd into the archbishop's open house, the three escaped to sit by the river with a meal of bread and cheese.

"I would not have in my wildest dreams imagined such a time as we have been having. The journey, while interesting, is utterly exhausting. I wonder how Meg endures it, but the Countess of Surrey thinks I am not worthy to associate with the Queen of the Scots. I hope I will have the opportunity to bid her farewell," Rosamund said.

"We leave the progress at Newcastle," Owein said. "Be glad we are not accompanying the bride all the way to Scotland, lovey. If you think the procession is bad now, just wait until it crosses over the border and the Scots begin to join the train." He chuckled. "It would almost be worth it to continue on and watch while they all jockey for position with the new queen."

"Well," Maybel said, "our departure for home can't come soon enough for me. All us serving women have been sleeping in haystacks and barns, wherever we can find accommodation," she grumbled.

"So have the knights and yeomen," Owein admitted.

"Only Meg's intervention with that overweening Countess of Surrey has saved me," Rosamund admitted, "although I have slept more on the floor of the halls we've visited than anywhere else. Even a convent's straw pallet will be an improvement."

"So we are agreed," Owein teased the two women, "that we will all be happy to be home at Friarsgate again?"

"Aye!" they chorused, and then they laughed.

Maybel arose from her place on the riverbank. "I need to move these old bones of mine a bit. Call me when you are ready to return to the general hubbub." Then she moved off slowly.

"She has done it to leave us to ourselves," Owein said.

"I know." Rosamund smiled at him. "Do you really think of Friarsgate as home, Owein?"

"Aye, strangely I do," he admitted, reaching out to take her hand in his. Lifting it to his mouth he began to kiss her fingers one by one. "I liked it from the start, even as I liked its lady," he told her.

"Now it is you who are flirting with me,

sir," she told him with a smile. "I quite like it, Owein."

"I am only slightly more experienced in the matter of courtship than you, Rosamund," he admitted. "You know I never thought to have a wife to cherish, or the hope of children of my own. I have as I told you flirted with the ladies, but this is different. It never mattered before if a lady cared for me, but it matters now." He laughed nervously. "Rosamund, I fear I wear my heart on my sleeve where you are concerned. I find I am not brave in your presence, but rather a little afraid."

"But why would you be afraid?" she cried, her hand reaching out as if she would comfort him.

"I have been given a great gift in you, Rosamund. I want you to be happy, but do I know how to make a woman, *a wife,* happy?"

"Owein," she reassured him, touched by this strong man's vulnerability, "I am happy. I swear it! My marriage to you is the first real marriage I will have. John Bolton and I were babies. My dear Hugh more grandsire than husband, and I far too young at any rate. Now I am not too young, nor are you too old. We are friends, and comfortable with each other. Friendship is important between a husband and a wife, or so the

Venerable Margaret told me. I trust her. I believe that we are starting off better than many."

"But lovey, there is more to marriage than just friendship," he said softly.

"There is passion I am told," Rosamund answered him. "How lovely that I shall explore that side of my nature with my best friend, Owein. You will lead, and I will follow. Perhaps we will learn to love each other, but if not, we will surely respect each other."

He shook his head in wonderment at her words. "You reason like a London lawyer," he teased gently. "You are young and inexperienced, but God's boots, lovey, you are wise!" Reaching out, he cupped the back of her head in his palm and pulled her forward to kiss her lips.

"Mmmm," Rosamund approved his actions. "I like your kisses, Owein Meredith. They are delicious. Not at all like Prince Henry, whose kisses seem to demand everything of a lass, especially that which she should not give him." Then she leaned toward him and kissed him back enthusiastically.

After a few breathless moments he broke the embrace between them, saying, "I want the church marriage performed between us as soon as we return to Friarsgate,

Rosamund. I do not think I can wait to love you, my betrothed wife."

"Why must we wait?" she asked him candidly. "We are formally betrothed. It is legal if we decide to enjoy each other, is it not?"

"I will have no hasty first coupling with you, lovey," he told her, "and in this you must defer to my wisdom. Besides, when we come together at last 'twill be in our own bedchamber, not upon some riverbank where we might be discovered by any low peasant." He took her chin between thumb and forefinger. "The first time must be perfect for you, Rosamund, for it will surely be perfect for me, my beautiful bride."

God's boots! How this man set her heart to racing when he said things like that, she thought. Her breath grew short, her mind reeled with an elusive pleasure she didn't quite understand, but certainly enjoyed. "Owein Meredith," she teased softly, "I believe that you have already begun to make love to me, and I find it most pleasant."

The afternoon had become an idyll, but it had to end. Maybel returned from her stroll, and they rejoined the wedding party. Margaret Tudor departed York on the seventeenth of July, traveling to Durham next. It was there that a new bishop was to be installed. The bridal progress remained three days, entertained by the bishop, who gave an enormous feast for all who might come, and his hall was filled to overflowing with all the guests who arrived, each eager to see and be seen.

They next traveled to Newcastle where the young Queen of the Scots made another state entry into the town. She was greeted at the city's gates by a choir of fresh-faced children singing happy hymns of joy to her. On the quayside of the river Tyne the citizens scrambled into the rigging of the moored ships in order to get a better look at the wondrous public display. The young queen rested that night at the Augustinian monastery in the town. It was there that Rosamund came to bid her friend farewell.

When the officious Countess of Surrey attempted to prevent Rosamund's entry into the queen's rooms, Tillie, Margaret Tudor's faithful tiring woman since her birth, said boldly, "This is the Lady Rosamund Bolton, the heiress of Friarsgate, who has been my mistress' dearest companion these last months. She is much in both the Queen of the Scots favor and that of the Countess of Richmond, even as she was with our dear queen, God assoil her soul. Tomorrow this lady departs the progress for her own home with her betrothed husband, Sir Owein

Meredith. My mistress will want to see her before she goes, your ladyship." This last was said with a rather strong emphasis.

"Oh, very well," the Countess of Surrey said, bested. "But do not remain too long with her highness, Lady Rosamund."

Rosamund curtsied. "Thank you, madame, for your kindness," she said with innocent malice.

"Well, at least she has manners," the countess sniffed as Rosamund disappeared into Margaret Tudor's apartments, while Tillie swallowed her laughter.

"Meg!"

"Oh, Rosamund!" Meg cried, "I was fearful the old dragon wouldn't let you in to see me before you left us." The two girls embraced.

"Thank your Tillie. She is a far fiercer dragon than the Countess of Surrey." Rosamund laughed. "You look tired, Meg." She took her friend's hand, and they sat together.

"I am," the young queen admitted, "but I cannot show it. Such a great to-do is being made over this marriage. Everyone is so anxious to please my father with their entertainments. John Yonge is keeping a most careful chronicle of the entire journey. I have seen some of his writings. He has written in copious detail of the Earl of Northumberland's wardrobe, which is, of course, magnificent. I do not know if Harry Percy means to do me honor as they all say, or make himself look royal." She laughed. "I am gaining the first prerequisite of a queen. A suspicious nature." And she laughed again, this time almost ruefully. "When will you leave us?" she asked.

"Tomorrow," Rosamund said. "We must ride cross-country in order to reach Friarsgate. It will take us two or more days."

"Then you will miss Percy's great banquet tomorrow on St. James' Day. There will be games, another tournament, dancing, and a great deal of food. Then we will go on to Alnwick Castle so I may have a few days of rest before going over the border at Berwick. Lord Dacre, who is my father's representative there, and his wife, will meet us with even more lords and ladies. They say my train as it enters Scotland will be at least two thousand people strong. I almost envy you your quiet ride across the summer countryside to your little home."

"I wish you could see Friarsgate, Meg," Rosamund told her enthusiastically. "The hills will be so green now, and the lake in our valley blue-blue. It is all very peaceful, and the people are so good," Rosamund told her.

"When will you wed Owein Meredith?" Meg asked, her blue eyes twinkling. "Grandmother said he was so surprised when she said he was to be your bridegroom. He loves you, I believe. I pray that James Stuart will love me, Rosamund. I know that such an emotion is not supposed to matter in a marriage such as mine, but I want it so!"

"I will pray for you, Meg," Rosamund promised. "As to your question, Owein wants to be married almost immediately, but I must really inform my uncle Henry of my betrothal first. He cannot stop my marriage, of course, but if I do not tell him, he will cry insult all over the district. I would not have my husband slandered unfairly."

"You will love him one day," Meg predicted.

"I hope so," Rosamund said, "but if I do not, at least I like him. He is very kind to me. But now, before the Countess of Surrey comes bustling in to eject me, I must bid you good-bye, Meg. There is no way in which I can thank you for all your kindness to me. I do not know what I would have done without you. You, and the Princess of Aragon, but mostly you."

"You saw Kate before we left?"

"Aye. I gifted her with the remainder of

my account at the London goldsmith's. I spent little of it. She will, I suspect, have need of those funds in the months to come. But tell no one," Rosamund added.

"Aye, she will, if her father does not pay the rest of her dowry portion," Meg said. "That was kind. I shall keep the secret."

"Our carefree days are over with now, your highness," Rosamund said, rising and curtsying to the young Queen of the Scots. "May your marriage be a happy and fruitful one."

Margaret Tudor stood straight, accepting the simple homage of her friend, "And you, Lady Rosamund of Friarsgate, I wish the same to you and a safe journey home."

"Thank you, your highness." Rosamund curtsied again. Then she backed slowly from the room, stopping briefly at the door to raise her hand in a final farewell. Her last glimpse of Margaret Tudor as the door closed and Tillie escorted her out of the queen's apartments was of a smiling girl. "Tillie, I thank you," Rosamund told the tiring woman. She put a silver piece into Tillie's hand.

The serving woman nodded quietly, slipping the coin into her pocket without looking at it. "God bless you, lady. You've been given a good man. Take care of him now.

Your Maybel will guide you."

Rosamund nodded. Then she hurried off to find her own faithful serving woman and her betrothed husband. Tomorrow they would begin the final leg of their long journey back to Friarsgate.

They departed from Newcastle just after the early summer's dawn. Owein had inquired of the monks at the monastery and learned that their order had a small establishment near Walltown that they could reach by very late afternoon, provided that they did not dally. They followed a track that paralleled the Picts Wall, which Owein explained had been built by Roman soldiers. The wall had been constructed to keep the wild northerners from coming south into the more civilized areas. Several hours along their route they stopped to rest themselves and the horses briefly. Built into the wall was a stone tower. Rosamund and Owein climbed the stairs of the tower and were rewarded with a splendid view of the countryside. Around them the rough landscape spread out in every direction. Cattle and sheep dotted the hillsides.

They finally reached the monastery, which was located on the east side of Walltown, in late afternoon. Owein knocked upon the great wooden gates of the establishment. Very quickly a barred aperture slid open to reveal a face.

"Yes?"

"I am Sir Owein Meredith, traveling in company with my betrothed wife, Lady Rosamund Bolton of Friarsgate, and her servant. We have come this day from Newcastle, where we were with the Queen of Scots' wedding progress. We were informed by the monastery in Newcastle that we could find shelter here for the night."

The vent shut with a slam, and after a long moment the small door in the gate was opened by a young monk. "You are welcome, Sir Owein," he said, and ushered them into the courtyard after they had dismounted their horses. "We must have a care here so close to Scotland. Even our calling does not necessarily protect us. I will take you to the abbot if you will please to follow me," the young monk said.

They followed the monk into the abbot's receiving chamber where they were greeted by the elderly religious. Sir Owein once again explained who they were and from where they had traveled.

The abbot waved them into the chairs set about the chamber. "We do not often get guests or hear news from the outside world," he said in a quavery voice, "You have traveled with the Queen of the Scots, our own Princess Margaret? When did you join her train?"

"At Richmond," Sir Owein replied, "I have until recently been in service to the House of Tudor, good father. Lady Rosamund has been a companion to the young queen for almost a year. We are now returning to Friarsgate to have our union blessed by the church and to begin our life together."

"Would you be related to Henry Bolton, the squire of Friarsgate?" the abbot asked.

"Henry Bolton is my uncle," Rosamund said stiffly, "but I am the heiress to Friarsgate, holy father. When I was first orphaned my uncle was my guardian, but after my second marriage to Sir Hugh Cabot, my uncle returned to his own home at Otterly Court. When Sir Hugh died his will gave my wardship to the king. The king has effected this new union to Sir Owein. My uncle has no control or authority at Friarsgate. He is certainly not its lord."

"Perhaps I am mistaken," the abbot said slowly, "I am old, and my mind often becomes confused."

"I doubt your mind was confused on the matter, good father," Rosamund replied, half-laughing. "My uncle has always desired what is mine, and I have no doubt hoped to gain it one day."

The old man nodded. " 'Tis often the case with a prosperous estate, my lady. Now let me bid you welcome to our house. We are a simple place, but we should be able to make you comfortable this night. Another day's ride and you will be home."

They were invited to join the abbot in his private dining room that evening. Expecting a pottage of root vegetables, they were delighted to be served a roasted capon stuffed with apples and bread, a platter with slices of fresh trout on a bed of watercress, a bowl of onions in milk and butter, bread, freshly baked and still warm, butter, and a fine aged cheese.

" 'Tis the feast of St. James, the patron of travelers," the abbot said with a twinkle in his eye, seeing their surprise, "It is a good feast to celebrate, and tomorrow is St. Anne's Day. She is patron to housewives and unmarried girls. You would, it seems, my lady, stand now between the two." And the old abbot chuckled.

A young monk filled their pewter goblets with a rather fine wine.

"It is important to keep up your strength here in this desolate location in which this house is set," Sir Owein said with a smile. "Where do you find such excellent wine?"

"The mother house in Newcastle sends it to us. It is part of our payment for the wool we harvest from our sheep each year. We support our little monastery in that way, sir. They send the wool to the Low Countries where it is turned into cloth that we then sell."

"You would do better to card your own wool and spin your own cloth," Rosamund said. "You lose good cloth when you have to ship it and then use a middleman to obtain the results that you could obtain yourselves here at your monastery. Why do you not do it?"

"We have no knowledge of the process other than caring for our sheep and shearing them," the abbot admitted.

"If you want to learn I will send someone to teach your monks," Rosamund offered. "You will find it far more profitable, I guarantee it, than sending your wool to the Low Countries."

"I must ask permission of the abbot at our mother house," the old man said, "but I see no reason why he would refuse me. Thank you, my lady Rosamund."

"The king's mother, who is called the Venerable Margaret, is patron to many good causes, but particularly to the church. I have learned from her, holy father. I am not a great lady so I cannot hope to equal her many accomplishments, but I can do something. This is what I choose to do, and I know that my betrothed husband would agree."

Owein smiled. He was going to have to speak to Rosamund about asking first and not simply assuming it would be all right, although in this particular case he did indeed agree with her. "My lady knows my mind in such matters," he agreed, putting the old monk's concerns at ease.

They were separated to sleep, but in the morning they again departed easily. The monks served them a good breakfast of oat stirabout, sweetened with bits of apple and honeycomb, and awash with heavy golden cream. The hot cereal was placed into small individual trenchers of new bread, and mugs of apple cider accompanied the meal. The mass prior had been beautiful, the pure voices of the monks rising in the quiet morning air. They left St. Augustine's well-fed and feeling surrounded by the notion of peace. The day, however, was gray and drizzly as they rode along. The monks had given them bread, cheese, and apples to eat on their journey. They did so, sheltering within another of the Roman towers during a late-morning downpour.

Rosamund knew instinctively when they passed into Cumbria from North-umberland. There was something about the hills. There was a familiar smell to the clean and crisp air. She could feel her anticipation mounting with each passing mile. It didn't matter that it was wet and gloomy. She was coming home! Home to Friarsgate. She had believed when she left it almost a year ago that this day would never come, but it had. Tonight she would sleep in her own bed. And then they reached the crest of a steep hill. Below them, to her surprise, was her lake — her home! At that moment the clouds parted. The sun came out, spreading its golden rays over the entire valley.

"Maybel!" Rosamund cried, her voice breaking with happiness.

"Lord bless us, my sweet bairn. Some nights I never thought to see that sight again," Maybel admitted. Then she kicked her gelding into a trot. "I'll not wait another moment to see my Edmund," she said.

"It's beautiful," Owein told Rosamund, "I had almost forgotten how beautiful, lovey."

" 'Tis home," Rosamund said simply. *"Our home,* Owein."

Reaching out, he took her gloved hand and kissed it. "Let us go down, sweetheart, for Maybel will have surely aroused the whole manor by the time we get there." He laughed, and releasing her hand, he moved his horse into a trot while Rosamund followed behind.

Maybel had indeed aroused the manor, and as they reached the bottom of the hills surrounding Friarsgate the people were coming from the fields to welcome their mistress home again. They brought their mounts to a halt before the house, and Rosamund said, "Good people of Friarsgate, I am returned to you with my betrothed husband, whom you already know. Sir Owein Meredith will be your new master. I would have you respect and obey him even as I do. Father Mata will bless our union in a week's time after my uncle at Otterly has been notified."

The Friarsgate folk cheered her words and pressed about them as they dismounted their horses, wishing them long life and happiness. Escaping into the house both Owein and Rosamund were rosy and laughing. Edmund Bolton met them, his smile warm as he congratulated them.

"Henry will not be pleased," he said with a wicked chuckle.

"Send a messenger off to him at first light," Rosamund said. "It is time to end his schemes for good and for all. This time I will not only be wedded, but bedded, uncle!" And Rosamund Bolton laughed aloud with her happiness.

Chapter 9

Rosamund consulted with the young priest Father Mata, and it was decided that the church formalities involving her betrothal and marriage would take place on Lammastide, August first. The manor folk would have the day for a holiday no matter, and home again, Rosamund's practical nature came forward. No need to give two days of holiday when one would do.

" 'Tis harvest," she said to the priest. "We cannot afford two days. You have had no difficulties while I was away?"

"No, lady. I celebrate the mass daily, and minister to the spiritual needs of the manor folk. I am honored to celebrate the sacrament for you and Sir Owein."

"Tell me what my uncle has not," Rosamund said craftily.

"Lady, I practice only my spiritual duties," Father Mata replied cleverly, a small smile upon his face.

"Then there is something," Rosamund mused. "I thought as much! Even a place as remote and quiet as Friarsgate cannot go a year without something happening. Thank you, good father." And she hurried off to find Edmund Bolton.

He was in the hall with Owein. The two men were conversing in low and somber tones. "What has happened?" she demanded.

Edmund Bolton looked at his niece. She had grown in the ten months she had been away from them. Not only had her height increased, but there was a new maturity about her young face. "What do you mean?" he countered, his blue eyes meeting her amber ones.

"Uncle, I spoke with the priest. Now tell me what has happened that was unusual while I was gone," Rosamund repeated. She sat down in Owein's lap, her blue skirts covering his long legs.

Edmund sighed. "I think it may be naught," he began, "but the Scots have been seen hereabouts. We have had horsemen on the heights above our valley in recent days. They just stand and watch. Nothing else."

"Has anyone ridden out to speak with them?" Rosamund asked.

"Nay, niece, we have not. They have done naught. They just observe," Edmund Bolton replied. He ran a nervous hand through his silver-gray hair and shifted in his chair.

"I want to know the next time they come," Rosamund said. "I will ride out myself to question these intruders."

"Rosamund, it is too dangerous!" Edmund cried. "Your husband should go, not you.

"Nay, uncle, I am the lady of Friarsgate. It is my duty and my responsibility to investigate this. And I must go alone. They will not, whoever they may be, attack a woman, particularly if her menfolk remain below, watching over her. Remember, I am a friend of the Queen of the Scots."

"As if that would matter to a pack of ravaging borderers," Edmund muttered irritably. "Owein, you must speak with your wife!"

"What would you have me say?" Owein Meredith demanded. "She is perfectly correct. She is the lady here. I am only her husband. The land is not mine, and will most likely never be. I am not of a mind to inherit, for to do so my Rosamund must die. I am not Henry Bolton."

"But if you allow her to ride out alone, do you not put her in danger?" Edmund asked the younger man.

"Have these borderers stolen anything belonging to Friarsgate, or even attempted to
steal anything?" Owein queried him.

"Nay, they have not. They but sit upon
their horses on the hills about us," Edmund
replied slowly.

"They have always remained atop the
hills? They have never come down, even a
little ways?" Owein continued.

Edmund Bolton shook his head in the
negative.

"And other than looking back you have
made no move toward them?" Owein asked.

Again Edmund Bolton shook his head in
the negative.

"Friarsgate's wealth is well-known,"
Owein noted. "But so is the difficulty in escaping from here with livestock known as
well. These borderers have most likely come
to see if there isn't a way around the challenges our natural defenses present them. I
suspect that if Rosamund beards them face-
to-face they will decide it isn't worth it.
Particularly if they learn she is a friend of
their new queen," he concluded.

Rosamund broke into their conversation,
"I am curious. Have you any idea of who
they might be, uncle?"

"I do not," he admitted. "I haven't gotten
close enough to see their plaids or their

badges, niece." He stood up. "We're beginning the harvest in the pear orchard today. I must go." Then he smiled. "I think you will entertain each other in my absence, eh?" Then he departed from the little hall, chuckling to himself.

"I like it that you respect me," Rosamund told Owein.

"I indeed respect your position as this manor's lady," he replied as he began to fondle her full young breasts. "What date have you decided upon for our church marriage, lovey? I fear I grow more lustful to possess you as each hour passes. We have already been home a full day."

"August first," she murmured, enjoying his hands and leaning forward to kiss his ear. "You have such beautiful ears, Owein. They are long and narrow, and I find the lobes most delicious," she told him, nibbling upon the flesh.

"I am beginning to regret my nobility in refraining from your bed until the church has formally blessed our union with the sacrament of marriage," he told her. The hand that had been fondling her breasts now slipped beneath her skirts. His knuckles grazed along the soft, satiny flesh of her inner thigh. He cupped her mons in his big hand and squeezed, feeling the moisture suddenly crown his broad palm. The knowledge that he was exciting her began to arouse him, and he felt himself growing hard. Their lips met, their tongues playfully teasing at each other, as the kiss between them deepened and grew more passionate. He pressed a single finger against her slit, and it slid between her nether lips. With little difficulty he found her untried love bud and began to bedevil it, the rough ball of his finger harrying and tantalizing the tiny nub of sentient flesh until he felt it swell and heard Rosamund moan against his mouth with a sound of distinct and open pleasure. She shuddered against him, sighing, and he ceased the delicious torture, moving the finger slowly over her again and again until he finally thrust the long digit into her love sheath carefully and gently.

"*Oh!*" She sighed again, and shifting her body, attempted to make his penetration deeper.

The finger moved swiftly back and forth within her until she gasped, and he said softly, "This is just the beginning, lovey. Now you have a sweet inkling of what is to come." He kissed her tenderly.

"I want more," Rosamund said demandingly. "*More!*"

"On Lammas Night I shall give you more

than you can even anticipate," he told her, taking his hand from beneath her gown.

"I think you are ever so mean to tease me thusly," she complained.

He grinned mischievously at her. "I am beastly," he agreed cheerfully. "But there will come a time when you may repay me in kind, my sweet Rosamund. I cannot explain it, but you will see."

There would be the traditional feasting on Lammas Day, of course, but there would also be a special feast for all the manor to celebrate the lady's marriage to Sir Owein Meredith. Twin sides of beef would be packed in rock salt and slowly roasted. There would be sweets as well, candied rose petals and pear tartlets. And of course the usual products of the first grains harvested and milled.

On the twenty-eighth of July the mysterious riders appeared on the hill for the first time since Rosamund's return home. Notified, she immediately went to the stables and mounted her horse to ride up the hill where not one but three riders stood. Below, Owein and Edmund watched her progress.

Reaching the crest of the hill she brought her horse to a stop even as she said, "I am

Rosamund Bolton, the lady of Friarsgate. You are, sirs, trespassing upon my lands."

"You stand on your lands, lady, but where we rest 'tis not," the spokesman for the group said. He was the biggest man Rosamund had ever seen, well over six feet and sitting very tall upon his horse, which he gripped with legs like tree trunks. To her surprise he was clean-shaven although most borderers were not. "I am the Hepburn of Claven's Carn," he announced in a deep voice that seemed to thunder up from within his broad chest.

"What is it you seek, my lord?" Rosamund queried him. "Your clansmen have been observed upon the hills about my home for some weeks now. If your purpose is honest, you have always been welcome here."

"I could hardly come courting until you had returned, lady," the Hepburn of Claven's Carn replied. His thick black hair was cropped close, and he had the bluest eyes she had ever seen. Even bluer than Prince Hal's.

"Who would you court?" she queried him.

The two clansmen with the Hepburn laughed aloud.

"Why you, lady," the Hepburn replied.

"*Me?*" Rosamund was genuinely surprised.

"My father, God assoil him, tried to make a match between us when you were but a youngling, but your uncle instead married you to his cat's paw so he might keep your estate in his hands. Several months ago I learned that your husband had died but that you had been taken south. I have had men posted on the hills about Friarsgate awaiting your return," the Hepburn explained. "Now I have come to court you, lady, and I intend to wed you whether your uncle will or nay." He looked directly at her when he spoke.

Rosamund's cheeks grew warm, but she held her ground and stared straight back at him. "I am betrothed," she said quietly, "and at the king's command, not my uncle's. The cat's paw had claws and was not the toothless lion my uncle believed."

The Hepburn laughed. "You have spirit, lass," he said. "I like it. And is your betrothed the English coward who sits his horse at the bottom of the hill with your steward?"

"Owein sits his horse at the hill's bottom because he is not the lady of Friarsgate, and I am," she replied. "I speak for myself and my people. No one else does." This Scot was arrogant, but she would not be cowed by either his size or his manner.

The Hepburn laughed again. "One of

Henry Tudor's Welshmen, is he? When is the wedding, lass?"

"Lammastide," she answered.

He nodded. "Aye, 'tis well done, for they will have a day for the holiday no matter." Then the blue eyes narrowed. "I could steal you away right now, Rosamund Bolton. Bride stealing is considered an honorable pastime in the borders." He moved his mount up next to hers, so close that she could scent him, and her nostrils twitched.

But she did not flinch, saying instead, "And would you take me to King James' court to show me off, my lord?" Her dark lashes brushed against her cheeks in a most flirtatious manner.

"Aye, I would," he replied, reaching out to finger one of her auburn braids.

"Then my friend, *the Queen of the Scots,* would be quite curious to learn why I was not with the man she personally chose to be my husband," Rosamund told him with a wicked grin.

The Hepburn's jaw dropped in surprise, "You know Jamie Stuart's new queen?" he said, astounded.

"I have been her companion for the last ten months," Rosamund told him in dulcet tones. "My betrothed and I traveled as far as Newcastle in her wedding train, my lord.

Aye, I know Meg Tudor very well."

"Well, I'll be damned," the Hepburn of Claven's Carn said.

"Aye, sir, I have no doubt that you will," Rosamund replied with a small grin. "Now, tell me, why on earth did your father offer for me? You're a Scot and his heir. I am English, as are my lands."

"We're borderers, my lady," he said, "no matter which side. I saw you when you were just a wee lass. It was at a cattle fair, and you had come with Edmund Bolton."

"I must have been six then," Rosamund recalled. "It was on the Scots' side of the border in Drumfrie, was it not? Aye, I was six that summer. How old were you, sir?"

"Sixteen, and my given name is Logan," he answered her.

"Sixteen, and you had no wife?" she queried him, curious.

"My father was still alive. I chose not to wed until I was the Hepburn of Claven's Carn," he told her.

"And by not marrying, Logan Hepburn, you have been able to bestow your affections generously *and* on both sides of the border, I have not a doubt," she replied tartly.

"Jealous?" he teased her, "You need not be, lass, for I have been saving my heart only for you."

She blushed again. "I am, sir, to all intents and purposes, a married woman," Rosamund snapped.

"The Welshman looks old, yet young enough to bed you," Logan Hepburn said boldly. " 'Twill be more a marriage than the other two you have had, Rosamund Bolton. I envy the man. And does your greedy uncle approve?"

"His approval is not necessary," she answered.

"And has he been invited to the wedding?" he taunted her.

"Aye, he has!" she said.

"And will you invite me?" The blue-blue eyes danced wickedly.

"No, I will not!" Her foot stamped against her stirrup, and the mare danced nervously.

"I may come nonetheless," he said seriously.

"You would not dare!" she cried.

"Aye, I would," he drawled.

"We have no business between us, Logan Hepburn. I will bid you good day," Rosamund told him. Turning her mare about, she rode off down the hill without even looking back.

"You could take her," his brother Colin said softly.

"And have our cousin Patrick, the Earl of

Bothwell, come calling? If the lass is the queen's friend then I have no choice in this matter," Logan Hepburn told his two companions.

"How did an unimportant little northern heiress become friends wi King Henry's daughter?" Colin Hepburn wondered aloud.

"I do not know," Logan replied, "but I believe her. She is very outspoken. I do not believe she would lie about such a thing, but when I see Patrick Hepburn again, I will ask, you may be sure."

"So who will you marry now, Logan?" his youngest brother, Ian, asked him. "There's plenty who would have you," he chortled.

"Aye, but I don't want them," Logan said. "There is the lass I want for my wife, and one day I'll have her."

"Claven's Carn needs an heir," Colin carefully pointed out.

"You and Ian can have them," Logan replied.

"I don't know whether you are a fool or — worse — a romantic," Colin said. "Perhaps both, brother."

Logan Hepburn chuckled.

"Will you really go to her wedding to the Welshman?" Ian said.

"Aye, I'll come, and I'll bring my pipes. We all will." Then with a great shout of laughter he turned his stallion from the overlook to Friarsgate and galloped off, his two brothers riding in his wake.

Rosamund heard the laughter as she descended the hill. The very sound of it irritated her greatly. She had never before met such an insolent, irritating man as Logan Hepburn. But at the same time she was rather fascinated by what he had told her. She would ask her uncle Edmund if it was indeed true. It was flattering to think that someone had made an offer for her. She wondered if Hugh had been aware of the Hepburns. *Dearest Hugh.* He would, she knew, be very happy for her, and he would certainly approve of Owein Meredith. She had now reached the bottom of the hill. She drew up her mare before Owein and Edmund.

"You are flushed, lovey," Owein noted, curious.

"I have just met the most annoying, aggravating man," Rosamund said. "Edmund, do you know the Hepburns of Claven's Carn?"

"Their holding is on the other side of these hills," Edmund replied slowly. "Which of them was it, and why have they been spying upon us these past weeks? Did they tell you?"

"It was the laird himself," Rosamund began.

"Old Dugald? I thought him too ill to sit a horse any longer," Edmund remarked.

"The old laird is obviously dead. 'Twas his eldest son, Logan Hepburn, and from the look of them his two companions were his brothers," Rosamund told her uncle. "Let us go back to the house, Edmund, and I will tell you both everything, but I must have a cup of wine. I do not know when I have been so vexed." She walked her mount toward the stables, followed by her two puzzled companions.

"This man has admired her," Owein noted softly to Edmund.

"He would not dare!" Edmund said quickly. "He has no right!"

"Nonetheless he has," Owein said with a knowing smile. "I have not lived at a Tudor court for most of my life not to know the signs of a woman complimented, confused, and angry over it. Remember that Rosamund is really quite innocent in the games men play with women."

"And you, my friend, how do you feel about the possibility that another man would pay your betrothed court?" Edmund asked, curious.

"I love her," Owein said quietly, "but if

317

another would make her happier than I will, then I should step aside, though it would break my heart, Edmund Bolton. However, our marriage is set for Lammas, and I do not intend giving her up."

"You would fight for her?" Edmund wondered.

"Aye, I would if necessary," Owein admitted softly. "She has become my world, Edmund. I cannot help myself."

"So that is why you defer to her in matters pertaining to Friarsgate?" Edmund said.

"Did not you and Hugh Cabot teach her to be independent?" Owein countered. "She is made in the same mold as the Venerable Margaret. It is not fashionable for a man to admire such a woman, I know, but I do. We will make strong babies together, Edmund. I would instruct both sons and daughters to be as strong as she is."

"My niece has not been fortunate in her family," Edmund said, "but by God's blood she has been lucky in her husbands."

"She is fortunate in you, and I suspect your priestly brother, too," Owein said. "I shall look forward to meeting all your siblings."

They dismounted their horses, which were led off by the stable lads, and they entered the hall where Rosamund was already awaiting them, a pewter goblet of wine in her hand.

Owein took her other hand and kissed the palm softly. Then he led her to a chair by the afternoon fire, saying, "Tell us, lovey, what has distressed you so very much?" He sat himself with Edmund Bolton upon a settle facing her, accepting the wine the serving wench offered him.

Rosamund looked directly at her uncle. "Did the Hepburns of Claven's Carn offer for me the summer I was six? Do you recall, Edmund? You took me to a cattle fair at Drumfrie. We were yet mourning John's death, but Uncle Henry let me go at my aunt's behest."

"Aye, they did," Edmund said. "I remember returning home with you and speaking with Henry. The knowledge set him into a frenzy, however. All he could see was that he might lose Friarsgate through your marriage to someone who wasn't related to him. Shortly afterward he settled upon Hugh Cabot. But he lived in fear for the rest of the summer that the Hepburns would come over the hill and steal you away. I had quite forgotten about it, Rosamund."

"So the young Hepburn has come courting, has he?" Owein said softly, noting Rosamund's blush when he spoke.

"I set him aright," she quickly replied, "I told him I was to be wed at Lammas, and was content to be so. The devil said he would come and dance at my wedding!" Rosamund cried, outraged with the memory.

Owein laughed. "Then we shall welcome him, lovey. Are you having second thoughts with this new knowledge you have obtained?"

"Never!" she declared passionately. "I would be your wife and no other's, Owein!" She slipped from her chair and knelt by his side, looking up into his face. "Do you not still want me? Perhaps 'tis you who are having second thoughts. Mayhap the thought of marriage to an unsophisticated country girl like me, a life here in the north with no excitement, does not appeal to you any longer, now that we are returned." Her gaze was anxious.

He reached out and touched her face gently. Then, taking her hand, he drew her up and into his lap. "I will have no other wife but you, Rosamund Bolton," he assured her. "And life at Friarsgate seems like paradise to me after a lifetime in other men's houses. Besides" — and here Owein smiled tenderly at her — "I seem to have developed a strong weakness for an auburn-haired wench with amber eyes that melt my heart each time I look into them." Then he kissed her soundly, and Rosamund sighed happily, feeling safe and secure again in his strong arms, wishing her uncle were not there so Owein might touch her as he had before. Only three more days, she considered.

Their wedding day dawned unusually hot even for summer. A haze hung over the landscape. The blue sky had a milky look about it. Still dressed in her night garment Rosamund came into the hall at first light. Edmund brought her the year-old quarter loaf, and following the traditional Lammas customs, she carefully broke it into pieces, which she then crumbled, filling a small earthenware dish. She walked barefooted from the hall and out into the morning light, spreading her crumbs for the birds as she came. Having followed the age-old tradition, Rosamund then returned to the house to prepare for her wedding, which would be celebrated immediately following the mass. Her uncle Richard, who had arrived the day before, would assist her own priest.

Maybel had brought Rosamund's oak tub into her bedchamber. It was already filled with hot water. "Hurry, child," she encouraged Rosamund, pinning up her hair, which had been washed the afternoon before, so it would not get wet again, "Ah, this will be the last time you use this chamber. I remember you as just a wee lass in this room." She sniffed and wiped her eyes with her sleeve. "I believe I always shall."

"Why? Will I not use my room again?" Rosamund wondered aloud as she stripped off her night garment and stepped into the water, seating herself. Then the answer dawned upon her. *"Oh,"* she said with a nervous little laugh. "Tonight I shall sleep in the master and mistress' chamber with my husband. The room is ready?" She picked up the flannel and soap and began to wash herself.

"Of course," Maybel said, her tone just slightly aggrieved.

"I think I shall wear my Tudor-green gown today," Rosamund replied, pretending that she hadn't noticed.

"You most certainly will not!" Maybel said indignantly, "You're a bride, my lass. *A real bride.* The gown your mam wore has been packed away in the attics for years. I have spent these past few days altering it for you. Tillie showed me how to take an old-fashioned garment and remake it in the latest style. She said the king, may God assoil him, is very tight with a penny. He would not waste good coin on new gowns when the old ones were not worn out. And I can't say I disagree with him. Tillie had to learn how to make do because her mistress insisted on always being dressed in the latest styles."

"Aye, she did," Rosamund recalled. "And how Meg hated to wear mourning so much. Oh, Maybel, thank you! To have a proper gown for my marriage to Owein is more than I could have hoped for ever. What would I do without you?" Her amber eyes were filled with tears that slipped unbidden down the girl's face.

"Wash your face, lass!" Maybel responded in a husky voice, for she, too, was near tears. Rosamund had been in her charge since her birth, for her mother had never been very strong. Maybel's own child with Edmund had died before its first birthday. So she had nursed Rosamund at her own milk-filled breasts, with scarcely time to even mourn her own Jane. Rosamund had become her daughter in every sense except that she had not birthed her. "And do the back of your neck!" she half-scolded, a small smile on her lips.

Rosamund giggled happily, vigorously scrubbing the back of her neck with the soapy flannel and rinsing it. Then, standing up, she stepped from her tub, drying herself with the towel that Maybel had been warming by the hearth. She was very eager to see her wedding gown.

Maybel first handed the girl a fine linen chemise with its ruffled lace neckline, which was not high like her everyday chemise, but low to fit the square neckline of the white silk bodice that Maybel had embroidered in silver threads with a design of pendant flowers and small roses. The lace of the chemise would show from beneath the top of the bodice. Her sewn silk stockings were fastened just above her knee with garters of white rosettes. Her round-toed shoes were made of white kid. Some things had not been changed on the dress. The sleeves of the gown were long and tight as they had been on the original dress, and the long skirt was still gracefully pleated.

"Oh," Rosamund complained, "I wish we had a large looking glass like Meg's so I could see what I look like." She twirled and preened, skirts ruffling out. "This was my mother's? She wore it on her wedding day?"

"Aye," Maybel said. "The skirt was longer because it was held up to reveal a fancy brocatelle underskirt. The neckline wasn't as low, and there wasn't any embroidery on the bodice. Still, it was the finest gown anyone had ever seen in these parts. They say your mother's father sent all the way to London for it when he betrothed his only daughter to Guy Bolton, the heir to Friarsgate. I remember your mam well, for we were of an age. She looked lovely. She would be so pleased to know you are wearing her gown on your own wedding day."

"I wore green for Hugh, and I think it brought me luck," Rosamund said thoughtfully. "I remember that October day well."

Maybel nodded. "Henry Bolton thought to bind you to his branch of the family forever with that marriage. You were fortunate in Hugh Cabot, my lass, but then I need not tell you that."

"And I will be fortunate in Owein, as well," Rosamund said. "Meg says he loves me. Do you think it is so, or was she just saying it so I would not be afraid or angry again?"

"Gracious, lass, can you not see it?" Maybel exclaimed. " 'Tis as plain as the nose on your face. Aye, he loves you. And from today you had best learn to love him. 'Tis better when there is love."

"Do you love Edmund?" Rosamund asked boldly. "Has he ever told you that he loves you?"

"My father was the miller here at Friarsgate when I was a lass. Like you, I was an only child, and he wanted a good marriage for me. He set his sights on Edmund Bolton, whose own da had made him the steward here, for he could not inherit Friarsgate, you know. Still, your grandsire loved all his lads and tried to provide for them all. I was pretty in those days, like all young girls are pretty. Everyone knew I was a hard worker. My father set a generous dowry on me of five silver pieces, a chest of linens, four gowns, four chemises, caps, a wool cloak, and a pair of sturdy leather shoes. He went to the lord of Friarsgate and asked his permission to betroth me to Edmund, for I was a proper lass with a fine dower portion. The lord knew when my da died I'd inherit what was left for my own. Ma was already gone. Your grandfather gave us our cottage as a gift. Did I love him? Not then. But your uncle's a man who grows on you. One day out of the blue, and I don't know why because I never dared to ask him why, Edmund says to me, 'I loves you, Maybel. Do you love me?' 'I do,' I answered him, and that was the end of it. We've never spoken on it since, nor is it necessary, for neither of us has ever been the kind of folk who dissemble. He said it, and I said it, and there's the end of it. Now, hold still, lass while I brush your hair. Margery has made

you a lovely wreath of flowers to wear in it."
She wielded the boar's bristle brush, sliding
it down the long length of Rosamund's hair
until the auburn tresses shone with golden
lights. Rosamund's hair would be worn
loose and unbound, for she was a virgin.

"Has Uncle Henry arrived yet?" the nervous girl asked.

"Not yet, and just as well, I'm thinking,"
Maybel said tartly. "I wondered if he could
bear to see all his scheming go for naught,
but then he may show up yet, lass." She put
down the hairbrush, and taking up the floral
wreath, set it on Rosamund's head. "There!
You're ready now, and a prettier bride I have
never seen."

Rosamund turned and hugged Maybel
hard. "I love you," she said, "and I shall
never be able to thank you enough for your
mothering, dearest Maybel." She stepped
back from the older woman. "How pretty
you look," she told the beaming Maybel. "Is
that the gown Tillie helped you make?"

"Aye," Maybel said, "and perhaps a bit
grand for Friarsgate, but I wanted to look
special for you on this day." Maybel's gown
was a dark blue in color, her round-necked
and ruffled white linen chemise showing
above the gown's square neckline. Her long
tight sleeves had turned-back cuffs in a con-

trasting lighter blue. She wore a short blue velvet hood with a snow-white veil over her neat white cap.

Outside they heard the little church bell begin to toll, calling them to the mass. Together the two women descended the staircase of the house to where Edmund and Sir Owein Meredith awaited them. Both men were wearing hose attached to their doublets, and overgowns. Edmund's was a dark blue, matching his wife, but the bridegroom had parti-colored silk hose of black, white, and gold. His overgown was a rich burgundy wine color trimmed with dark fur, and his round-toed shoes were of black leather. On his dark blond head he wore a soft fabric hat that had been gathered into bands. Its color matched his gown.

Owein's face lit up at the sight of Rosamund in her bridal finery even as she looked surprised upon him. She had never seen him in such elegant garb, even at the court. His clothing had run, as hers had, to the more practical.

"How handsome you are," she said almost breathlessly.

Reaching out, he took her hand, bringing her down the last few steps. "And you are surely the most beautiful bride any eyes have ever seen, lovey. If I went blind this moment

I should always have the sight of you now in my memory no matter." Gallantly he kissed the hand in his. Then, tucking it in his arm, he led her out the front door of the house.

Suddenly, and to her great surprise, three kilted borderers appeared, playing their pipes, and prepared to lead the bridal party to the church. "What is this?" she whispered to Owein.

"The Hepburn of Claven's Carn and his brothers have come to kindly play for us," Owein said calmly. "You will, I hope, thank them at the feasting later, lovey."

"It is intolerable!" she hissed back at him.

Owein chuckled. "He does it partly to make his peace with us and partly to tease you, Rosamund," her bridegroom explained.

"I told him he was not to come!" Her color was high now.

"But surely you knew he would under the circumstances?" Owein replied. "Be gracious, lovey. Logan Hepburn cannot resist a challenge, and you have surely presented him with one by being so firm in your resolve. I doubt he has ever met a woman who didn't fall swooning into his arms. He is, after all, an outrageously handsome fellow. He would be a huge success at court with his wavy black hair, his blue eyes, his strong jaw, and his great height." Owein chuckled.

"It is plainly obvious that he was never disciplined or taught the virtues of restraint growing up," Rosamund grumbled.

"Very shortly you will be my wife, lovey, and naught can ever separate us except death," Owein told her quietly. "My life, my sword, and my heart are yours, Rosamund. What could Logan Hepburn possibly offer to tempt you from my side? Do not be afraid, lovey. I will protect you, but be certain before we enter the church that this is what you really want. *Is it?*"

"Aye," Rosamund answered him without hesitation. "I want only you for my husband, Owein Meredith. I do not know why Logan Hepburn annoys me so greatly."

"It is his youthful arrogance. Much like Prince Henry's," Owein remarked. "It is that air of entitlement that vexes you very much, as it did with the prince," Owein explained to her.

"Their music is festive," Rosamund grudgingly admitted as they walked the path to the church.

"Tell them afterward at the feasting," Owein said. "The Hepburn has come to taunt you, but if you do not rise to his bait, but rather thank him prettily as if he were a dear friend and neighbor who has done you a kindness, you will, I promise you, Rosamund, get your own back on the laird of Claven's Carn."

She laughed. "There is much, I can see, that I can learn from you, my lord. Your years at the Tudor court were not entirely wasted."

He grinned down at her. "We Welsh can be as canny as yon trio of Scots," he replied.

Their path was bordered by Friarsgate folk, who having gotten a good look at the bride and her groom now followed along behind the bridal party into the church. The small building had been decorated nicely with sheaves of wheat and late-summer flowers. There were real beeswax candles in polished brass candlesticks upon the stone altar. Unlike the large churches in the towns that often had carved screens between the congregation and the priest, Friarsgate church had no such barrier between its people and God's representative. There were even some oak pews within the country church. The bridal party now took their places in the first of them, while everyone else who could crowded into the pews behind or stood.

The two priests emerged from the sacristy. Father Mata was garbed in a white linen surplice embroidered with golden sheaves of wheat. It was a special garment that he wore only at Easter as a rule. Usually he celebrated the mass in the simple brown robes of his order, such as Richard Bolton was wearing this day. The candles upon the altar flickered in the morning sunlight filtering through the plain arched gothic windows with their leaden panes.

One day, Rosamund thought, she would have stained-glass windows in this church as they did in the royal chapel and the churches she had seen in the south. Then she settled down to listen intently to the words of the mass. When it was over Father Mata beckoned her and Owein forward to stand before him. In a quiet voice he spoke the words of the marriage rite. When he questioned their intent, both bride and groom answered in a clear voice heard throughout the church. There was no shyness or uncertainty in either of them this day. Finally the young priest pronounced them husband and wife. Richard Bolton stepped forward to bless the couple, smiling warmly at them. Owein Meredith kissed his bride rosy, and the Friarsgate folk erupted into cheers.

They were led from the church back up the path to the house by the Hepburn pipers. Tables had been set out in front of the building, benches upon either side but for the bridal table, which was the high board brought from the hall along with its carved, high-backed oak chairs. The kegs of ale and cider were broached. The servants began to come forth from the house with platters and bowls of food. In a nearby pit the two sides of beef in their rock salt were turned slowly by four young turnspits. All the traditional wheaten products connected with Lammastide were served as they had been the previous year, but because this was a wedding feast as well, there was the beef, fat capons stuffed with bread and apples that had been mixed with sage, a thick rabbit stew with chunks of carrot and pieces of leek floating in the wined gravy, game pies, and roast mutton. When a platter of thinly sliced salmon lying upon a bed of crisp green cress was presented, Rosamund asked, "From whence came this fine fish, Edmund?"

"The Hepburns brought it, my lady," Edmund answered.

Rosamund turned to Logan Hepburn, who because of his rank was seated at the bridal table, and said sweetly, "We are truly fortunate in you as a neighbor, my lord. Your gift of music to liven our feast was more than generous, but to bring us salmon, too!

I do indeed render you my thanks." And she smiled brightly at him.

He bowed from the waist in his chair, an amazed smile upon his handsome face. "I am delighted I might bring you pleasure, lady," he told her, his blue eyes dancing.

" 'Twas salmon you brought, my lord, only salmon. And I shall not ask from whence it was poached," Rosamund teased him wickedly. "The evidence will be so quickly devoured that you should be safe."

Everyone at the table laughed, including Logan Hepburn who was wise enough to know when he had been bested. Target butts were set up in a nearby field, and long bows in hand, the men took turns shooting. Very quickly it became an open contest between Owein Meredith and Logan Hepburn. Arrow after arrow was shot, each man bettering himself with his next turn. When Logan Hepburn's arrow split Owein's previous shaft a gasp of surprise went up among the onlookers.

The Scot grinned, saying, "You cannot better that, Owein Meredith."

"Perhaps I can," the Englishman answered softly, and he notched his arrow, letting it fly toward the target.

A shout of amazement went up, followed by a great cheer as Owein's arrow split the

Scotsman's. Logan Hepburn's jaw dropped with astonishment as the Englishman, hands on his hips, grinned at him.

"Well, I'll be damned!" he exclaimed.

"I keep telling you that you surely will, my lord," Rosamund said, coming up next to Owein. Standing on her tiptoes she kissed his cheek. "Well done, husband!" she congratulated him. "Now, come and sit by my side. Cook has made a fine pear tartlet to celebrate this day. You, too, Logan Hepburn. You look as if you could use something sweet right now. And perhaps a bit of wine?"

"I could," he admitted. "Sir, you must teach me how to shoot like that. I thought I was surely the best archer I have ever known, but I admit that you outshot me easily."

"There is no trick to it, my lord," Owein said, "and I will gladly share my skills with you. But not today. I shall need my strength and skill for *other* sports shortly." Then putting an arm about Rosamund, he went with her back to the high board.

"He taunts you," Ian Hepburn said softly.

"Aye, I know," Logan replied, "but I deserve it. He is no fool and knows I covet his wife. I may not have the first taste, Ian, but I shall have the last one day. She will be mine, I vow it."

"You're a fool," Colin Hepburn sneered at his elder. "Find another lass and marry her. 'Tis your duty as our laird."

"You find a lass, Colin. If I die without heirs, 'tis your sons who will inherit. I don't care. The lass who was wed today is the only bride I want."

"You should have taken her the other day when you had the chance," Ian remarked.

"Perhaps I should have, but 'tis too late now," Logan Hepburn replied. "This is not the end of it, brothers. I will have another chance, and when it comes I will take it without question."

The Friarsgate folk ate until their sides were sore. The men played their rough games, kicking the sheep's bladder in the mown field beyond the house. The three Hepburns, having regained their honor by besting the English on that field, now took up their pipes and began to play. They were joined by several of the local men upon the double reed pipe, a fiddle, bells, a tambourine, and a drum. The people began to dance, holding hands in a circle. They danced other dances in a long line, weaving amid the tables, led by the bride and the groom. The day began to wane. At Rosamund's signal loaves of bread were given to each guest. Each loaf had a lighted candle in it. Led by Edmund Bolton, Friarsgate's steward, the bridal party and its guests circled the house three times. The candles were then snuffed, and each loaf was devoured but for a quarter of the bread, which would be saved for the following year's Lammas-morning celebration.

The sun beginning to sink in the west, the guests departed back to their own cottages. The Hepburn of Claven's Carn and his brothers bid their hostess and her bridegroom their thanks and farewell. Logan Hepburn bowed over Rosamund's hand.

"We shall meet again one day, lady of Friarsgate," he told her.

"I shall look forward to it, my lord," she told him, her gaze never flinching from his bright blue one. Then she drew her hand from his and wished them a safe journey home.

"You will not remain the night?" Owein asked hospitably.

"Nay, my lord, but thank you," Logan said. "There is a fine border moon coming that will guide us home."

Owein and Rosamund watched the three Scots ride off. The bride had to admit, if only to herself, that she was relieved to have seen the last of the Hepburn of Claven's Carn. He fascinated her in a rather wicked way, but she would tell no one of her secret thoughts. Not even Owein. She had a good man for a husband, and she was going to love him.

They stood silent for a time, watching the sunset over the hills to their west. Then hand in hand they reentered the manor's hall. There were candles lit as usual, and the fire burned brightly, taking the chill off the evening, which after the unusually warm day had turned cool. Together Rosamund and Owein sat before the hearth on a small cushioned settle. A lute lay by his feet, and Owein picked it up and began to sing to his bride in his clear Welsh tenor. She was both surprised and charmed, for she had never heard him sing or play before; nor had she ever realized that he could.

Look on this rose, O Rose,
And looking laugh on me,
And in thy laughter's ring
The nightingale shall sing.

Take thou this rose, O Rose,
Since Love's own flower it is,
And by that rose,
Thy lover captive is.

The music died, leaving her quite breathless. He took her small hand in his as he lay the lute aside and kissed it tenderly. Their eyes met, and Rosamund felt a strange stirring within her heart.

"I have never been serenaded before," she said softly. "Did you write the song?"

"Nay," he admitted, realizing that he might have lied to her, and she would have never known. "The poem is said to have been written by Abelard, a French philosopher and sometime poet. The tune, however, is mine. Like most Welshmen I have a knack for music. I am glad that I have pleased you with my small effort, lovey."

"My uncle Henry did not come. I thought surely he would," Rosamund said after a small silence.

"He knows there is nothing he can do now," Owein replied. "He has had a year to grow used to the idea that Friarsgate will belong to your children and not to his grandchildren."

"But I thought surely he would come, if only to complain at us for *stealing* the manor from him," she said with a small smile.

Owein laughed. "He will be here eventually, and before the winter I am certain," her bridegroom assured her. "Are you tired, Rosamund? It has been a very long day for you, and neither of us is quite recovered from our journey with the Queen of the Scots."

"I will call Maybel to help me," Rosamund answered him, and she stood up. She was relieved that their guests had departed and forgone the traditional putting to bed of the bride and the groom. *I am brave, but if they had made a fuss I should have grown quite embarrassed. I am not certain that I am not frightened.* She turned to her husband. "I will send Maybel to fetch you when I am ready," she told him.

He stood, and kissing her hand, said, "I will wait here." He watched her hurry from the hall, and he sat back down before the fire. She was nervous. Of course she was. She was a well-brought-up virgin, and he was a man of experience. But I have never made love to a virgin, he thought. He struggled to recall what he could about virgins. They must be treated gently and not hurried. That much he knew. But he would be firm with her, for the marriage must be consummated in order to be completely legal. He heard a discreet cough and looked up.

"The Hepburn brought us a small keg of whiskey, my lord," Edmund Bolton said. "I suspect you could use a dram or two now, eh?"

Owein Meredith nodded and gratefully accepted the cup. He swallowed down a great gulp, savoring the smoky taste and the heat that suffused him from throat to belly. "I love her," he said, almost despairingly.

"I know," Edmund answered him.

"She doesn't understand love," Owein said.

"Nay, not a love between a man and a woman," Edmund agreed. "But she will, and sooner rather than later I believe, my lord."

"I am Owein when we are together," the new master of Friarsgate said to Edmund Bolton. "Have a dram yourself, man."

Edmund nodded. "I thank you," he said. "The whiskey from Claven's Carn is reputed to be excellent."

"And sit down," Owein told him.

Edmund Bolton poured himself some whiskey and then sat next to Owein Meredith. He sipped the brew appreciatively. " 'Tis excellent," he pronounced, a smile lighting his features.

"I'll be good to her," Owein promised.

"I know you will," Edmund responded.

"I don't know what a husband does, Edmund," Owein said. "My father never remarried, and all the men I've known in the Tudor household have been soldiers. A man doesn't love a wife like a whore. The king loved his queen, but I never knew what they were about when they were alone, which was rare, I tell you. You are a husband. What do I do?" His look was slightly despairing, and his voice now bordered on panic.

Edmund chuckled. "Husbands mostly do as they are told, Owein lad," he said. "At least that has been my experience. Rosamund was raised by Hugh and me to be independent. We both hated Henry's lust for this manor. We wanted our lass to be free. What does a husband do? Well, he must be strong where a wife is not, or when she needs him to be. He must be a lover, a friend, and a companion. She will want to spoil the bairns. You will know when she must not, and you will make certain your will prevails in that matter. You must be the strength and moral compass in your family, Owein Meredith. You will be loyal to her and to Friarsgate. 'Tis the best I can tell you. But for tonight, be gentle, be patient, and show her the pleasures of the marriage bed. Tell her what is in your heart so she may feel free to tell you what is in hers. Women like Rosamund never like to admit to love unless they are loved in return. I have never understood it, but there it is."

"Thank you, Edmund," Owein said quietly, and he put the dram cup aside. "I shall try to follow your advice."

"You'll learn along the way, Owein lad, but as I said, for now just love the lass. The rest will come."

"Will you keep the man talking in the hall all night when his bride awaits him?" Maybel demanded as she bustled in. "Go on with you, Owein Meredith. Your bride is already in your bed waiting for you. Do not be a laggard now!"

The lord of Friarsgate jumped up from his seat and hurried from the hall, a smile upon his lips.

"You're a wicked old woman," Edmund teased his wife. "I had him all calm and quiet, and you come shouting orders." He pulled her down into his lap and kissed her soundly.

"You've been drinking," Maybel scolded.

"Would you like a dram yourself, old woman?" he asked her.

"Aye, but kiss me again before you get it for me," Maybel said. "We may not be a bride and groom, but you've never been a loiterer in love, Edmund Bolton."

He grinned at her. "And after all those

months away from you, Maybel, I'm ready to prove my heart is yours once again tonight, as I have proven every night since you got home." Then he kissed her.

Chapter 10

He slowly opened the door of their bed-chamber and stepped into the room, almost jumping as the door clicked loudly behind him. The draperies were drawn over the leaded paned windows. At one end of the chamber a large fireplace blazed brightly, warming the place. The room was nicely furnished with sturdy oak furniture, but it was the large draped bed that caught his immediate attention. The curtains about the bed were almost completely drawn.

"Owein?" Her voice sounded young and small.

"Aye, 'tis me, Rosamund," he answered her, coming around the bed to where the hangings opened slightly to give him a glimpse of his bride sitting straight up against the pillows, clutching the coverlet to her chest. Her hair was loose about her bare shoulders.

"Come into the bed," she invited him, her voice a bit stronger now.

"Are you so impatient, then?" he teased her as he began to disrobe.

"Aren't you?" she countered mischievously.

He laughed. "You are a bold wench for a virgin." He pulled his garments off as quickly as he might without seeming over-eager, although the truth was that he was more than anxious to join her in their bed. His back was to her as he undressed.

"Oh, you have a fine rounded bottom," she said wickedly as he pulled his sherte off, "but such hairy legs, sir. Is the rest of you so wooly? You are like one of my fine sheep."

He turned. "I shall be the ram to your sweet little ewe sheep," he said. He was fully naked now.

"*Oh, my!*" Rosamund said upon viewing her first unclothed man. Her amber eyes carefully examined him, taking in his wide shoulders, the broad chest with its mat of golden fur, his long legs, his — "*Oh, my!*" she repeated as her eyes encountered the first manhood she had ever beheld. "That is your . . ." Her voice trailed off, but her gaze was fascinated, curious.

"Aye, that is the object of your downfall, lovely," he told her. "Now move over, lass. I am freezing out here despite the fire. Can you not hear the rain against the windows? 'Tis August, yet the autumn is already coming."

She flung back the down coverlet and slid over, inviting him to join her as she did. "How do you use it?" she asked naively.

He put his arm about her as they sat together in their bed. "It will grow larger as my desire for you grows," he explained. He began to fondle her small rounded breasts.

She turned her head to look up at him. "And then?" His hands on her flesh were exciting.

He bent, kissing her softly. "Let us not get ahead of ourselves, lovey," he told her. "I promise I shall explain as we go along." His thumb began to rub a nipple, and he drew her deeper into his embrace, lowering her back against the pillows. "A woman's breasts are very enticing," he told her as he lowered his head to kiss the rounded flesh.

His lips were warm against her skin. Rosamund's heart began to beat quickly within her chest. She murmured softly as he licked first one nipple and then the other. The velvet of his tongue sent a tingle through her. Then his mouth closed over a nipple, and he began to suckle upon her. *"Ohhh!"* The gasp of surprise escaped her.

He raised his dark blond head, and his eyes were almost glazed with something she did not understand. "*Ohhh* good? Or is it distasteful to you?" he asked her softly.

"No! No! It is good!" she assured him.

He lowered his head once more, this time moving to her other breast. His mouth pulled strongly upon the sentient nub of flesh. And after a brief time his teeth grazed the nipple gently.

"*Oh, yes!*" Rosamund said as ripples of new pleasure began to wash over her. The teeth were sharp, but not hurtful. She found his actions very thrilling. He moved to suck upon her other breast, and Rosamund sighed. His sensuous actions were sending ripples of shivers down her spine. It was pleasurable and exhilarating, she decided.

She had a fragrance about her, he considered as he nuzzled her. She smelled of heather. It was the perfect scent for her, he thought. He began to kiss her sweet warm flesh, his lips moving from her breasts down her torso to her belly. He was surprised to find that he could feel her pulses jumping nervously beneath his mouth. He stopped at her navel, not certain how far he might proceed, but realizing once again that she was young and untried.

He lay his dark blond head upon her belly,

and his fingers stroked her thigh. How did a man make love to a wife? he asked himself once more. If she had been older, more knowledgeable, *a whore,* he would have been surer of himself. But she was not. And therein lay his dilemma.

Why had he stopped? Rosamund wondered. Was something wrong? Had she done something she should not have done? "What is the matter, Owein?" she asked him softly. "Have I displeased you in my ignorance?"

Her voice. The innocent question she asked brought him back to reality. "I am not certain how to proceed with you," he told her candidly. "I have never made love to a virgin, or to a wife, Rosamund."

"Whom have you made love to then, sir?" she queried, genuinely curious, and perhaps even a bit jealous.

"Women of the court seek diversion . . . courtesans and whores," he admitted. "You are so different, lovey. You are clean and sweet. You are my wife."

"Do not all women have the same desires and lustful longings, Owein?" she wondered aloud.

"I don't know," he admitted. "I have spent my life in loyal and royal service, Rosamund. My couplings have been mostly hurried, and for the sole purpose of pleasure. You, however, are my wife. Our couplings are meant to produce children of our loins and our blood, not for sport or amusement."

"Why not?" she demanded. "Why should we not disport ourselves for our mutual enjoyment in the getting of our bairns, my husband? Should our bairns not come from love? Why should our passion be sober?"

"It shouldn't," he agreed as her wise words penetrated his brain. Then he raised his head up to look into her warm amber eyes. "I love you, Rosamund. Do you, can you, love me?"

"I do not love you yet," she told him honestly, "but I believe I can love you, Owein. Do you really love me?"

"Aye, I do. I probably have loved you since we first met. I admired how well you conducted yourself in the face of your uncle Henry's behavior and greed, and Hugh Cabot just in his grave."

"Your timely arrival saved me," Rosamund said quietly.

"I know," he replied.

"Owein, I do not want to talk anymore," Rosamund told him. "I want to become a woman this night, and I want to know the pleasures of the marriage bed. Are you shocked?"

He thought a moment and then he said, "Nay, I am not shocked. I think I am relieved, for I am mad with love for you, my bride, and beginning to be filled with lust." He bent and kissed her until she was quite breathless and rosy.

"I want your manhood inside me," she whispered hotly, sending a bolt of raw desire through him. "Will you mount me like the ram mounts his ewe sheep, Owein?"

"I could," he said, "but I will not. The more common way for a man and a woman to mate is face-to-face. Ask no more questions now, Rosamund. Just let me show you how much I love and desire you." Now he began to kiss her again, his mouth fusing with hers, their tongues playing hide-and-seek with each other. The blond hair on his chest tickled her young breasts. He felt the smooth mounds giving way beneath his weight.

Her head began to spin in a most pleasurable way, Rosamund thought. Her nipples tingled as the soft fuzz on his chest taunted them. She let her fingers caress the nape of his neck, smooth over his broad shoulders. She closed her eyes and enjoyed the plethora of delicious sensations sweeping over her body and spirit. His lean body was hard against her. She felt a ripple of unfamiliar sensation rising up. Was it desire? It had to be! She was experiencing desire for the first time! *"Ohhh, husband!"* she murmured against his ear, and then her teeth nipped at the fleshy lobe, for she was unable to constrain herself.

Her obvious rising and newly discovered lust thrilled him. He had been afraid as to how she might react to his own burgeoning passion. Catching her head in his hands again he kissed her once more. The auburn tresses were soft beneath his fingers. Her dark eyelashes lay spread across her cheeks like summer moths. Those lashes were gold tipped he noticed. There was so much he was going to discover about her now that she was his wife.

Rosamund felt the hardness against her thigh. A long and very firm hardness. His manhood had ripened and was ready to penetrate her. Her heart began to beat even faster. Now his hand was covering her mons and pressing down upon it. *"Oh,"* she cried out with the sensation he produced. A single finger began to move along her slit, sliding through to find her love bud, which was already tingling in anticipation. He played with it but briefly, instead sliding the long finger within her wet love sheath. Then he pressed a second finger forward, moving the two digits slowly back and forth. *"Yesss!"* she hissed. She was ready.

Without a word Owein mounted his wife, his love lance pushing forward through her nether lips, gently, gently, entering her eager body. He paused a moment, allowing her the opportunity to become used to this first invasion.

"Are you ready to become a woman, lovey?" he murmured against her love-swollen lips.

She nodded, and then her amber eyes widened as he thrust deep within her. She cried out as her maidenhead was torn asunder, quick tears slipping down her cheeks, which he swiftly kissed away, but to his relief she clung to him as he pistoned her until he could bear no more of the sweetness that possessing Rosamund's body had given him. To his delight he heard her cry out, but this second cry was one of pleasure and not pain. His love juices thundered into her love bower even as her fingernails dug sharply into his shoulders and raked down his broad back.

There had been pain, and then it had dissolved almost magically. The fierce driving, repetitive motion of his loins had had a strange effect upon her. She seemed to lose all control over herself, living only for the delicious sensations that poured through her straining body. With each thrust of his love rod she had grown more dizzy until finally the passion erupted within her, and she had actually lost consciousness for a brief moment or more. *"Owein! Owein!"* she heard her voice calling out to him from a very far distance.

He enfolded her within his arms, kissing the top of her auburn head. Warmth streamed through them both. "There, lovey," he whispered. "You are a woman now, and perhaps this night we have made a child."

She sighed and snuggled against him. "I should like that," she told him in a low voice. Then she looked up at him saying, "It was wonderful, sir knight. Even the pain was good, I vow. I am relieved to be a maid no more, and a true wife at last, Owein. Thank you."

He could feel the tears pricking against his eyelids and forced them back. Men did not cry. "Nay, lovey," he told her. " 'Tis I who must thank you for the magnificent gift of your virginity. I shall always be true to you, Rosamund. This I swear to you on our wedding night."

In the morning Henry Bolton arrived at Friarsgate early, even as Maybel brought down the bloodied sheet from the bridal bed. Boldly she waved it at him.

"She's wed good and true this time," Maybel said with a grin.

"He could die," Henry Bolton said grimly.

"She could already be with child," Maybel snapped. "You'll not have Friarsgate now, Henry Bolton. Hugh Cabot, may God assoil his good soul, outfoxed you!" And Maybel laughed aloud.

"He could die, and children perish young in this country, as you and I well know," Henry persisted. "Then she would have no choice but to wed my son."

"The Hepburn of Claven's Carn came courting, and only went away because he is an honorable man," Maybel replied. "God forbid anything happen to Sir Owein, but if it did, the Hepburn would be over the hills and into this house as quick as a wink."

"That Scots bastard had the temerity to come courting my niece?" Henry Bolton demanded angrily.

"Aye, he did, and he's a good man, too," Maybel answered. "He came to my lady's wedding and played his pipes for the bridal couple."

"He came to get the lay of the land," Henry Bolton snarled.

"He brought salmon and whiskey, uncle,"

Rosamund said entering the hall and over-hearing the conversation. "The salmon was delicious, and we will enjoy the whiskey this winter. We are sorry that you and Mavis missed the wedding. Did she not come with you, uncle?" She smiled at him, smoothing her russet skirts of an imaginary wrinkle.

"My wife is not well, which is why I missed your nuptials," Henry Bolton said.

"Good morning, brother Henry," Richard Bolton said as he entered the hall. "We missed you at the mass, niece, but under the circumstances you are forgiven." He chuckled. "I will break my fast and then depart."

Rosamund colored becomingly, but then she laughed lightly. "We shall be sorry to see you return to your monastery, uncle."

Richard Bolton grinned, then turned to his youngest sibling. "Henry, you do not look well yourself. Too much rich food and too much wine, I will vow. Abstinence in your excessive habits is to be advised, I think."

"Mind your business," Henry Bolton snapped. "I will not be preached at by a bastard, even if he is a priest. Niece, will you offer me no food, and after I have ridden from Otterly Court since before the dawn? It was chill for August. I have no wine. Your servants are lax and need a firm hand. 'Tis to be hoped that your husband can manage them, since you cannot."

Owein Meredith entered the hall at that moment. "Good morning, *uncle*. Certainly I may now call you uncle as I am Rosamund's husband." He nodded to Richard with a small smile of shared conspiracy.

The priest nodded back, a twinkle in his eye.

"Ten months at court, and you could do no better than this common, landless knight?" Henry said ungraciously, not answering Owein's mockery. "You might as well have remained right here and wed with my lad."

"I should have hardly been as happy and content the morning after such a marriage, as I am this morning," Rosamund replied pertly.

Owein and Richard laughed aloud at this remark, but Henry Bolton scowled sourly.

"And, *uncle*, I would have you know that the Queen of the Scots, Margaret Tudor, with her grandmother, the king's gracious mother, chose my husband for me. The king himself announced our betrothal in his hall before the entire court and was cheered for it. My husband has been raised in the House of Tudor. The king knows he can trust him to manage this small piece of his borderland

and not betray him. My husband is respected by the most powerful and mighty man in England, King Henry. My husband is loved and well-regarded by men of consequence. I am proud to be his wife, uncle. I would have gone into a convent and deeded Friarsgate to my order before I would wed with another of your offspring!"

"But you did not have to, lovey," Owein soothed his wife. "Come, uncles, and let us break our fast." He led Rosamund to the high board and seated her, placing Henry Bolton on his right and Richard Bolton on Rosamund's right.

The servants brought the food. Oat stirabout, boiled eggs, ham, bread, butter, and cheese. There was wine and cider. Henry Bolton spoke not a word once the food had been set before him. He ate with both hands and drank three goblets of wine. And when the servants had cleared away the few remnants of the meal, Richard Bolton spoke up.

"When you are ready, brother Henry, I will ride with you."

"*Ride with me? Where?*" Henry snapped.

"Home, brother Henry. You have paid your respects to the bridal couple, but surely you will not intrude upon their connubial bliss? Especially as your good wife is ill. You will want to be with her."

"As you are leaving, *uncle*," Owein said, "I will bid you my farewell. I must ride out today to inspect our livestock. The herds need to be culled and the culls taken to market. We cannot afford to feed useless beasts this winter, eh?" He stood up, and taking Henry Bolton's fat hand shook it heartily. Then he turned to Richard. "I thank you, Richard, for all your help. Travel safe and return often." He shook the older man's slender and elegant hand. Finally he bent and kissed Rosamund, his lips lingering just long enough to set her pulses racing. "Are you making soap or conserves today, lovey?" he inquired solicitously.

"I have not decided," she replied with a grin. "A woman's work is never done. Perhaps I shall make medicinal salves, my lord."

"Well," Henry Bolton said, "I am pleased to see that at least you are finally behaving like a proper and docile wife, niece."

"Thank you, uncle," she replied demurely, arising. "Let me go with you to bid you both a proper farewell." She curtsied to Owein, "I will see you tonight, my lord," she told him, and he departed the hall. Rosamund turned to a young serving girl and told her, "Go to the kitchens and see that my uncles have sustenance for their travels today."

"Yes, lady," the girl responded, bobbing a curtsy before hurrying off on her mission.

Rosamund then sent a serving man to the stables to be certain her uncle's mounts were fed, watered, and ready to travel. He returned at the same time the serving girl came from the kitchens carrying two squares of cotton cloth, carefully tied. Rosamund took them from her, smiling.

"What is in them?" she asked.

"Fresh bread, cheese, a small joint, and an apple, m'lady," the girl replied quickly.

"Feel free to fill your flasks, uncles," the lady of Friarsgate invited. "The sun will eventually grow hot, and you will welcome a drink."

When the brothers were finally ready, their niece escorted them outside the house where two stable lads were holding their mounts. Richard Bolton bounded lightly into his saddle, his dark homespun robes riding up just slightly to show his well-muscled white calves and his slim feet in their leather sandals. Henry, however, needed a mounting block, and even so had to be pushed and pulled into his saddle. His own gown rode up, revealing his fat thighs straining in their dark hose. No, Rosamund thought, he did not look well, but it was not just his weight, she suspected.

"God go with you both," she said, bidding them farewell.

"God grant you a son, niece," Richard Bolton said. "We shall pray for you at St. Cuthbert's."

"Thank you, uncle," she replied.

Henry Bolton grunted. "Can we get going?" he grumbled. Then, as an afterthought, he said, "Farewell, niece."

Rosamund watched as the two men rode off and then turned and went back into the house where Maybel was awaiting her in the hall.

"I did not think my uncle Henry looked well," she noted.

Maybel chuckled. "I have just had the gossip from the cook who has a sister at Otterly Court. Madame Mavis has grown a big belly, but it ain't your uncle's get. 'Tis said your uncle's wife has been futtering a brawny young stableman. He caught them at it himself and sent the devilish lad packing. Then Madame Mavis announced to all at Easter dinner that she was with child again. Your uncle dares not deny he is the father, for he would sooner die than be made a public cuckold, though most know he is. Now, 'tis said, he questions the paternity of all her bairns, but for the eldest who is so like him that there is little doubt as to who sired him."

"Poor Uncle Henry," Rosamund replied, "I almost feel sorry for him, for he is so very proud of being a Bolton, born on the right side of the blanket unlike my uncles Edmund and Richard. Still, he is so avaricious and unpleasant one cannot help but have sympathy for Mavis. Uncle Henry is not easy to live with, Maybel, as we both well know. But adultery? 'Tis a fierce vengeance she has taken on him, I fear, and the poor bairns will suffer the most for her indiscretion and his overweening pride."

"You have a kind heart, my lass," Maybel said.

"Will you see to the household today, Maybel?" Rosamund asked her. "I am still tired from our travels and would retire to my chamber to rest a while."

"Run along, lass," the older woman said.

"I think I should like a bath brought to me," Rosamund murmured.

"I'll send the lads up with hot water," Maybel answered. "They'll get the tub out for you, *m'lady.*"

"How grand that sounds," Rosamund said.

"Well, you're a knight's wife now, and should be addressed as thus," Maybel said.

"Now, go along, *m'lady*."

Rosamund entered the bedchamber, smiling immediately at the man lying upon the bed awaiting her. "My lord," she curtsied. "I have ordered a bath, and you must secrete yourself when the servants come, for I would not have it known you are not in the fields culling the livestock, but rather in our bed pleasuring me." Her amber eyes twinkled. "I have seen my uncles off with picnic lunches to sustain them."

"Come here, wife, and kiss me," he said, his hazel-green eyes narrowing speculatively.

Rosamund teasingly kept her distance. "Maybel says that the cook, who has a sister at Otterly, says that Mavis has a big belly and that it isn't my uncle's. That is why he looks so dyspeptic. He dare not deny the bairn without bringing scorn upon himself, and you know how Uncle Henry is."

"Come here," he repeated, and with more emphasis this time.

"I think I hear the serving men," Rosamund responded mischievously. "You must hide in my little garderobe, husband."

Reluctantly Owein arose from their bed and walked to the small sheltered alcove. Turning, he reached out and yanked her to him. "Madame," he growled at her, "you are in danger of being spanked, for you are, I fear, a wicked little cock tease." He kissed her a slow kiss.

Breathless, she pushed him away, but not before she had reached down to caress his love rod, which was in very obvious need of her sweet attentions. "We will decide this among ourselves after the tub is ready. Take off your clothing, sir, for I mean to bathe you myself."

"Ah," he murmured, "so you are quite as disobedient as I thought, madame. I will obey you, lovey, and look forward to your tender ministrations." With a chuckle he went into the garderobe.

"Enter," Rosamund called out to the rapping on the bedchamber door.

It opened to admit several serving men carrying oak buckets of steaming water. One of them, putting his burden down, went to the tiny recess by the fireplace and drew out the tub, which he placed before the hearth. Then the servants began to fill the tub with the hot water. Rosamund splashed a dollop of her precious bathing oil, a gift from the Queen of the Scots, into the water, and immediately the room was filled with the fragrance of white heather. Picking up their empty buckets, the serving men departed the chamber.

"Humph." The sound came from the garderobe.

"Not yet, my lord, but a moment more," Rosamund called to her husband, her fingers hurrying to unlace her garments as she quickly shed them. Finally she was as naked as the day she had been born, and she called out to him in dulcet tones, "Come forth, Owein. I am ready for you now."

He stepped from the shelter of the deep alcove, equally naked. Seeing her as unclothed as he was, Owein smiled. "I shall not cull you from the herd, lovey," he gently teased her. "God's blood, Rosamund, you are surely the most beautiful creature I have ever seen. I do not believe I have ever seen a woman entirely denuded of her garments." His glance was openly admiring.

Her own eyes swept over his tall, lean body. In the sunlight filling their bedchamber he was magnificent. His shoulders were so very broad, yet his waist was narrow, his long legs slender yet shapely. A light golden down covered his legs and his chest, a slim ribbon of the fur descending his belly to enter into a thicket of golden curls where his manhood lay resting. "And you are the most beautiful creature I have ever seen, my lord," she answered him softly. Then she blushed with the boldness of their actions and turned away from him, suddenly shy of this big fellow who was her husband. Did all wives behave thusly with their lords? She wondered.

He came up behind her, sliding an arm about her waist to draw her back against him. His other hand cupped a breast and began to play with the nipple. His warm lips brushed the nape of her neck, her shoulder. Then he began to speak softly in her ear, the heat of his breath exciting her as did the words he whispered to her.

"You asked me last night if we would make love as the ram and the ewe. I told you that we should, but not the first time. I have sheathed myself within you thrice, Rosamund. Now I shall show you how the ram sheep takes the ewe sheep." His fingers closed about her breast and squeezed.

She could scarcely breathe with the effect his words had on her. She shivered with arousal as he gently pushed her toward the table by the fire.

When the table was pressing against her thighs he murmured again in her ear. "Now, lovey, bend forward, bracing yourself with your hands upon the table. Thus you are positioned like the sweet little ewe sheep in her meadow. The lustful ram will cover you with his own body, mounting you, and thrusting himself within your wet, hot love sheath . . . *so!*" He drove himself forward into her with a single movement.

Rosamund gasped to feel him filling her so fully. He was so very big, and she could swear that his love lance was throbbing inside her. *"Ohh, Owein!"* she cried softly. *"Ohh, yes!"* she encouraged him as he began to move upon her with sharp, fierce strokes of his weapon. His weight pressed her breasts flat upon the table. His fingers held her hips tightly. She gasped with her pleasure as he drove himself forward as far as he might go. And then drew himself almost all the way from her body with a slow, sensuous, and majestic stroke of his manhood. *"Please!"* She could feel the excitement building within her. *"Ohh, please don't stop! Don't stop, Owein!"* She arched her back to allow him greater access. *"Oh! Oh! Ohhhhhh!"* she cried, and then she reached her peak, falling away, disappointed that there was no more.

His love juices thundered into her eager body. He hadn't meant to give in to her so easily, but she was impossible to resist. And now he knew. You made love to a wife like you made love to any woman. With passion, with skill, and in Rosamund's case, with love. He kissed her ear, murmuring into it, *"Baaaa!"*

Rosamund giggled. She couldn't help herself. He had just made love to her in a most exciting way, and she felt wonderful. "Let me up, my lord. Now we must both bathe, I fear." She felt his bulk remove itself from her, and straightened up. "Come. The tub is cooling. You first, and I will wash you." She took him by the hand and led him over to the round oak bath.

He climbed into it, seating himself carefully. "I don't suppose there is much room for two," he suggested hopefully.

"Not in this tub, although I have heard there are larger ones. Shall we have the cooper make us one, my lord?" She knelt by him, and began to bathe him with her flannel cloth and a bar of soap.

"Yes, madame, we must have the cooper make a tub in which we may both bathe together. In fact, I like the idea very much!"

She washed his face, gazing into his eyes and feeling her heart melt within her. Was it possible that she was going to love this man? She certainly liked him a great deal, and their lovemaking was wonderful. Of course she had no basis of comparison, but he gave her such incredible pleasure that surely meant something. Didn't it? Rosamund slicked the flannel across his chest. She washed his long arms and his big back, his neck and his ears. "You must do your own legs and feet," she said, "for I fear if I do" — she blushed — "we may spill water upon the floor in our enthusiasm for each other." She handed him the washrag.

"I agree," he said, and took it from her.

She waited patiently until he had finished, and when he stood up she wrapped him in a warmed towel. "You must dry yourself, my lord, else the water get too cold for me," she told him. Then she plopped herself into the tub and began to quickly wash, for the water was indeed cooling. When she was finished and arose, Owein wrapped her in a second warmed towel that he had taken from the rack before the fire. Rosamund yawned as he dried her off.

"We will sleep a while now," he said. "We have been home scarce a week, and you are not used to such traveling, lovey." He picked her up and tucked her into their bed, climbing in beside her.

"Aye, my lord, I am tired," she admitted, and nestled within the curve of his arm she was quickly asleep.

It was late afternoon when they awoke, and it was to a discreet rapping upon their bedchamber door.

Maybel's head popped around the open door. "Ah, good, you're awake," she said, apparently not in the least surprised to find the master of the house with his wife. "Will you be coming down to the hall for the meal, or shall I bring it upstairs?"

"I will come down," Owein said, "but my lady must remain abed and rest. Bring her a tray of something nourishing."

"I'll send a lass up," Maybel said, "and I'll send the lads to empty the tub and put it away." Then she was gone, closing the door behind her as she went.

"I am rested now," Rosamund protested.

"Nay, lovey, you are not." He opened the trunk at the foot of the bed and drew forth a delicate linen chemise, which he handed her. "Put this on, Rosamund. You should not be *au natural* beneath your coverlet when the lads come to remove the tub." He was dressing as he spoke.

Meekly she obeyed him, realizing as she did that he had begun to look after her as a husband should. It was comforting. "Give me my brush," she said, and when he had handed it to her she began to brush her long hair. Then she fixed it into a single plait, which she tied with a blue ribbon that she found in the pocket of her chemise. "Am I respectable enough to receive the lads now?" she teased him.

"Except for that well-satisfied look in your eyes and your pretty bruised mouth, aye," he said. "I think I shall remain until the lads have gone."

"Are you jealous then, my lord?" she flirted with him.

"I am jealous of every minute of your life that we have not shared, Rosamund," he told her.

"*Oh!*" She was quite overwhelmed by him. He was so romantic, and she would have certainly never expected it when she first met him.

"You are not the man I thought you were," she told him.

"Are you disappointed, then?" he asked.

"Nay! You are wonderful, Owein Meredith!" Rosamund said.

"I never thought I should be a fool over a woman," Owein admitted to her, "but I fear I am one where you are concerned, lovey. I love you quite shamelessly, and I want you to love me back one day."

"I will," she promised him. "I think I am already falling in love with you, husband. How could I not love a man who has been so gentle and kind with me? A man who respects my small position as the lady of Friarsgate. You are unique among men, and much like Hugh Cabot might have been had he been a younger man."

"High praise indeed," Owein responded with a smile. "I know how very much you cared for Sir Hugh. I know how much you respected him. Would you be offended if I said I think I feel his spirit in this house, and I believe he approves of me?"

"Nay, and I feel it, too, and I think he does approve of you," she said.

It was a new world in which Rosamund now found herself. She was actually a married woman, even as other married women. The days became weeks and the weeks months. The harvest was now all gathered. The grain had been threshed and was stored in her stone granaries. The apples and the pears had been picked. The manor folks were surprised when Sir Owein climbed to the top of each tree in the orchards, harvesting the fruits from the very tops of the trees. In past these fruits had been left to rot or fall to the ground for the wild beasts.

"It is not right to waste," he explained to them quietly.

The flocks and the herds had been culled. Some of the beasts were slaughtered for the winter meat supply, but most were taken to market to be sold. The proceeds were then used to purchase those things that the manor could not produce itself, like salt, wine, spices, and thread. The remaining coins were placed into a leather bag and hidden behind a stone in the master and mistress' bedchamber fireplace.

On Martinsmas Rosamund was certain that she was with child; a fact that Maybel and the manor midwife both confirmed. The bairn, both agreed, would be born in mid-spring, probably in the month of May.

"I should like to call a lad Hugh," Rosamund ventured after she had told her pleased husband.

He nodded. "Aye! 'Tis a good name, but what if we have a lass, lovey?"

"Do you think it could be?" Rosamund was surprised that he would even suggest such a possibility. Most men wanted sons, and they were not shy about saying so. A daughter later, perhaps, but sons first.

"Anything is possible, lovey," he answered her. "I will be content with a healthy bairn, lad or lass — and a wife who survives the rigors of childbirth."

Rosamund laughed then. "For a woman to give birth is a natural event, Owein. And I am older than the Venerable Margaret when she birthed our good King Henry. The women in my family do not die in childbed."

"And if the good lord favors us with a daughter what shall we call her?" he asked once more.

Rosamund thought a moment, and then she said, "I do not know. Every girl in England born in the next few months will be named Margaret after the Queen of the Scots. I shall, of course, use Margaret as one of our daughter's names, but she must have her own name first."

"There is plenty of time for you to consider it," Maybel noted wisely. "The bairn will not come before the spring, and it is just now but the beginning of winter. Besides you may well have a son."

They celebrated the Twelve Days of Christmas in the traditional manner, a large Yule log being found in the forest nearby and brought into the house. There was roast goose, and at the manor court Rosamund forgave the miscreants before her their offenses and passed out gifts to all of her tenants. In addition they would be allowed to hunt rabbits twice monthly during the winter, on a Saturday, but for the Lenten season when they would be allowed to take fish from the Friarsgate streams on those same days. Rosamund Bolton was a good mistress all agreed.

January passed in relative quiet. The ewes,

of course, began to birth their lambs as usual during the February storms, causing a frenzy among the shepherds to find the newborns before they and their mothers froze to death.

"Sheep are not the most intelligent of beasties," Rosamund observed. Then she told her husband, "You will have to go to Carlisle in the spring to treat with the cloth merchants from the Low Countries, my lord, as I will be unable in my condition to do so." Her hand instinctively smoothed over her rounded belly as she spoke, calming the child within her who was a most active creature.

"We may go together if the bairn is already born," Owein said. "It is not until the end of May, or early June that they come, for the seas are not hospitable before that."

"You must go," she insisted, "I am not a high-born court lady who will dry up her milk and put her infant to suck at the breast of some farm woman. I am a country lass, and we nurse our own bairns, husband. But that my mother was frail I should have sucked at her teats. Thank God for my Maybel! But Maybel agrees with me that a bairn belongs at its mam's breast first."

"I have no experience with bairns or their

mothers," he told her. "I must accept your judgment in the matter." He wrapped his arms about her, a more difficult task these days, and kissed her softly. "I shall envy the bairn, lovey," he admitted in meaningful tones.

"*My lord!*" Rosamund could still blush, and she did.

He chuckled. "You cannot blame me, lovey. I never thought to know the joys of connubial bliss with any woman, yet the fates have given me you. I never believed I should father bairns of my own blood, and yet here you are ripening before my very eyes with our child. It is all wonderful and very new to me, wife."

They were seated companionably in their hall, the winter snow beating upon the few windows, a fire blazing merrily in their hearth. Two cairn terriers, a greyhound, and a smooth-coated black and tan terrier lay sprawled by their chairs. A fat tabby washed its paws by the fire, preparatory to a long winter's nap.

"I wonder if Meg is as happy," Rosamund said.

"She is a queen," he replied. "Queens have little time for happiness, I fear; their other duties get in the way. But knowing Margaret Tudor as I do, I suspect she is not unhappy. She has beautiful garments to wear, jewelry to flaunt, and if the stories are to be believed, a lusty husband to keep her content in their bed. All she must do to continue to merit these pleasures is to produce an heir for Scotland. Given her mother's success in such endeavors I think she will do well."

Rosamund laughed. "You are cynical, my lord. 'Tis a side of you I had not expected you possessed."

"I prefer to believe I am a realist," he said, chuckling. "I grew up in the Tudor household, lovey. I know them well. I think it would disturb the mighty to discover how well their loyal retainers know them."

March arrived, and the snow on the hills began to melt away as the winds began to come more from the south and the west. The land grew green again, and was dotted with the ewes and their new lambs who gamboled carelessly through the grass. The sky above was bright and blue one minute, only to be filled with rain clouds the next. But it was spring. Easter came and went. The time drew near for Rosamund to deliver her first child. She was elated and irritable by turns.

"I am bigger than a ewe sheep with

twins," she grumbled. "I cannot find my feet, and when I do they are swollen like sausages."

"If our Blessed Mother could bear her son with fortitude," Father Mata remarked innocently, "then so can you, my lady."

Rosamund glared at the young priest. "Only a man would say something that foolish, good father. Until you have carried new life within you and had your belly and breasts stretched beyond reason, you cannot know what our Blessed Mother, or any other woman goes through in matters such as this."

Owein burst out laughing at the discomfitted look on Father Mata's young face. "You cannot know," he said, "being a man of God and not a husband. Women, I have discovered, are extremely irritable at this time in their lives."

"Rosamund, give over," Maybel gently scolded. "He could not know now, could he?"

"Then he shouldn't mouth churchly platitudes," she grumbled. She arose from the board, and a sudden look of dismay crossed her face.

Maybel saw it and quickly asked, "The bairn?"

"I have no pain," Rosamund said slowly,

"but water has gushed forth from me, yet it isn't pee." She looked extremely perplexed.

"Some start with the pains and others with the water," Maybel said calmly. "The bairn has decided to come, and it is its time, lass. You must walk the hall while we set the birthing chair up by the fire." The older woman turned to Owein, "You and Edmund know what to do, my lord. As for you, my fine priest, a few prayers will help us all along."

Rosamund began to walk about the little hall. *I am having my child now,* she thought, suddenly excited. By morning I shall hold my son in my arms. A new generation for Friarsgate. Come, my wee Hughie, and be born. Aye! Hugh for Hugh Cabot. Edward for my lost brother, and Guy for my father whom I barely remember. Hugh Edward Guy Meredith, the next lord of Friarsgate. And suddenly the first pain struck her, and she stopped dead in her tracks. *"Ohhhhh!"* The wave washed over her, and then was as quickly gone.

"Keep walking," Maybel instructed her.

The birthing chair was set up by the hearth upon a bed of straw. A large cauldron of water bubbled over the fire. A small table was piled with linen cloths. Another table held a brass ewer and a small flask of oil.

The cradle was brought along with the swaddling clothes.

"Now get out, all of you," Maybel instructed.

"Owein must remain!" Rosamund cried as her uncle Edmund, the priest, and the servants exited the hall.

"Birthing is woman's work, lass," Maybel said.

"I'll stay," Owein said quietly, and Maybel nodded.

Rosamund walked about the hall until her legs grew weak and she could no longer stand. Owein caught her before she fell, and carried her to the birthing chair. He seated her, and she clutched the sturdy wooden arms of the chair as her pains grew closer and closer. It finally seemed as if there was no respite from her agony at all.

"Push, lass," Maybel instructed her. "You have to push the bairn from your body."

"I cannot," Rosamund wailed. Her brow was dotted with perspiration, and she could hardly catch her breath now.

"*You must!*" Maybel said fiercely.

The long spring twilight turned into blackest night. The night wore on, and Rosamund grew more tired and weaker as she labored to bring forth her child, the heir to the Friarsgate inheritance. Owein stayed by her side, encouraging her, moistening her dry lips with a rag soaked in wine, smoothing her now lank auburn hair from her moist forehead.

Finally, as the sky began to lighten with a new day, Maybel cried out, " 'Tis almost done, lass! The bairn is almost here. With the next pain you must push with every bit of strength in you!"

And Rosamund clutched the arms of the chair, gritting her teeth and grunting as she pushed with all of her might. A cry rent the dawn, and Maybel on her knees before the birthing chair drew the howling infant the last bit from its mother's body.

" 'Tis a lass!" Maybel cried, "and every bit as pretty as you were when you were born!"

"But I wanted a son!" Rosamund wailed.

"Next time," Owein said, his hazel eyes shining as he looked upon his daughter for the first time.

"*Next time?* You must be mad," Rosamund told him, but Owein and Maybel only laughed.

"What shall we name her?" he asked his now exhausted wife.

"What is the day?" Rosamund replied, feeling so very tired and almost unable to keep her eyes open now.

"April the twenty-ninth," he said.

"Tomorrow is my birthday. I shall be fifteen. Today, however, is St. Catharine's Day. We will name her after my mother, the saint, and the Queen of the Scots," Rosamund decided.

Maybel had finished cleaning off the child, whose previously loud cries were now subsiding. She wrapped the baby in clean swaddling clothes and handed her to her mother. "She has your auburn hair, lass."

Rosamund looked down at her firstborn. "Welcome to the world, Philippa Catharine Margaret. We almost shared a birthday," she said, and then she laughed as her daughter yawned and closed her eyes in sleep, as if to say, *Well now that that's settled we can get some rest.*

Owein's slender finger touched the infant's silken cheek. "Our daughter," he murmured softly.

"I am sorry, my lord," Rosamund told him. "I did try to make you a son."

"She is perfect," he responded. "I could not be happier, lovey."

"Truly?" She searched his handsome face.

"Truly," he replied. "Now I have two beautiful women to love and to spoil."

Chapter 11

If there was one thing Rosamund had learned in her brief stay at court, it was the value of having connections with important people. She had not considered the lesson seriously until the birth of her daughter. For now Philippa was the heiress to Friarsgate, but even when she was supplanted by a brother, she would still be the sister of the heir. Rosamund knew that in their sparsely settled region good matches were difficult to make. Her daughter's dowry, looks, and connections would all be taken into account. Philippa was not of noble birth, but neither was she a peasant. Consequently, it was up to her parents to maintain their fragile ties with the Tudor court if only for their children's sakes.

Rosamund wrote to the Venerable Margaret and to her former companion Margaret, Queen of Scotland, announcing the birth of her daughter. As an afterthought she also wrote to Katherine of Aragon who would probably one day be Queen of England. It could be extremely useful to be acquainted with a queen. To Rosamund's delight, correspondence arrived from all three women. The king's mother sent her congratulations along with a small broach of emeralds and pearls for Philippa. The Queen of the Scots sent with her correspondence twelve silver spoons and a gossipy letter written in her own hand. The widowed Katherine's missive had been dictated to a secretary, for her English was still poor. In it the Spanish princess sent her loving wishes for Philippa's good health and apologized that her gift, a small leather-bound missal, could not be more grand. Her funds, she explained, were low, and the king would not help her.

Rosamund was appalled, but Owein was not in the least surprised. He explained to his wife that Henry Tudor would not feel responsible for Katherine until she was wed to his younger son. He would consider it her father, King Ferdinand's, obligation to support his daughter. While it was expected that this new match would eventually take place, Prince Henry was still too young to be married. There might possibly be a more advantageous match for the heir to England's throne, and until the king could decide one way or another, he would retain custody of the Spanish princess.

The gentle and obedient princess was now at the mercy of both her father and her father-in-law, neither of whom considered that Katherine needed funds to pay her servants, to clothe and feed and house them. Her own garments, the magnificent wardrobe she had brought with her when she had first come to England several years ago was now beginning to show wear. She possessed only two damask gowns still in good condition. And, too, the unfortunate princess was suffering from poor health. She had grown pale, wan, and listless, she wrote to Rosamund. The doctors claimed it was her inability to adjust to English food and the English climate.

"I wonder if that is so," Rosamund said to her husband, "or if it is her fears for her future that trouble her. She was not ill before Prince Arthur died, or indeed after it, while she was with us. She had been at Greenwich but now says they have brought her to Fulham Palace in the countryside, but even there she is worse rather than better."

Rosamund wrote the princess back. She would pray for Kate's health. She wrote about Philippa, and how each day brought about new changes in her baby daughter. How her daughter would, when she had grown enough to understand the honor done her, cherish the beautiful little leather missal. And the lonely Katherine of Aragon responded, and thus was their correspondence born. The pope, Kate wrote, had given the dispensation for her marriage to Prince Henry. It would take place when he was fourteen and she nineteen.

When Philippa Meredith was seven months old, Queen Isabella of Spain died. Her youngest daughter in England was devastated by the loss of her mother. What she was not aware of was that her social position had changed drastically with the death of her mother. Isabella had been the Queen of Castile in her own right. Her husband, the King of Aragon, had only been the consort. Between them, however, they had ruled almost all of Spain. It was her oldest daughter, Juana, who was the wife of Philip the Fair, Archduke of Austria, who inherited her mother's throne. When Juana became the Queen of Castile, her youngest sister's social status was greatly diminished, for now Katherine was merely the daughter of the King of Aragon, and not the offspring of Ferdinand and Isabella of Spain. Henry

Tudor began to seriously reconsider the marriage between his surviving son and the princess. And Katherine, being no fool, was suddenly very aware of her now precarious position.

It seems, she wrote to Rosamund, *that there is no one to champion me any longer. How I wish I had a strong arm like that of your good Sir Owein. While I am grudgingly housed and fed at the court, I have no monies for the bare necessities now. My father and King Henry haggle over the matter while my poor servants grow more shabby with each passing day. The king barely acknowledges me, and though I have petitioned my father's ambassador, Dr. de Puebla, to intercede for me, he is a useless creature, only interested in feathering his own nest. I have written to my father of this, but he does not address it in his correspondence to me.*

I am very displeased with my duenna, Dona Elvira. Here I am in financial straits, yet she fusses and harries me about my decorum. Having tasted the freedom of Englishwomen, I can never again be truly Spanish. Yet this meddlesome creature went and wrote to my father that my behavior was not that befitting a princess of Spain. My father in his turn wrote to King Henry, and now I am told I must obey my father's wishes. I am forbidden from such small pleasures as singing and dancing with others of the court. I would send the old witch back to Spain if I but could!

"Poor Kate," Rosamund said to Owein as she finished reading this particular letter. "Would she be offended if we sent her a purse to sustain herself? I cannot bear to think of Kate being so mistreated."

"I agree," Owein said, "but let me think on the proper amount, lovey. We do not wish to offend the princess, for she is a proud lady."

Owein did not tell his wife that he had heard from old friends at court that the king had entered into secret negotiations with the new King and Queen of Castile, for a marriage between Prince Henry and their daughter, six-year-old Princess Eleanor, whose social standing was now greater than that of her nineteen-year-old aunt. Everyone was whispering about it, though it was certainly not public knowledge.

Though the prince had turned fourteen in June, the marriage between him and Katherine had not been celebrated, nor had it even been mentioned. Katherine of Aragon was beginning to realize her situation. She understood that her father's failure to hand over the second installment of her dowry might very well be a sticking point, and she wrote him to that effect, begging him to substitute a payment of gold for the plate and jewels in her possession, which were meant to have been the final payment to Henry Tudor. Ferdinand promised his daughter he would send the remainder of her dowry.

By the spring the payment had not arrived, and the English king began to complain publicly and bitterly. Katherine's position at court grew even more precarious. Ferdinand was technically within his rights to refuse payment until the marriage had been formally celebrated and consummated. But unless it was formally celebrated it would not be consummated, and it would not be consummated until the Tudor king had all of the princess' dowry in his hands.

Rosamund birthed a second daughter in March of fifteen hundred and six. Her new daughter was christened Banon Mary Katherine. Banon had been her husband's mother's name. It meant *queen* in the Welsh tongue. Mary was for the Blessed Virgin, and Katherine for the Princess of Aragon who was asked, and agreed, to be Banon's godmother. It was quite a coup and an honor for Friarsgate.

As they sat in their hall one spring night

Rosamund said to her husband, "You must go to see the princess. And you will bring her the small purse we discussed to help defray her expenses. She is very poor right now, and it is not right. I do not understand why her marriage has not taken place. Prince Henry is old enough."

"It is a long way to court," Owein reminded his wife. He had chosen not to tell Rosamund of Henry Tudor's duplicity.

"But riding alone you can reach the south far quicker than when you had to escort me," Rosamund reasoned. "We cannot trust this matter to a stranger, Owein. I cannot bear the thought that someone as kind and gentle as Kate is so abused. Please go. If not for her sake then for mine. If I am distressed, my milk will not flow, and surely you do not want me to put Banon out with a wet nurse."

" 'Tis spring. There is planting to be done and lambs to be culled, and the manor court must be held soon now that winter is over," he told her with a small smile.

"Edmund will see to the planting and the lambs and all the other things that need doing. And I oversee the manor court, my lord, as you well know. Go south for me, *please.*"

He agreed, though reluctantly, for he had

grown comfortable with his life at Friarsgate, with Rosamund, and with their family.
Owein Meredith had to admit to himself
that he was happier now than at any other
time in his life. Still he rode south, finding
the princess at Greenwich and seeking an
audience with her. She received him immediately, for few people but her creditors
sought her out.

"Sir Owein, I am happy to see you again,
and looking so well," Katherine of Aragon
said slowly in her careful but accented
English.

He bowed and kissed the outstretched
hand, noting that it was thin, almost bony,
and ivory in color, "I have brought you a
small gift," he said, tendering the small
leather bag. "I am happy to tell you that
your goddaughter thrives, and like her sister
and her mother, has auburn hair." He
smiled at the princess as Dona Elvira discreetly took the pouch from him.

"Sit down, Sir Owein, and tell me everything," Katherine of Aragon said, ignoring
the scandalized look that Dona Elvira shot
her. "How is Rosamund? And does her
beloved Friarsgate thrive?"

"She is well, your highness. Indeed, she
blooms more with each child she bears. And
Friarsgate, I am pleased to say, is prosper-

ous. Our wool and our cloth, particularly the special blue we make, is greatly sought after by both English mercers and those from the Low Countries who come to Carlisle."

"God has blessed you, Sir Owein. I hope you realize it and give thanks to our dear Lord, and his Blessed Mother," Katherine said piously.

"We do, your highness," he assured her. "Indeed, our priest, Father Mata, says the mass daily, and twice on special feast days. We make certain that each babe born at Friarsgate is baptized immediately, and we send alms to the bishop at Carlisle regularly."

The princess smiled. "I am pleased to know that your household is a good Christian one, Sir Owein." Then she turned to Dona Elvira, saying, "Fetch some refreshment for us. Would you have Sir Owein say I am a poor hostess when he has come so far to see me?"

"And leave you alone with a man?" the duenna said furiously in their native Spanish. "Are you mad?"

"Maria is with us, duenna," the princess replied in the same tongue. "Now go and do as I have instructed you."

With a swish of her black skirts Dona Elvira stamped from the room.

"She pretends to have no knowledge of English," the princess said, "but she understands the language perfectly even if she does not speak it any better than I. First I would thank you for the purse. I will not dissemble with you. I am in desperate need."

"We wish it could be more, your highness," Owein said, noting that the princess' sleeve cuffs were badly worn. "If I would not offend you, could you send one of your people to us in the autumn? If you do, we will see he returns with another small purse for your highness."

"Maria, see it is so, and do not tell the old dragon," Katherine of Aragon said.

"I will arrange it, your highness," Maria de Salinas, the princess' close companion, responded.

"Poor Maria," the princess told Sir Owein. "Her family had arranged a marriage for her with a wealthy Fleming, but it was my responsibility to dower her, and I could not. I hope one day to be able to make it up to her." She sighed deeply. "Tell me what you hear, Sir Owein."

"Madame, I live in Cumbria. I hear little of the court," he replied.

"You have friends, and they write, I know. What is being said about my marriage to Prince Henry? I have not seen him in many months now, though we both live at court." Her fingers nervously plucked at her dark claret silk skirts.

He hesitated, but then decided that the truth was best in this difficult situation. "There is a rumor come to my ears in the north, and mind you, as far as I know it is just a rumor. It is said that the king considers another alliance for his son."

"With whom?" she queried.

"Your niece, Princess Eleanor," he replied.

Katherine of Aragon shook her head in despair. "She is a child, God help her. But how like my brother-in-law to even involve himself in such a negotiation. I knew he hated my father, but I did not think he hated him enough to harm me. And Juana! My poor mad sister! She is so jealous of Philip that she has driven him away with her suspicions. A wife must overlook her husband's peccadilloes no matter her own pride. My sister does not understand that being the archduke's wife makes her important, and no mistress can take that away from her. Do you know if anything has been signed?"

"Not to my knowledge, your highness, but they can sign nothing unless your own betrothal to Prince Henry is repudiated," Owein reminded her hopefully.

Katherine shook her head sadly. "I am in such difficult straits," she said. "King Henry regards me as bound, but his son as free. I do not know what I shall do if I am cast off."

"You will not be!" Owein Meredith said strongly. "It is your sister who inherited Aragon, not Archduke Philip, your highness. Your father will find a way to make this satisfactory. He can surely reason with Queen Juana in this matter. Everything will be all right, your highness. I am certain of it! We pray for you at Friarsgate, and we will continue to pray for you."

"How odd," the princess said softly, "that an unimportant girl from Cumbria and her knightly husband should be my champions. I have few friends here, Sir Owein. I am content to know that you are on my side, though you be far away."

"You will be Queen of England one day, your highness," he told her quietly. "A Tudor queen. From the age of six I have served the Tudors, and I will serve you, too, as will Rosamund." He knelt and kissed her hand once again. "King Henry can be hard, and I know from my friends that he is not well. But he is no fool. The match he made with your parents will stand in the end, your highness. Of that I am certain." He arose. "With your permission I will withdraw from you now. I have had a long journey, and I should like to see some of my friends before I must return home to Friarsgate." He bowed to her.

"See me one more time before you go," she said, and he nodded.

He left the princess' apartments and sought out some of his former companions. They were pleased to see him, and teased him that he had sired only daughters so far. Over their wine cups, however, they were filled with gossip, and Owein learned it was even worse for the poor princess than he had imagined. Katherine of Aragon was virtually destitute. The king had stopped her allowance entirely. She lived with the court because she could no longer afford to live at Durham House, which belonged to the Bishop of London.

Before she had been forced to give up her house she had been driven to economize to such an extent that her servants had to buy day-old fish, bread, and vegetables in the market. Many of the young women who had come with her from Spain in hopes of making good English marriages had been sent home because the princess could not afford to keep them, let alone dower them. Maria de Salinas had refused to leave her friend, however. Katherine was in debt to several

London merchants who were not in the least shy of dunning her. Katherine, it was said, disliked Dr. de Puebla, the Spanish ambassador. She preferred the other envoy from Spain, Hernan Duque de Estrada, who was *simpatico* toward the princess and wrote the king on her behalf, though it did absolutely no good.

The princess, Owein's friends told him, was constantly ill now with one complaint or another. She suffered from tertian fevers, an irregular flux, and headaches that left her so weak she was often unable to arise from her bed or leave her chamber for days at a time. Her nerves were not good, and she was suffering depression. Feeling alone and virtually friendless, she was frequently near collapse. Owein's friends wondered aloud to him if she were indeed the right wife for Prince Henry.

"Will a girl of such delicate sensibilities be able to make princes for England?" one said bluntly. "And she is no spring chicken any longer at nineteen. Perhaps the king is correct when he seeks a younger girl."

"Princess Katherine will make England a fine queen one day," Owein said loyally. "She is yet young enough, and I suspect the prince will do better with a wife a bit older than he."

"You should see him," another knight said. "He has grown from a big boy into a large man. Why, Owein, he stands at least six feet four inches in height, and has limbs like tree trunks. He has a man's body, but yet a boy's mind. The king hardly allows him any chance to rule. At least they sent poor Arthur, God assoil his soul, to Wales to learn kingship. The king will not part with Prince Hal though. He keeps a tight rein upon the lad."

"Not so tight that the prince doesn't get to lift a few skirts now and again," said a third man with a chuckle. "He's got a satyr's appetite for female flesh, he does. If the princess does wed him, she'll have to look the other way when his highness' eye begins to roam, as it undoubtedly will."

"It is to be hoped that Prince Hal will not make a public spectacle," Owein noted. "The princess is a proud girl."

He remained drinking and learning the court gossip with his friends until they all bedded down in the king's hall for the night. In the morning, his head a bit the worse for wear, he again sought out Princess Katherine and bid her farewell.

"Please tell Rosamund to continue to correspond with me, Sir Owein," the young woman said. "I like her letters so filled with

your domestic details, the news of Friarsgate, and your daughters. And you will pass
on to me any information that you learn
from your friends here."

"I am your highness' loyal servant,"
Owein Meredith said, bowing as he kissed
the regal hand a final time and then withdrew.

He hurried his horse northward over the
next few days. The spring sunshine cheered
him as he rode and thought of Rosamund.
He could scarce wait to tell her all the
news. She would be distressed by
Katherine of Aragon's pitiful plight, but
they would continue to aid the princess as
best they could. Owein firmly believed that
Katherine would one day be England's
queen, and she was not a woman to forget
her friends.

Finally he sat his horse above the hills
overlooking Friarsgate. The lake below was a
bright blue in the late May sunshine. The
green hills were dotted with their sheep, and
the pastures were filled with the cattle and
horses. He could see the folk working in the
fields, tending the new crops of grain and
vegetables. He moved his mount slowly
down the hill road, knowing that his wife
and children awaited him this day and was
very glad to be home once again.

A stable lad came to take his horse as he dismounted.

"Give him a good brushing, Tom, and an extra measure of oats. He has traveled a long way and back these last two weeks," Owein instructed. "And turn him loose in his own pasture to run and graze afterward."

"Aye, m'lord," the stable lad said, "and welcome home!"

Owein nodded at the boy's greeting, and hurried into the house.

Alerted by a servant, Rosamund ran to greet him, flinging her arms about his neck and kissing him with great enthusiasm.

Laughing, Owein picked her up and carried her into the hall, setting her down gently as he said, "God's blood, lady, 'tis a goodly greeting you give me. Have I been missed that much?" But he was pleased, for it was the first time since their marriage that they had been separated.

She looked up into his face, her eyes shining with her love for him. "Aye, sir, you have been very missed!" she assured him.

"Papa! Papa!" He felt the insistent tug at his doublet.

Looking down, he saw Philippa. He bent down and picked her up with a smile. "How is papa's precious princess?" he asked her and he kissed her rosy cheek. "Have you been a good lass, Philippa, and helped mama with your baby sister?"

Philippa looked at her father and lisped, "Yeth." Then her brow furrowed. "Bannie stinkth," she told him.

"Bairns sometimes will," he agreed, "but your sister doesn't always smell, does she? Be truthful now."

"Nay," Philippa said reluctantly.

Owein put his daughter down. "Rivalry already?" he asked his wife, as Philippa toddled off with a twinkle in her eye, satisfied to have been noticed and fussed over by her father.

"We need another," Rosamund said. "That will put an end to it." She smiled seductively at him. "And did you miss me, sir?"

"The bairn is scarce out of your belly and you want another, madame?" he teased her. "I think we should wait a bit."

"We need a son," Rosamund reminded him.

"In God's good time," he answered her. "Now, woman, where is my supper? I have eaten little but swill since I departed here. I am tired and I am ravenous."

"At once, sir," she replied, calling to the servants to bring the food. "And you will tell me of all you have seen and heard after you have eaten your fill."

He nodded and then sat himself down at the high board.

They brought him a capon, roasted golden and stuffed with bread, apples, onions, and celery. A fine trout, sliced, set upon a bed of bright green watercress. There was a bowl of mutton stew, the chunks of meat swimming in a cream gravy with pearls of barley and slices of carrot and sweet leeks. There was fresh warm cottage loaf, a crock of sweet butter, and a wedge of yellow cheese. They both ate heartily, mopping the gravy from the stew with pieces of the bread. They drained several cups of ale. And when they were sated with their supper a servant appeared to place a bowl of strawberries and another bowl of clotted cream upon the high board.

"Now," he said, dipping a berry into the cream and popping it into his mouth, "I will tell you all, my love." And he did.

Rosamund listened, not interrupting him until he had finally concluded his recitation. Then she said, "Poor Kate has even less control over her life than we do. She is a princess, and I should not have thought such a thing possible. I cannot believe the king so cruel. What kind of example does that set for the prince?"

"He is not being cruel deliberately,"

Owein explained. "He and King Ferdinand play a game of power. It is something like chess. Unfortunately, the princess is their only pawn, and she suffers for it."

"We must continue to help her, Owein. We have so much, you and I, here at Friarsgate. She has little but her hopes," Rosamund told him. "I know we have not a great deal of coin, for we country folks live by barter and trade, but we must find the coin to send her when we can. Please do not deny me this, my lord." She looked anxiously at him.

"You are the lady of Friarsgate, lovey, and I but your husband," he told her. "Still, we are of one mind in this matter, Rosamund. Sometime in the autumn there will be a visitor from Princess Katherine. We will send him back with what we can."

"Aye! We can sell some lambs or two young heifers. There is a yearling in the pasture not yet gelded that will give us a profit, for he was sired by ShadowDancer, the best sire of warhorses in all the north of England. I call him Tatamount, for he is his sire's twin. If we put it out that we have him for sale, we can take the monies from such a sale and send them to Princess Katherine," Rosamund said enthusiastically. "He should bring us a pretty penny."

"Let him remain the summer in our pastures, fattening," Owein suggested. "We shall sell him after Lammastide."

She nodded. " 'Tis a good plan, my lord." Then she said, "You must have a bath, sir, for you stink right well of the road. I shall go and prepare it now. Maybel will come for you."

"Perhaps you will join me, madame?" he said softly. "That fine new tub the cooper made for us has seen little of us in these last months. Now that Banon is safely born we must put it to good use again." He heard her laugh softly as she ran from the hall. His eyes now strayed to his daughters. Philippa played on the floor beneath the watchful eye of her nursemaid. She was well past two now, and very active. She had Rosamund's auburn hair, but her baby-blue eyes had darkened to his own hazel green. By the fire the rocker's foot moved rhythmically as she gently agitated Banon's cradle. There was little he knew of this second daughter yet but that her look was lively.

Rosamund seemed to be a good breeder. Her confinements appeared easy, with little sickness. She birthed her children readily and without great difficulty. The bairns seemed healthy. But she wanted to give him a son, and the truth was that he longed for a son. But he would never admit to it, for he knew his wife well by now. Rosamund loved him every bit as much as he loved her. If he announced he wanted a lad, she would keep trying to birth a son until she either had one or could no longer conceive. Owein Meredith was no fool. He knew that too many bairns could kill a woman. His own mother had died that way. He should rather have his sweet Rosamund than a son any day.

Maybel interrupted his thoughts. "Your bath is ready, my lord," she said. "I have not yet had the opportunity to welcome you home, but I do so now."

"Maybel," he said bluntly, "how do you keep a woman from conceiving a bairn?"

"My lord! Such a thing is forbidden," she told him.

"Aye, but there are ways, I know, and I suspect that you know them, too. Listen to me. Rosamund wants to give me a son, but I think to have another bairn so soon after Banon might harm my wife. Can you help me, Maybel?"

"You'll not refrain from your passions, I know," Maybel said quietly, but there was a twinkle in her eyes.

"The lass will not leave me in peace," he

chuckled, "and I am weak where she is concerned. I admit it."

Maybel laughed, but then she grew serious. "My lord, do not be angry, I beg of you, but I have already taken the matter in hand. I did after Philippa was born. Rosamund does not know, but she must rest between her confinements, and she will not if given the choice. Each day I bring her a *strengthening* drink that she drinks down because she trusts me. It is actually a brew I make from the seed of the wild carrot and a bit of honey to take away the bitterness. This should allow your seed to fall on unfallow ground, my lord. A child every two years or more is enough. We must have a son for Friarsgate one day."

"Agreed, but not too soon." He smiled at the older woman. "I will go to my bath now easy in the knowledge that we are free to love each other, for my lass will not be denied, wicked wench that she is."

" 'Tis that same spirit that kept her safe from her uncle Henry and his machinations," Maybel replied, smiling back at Owein.

He hurried upstairs to their chamber and entered it to find his wife awaiting him. After closing the door to the chamber, he threw the bolt. "And will you join me, madame?

You did not answer me when I asked you in the hall earlier." He sat down and offered her a booted foot.

Rosamund pulled the boots from his feet and peeled his sewn stockings off, her nose wrinkling as she did so. "Jesu! Mary!" she exclaimed. "Never have I smelled such a stink, and in answer to your query, my lord, aye, I will join you. How else can I scrub the dirt from your body and pick the nits you have undoubtedly acquired at court from your head? I can but imagine you in the king's hall with your cronies, drinking and gossiping all night. As I recall, your companions are none too fastidious in their personal toilet."

"A simple knight does not have many opportunities to bathe," he admitted to her as she undressed him.

"Did you see Prince Henry?" Rosamund wondered.

"In the hall at dinner, aye, but not to speak with, lovey. He's grown into a man — tall, big boned, and much like his grandfather, King Edward IV they say. He is wondrous handsome, with skin almost as fair as a maid's, red-gold hair, and bright blue eyes. He is in some ways like his late brother, Arthur, though that prince had not this prince's size, or height, or robust health. He is very boisterous and amusingly clever. The people seem to adore him every bit as much as they dislike his father."

"Get into the tub," she instructed him, and he obeyed her while she slid out of her chemise, joining him in the warm water.

"You must kiss me, madame, before you take a brush to me," he said with a grin. "God! This water feels wonderful, lovey. No one can prepare a bath like you can." He sniffed. "White heather."

"It will not linger on you, sir, but considering your journey I thought it best to add a bit of scent." She kissed him quickly on his lips, but he was not satisfied.

He pulled her back into his embrace, his lips pressed firmly against hers, and beguiled as she always was by his kiss, Rosamund sighed. Their tongues played a game of hide-and-seek. His hands began to roam her firm body, fondling her buttocks, caressing her breasts. His very quick arousal surprised even him. They did not speak. Instead, he pushed her back against the oaken walls of their tub, and lifting her up, impaled her on his love rod.

"*Ahhhhh!*" They both sighed with pleasure together.

Her arms slipped about his neck as she pressed against him.

He took her face between his two palms. "Do not ask me to leave you again, Rosamund. I missed you greatly."

"And I you, my lord. Ah, oh, that is nice, Owein."

His buttocks contracted as he thrust into her. "Aye, 'tis heaven, lovey."

Their lips met in a burning kiss that but intensified the passion felt between them. He could feel the crisis approaching as could she. His desire exploded as her sharp little teeth sank into his muscled shoulder. Then her legs unwrapped from about his waist, and she clung to him weakly, their breath coming in short quick pants that gradually died away to slow deep sighs of satisfaction.

Finally Rosamund opened her eyes once again. Her legs still felt a bit wobbly, but gamely taking up the flannel cloth, she began to wash her husband. Owein had a small smile upon his lips, and she laughed softly to see it.

Hearing her mirth he opened his hazel-green eyes and said, "You find something funny, madame?"

"You really did miss me, Owein," she teased him. "Did no lady of the court offer her charms for old times' sake, my lord? You were most eager to couple with me."

"You did not naysay me, lovey," he teased back. "I do not believe we have ever before made love in our tub. I found it quite stimulating. I wonder if all husbands and wives enjoy each other as we do. We have certainly made the best of the bargain given us."

" 'Twas not a bad bargain," Rosamund admitted. "You loved me before we even wed, and I have come to love you with all my heart. I can only hope that poor Kate will one day have the same good fortune. Now, stand still, Owein. I have never seen such filth as is on your neck and in your ears, sir. I wonder if I shall ever get you clean."

"Whether you do or not, lovey, I beg you to hurry. I long for our bed, and I long to hold you in my arms again."

"We shall make a son sooner than later if you continue to behave with such enthusiasm," she crowed, pleased.

"We shall make a son in God's good time, lovey," he answered her, feeling just a trifle guilty about the deception he and Maybel were involved in, but he really did not want to lose her now — or ever.

The summer passed peacefully. They heard little news from the south. The king would be on his progress, and he never came this far north. The weather was not as clement as they would want, and so the harvest was not as bountiful as the previous year. Still, they would survive the winter. The word was put about by Edmund Bolton that Friarsgate would be selling a fine young stud after Lammas. The sale was set for the first day of September.

Tatamount was a dappled gray animal with a coal-black mane and tail. He pranced and snorted and tossed his mane about as he was brought into the enclosed area where he was to be displayed to the prospective buyers.

"Has he been trained to fight?" asked the Earl of Northumberland's representative.

"He's too young," Sir Owein answered, "but if the buyer wishes him trained, we will train him. However, we left him ungelded because his value is in his ability to sire. His own sire is ShadowDancer."

"The earl wants a fighting mount," came the reply.

"This is not the animal for him, then," Sir Owein responded. "But we do have a well-trained gelding that might interest you. If you will follow Edmund Bolton to the barns he will display the animal to you."

The earl's man nodded and trailed after Edmund. This left but two other bidders. A representative from Lord Neville and Logan Hepburn. Owein was surprised, for he did not think Logan Hepburn had the funds for such a purchase. Yet the Hepburn of Claven's Carn bid heatedly against Lord Neville's man. It finally reached a point where Sir Owein had to say, "Gentlemen, I must see your monies before we can proceed further."

Each man held up a heavy bag. Lord Neville's man topped Logan Hepburn's bid. Now it was the Hepburn who bid the price even higher, adding, "I am bidding for my cousin, the Earl of Bothwell, who seeks the beast as a gift for his queen."

Lord Neville's man laughed ruefully. "Then I must decline to bid further, for I will not bid against a man who seeks to gift Margaret Tudor, my own king's daughter. The beast is yours, my lord."

Logan Hepburn bowed. "Thank you," he said.

"We will conclude our business inside the house," Owein said. He turned to Lord Neville's representative. "Will you join us and have some wine, sir?"

"Nay, but my thanks, Sir Owein. I must return to give my master the disappointing news." He bowed to the two men, and mounting his own horse, which had been tethered nearby, he rode off with a wave of his hand.

Owein led the Hepburn into the hall where Rosamund was waiting. Her eyebrow arched in surprise as she saw their guest.

"Logan Hepburn has bought Tatamount for his cousin, the Earl of Bothwell, who wishes the beast for the queen."

"It will not prove a good gift, Logan Hepburn," Rosamund said. "The Queen of the Scots likes only well-mannered palfreys. What would she do with a stud like Tatamount?"

Logan Hepburn handed his bag of coins to Owein. "I lied," he said, his blue eyes dancing. "Lord Neville's man was beginning to irritate me, and I had only so much to spend. You shall have it all if you so wish. I want the stallion for myself." The defiant look he gave them dared them to argue with him, but Owein did.

"You have acted in a dishonorable manner, my lord," he said. "I should send after Lord Neville's man and let him have the animal."

"But you will not," Logan Hepburn said. "Neville does not treat horses well, and you have heard the rumors yourself. I have simply saved you from an unhappy ending of this auction. The earl's man wants a fighting horse. I want a stud. I would have outbid Lord Neville's man in the end at any rate. Are my monies not as good as an English-man's, my lord?"

"It is not your monies I question, but your manners," Owein replied. "Open your bag and spread the coins before me."

Logan Hepburn carelessly spilled his monies onto the high board. Owein counted out the amount agreed upon. He was about to return the remaining coins, but to his sur-prise Rosamund stepped forward and swept the balance into her own hands.

"Since, my lord, you were willing to bid your entire stash, you shall indeed forgo it all for your duplicity. You see, I find your Scots' coin every bit as good as English coin, being a sensible woman."

Logan Hepburn burst out laughing.

"Rosamund, we cannot," Owein said.

"Aye, we can!" she replied. "Remember what it is for, my lord. Yon canny Scot would have cheated us if he could. He deserves to forfeit all of his monies."

"Keep it," Logan Hepburn said, wiping his eyes of the tears that his laughter had brought forth. "Each time, lady of Friarsgate, that I think you are as meek and mild as the lambs dotting your hillside, you surprise me with your claws, which are still very sharp. You are a most worthy opponent." He bowed to them both. "I know my way out. I shall take the animal with me if you will prepare the bill of sale."

"Edmund Bolton will see that you have it," Owein said shortly.

The Hepburn of Claven's Carn bowed again, "I will bid you both a good day then. I look forward to our next encounter, lady." Then, with a wave, he was gone from their hall.

"I am beginning to understand your dislike of the man," Owein said through gritted teeth. "He looks at you as if you were the next meal he anticipated devouring."

Now it was Rosamund who laughed. "Are you jealous, my lord?" she teased him, stroking his clenched jaw. "He did not cheat us, Owein. He paid full price for the beast and a bit more. We shall send it south with Kate's man when he visits us this autumn. I am content, and I would have you be, too."

He bent and kissed her hard. "Aye, I find I am jealous, lovey. Each time we meet I remember that Logan Hepburn wanted you for his wife before we wed. He has not yet married I am told."

"But you are wed, and to me, my lord. Let us put this rude borderer from our minds, and enjoy each other," she said softly, seducing him with a smile and a caress.

He nodded. "Aye, lovey. I must remember. I have you. He doesn't."

Chapter 12

Rosamund received but one letter from Katherine of Aragon after the summer of fifteen hundred and six and Owein's visit to court. In it Kate began joyously writing that the king was permitting her to spend more time with Prince Henry. It would appear the difference in their ages was smoothing itself away as he grew into manhood. The prince was attentive. He was kind, the princess wrote, continuing to refer to her in public as "my most dear and beloved consort, the princess, my wife." The bond of affection began to grow between Katherine of Aragon and young Prince Henry Tudor. The king, however, seeing what was happening, decided to separate the couple, for he had still not determined that the marriage take place.

I believe, the princess continued, *that he now thinks the marriage between his son and I*

*will not take place. I have been sent to Fullham
Palace again, although the king has said if I
prefer any other of his houses I may have it. I
cannot afford to maintain Fullham, and have so
written to the king. Why does he not understand
my plight? I am now told I will return to court
come autumn. Oh, Rosamund, what will happen to me? I am beginning to be afraid, but I
must trust more in God and his Blessed Mother
to protect me and keep me from all harm. Of
late I have felt my faith wavering and must
make amends for it lest I be punished.*

"It is intolerable that they play this game
of cat and mouse with her," Rosamund said
indignantly.

Then in November a messenger arrived
from the Princess of Aragon with stunning
news. Kate's brother-in-law, Archduke
Phillip, had died suddenly at the age of
twenty-eight. Her sister, Juana, the Queen of
Castile, was devastated. Never stable, Juana
had collapsed, resolutely refusing to believe
that her husband was dead. She would not,
at first, allow his body to be buried, opening
the coffin and kissing the decomposing remains passionately before falling into great
bouts of hysteria and weeping. Finally her
attendants were able to convince her to per-
mit her husband a decent Christian burial.

King Ferdinand immediately moved to take possession of Castile, as it was very obvious to everyone that Queen Juana, never strong under the best of circumstances, would not ever again be entirely sane. She could not govern, and her eight-year-old son Charles was declared Carlos I of Castile, his grandfather of Aragon acting as regent for the boy. Now Ferdinand had all of Spain back in his hands. It did not, however, help Katherine's position, as her nephew should one day be ruler of Castile.

Rosamund and Owein gave the princess' man the proceeds from the sale of Tatamount and enclosed a loving letter of support with the instructions to have the messenger return in the spring with news and they would try to help further.

"We will sell lambs," Rosamund said, determined. "Oh, Owein, that I were a wealthy heiress with bags of gold in my vault! But I am just the lady of Friarsgate. My wealth is in my lands, my flocks, and my herds. Do you think poor Kate will ever be Queen of England now?" She sighed. "Poor lass for all her fine title."

In the late spring of fifteen hundred and seven, Rosamund's two daughters celebrated birthdays. They were, to their parents' relief, strong and healthy little girls.

Wherever Philippa would go, Banon was sure to be found toddling on fat baby legs right behind her. By late summer Rosamund knew she was once again with child, and she despaired.

"Another daughter, I am certain of it!" she wailed. "Why can I not make you a son, Owein?"

"You cannot know until the bairn is born," he said, "and if it another lass I shall be content as long as you are both safe and well. Besides, it will give me great pleasure to match my girls while your uncle Henry sits by gnashing his teeth that I overlook his sons."

She laughed in spite of herself. "Aye, it will drive him quite wild to see my female progeny inheriting Friarsgate," Rosamund agreed. "I hear that Mavis has whelped another bastard, although my uncle must claim it as his own."

"What shall we name another daughter, if indeed it be a lass?" he asked her.

"Well," Rosamund considered, "we have named the first after my mother and the second after your mother. I think I shall call this one after the king's late wife, Queen Elizabeth, who was so good to me when I first arrived at court. It is a lass, Owein. I quicken the same way as with the others and am as healthy as a sow." She sighed, then said with a grin, "We do have a great deal of fun producing these daughters of ours. Yet we must be doing something wrong. After I have birthed Bessie we must consider it well, for I will have a son, dammit!"

Rosamund birthed her third daughter, Elizabeth, on May the twenty-third, fifteen hundred and eight. The child was also given the names of Julia, for her birth date was the saint's day, and Anne, for the mother of the Blessed Virgin, who was said to be the patron of expectant mothers. Like her sisters, Bessie was a strong and healthy child, but unlike them she had blond hair like her father, and Owein was visibly pleased.

The princess' messenger arrived from Greenwich and was filled with gossip. Rosamund insisted upon being carried into the hall so she might greet him and learn all the news. It was not good. The Princess of Aragon's few remaining servants were the joke of the king's court. Those proud Spaniards walked about now, their clothing and livery virtually in rags. Not only that, but the king was in negotiations with Emperor Maximilian of the Holy Roman Empire, to betroth the emperor's grandson, Archduke Charles, the mad queen of Castile's son, with his youngest daughter,

Princess Mary. As the boy archduke was heir to the Low Countries, this would very much be to England's advantage regarding the wool and cloth trade it had with that part of the world. It would also act as a counterbalance to a surprising political alliance only recently made between King Ferdinand and France.

The English king had decided that Ferdinand was no longer necessary to his plans. The Princess of Aragon was made very aware of Henry Tudor's *want of love for her* as she delicately put it. She had written to her father, begging him for aid. Her few remaining servants were her responsibility, she pointed out again. She was not asking for luxuries, but the simple ability to sustain them. Like all the women of her family, Katherine had been taught from the cradle to submit to the men in her life. Hence she would not criticize, but she would beg. Yet her great pride sustained her somehow, especially when she was being constantly dunned by her creditors. They were aware of the gossip regarding the king's manner toward the Spanish princess. They feared she would be removed to Spain before they might be paid what was owed them. They did not understand that even a princess may be destitute.

Rosamund wept at her friend's plight, but as Owein wisely pointed out to her, there was nothing more she could do for Katherine than she was already doing. These were the affairs of the mighty, not of a small landowner in Cumbria. The coins they sent to the princess were great for them, although they would probably sustain the lady for little more than a few days, and poorly at that. Still Rosamund set aside what she could to send to Katherine of Aragon whenever her messenger came to Friarsgate.

The princess' messenger did not return to Friarsgate for over a year, but when he came the tale he told was worthy of a bard. King Henry Tudor had gotten it into his head that he would marry the mad Queen Juana of Castile. Her mental state meant little to him. What counted was that she was a breeder of healthy children. The king suddenly decided he must have more heirs. Katherine favored the plan, for she was wise enough to realize her own future depended on it. She had managed to convince her father to recall his ambassador, Dr. de Puebla, who was now ill. King Ferdinand, his conscience finally troubling him, sent his daughter two thousand ducats and appointed her his ambassador until he could send another man. The sum of money was not great, but it did allow

Katherine to clear many of her more serious debts, pay her servants, and see to their welfare. Her new ranking as ambassador from Spain again increased her status with Henry's court. She found herself briefly in favor once more.

Good-hearted and loyal and lacking in malice, the princess had finally learned the hard lesson that the morality practiced by men good or bad was far different from that practiced by women. She grew more assured in her dealings with the king, charming him one moment, learning how to look at him directly and lie facilely. The king even began paying the princess a small allowance once again, but the goodwill did not last long.

Henry Tudor quickly realized that King Ferdinand had no intention of giving up Castile, or Juana, who was totally mad now and confined. He began casting about for another wife. Katherine's star once more descended into the depths. The king again attempted to make a match for Prince Henry with Eleanor of Austria, but the negotiations quickly collapsed.

Now he turned to France for a bride for his son, but as the year fifteen hundred and nine began, the king was growing sicker. A group of his nobles approached him to beg that he honor the match with Katherine.

The last of her dowry was finally ready for payment. He was ill. They feared for the succession if the prince were not quickly wedded and bedded and producing heirs for England. Convinced by his mother, the Venerable Margaret, that he was growing sicker by the day, the king agreed to consider it. But now there was serious talk of Katherine returning to Spain to await another match. She was twenty-three, a bit long in the tooth to begin breeding heirs according to the standards of their day.

Katherine was yet again in financial straits. The tension within her little household was fierce. She had dismissed Dona Elvira at long last, but now there was no one to run her household. Her chamberlain treated her boldly and impertinently. She could not dismiss him because she could not pay him. Her confessor, Fray Diego, an extraordinarily handsome Franciscan, had too great a hold over her and a wicked reputation for lechery among the ladies of the court. Katherine would hear nothing against him, for she adored him, and was frankly besotted. The new Spanish ambassador, Don Guitier Gomez de Fuensalida, noted the princess' frightening dependence upon the young priest. He wrote of his genuine concern to her father, sending his own personal servant with the details and asking that the king replace Fray Diego and send the princess an "old — and honest — confessor."

Learning of the ambassador's correspondence with her father, the princess cut him dead from that moment on. The ambassador was recalled at her insistence, and Katherine refused to do anything without her confessor's consent. Then on the twenty-second of April Henry VII finally died at Richmond. After his funeral the court moved to Greenwich, and the new king's intentions were soon patently clear. He intended honoring his betrothal to Katherine of Aragon, although for a brief few days he hesitated, troubled by his scruples of conscience. Would he, he wondered aloud, commit a sin by marrying his brother's widow? Or was the pope's dispensation all right? Some churchmen were not happy with the dispensation, but as King Ferdinand pointed out, two of Katherine's sisters were wed to the same King of Portugal, and each bore him healthy children.

The Privy Council pressed the new king to marry the princess. Despite his qualms, he admitted to them that he loved Katherine and desired her above all women. He had admired her since he was a boy of ten, and now he was eighteen. He respected her and thought her courage these past five years admirable. The Venerable Margaret agreed, and her influence with the young king was considerable. Without further hesitation Henry proposed to Katherine. They were married privily on the eleventh of June in her apartments.

I am happier now than I have ever been in all my life, dear Rosamund. Happier than I could have ever imagined. My lord husband is the finest and gentlest of men. I shall always love him. As for you, my dear friend, I cannot thank you enough for your kind sustenance and especially your prayers these last years. I do not know if I shall ever be able to repay you. . . .

Rosamund read the missive, tears streaming down her face.

"Tell the queen," she said to the royal messenger, "that the little I did warrants no repayment. I was honored to serve her highness. I will serve her again given the opportunity. You will tell her my exact words? I will not write them, for they would only be seen by some secretary and probably filed away."

"I will tell her, m'lady," the messenger said, "and if I may say it, I shall miss my visits to Friarsgate. I have enjoyed watching your daughters grow. May God watch over them." He bowed.

"Thank you," Rosamund said with a small smile.

"So there is an end to it," Owein said quietly that night as they lay abed. "The Henry I served is dead and buried. The young king has done the honorable thing and married Princess Katherine. Now we have but to wait for their heirs."

"And speaking of heir," Rosamund murmured in his ear, "it is past time we tried to make a son again, my lord." She nibbled at his earlobe mischievously.

"Bessie is just a year," he demurred. "It is too soon."

"I am twenty years old now, Owein," she reminded him. "Let us make a son or two, and I will cease my maternal natterings. Besides, the bairn would not be born until next year, and by then Bessie will be two. It is time enough." She looked down into his face. "Do you not desire me any longer, my lord?"

"You are becoming a very wicked woman, madame," he told her.

"It is obvious I must be if I am to arouse your passions for me, Owein," Rosamund said. Then she astounded him by mounting him. "If a man may bestride a woman, why not a woman a man?" she demanded to know, looking down into his surprised face.

He thought a moment, and then, reaching up, he began to fondle her rounded breasts. "I know of no admonition against such a thing," he considered thoughtfully. His thumbs rubbed against her nipples.

It was startling. That delicious feeling that always began when he played with her breasts. She shifted atop him, "I remember saying to you that we must do something different if we were to have a son, my lord. Perhaps this will be the charm for us." She bent and brushed his lips with hers. "You shall be my stallion and I your rider."

Her new and brazen attitude was incredibly arousing. He had never imagined his sweet Rosamund would be so bold and forthright. She had always welcomed his advances, lying contentedly beneath him, taking her full share of their pleasure in each other but doing little else. He felt himself harden with amazing rapidity. For a moment he closed his eyes and simply enjoyed the sensation, but then he opened his eyes again and reached out to tease at her little love jewel with a fingertip, and finding her already wet with her own lust he laughed aloud. His fingers tightened about her waist, lifting her up, then lowering her so that she

429

was impaled upon him. He groaned as her warmth surrounded him, struggling to gain a firmer control over his own desire.

He slid so easily into her sheath, and Rosamund's tongue encircled her dry lips, moistening them. Bracing herself with her hands, she leaned back, shamelessly enjoying the full length of him. Then, her thighs tightening about him, she began to ride him, slowly at first, but as their excitement mounted she plunged faster and faster until she could not restrain the little cries of pleasure that leapt from her throat. Suddenly Owein gave a great cry, and she felt his juices thundering into her own eager body. She collapsed upon his broad chest, suddenly exhausted and close to tears. They had finally made a son! She knew it!

His arms wrapped about her. " 'Tis a bold baggage you are, Rosamund, my bonny wife. I love you."

"I know," she responded. "Is it not fortunate that I love you as well, my Owein?"

He felt her tears upon his chest and smiled to himself. He did not care if she ever gave him a son. He was content just to be with her. His sweet rose. His own true lovey. She had fallen asleep atop him, and he gently rolled her onto the mattress, drawing the coverlet up over them both, still smiling as he looked down at her. She was so fair. He could understand the prince wanting to seduce her all those years ago. He had wanted to seduce her, too, if the truth be known, but his own code of chivalrous behavior would not allow him to dishonor an innocent girl. Any girl. Owein closed his eyes and drifted into sleep. Thanks to the kindness of the Queen of the Scots and her grandmother, he had been given the fair Rosamund, and for that he would always be grateful.

By Lammastide Rosamund knew she was again with child, and this time her confinement was very different. For several months her belly was extremely sensitive to everything, but especially to the smell of roasting meat. The slightest odor would cause her to disgorge whatever was in her stomach. And then as suddenly as her sickness had begun she was fine once more. But she was growing larger with each day. She had never been quite so big with her girls, but then this, she assured everyone, was her first lad. And he would be named Hugh after her second husband, she reminded them.

"Henry will not be pleased to have that memento presented him," Edmund Bolton chuckled as they all sat in the hall, a

February storm beating at the windows. The fire in the hearth crackled loudly.

"I should hardly call my son Henry," Rosamund said, reaching for a sugared rose petal that she had put up the previous summer.

"You must have a girl's name, too," Maybel said.

" 'Tis not a lass," Rosamund said firmly.

" 'Twill be what God wills, Rosamund," Maybel replied. "Choose a lass' name just in case."

But Rosamund could not, nor did she want to. "He is Hugh," she told them implacably.

Then several days later Rosamund went into labor.

"It is too soon!" she cried. "Oh, God! It is too soon!" She crumbled to her knees, doubled over with the terrible pains racking her.

Owein picked up his wife and cradled her in his arms as the servants ran for the birthing chair. Her waters broke, soaking them both, but he would not leave her, instead kneeling by her side and speaking in soothing tones to her as she labored to birth the child within her. He moistened her lips with a napkin soaked with wine. He kissed her brow and mopped away the beads of perspiration that dappled it. And Rosamund wept wildly, for as she had known this child was a son, she also instinctively knew she would lose him before she even knew him. It broke her heart, but she was not prepared when the perfectly formed little boy slid from her straining body in a rush of bloody fluid, the cord wrapped tightly about his neck, his little face and limbs blue. No sound issued forth from the baby, and Maybel, tears running down her own face, shook her head wearily.

"He is dead, poor wee bairn," she announced. Then she said, attempting to cushion the tragedy, "But you will live, my dearest lass, and you will bear Friarsgate another heir."

"Let me see him," Rosamund said. "Let me see my Hugh."

Maybel wiped the birthing blood from the infant, and after wrapping him in a white swaddling cloth, handed him to Rosamund.

The grieving mother looked down at the child in her arms. The baby was his father's image, his miniature features mimicking Owein's: a tiny fuzz of blond hair upon his rounded skull, the almost invisible minuscule sandy lashes upon his cheeks. Her silent tears fell upon the tiny corpse as she clutched him to her aching breasts. Maybel had cut away the cord from the child's neck, but he was still pale blue in color. The older woman reached out now to take the baby, but Rosamund gave Maybel a fierce look. "Not yet," she said. "Not yet."

Finally Owein said in a quiet voice, "Give me my son, Rosamund," and kissing the baby's cold brow she handed him to his father. Owein studied the small scrap of humanity in the curve of his arm. "He's perfect, and considering he was early by a month, every bit as large as his sisters were when they were born. We made a fine son, lovey. We will make another, I promise you." Then he handed the baby to the young priest.

"I will baptize him, m'lady, before we bury him," Father Mata said softly. "I know he is Hugh. May we add Simon, for today is St. Simon's Day?"

She nodded, then asked sadly, "How can you bury him with the snow on the ground, good father?"

"The earth is softer by the church itself, lady," he said.

Rosamund nodded again. "Go then," was all she said.

The priest departed the hall with the dead infant.

"Why can I not give you a son?" Rosamund said despairingly.

"You gave me a son," Owein replied.

"But he is dead!" she cried. *"Our son is dead!"*

He put his arms about her and let her weep until finally she could weep no more. Her eyes were almost swollen shut with the burning, stinging salt from her tears. She was exhausted with her labor, and finally collapsed with her sorrow and weariness. He picked her up after Maybel had cleaned away the evidence of the unfortunate birth, and carried her to their chamber. After tucking her into their bed, he brought her a cup of warmed, mulled wine, and supporting her shoulders, he helped her to drink it all down. He knew that Maybel had doctored the wine with poppy juice. Rosamund fell quickly into sleep.

"I will see she sleeps for several days," Maybel told Owein when he returned to the hall. "Sleep is a great healer, though she will grieve a long time for the bairn's loss. What a pity, Owein, for the lad was perfect."

"Then why did he come early, and why was he born dead?" Owein said bitterly. He was angry, though Rosamund should never know it lest she blame herself. "Aye, he was beautiful. Every bit as his sisters."

"He was born dead because the cord twisted about his wee neck and strangled him. He was dead in her womb, and who knows for how long. Why? The priest will say 'tis God's will, though why God would will a sweet bairn to be born dead I do not know," Maybel responded. " 'Tis a mystery, but she has proven she can birth a son. You will make another, and next time 'twill be all right. This was an accident. Nothing more, no matter what the priest will say."

"Aye," he agreed, "but she will grieve hard, Maybel." He sat down in his chair by the fire, one hand going to pat the greyhound and accepting the goblet of wine she handed him with the other.

"Of course she will grieve. She is a loving woman, a devoted mother," Maybel retorted.

"What am I to tell our lasses?" he wondered.

"You will tell them that their brother decided to remain with the angels," Maybel said. "Only Philippa will really understand. Banon and Bessie are too young."

"Aye," he said, and sipped thoughtfully at his wine, not even noticing that she left him to his thoughts in the empty hall, the fire warming his feet. He had not felt such sadness since that time long long ago that his own mother had died and he was left alone for the first time in his life. He had remained alone until he had married his Rosamund. They would grieve Hugh's loss together, each giving the other comfort and love in their sorrow. It would be easier for them having each other.

Rosamund slept for several days, waking for brief times to eat lightly and be consoled by her husband. Then she would drink from the cup and sleep again. After a week she could sleep no more. Her three daughters climbed into their bed, cuddling with her and chattering how their brother had decided to stay with the angels. Rosamund swallowed back her tears upon hearing that and hugged her girls tightly. After a second week she arose from her bed, discovering that the snow was melting away, and the hills were beginning to green up again. Her first foray outside took her to a small grave where her son lay buried. She stood over it for what seemed to Owein a long time, and then, turning away, she announced, "I am hungry."

Relief poured through him. "Then let us go to the hall and eat," he said to her.

She slipped her hand into his. " 'Twas an accident, I know. It will not happen again, and we shall have another son, Owein."

"Aye, we will," he agreed, but when she

was not within his hearing he instructed Maybel to see she was given the potion that would prevent her conceiving again for the present. "Whether or not we have a son is God's will," he said, "but I will take no chances and lose my lovey."

"Aye, she needs to recover her strength fully," Maybel concurred.

The rhythm of their life continued as it always had. The fields were plowed and planted with grain. The kitchen gardens were restarted. The herbs began to green up under their mulch of straw. Spring had come in full force. The orchards bloomed, and never had Rosamund seen them so beautiful, the pink and white blossoms that covered the trees emitting a faint odor of sweetness.

Henry Bolton paid them a visit from Otterly, professing sorrow for their loss and then suggesting a match between his eldest son and Philippa.

"I am not of a mind to match any of my daughters yet," Owein told Rosamund's uncle, "but if I were, I should seek farther afield. Fresh blood always improves and strengthens a line, Henry. Find another lass for your lad. You shall have none of mine."

Henry Bolton rode away, shoulders drooping.

"I think he is defeated at last," Rosamund said, watching him go. "I never thought he should give up on possessing Friarsgate, but I truly believe now that he has."

"He is a broken man I can see," Owein said. "His wife's brazen behavior has destroyed him. If he were truly a brave man he would put her from his house, but he is not brave. He is a bully and a coward, and always was so."

For a moment Rosamund almost felt sorry for Henry Bolton. He had fancied himself so superior to his two half-brothers, scorning them because of their illegitimate birth. Now he was forced to accept his wife's infidelity and her two bastards. He dared not do otherwise else he be publicly made the fool, and that Henry Bolton could not tolerate. So he gritted his teeth and accepted what he could not change.

Now that Henry VIII reigned in England the news came more frequently, especially as the weather was warm. The peddlers were out in force, and they came to Friarsgate knowing of its prosperity.

They heard that the king and queen had been crowned on June twenty-fourth, Midsummer's Day, at Westminster Abbey. The royal couple had come from Greenwich by barge the twenty-second and had been housed in the Tower of London as was customary. The city of London was one huge festivity. The young king was magnificent in his rich garments.

The harvest came once again, and it was more than bountiful. Friarsgate's granaries overflowed, and the fruit was being harvested by the bushel from the apple and pear trees in the orchards. Owein was right in the middle of it all. For some reason Rosamund had never understood, he enjoyed climbing to the tops of the trees for those fruits that no one else could reach. He would pick them by hand and toss them down to those women waiting below. Nothing pleased him more than to go to the cellars in the deep of winter and return with a crisp apple or pear. The ones at the top of the baskets, he told Rosamund, were those very same ones he had climbed up to reach. Then he would eat his fruit with a pleased grin upon his handsome face.

He was in the orchards one September afternoon when Edmund entered the hall where Rosamund was sewing a hem into Philippa's new skirt. She looked up and smiled her greeting at him. He was suddenly beginning to look old, she thought.

"Rosamund," he said.

"Aye?" It was then she saw Maybel just behind Edmund.

"Rosamund," he repeated, and then to her amazement he began to weep in great gulping sobs of genuine sorrow.

"Jesu! Mary!" Maybel swore softly, and then pushed past her husband. Men could weaken at the worst possible moment. "There has been an accident," she began.

Rosamund leapt to her feet, the little skirt falling to the floor of the hall. She said one word. "Owein?"

Maybel drew a deep breath. "He's dead," she said.

"*Dead?*" Rosamund looked at the older woman as if she had lost her wits. "*Dead?*" she repeated.

"He fell from a tree, lass. Broke his neck, he did," Maybel said bluntly. "Dead the moment he hit the ground." She was fighting to hold back her own tears.

Rosamund began to scream, the sound so pitiful that the dogs in the hall started to howl and the two cats fled beneath the high board.

Her husband was sobbing like a maid. Her lass was teetering on the brink of madness. Maybel stepped forward, tears now pouring down her own weathered face, and slapped Rosamund as hard as she could.

"Get hold of yourself, my girl," she said fiercely. "Remember that you are the lady of Friarsgate. There is nothing to do but accept what has happened! It is a dreadful calamity, but it cannot be changed. Remember how the queen bore her adversity, and follow her example."

Rosamund's amber eyes finally focused. Her hand went to her mouth as the men brought her husband in upon a board. She drew a deep breath to clear her head. "Edmund, you must cease your grieving now and speak with the carpenter. I want a casket in the hall before nightfall. My lord must be laid out properly for his burial. Someone fetch Father Mata, if they have not already. Annie," she addressed a serving woman. "Bring my daughters to the hall at once. They must know what has happened to their father." She walked over to look at Owein, "Put him upon the high board," she instructed the farm workers. Owein looked so odd, his neck at a strange angle, a look of surprise upon his lips. She turned away, feeling faint. Finding her chair, she sat down heavily. "Oh, God," she whispered, almost to herself, and she finally began to weep.

Annie brought the children into the hall. Philippa and Banon were holding hands, but Annie carried wee Bessie. Philippa's eyes went to the high board, but the younger girls noticed nothing except that their mother was crying. Rosamund held out her arms to them.

"What is the matter with papa?" Philippa asked.

"There has been an accident. Papa fell from a tree," Rosamund explained. "He has gone to be with the angels." It sounded so inadequate, but she could not think of anything else to say.

Warm water was brought, and they removed the clothing he had been wearing that day. Rosamund washed his lifeless body herself, redressing him in his good velvet gown, the one he had worn the day they were married. There was no need for a shroud. Owein Meredith was set in his casket, a linen band wound above his head and beneath his chin to keep his mouth from falling open. Two round copper pennies were placed upon his eyelids to keep them shut. She bent and kissed his lifeless lips, and then he was put into his coffin.

Footed candlesticks were placed at each corner of the coffin and the beeswax candles lit. The casket lid was placed atop it, leaving just the upper half of Owein's body to view. Father Mata came now, his arms full of late-summer flowers, which he strewed on the casket's oak lid. The two prie-dieux were brought from the church. The priest and the lady of Friarsgate knelt in prayer while about them the supper was brought into the hall. Rosamund sat at the high board with Philippa. Her appetite was gone, but she saw with relief that her eldest daughter ate her fill. Banon and Bessie were fed in their nursery. Afterward mother and daughter knelt by the bier and prayed beneath the watchful eyes of the priest, Edmund, and Maybel. Finally Philippa was taken off to bed, but Rosamund refused to go.

"I will stay here with my lord," she said in a stony voice.

It was agreed among the other three that they would each take a turn praying with her this night. Father Mata sent Edmund and his wife off to sleep while he knelt by Rosamund's side and prayed. The night was long, and it grew cold for the first time in many months. The priest remained by his mistress' side for almost the entire night, only giving way when Edmund returned to the hall to scold him that he had not been called.

" 'Tis almost dawn," Edmund said. "You must prepare for the mass, particularly on this sad day."

"When should we have the funeral mass,

Edmund?" the priest asked softly. "Will it be today?"

"Nay," he heard Rosamund's voice. "Tomorrow afternoon. I would have everyone be able to come and see my Owein for the last time." Then she smiled a weak smile at her uncle, "I am not poor mad Juana, Edmund, unable to give up the corpse of my lord. Owein is gone. There is nothing here but his mortal remains. What he was is now with God."

"Do you want to inform Henry?" Edmund said. "Or Richard?"

"Send to my uncle at St. Cuthbert's, Edmund, but not to Otterly. Henry will hear sooner rather than later, but I am not strong enough right now to dispute with him the merits of his eldest son as my next mate. I think I shall not wed again. Friarsgate has three heiresses, and surely that is good enough for the next generation."

Edmund nodded. "I'll ride to St. Cuthbert's myself, lass."

"Thank you," she told him, and then turned back to the coffin.

Richard Bolton arrived from his abbey late that afternoon. He immediately took his niece in hand, insisting that she sleep for several hours before keeping vigil once more. "If you grow ill you will be no use to your daughters," he advised her, "and you do not want them in Henry's tender care."

She obeyed him, but was awake once again to keep a night's vigil. The day of the funeral she slept in the morning, and then with her daughters, all garbed in black, she attended the funeral mass for her husband. The small church was overflowing with the Friarsgate folk, many of them weeping. Their grief became noisy as Rosamund and her children followed Owein's coffin into the graveyard by the church. Weeping openly now, the lady of Friarsgate watched as her husband's casket was lowered into the ground. Then to everyone's shock, she fell into a faint as the last shovel of earth was placed upon the grave.

They carried her back into the hall where she was revived by burning a feather beneath her nose. She opened her eyes to the anxious faces around her. "I'm all right now," she assured them.

"You're exhausted!" Maybel snapped, "and that's a plain truth."

"You should go to your bed, niece," Richard Bolton said.

"Not until after the feasting is done," she replied stubbornly. "It is my duty to appear as hostess to the people of Friarsgate."

They did not argue, but after the funeral

feast was served and Rosamund had been put to bed along with her daughters, Richard and Edmund Bolton sat in the hall with Maybel and Father Mata.

"He left no will," Richard said.

"Then we must see she is protected against Henry and his sons," Edmund said. "I fear she would turn to violence should Henry attempt to foist his will on her again."

"Then we shall make a will," Richard Bolton said quietly. "Henry cannot know Owein's hand. We shall write what we believe Owein would have wanted for Rosamund and the lasses, and you" — he looked at Father Mata — "shall sign Owein's name."

"*I?*" the young priest said.

"We shall say that Rosamund is charged with the care of her daughters and of Friarsgate. That you and I have been chosen to watch over her, and in the event of our deaths, she is to be in the king's care again, and her daughters with her."

"*I am to sign Sir Owein's name?*" the priest repeated.

"Aye," Richard replied, "You will sign the document that I write with Owein's name, and then you will confess your sin to me. I will, of course, absolve you, Mata." His blue eyes twinkled.

"In that case," Father Mata said, "let us get on with it. Henry Bolton will have heard of his niece's loss by now, and he will be with us in another day or two at the most. We'll need to rub a bit of dirt in the cracks of the parchment to age it."

"To age it?" Edmund looked confused.

"You don't want the document to look shiny and new, Edmund," Father Mata said seriously. "Dirt in the folds gives the appearance of aging. Do we have an old piece of parchment? That would help us, too." Now his eyes were twinkling.

Richard Bolton nodded, a faint smile upon his thin lips. "I foresee a bright future for you in the church, Mata," he said dryly. "Let us get started."

Part Three

FAIR ROSAMUND

ENGLAND 1510-1511

Chapter 13

The king and queen were having a rare quiet moment together in her privy chamber. While there were guards outside the door, and in the dayroom beyond the queen's ladies chattered away among themselves, Henry and Katherine were actually alone for a brief time. The young king loved his wife, and he greatly respected her, but he had a roving eye for a pretty face and a quick wit. He did not deny himself his pleasures despite his marital state. So far the queen was unaware of his forays into lust. And Henry knew her delicate sensibilities must not be disturbed. She had already lost one child. So he made certain to spend a half-hour alone with his Kate each day. She was content, bless her, just to be with him.

"Do you recall Rosamund Bolton of Friarsgate?" the queen asked her husband.

In her lap there was a parchment she had just read.

The king's broad brow furrowed in thought. Of course he most certainly did remember her. He had very much wanted to seduce her, but had been stopped by some damned knight of his father's who then proceeded to lecture him on chivalry, "I do not believe I do," Henry said to his wife. "Who is she?"

"She was here at court for a brief time," Kate answered him. "An heiress from Cumbria. She was your father's ward."

"He had many wards," the king responded. *But none with such rounded breasts and melting amber eyes.*

"She was a favorite of your sister's in the months before Margaret was married to Scotland," the queen persisted. "Your grandmother and your sister convinced your father to give her to Sir Owein Meredith as his wife. They were betrothed here at court and went north with Margaret's wedding train, although they left it before it got to Scotland," the queen further elucidated.

Sir Owein Meredith! Aye! That was the knight who had taken him so to task. The king smiled at his wife. "Did she have red hair, Kate, my love? I think I recall a lass with red hair. Or was it dark?" the king's brow wrinkled again as he appeared to ponder the matter.

"Her hair is auburn, and her eyes the same shade as good Baltic amber, Henry," the queen said. "She has that exquisite English complexion that I have ever admired. All cream and wild roses, which I always thought appropriate considering her name. Rosamund."

"Yes," the king said now. "I do believe I recall the lady. A pretty girl who had been widowed twice though she was but fourteen."

"Aye! That is right! Oh, I am so glad that you remember her, Henry! I want to ask her to court," the queen told him.

"What, sweetheart, have you not enough ladies to serve you that you must request the company of a Cumbrian lady? Her husband may have something to say about it, I fear. I should not want to allow *you* to go off without me," the king said with a broad smile.

The queen colored prettily. But then she responded, "She has been widowed once again, Henry. Her poor heart is quite broken, for she loved Sir Owein. They have three little girls, you know. I am godmother to the second lass, though I have never seen her."

The king was now intrigued. "How is it,

Kate, that you know so much about this country lady and are even godmother to her child?" he asked his wife. Sometimes, he thought, she surprised him, and usually when he least expected her to do so. He still had much to learn about his Kate.

"We have corresponded, my dear lord, almost from the time of her departure from court. You have no idea of how kind she has been to me, Henry, nor how loyal she is to our house. Rosamund Bolton is the best of women. If I can ease her sorrow in the least I should do it most gladly. Please say she may come. It will be such a treat for me."

"Of course she may come," the king said, even more curious now, "but tell me, in what way was she kind to you, sweet Kate?"

"She learned of my financial plight during that time when your father, may God assoil his soul," the queen said, crossing herself most devoutly, "was unsure whether our marriage would take place. And while he and my father niggled about my support, Rosamund Bolton sent me a purse. And not just one. Twice yearly she gave me what she could. It was not a great deal, no more than a few weeks' worth of coins, but she was faithful. Once, I am told by my messenger, she sold a young stud, a yearling, sired by a great warhorse, and sent me all the proceeds of that sale. Lady Neville, whose husband sought to have the animal but was outbid, confirms the tale."

"Damn me!" the king said, astounded.

"And her sweet letters brought me such comfort. She wrote me about her life at Friarsgate, her confinements, her children, but mostly about Sir Owein. She lost a son, born earlier this year, even as I lost our child. Now she is bereft of Sir Owein." The queen stopped and looked up at her husband. "You do see that I owe her a debt, Henry."

He nodded slowly. How interesting that his Kate had commanded such loving loyalty from an unimportant little girl she had but known briefly. Then he said, "How did Sir Owein die? He was not a young man, but neither was he a graybeard."

"He fell from a tree," the queen said, "though I do not know what he was doing in a tree. His age was thirty-eight years, poor Rosamund tells me."

"You may send an escort to Friarsgate to bring her to you, Kate. And send her a purse so she may purchase some materials to have a fine wardrobe while she stays with us," the king generously instructed his wife.

"Oh, Henry, you are so kind!" the queen cried, and flung herself into his lap, covering his face with kisses. "I do love you, my dearest lord!"

Henry Tudor chuckled and returned her kisses while fondling her breasts as her cheeks grew pink with both her pleasure and embarrassment.

The royal messenger arrived at Friarsgate carrying a bountiful purse for its lady as well as a letter from the queen. Rosamund was to take the purse and purchase fine materials from which she would make several gowns suitable for wear at court. She would be escorted in six weeks' time from her home to London. She could bring one servant with her.

"I cannot possibly go," Rosamund said to Maybel.

"Of course you can go!" Maybel said.

"How can I leave my bairns?" Rosamund wailed. "Bessie is barely weaned. I have responsibilities."

"Rosamund," her uncle Edmund said quietly, for he could see his volatile spouse was beginning to work herself up. "Dear niece, this is not a simple invitation. The queen of this realm has asked you to join her court. She will not expect you to remain with her long, but this is a royal command, Rosamund. The harvest is in, and all is in readiness for the winter. Tomorrow I will escort you and my good wife to Carlisle where you will shop for materials for your gowns. We have not a great deal of time to prepare, my dear, but you must go."

"How long do you think I shall remain?" Rosamund asked. "You know how very much I dislike being away from home, uncle."

"A few months at the most, my child. Remember, the last time you were at court you were a royal ward, but now you are a woman grown. Perhaps you might even find a fine new husband among the king's men," he said, chuckling.

"Jesu! Mary!" Maybel said despairingly, glaring at Edmund. Poor Owein was barely in his grave, and there was her husband going on about another man!

"Oh, uncle, I shall never wed again!" Rosamund told him.

"Well, be that as it may, my niece, you will certainly have a bit more freedom this visit. The young king is said to be quite merry, and his court a gay one. Owein would not want you mourning him for the rest of your life."

"Uncle, he is gone from me just two months," Rosamund said, tears springing to her eyes.

"Shut your mouth, old man!" Maybel hissed at Edmund.

They went to Carlisle and found rich materials for gowns to be worn at court. Rosamund would not choose bright colors in deference to her widowhood. She would wear quiet colors. Over the next few weeks she, Maybel, and many of the Friarsgate women sewed to make her a wardrobe that was suitable. She would take four gowns. Two were to be black, one of a deep hunter green, and the other a midnight blue. The skirts were bell shaped, for that, the mercer in Carlisle had assured them as he sold them a hoop, was the latest style at court.

" 'Tis the queen's Spanish influence," he said with a wink.

The bodices were difficult, for sleeves now were more intricate, the mercer's wife explained. She had a sister in London who had sent drawings of the latest fashions. She copied one for Rosamund, telling her as she did that the Spanish were very fashionable.

"Why, the queen has always looked better than any, my sister says. She says the gowns she brought from Spain were all magnificent."

If she only knew the truth, Rosamund thought to herself, but she nodded, thanking the mercer's wife for all of her help.

Her new wardrobe was completed but two days before her escort arrived. The gowns had square necklines. The bodices were all fitted, and the skirts came just to the floor. The black brocade was decorated with gold embroidery to relieve its severity, with gold embroidery on the deep cuffs as well. The green velvet was edged in soft brown fur, with wide fur cuffs on the sleeves. The blue brocade had a medium-blue velvet yoking about the neckline and deep cuffs that were embroidered in silver and gold, and the black velvet had a yoking of white velvet embroidered in silver and tight sleeves with fur cuffs.

"I've never wore such clothing," Rosamund said. "I shall certainly not shame the queen, my sponsor, though most of the gowns at court will be quite magnificent in comparison with mine." She looked at the garments laid out neatly for her inspection. There were chemises, six in all, more than she had ever seen in her entire life. There were two smocks for sleeping and an embroidered nightcap with pink ribbons. There were at least six pairs of stockings knitted from a fine wool that came from the first combing of the spring lambs. She had a beautiful new hooded cape of Friarsgate wool, dyed in the manor's famous and unique blue color. It was lined and trimmed in a pale rabbit fur, as were the tan leather gloves that matched it.

The manor's cobbler had made her new shoes and a pair of boots. There were chopines for her shoes should the weather be wet or muddy. He had also made her an elegant little needle case that fit into a beautiful kid pouch with small scissors.

Rosamund had little jewelry, but she packed what she had, for the ladies of the court would certainly wear jewelry. She possessed a single rope of pearls from which hung a gold and pearl cross. It had belonged to her mother and her grandmother. She had a broach that Owein had given her to celebrate the fifth anniversary of their marriage. It was silver and green malachite. She had a second broach of red jasper that had been her mother's. She possessed three rings in addition to her marriage band of red gold. One was pearl, one onyx in silver, and the third was a fine red garnet in gold. Then she remembered the beautiful emerald and pearl broach that the Venerable Margaret had sent to Philippa when she was born. Her daughter was too young yet for jewelry, and the king's grandmother had died but several months after her own son. No one would know, and the broach would be wonderful on her green velvet gown. Rosamund packed the jewel.

It had been decided that Annie, a young serving woman of whom Maybel was quite fond, would accompany Rosamund to court.

"I am too old now, my dearest lass, to go with you. Besides, you must leave someone behind who you know will make certain the bairns are well cared for, and I am that person. I have been training Annie myself, and she will do well for you. I will not always be here for you, Rosamund. You must have someone else to look after you."

"Do not even consider leaving me," Rosamund scolded Maybel, "but I will agree that it is better if a younger woman comes with me. You know the hours that they keep at court. If I am with the queen's suite then I shall not be allowed to seek my bed until her highness is safely tucked into her own chamber."

Rosamund prepared her daughters for her departure, but only Philippa seemed particularly interested. Banon was curious as to whether her mother would bring her something when she returned, and Bessie was too young to really know what was going on at all.

"Does the queen have a little girl?" Philippa asked.

"Nay, she has no children yet," Rosamund replied.

"You will not be gone long, mama, will you?" Philippa looked up at her, Owein's eyes searching Rosamund's face.

"I do not want to go at all," Rosamund said candidly, "and I would not, but no loyal subject can disobey the queen's command, my child." Rosamund smoothed her daughter's hair gently. "I should far more remain with my three girls than go to court. I am not a very social creature, I fear, my dearest."

"It is just that we have lost our father," Philippa explained, "and we do not want to lose you."

"You will not lose me, my child," her mother told her, "and you will have Maybel here to look after you. My own mama died when I was three. I barely remember her at all. It was Maybel who mothered me, and you may trust her to care for you and your sisters. But I will be back as quickly as I may. And I will write to you. I promise."

Philippa hugged her mother, and then went off with her sisters. Rosamund sighed deeply, but Maybel spoke up.

"No child likes to have its parent go away,

my lass. You must not worry. I will be here for them as I was for you. And Edmund will watch over Friarsgate." She patted Rosamund comfortingly.

"What if my uncle Henry comes calling?" the younger woman considered, "What if he steals Philippa away and weds her to his odious son? Oh, I do not like leaving my girls."

"Your uncle is not well, according to the cook's gossip, and he has his own troubles with that wife of his," Maybel reminded her. "Besides, Edmund wouldn't allow anyone to take the lasses. Now cease your fretting and finish your preparations for court. The queen's escort will be here in only two more days."

Rosamund sighed again. "I suppose that you are correct, as you always are, dear Maybel. There is nothing to be accomplished by my worrying. But I will far prefer the journey home."

The next day the Hepburn of Claven's Carn rode up to the manor house and walked boldly into the hall where Rosamund sat, polishing her few jewels. She looked up, startled, but did not arise until she had put her baubles back into their velvet bag. "My lord Hepburn," she said. "What brings you to Friarsgate?"

"Is it true?" he demanded to know.

She knew immediately what he meant, but said instead, "Is what true, my lord?"

"You are widowed again?" he replied, knowing that she had known what he meant. Was she being coy? Nay, not Rosamund. Which could only mean then that she was afraid of him. He softened his tone. "I am told that Sir Owein died in an unfortunate accident, lady. Had I known sooner I should have been here sooner to tender you my condolences." The blue-blue eyes looked directly at her.

"Aye," she admitted to him. "I am once more widowed. Is it not odd, my lord, that my husband who survived so many years, from the time he was but six years of age, in service to the Tudors, in both war and peace, should perish in so mundane an accident? He fell from a tree." She laughed softly. "From the moment he came here he was an integral part of Friarsgate. Each autumn he climbed every tree in the orchards, picking the fruit from their tops and tossing them into the women's aprons below. It was such an odd thing to do for a man who was a knight, but it gave him pleasure. The branch beneath him broke suddenly, and he fell." She shook her head wearily.

Logan Hepburn wanted to take the young woman before him into his arms and comfort her, but he knew he could not. *Not yet. Not now.* "I am sorry, my lady. Sir Owein was a good man."

"Aye," she responded, "he was."

There was a silence between them for a long moment, and then he said, "If there is anything you need, my lady, any way in which my clansmen can aid you . . ." His voice trailed off.

Suddenly Rosamund smiled. "You are kind, Logan Hepburn," she told him. "To come over the border to make such an offer says much to me about your character. Perhaps in the past I have misjudged you. I owe you an apology."

"Nay, madame, I am every bit the rogue and rascal you have accused me of being," he told her with a wicked grin. "I have come not just to tender my sympathies, as I suspect you know. But now is not the time to pursue a suit with you."

Rosamund blushed becomingly. Then she said, "Nay, it is not. I am leaving for court in a few days' time, Logan Hepburn. I shall not return for several months."

He was surprised by her revelation. She had said she was a friend of Margaret Tudor, but Margaret Tudor was Scotland's queen. Was it Scotland's court she meant? His heart beat faster. He had entrée into Jamie

Stuart's court through his cousin Patrick Hepburn, the Earl of Bothwell. "You go to visit your friend, my queen?" he asked.

"Nay," she replied, "I go to London."

"I would not have thought you a lass for court," he told her.

Rosamund smiled again, for she could not help herself. He was older than she. He was certainly bolder. Yet there was something about him that made her want to both kill him and kiss him. She blushed again. Now where had that thought come from? she wondered. "I am not a lass for court, my lord," she told him, "but the queen has commanded my presence, and so I must go. Edmund tells me that you do not refuse a queen's command, though I would if I could."

Now how did this little country girl know England's queen? But he could certainly not question her on the matter. He had no right, and she was not volunteering to tell him. "When you return from court, Rosamund Bolton, will you tell me so I may come and present myself before you?"

"My lord . . . ," she began, but then words failed her.

"I have waited since I was a lad of sixteen for you, Rosamund, and I am not known to be a patient man. I will consider your sensibilities, but if you return with a new husband from the English court, I swear to you that I will slay him, for I mean to have you for myself!"

Now she was angry. "Why would I marry you?" she demanded to know. "I am English, and have my home here at Friarsgate. You are a Scot, and live God knows where! *Why*, my lord, I repeat, would I wed with you? I am not of a mind to wed again anyway."

"You will wed me, Rosamund, because I love you, even as Sir Hugh and Sir Owein loved you. You take a man's love for granted, lass, and you should not. Besides, you have an heiress for your manor while I have neither heir nor heiress for Claven's Carn."

"So, my lord, you see me as good breeding stock, do you?" she snapped at him. Oh, he was absolutely insufferable!

"If I just wanted to breed up more Hepburns, lass, I should have wed long ago. God knows the lasses have been throwing themselves at my head and climbing into my bed since I was fourteen and attained my great height. But I want only you for my wife." He towered over her.

She glared up at him, hands on her hips, amber eyes blazing with her fury. "Am I supposed to be impressed by the knowledge that other women find you attractive, my lord?"

"You find me attractive," he told her, a wicked smiled beginning to take over his face.

"I?" she practically screeched the word. *"I find you attractive?* My lord, you have lost leave of your senses if you believe that."

He knew even as he did it that he shouldn't do it, but he could not help himself. He had to show this impossible lass the truth of the matter. Swiftly reaching out, he yanked her into his arms, his head spinning as the warm scent of white heather assailed his nostrils. He could feel the wondrous softness of her breasts against his hard chest. His mouth descended upon her sweet lips, and he kissed her as he had never before kissed any woman — with great depth of passion and with great tenderness. Then, as he looked down into the small heart-shaped face and the very startled amber eyes, he said, "Aye, Rosamund Bolton, you find me most attractive."

She pulled from his embrace and slapped him with every ounce of strength that she had. "Get out of my hall, you . . . you . . ." She struggled for the word. *"You Scots scoundrel!"* Her dainty index finger pointed the way, and her color was most high.

He rubbed his cheek, amazed that she could hit so hard, and indeed the blow had hurt. He bowed to her with an elegant flourish. "I will be back, Rosamund, when you return from London. You had best prepare yourself to become my wife, for my wife you shall be!" Then he turned and was gone.

If she had had something to throw at him she would have, Rosamund thought angrily. How dare he presume that she would marry him? She had no intention of ever marrying again, "I have grown weary of burying husbands," she muttered to herself.

Maybel came into the hall. "I saw a man riding in," she said. "Who was it?"

"Logan Hepburn," Rosamund answered her.

"The Hepburn of Claven's Carn? What did he want?"

"To pay his condolences," Rosamund said shortly.

"And to plead his case with you, too," Maybel responded with a chuckle.

"Do not speak on it!" Rosamund snapped. "I am glad now that I am leaving for court."

Maybel raised an eyebrow and did not mention to her mistress that she had also seen their guest heading for the church where he would speak with Father Mata, she had not a doubt. Rosamund was to be gone in another day. There was no reason to set her temper aflame any more than it was now.

In the church the priest and the Hepburn embraced.

"Thank you for sending to me, brother," Logan Hepburn said. "You did not tell me, however, that she was going to court in London."

"You have found out on your own, then," the priest answered, his eyes twinkling.

"What if they give her a new husband? And how does she know the Queen of England, too?" He wanted answers, and he was not going to obtain them from Rosamund. Mata was bound to him by blood. By the fact he was head of their clan branch. He would tell him.

Together the brothers sat in a narrow pew, and the priest began. "She met Katherine of Aragon when she was at court before her marriage to Sir Owein. She and Katherine and Margaret were just girls, but great friends. When Rosamund's eldest daughter was born she sent to Katherine, the king's mother, and the Queen of the Scots. All answered her, but her heart was touched by the Spanish princess' plight. She apologized for the poorness of her gift to the baby, but she explained she was in extreme financial straits. It seemed that old Henry and King Ferdinand were haggling over who should pay her allowance and her maintenance, so neither paid. The unfortunate princess was living from hand to mouth in the most abject poverty and her servants in rags because of it. The lady of Friarsgate was touched by the princess' difficulties. She sent her a small purse, and continued to send what monies she could twice a year. The two women corresponded. When the lady Katherine, England's queen, learned that her friend was once again a widow, she sent a very gracious purse, which she instructed the Lady Rosamund to spend on materials for court gowns, and she said she would send an escort for her. The escort should arrive tomorrow, Logan."

"I will kill any husband they give her," the Hepburn said quietly to the priest.

"And she ordered you from her hall, I am certain," the priest said, laughing. "I do not believe that this Tudor king will send my lady back with a new husband. His father did because it was expected of him that he do so. My lady is yet mourning her husband, and the queen will understand her delicacy of feelings. Nay, brother, this will just be a social visit, and the Lady Rosamund will return as quickly as she can, for she does not enjoy the court or its inhabitants. She is of no importance in the scheme of things. The court is filled with snobs who make her feel as unimportant as she indeed is. Nay, she will return in a few months' time to her beloved Friarsgate and darling daughters."

"Who will she write?" he asked astutely.

"Edmund and Maybel. They will share their letters with me, and I will send to you with what you should know, Logan."

"Good!" the Hepburn of Claven's Carn said. "Now bless me, Mata, for I know I am in strong need of it." He got up from the bench and knelt before his half-brother.

The priest stood, and placing both his hands on his older sibling's head, he gave him his blessing and then told him, "Go with God, Logan, and try not to kill anyone."

The Hepburn arose, chuckling, and replied, "I will try, Mata, but I dare not promise you, for you know how I am."

"I do indeed," the priest agreed as he walked with Logan Hepburn to the door of his church. The two men embraced a final time, and then, mounting his stallion, Logan Hepburn rode away from Friarsgate.

Rosamund watched him ride off from the

window of her bedchamber. She stood thoughtfully, her pearwood hairbrush in her hand, stroking her long hair which she had unplaited. She had told Maybel she had a headache and would eat in her chamber, but the truth was she did not wish to discuss the Hepburn of Claven's Carn with anyone. She was used to soft-spoken men who treated her gently. Logan Hepburn was not soft-spoken or self-effacing, as both Hugh and Owein had been. He was arrogant. There was simply no other word for it. He was bold, and he was arrogant. He did not use courtly language. Nay. He looked a person in the eye and spoke bluntly.

Yet was that a bad trait? Still, what right had he to come to her in her grief, and announce that he intended wedding with her? He had been waiting for her since he was sixteen, and had first seen her at age six at a cattle fair at Drumfrie. What nonsense! And women flung themselves at him. Well, perhaps that wasn't nonsense. He was devilishly attractive with his wild dark hair and his blue-blue eyes. She never thought of his eyes as just plain blue. They were bluer than blue, like her lake itself. Her brush caught on a tangle, and Rosamund swore softly to herself. "This time," she muttered as Logan Hepburn disappeared over the hill, "this time no one is going to plan for me or tell me who I will wed." Hadn't she already decided that there would be no next time? Rosamund swore again to herself.

Still, she couldn't help but wonder what marriage to such a bold man would be like. They would fight she had not a doubt. And what was this Claven's Carn like? There could surely be no place on the face of this earth that was as beautiful as Friarsgate. She knew enough of the Scots tongue to translate the meaning of his holding's name. *Claven's Carn*. It meant the *rocky hillock of the kites*. A kite was a bird of prey. She grimaced and wondered who had named it that. Nay, it would not be as beautiful as her own Friarsgate, named for an ancient, long-gone monastery.

Tracez Votre Chemin. Her family's motto slipped into her thoughts. Well, wasn't that what she was doing? She was making her own path, and it was past time that she did so. She had let other people make her decisions for far too long. But then, she was a woman, they kept reminding her, and women didn't make their own decisions. That was up to the men in their lives. *Says who?* Setting down her brush she began to rebraid her hair once again.

The following day the royal escort arrived, and at its head was a gentleman who introduced himself as Sir Thomas Bolton, Lord Cambridge.

"We are distantly related," Sir Thomas informed Rosamund as he looked around her little hall with a sharp eye. "Our great-grandfathers were first cousins," he explained, "I have always wondered what this Friarsgate looked like. I actually knew my great-grandsire. He died when I was seven, but he loved to tell stories of this Cumbria where he had been raised. It is beautiful, I will grant you, but my God, lady, how do you bear the want of civilized company?"

Under other circumstances Rosamund would have been greatly offended, but for some reason she wasn't certain of she had taken an immediate liking to Sir Thomas. He was of medium height and stockily built. He had beautiful blond hair that had been cut in a very elegant bob with bangs across his high forehead. His curious eyes were the same amber as her own. His clothing was simply gorgeous, and quite obviously the height of style. How he managed to look so perfectly turned out after his days on the road she could not imagine. But it was his manner that delighted her, for there was absolutely no malice in it no matter what he said. And Sir Thomas said a great deal.

"I am content, my lord, to live a quiet life," she answered him. "I take my responsibility to Friarsgate seriously."

"Indeed," Sir Thomas sighed, and he flung himself into a chair. "With the proper clothing, my darling, you would be simply spectacular." Then he pierced her with a sharp look, "I like you, cousin, and I am going to take you beneath my wing, but first you must give me something to drink, for I am perishing with thirst, and then you must tell me how you were invited to court. I am weak with curiosity, dear girl."

Rosamund giggled. She just couldn't help it. She had never in her whole life met anyone like Sir Thomas. She poured him a pewter goblet of cider, fearing her rustic wine would insult his palate, and handed it to him.

He sipped, looked at her over the goblet, and then drained it down, holding it out for more. "Excellent, and pressed just recently. Am I right, darling girl? When in the country . . ." he said with a smile. "Now, tell me the answer to my question, cousin Rosamund."

"I was at court as a ward of King Henry VII for a brief time. I met the Princess of

Aragon then. When I returned home, the wife of Sir Owein Meredith, we fell into a correspondence. After my husband died the queen called me to court. She means to cheer me, I know, but I should far rather remain here," Rosamund told him.

"Oh, I am sure you would, cousin, but the queen is right in this matter. A visit to court will help you through the worst of the doldrums. I remember Sir Owein. He was an honorable man, and loyal, if perhaps a bit dull. Now do not be offended. Many good men are dull, but it means naught unless you are bored to death by them, and you were obviously not bored, I can see." His gaze went to the end of the hall, where Philippa, Banon, and Bessie stood gazing in both awe and amazement at the sight of the beautifully fashionable Sir Thomas Bolton. "Are these your daughters? How charming they are," Sir Thomas said.

"We lost a son," Rosamund said as if to defend her lack.

"Ah, poor girl! Another tie with the queen," he remarked. Then he said, "We will depart tomorrow, cousin, if that is suitable. You are ready, I hope. The autumn is late, and I fear the road should the snows come early. The trip was far longer than I anticipated."

Rosamund had refilled his cup, which he now sipped. "How," she queried, sitting opposite him by the hearth, "is it that you were chosen to accompany me, Sir Thomas?"

"I overheard the king saying his wife was inviting the lady of Friarsgate to court. I immediately asked his highness, or his majesty, as he now prefers to be styled, and most recherché, I think, if the lady was a Bolton by birth, and this Friarsgate was in Cumbria. When he answered aye to both of my questions, I explained that I was your most distant cousin. When the queen learned of it, and of my curiosity about Friarsgate, she assigned me the task of coming north to escort you, dear cousin. And thank heavens she did! There is so much that has happened at court since you were there last. I shall catch you up on all the best gossip, some of which may even have a bit of truth in it. Now, take me to see your wardrobe, so I may decide what needs help before we depart. I hope what you are wearing isn't a sample of what you intend to bring to court, my darling."

"Nay," Rosamund said, laughing despite the insult, "I purchased material in Carlisle, and the mercer's wife had recent sketches from her sister in London."

Sir Thomas shuddered and made a face.

"I can but imagine," he said with a great sigh.

"But I am already packed, sir," Rosamund protested.

"My darling cousin, we can always repack. What we cannot do is erase the impression you will give the court with a bad fashion appearance. Lead on!" He set down his pewter cup and stood up.

Rosamund laughed again. Aye, she did like this cousin who had appeared out of the blue to bring her to court. "Come along, then, but be advised that my gowns are sober in both color and style. I am, after all, in mourning for my husband, Sir Thomas."

"Just Tom, or cousin," he told her, and as he passed the three little girls, he stopped, and reaching into his doublet, brought forth a handful of sweetmeats, which he casually gave them. Then he continued on, following Rosamund up the stairs of the house to her bedchamber.

They entered, and Rosamund said to Annie, "This is my cousin, Sir Thomas Bolton, who has come to escort us south, Annie. He wants to see my gowns. Unpack them now."

"Yes, m'lady," Annie said, eyes wide as she viewed Sir Thomas.

"What kind of jewelry do you possess?" he demanded to know.

Rosamund fetched the small velvet bag and poured it onto the bed so he might view it.

His long graceful fingers pushed the ornaments about, and then he pronounced, "The pearls and the broach with the emeralds and pearls are worthy of you. The rest is not. You will leave them behind."

"But I have nothing else," she told him.

"I do," he said. "My branch of the family is quite filthy rich, darling girl. I have jewelry to spare, and no wife to wear it."

"Why do you have no wife?" she asked him. "You would, I think, be considered a most eligible parti, cousin.

He smiled and patted her hand. "I do not wish a wife," he said simply. "A wife," he explained, "should encumber me. I am, I fear, a selfish man who prefers his pleasures to siring a brood of puling offspring, all waiting for me to die so that they can squander my wealth so carefully built up by my family. I am, darling girl, quite capable of squandering my wealth all by myself. I shall bedeck you in the family gems, and I shall probably have a slightly more fashionable wardrobe, in more cheerful hues, made for you after a short while." He eyed the gowns Annie spread out for him to view. "Not bad," he finally said. "A bit conservative, but not bad at all considering the source. The mercer's wife did well by you, and I am surprised. These will do for a start. Repack, Annie, for we are leaving in the morning, though not too early. Just early enough to reach St. Cuthbert's by sunset. Do you know it at all?"

"My uncle Richard has just been elected its new prior," Rosamund said. "Come back into the hall with me, cousin, and I shall tell you of the family's most recent history. In return you will tell me how a Bolton from Friarsgate ended up in the south a rich man."

He chuckled. "I am glad to see you are not some silly milk-and-water creature like so many of the women about the queen. All so very fashionable, all so very proper, all so terribly proud of their perfect breeding, and frankly not a bit of sense or backbone among them all." He followed her downstairs into the hall where Edmund had come in from the estate and Maybel was now directing the servants as they prepared for the evening meal. They would have sixteen extra mouths to feed this night, and the tables were already laid with bowls and spoons and polished wooden cups.

"This is Sir Thomas Bolton, Lord Cambridge," Rosamund said to them. "This is my uncle Edmund and his wife, Maybel, who raised me after my parents died."

Edmund came forward and shook Sir Thomas' hand. "You will be descended from Martin Bolton," he said. "You are welcome to Friarsgate, my lord."

"You know who he is?" Rosamund said. "Why is it that I have never heard of this offshoot of our family?"

"There was no need for you to know about them," Edmund said with practical sense.

"Come and sit at the high board," said Maybel, awed by the elegance of Sir Thomas.

They seated themselves, and Edmund continued. "Several generations back there were twins born into the family. Henry and Martin. Henry, the firstborn, was to inherit Friarsgate. Martin, the second-born twin, was to marry his first cousin, the daughter of a very wealthy London merchant, for Henry and Martin's mother had come up from London. Martin went down to London when he was sixteen, and at eighteen the marriage took place. A son was born, but then Martin's wife caught the eye of King Edward IV. The foolish lass, I am told, allowed herself to be seduced, then killed herself in shame. Has the story reached my ears intact, Sir Thomas?"

"Remarkably so, cousin Edmund. Now I shall finish it. The king was not a bad fellow, just amorous. He felt guilty for what he had done and what had happened to Martin's wife as a result, particularly as Martin and his father-in-law had supported King Edward and been most generous in forgiving his debts to them. So the king created Martin Bolton, Lord Cambridge, and gave him another wife, the daughter of minor nobility and a small holding in Cambridge. He withdrew from the business and left that to his former father-in-law and others who seemed to have a great knack for increasing the family wealth. We have lived to be amused ever since," he concluded with a grin.

Now it was Rosamund's turn to explain how Sir Thomas had ended up as her escort. She finished by saying, "We shall leave in the morning after the mass and after we have broken our fast."

When she had finished the evening meal, Rosamund departed to her chamber. Edmund took Sir Thomas aside and related the story of his niece's life to date. "She is wise in many ways," he explained, "but sometimes a bit too trusting, I fear, as she has been very lucky in her friends and husbands. You are our kin. Will you give me your solemn pledge to look after her?"

"I will," Lord Cambridge promised. "You have my word. Now tell me why you are not lord here. Was Rosamund's sire the elder? I understand her uncle is prior of St. Cuthbert's."

"I am the eldest of our father's sons," Edmund said. "My brother Richard was the second born, but we were on the wrong side of the blanket. Rosamund's father, our brother Guy, was the first legitimate born, and lastly came Henry. While Richard, Guy, and I were all as close as brothers can be, Henry always looked upon his two eldest bastard siblings with disdain, despite the fact that our father loved us all. He has never gotten over the fact that Rosamund survived the death of her parents and her brother to become the heiress to Friarsgate." Then Edmund explained the story further.

"Sir Hugh was a clever fellow to have outsmarted our greedy relation so well," Sir Thomas noted with a grin. "So that is how she came to court. I do not recall her, but then I would not have been in the slightest interested in a little maid in the queen's household. Besides, I lived in terror of the Venerable Margaret. She was a true dragon!"

"Rosamund was quite fond of her," Edmund said, "and grateful to her for arranging the marriage with Sir Owein."

"Of course," Sir Thomas said. He had heard enough. He yawned. "Show me where I am to lay my head, cousin Edmund. It has been a long journey from London, and the journey back, while more pleasant for Rosamund's company, will be long as well."

Edmund arose. "Come along, then," he said, and Sir Thomas followed him from the hall.

Chapter 14

Departing Friarsgate on the last day of November, they traveled south, stopping at St. Cuthbert's where Sir Thomas was introduced to his distant relation, Prior Richard Bolton. To Rosamund's surprise the two men were quite compatible. She would not have thought the flamboyant Thomas and the urbane Richard could have been friends, yet they forged an immediate bond that she had to admit was to her own, and the family's, good.

"Does Henry know you have gone to court?" Richard asked his niece as they supped in his private dining room that evening.

"It is not necessary that I inform him of my comings and my goings," Rosamund replied, "I thought it better he not be aware that my daughters are without their mother. Winter will soon set in, and he will keep to

Otterly, especially as Mavis is wont to roam. I should be back in the spring before he even knows I am gone."

"Mata will keep me informed," the prior answered her. "We will see the lasses are kept safe, dear niece."

"Mata seems to be a font of information for all," Rosamund said sharply. "He sent to the Hepburn of Claven's Carn that I was widowed. Just two days ago that brazen Scot came courting me," she said indignantly, her color now high.

"What is this?" Sir Thomas' eyes were leaping with curiosity, "You have a brazen Scots suitor? My dear, I am impressed!"

"He would be my suitor, but I will not have him," Rosamund responded, but she was near laughter. Her cousin Tom, it seemed, had the uncanny ability to make her laugh.

"Oh," his voice fell, and his look was most disappointed. "I have never met a brazen Scot," he said. "Is he *very* brazen?"

"Extremely," she told him. "He claims to have been in love with me since I was six and he saw me at a cattle fair at Drumfrie," Rosamund explained. "Have you ever heard such nonsense?"

"I think it wildly romantic, dear girl," Sir Thomas answered with a melodramatic sigh. "The man has waited for you through three husbands. What devotion! What fidelity! Why, I believe he is actually in love with you, Rosamund. How rare a thing is love. But you do not understand that with your practical heart, do you?"

"Hugh and Owein both loved me," she said heatedly, "and I loved them, cousin, I know love."

"Hugh Cabot loved you like a daughter. Owein Meredith loved you because he was grateful to you. This brazen Scot, as you style him, loves you only for yourself, dear cousin. Visit the queen at court, and then come back to him. Oh, play him like a salmon on a tight line if you will amuse yourself, but then let him catch you. You will never regret it, I suspect," Lord Cambridge said.

"The Hepburn of Claven's Carn is a bit wild," Prior Richard said, "but he is a good man, niece. A respectable woman such as yourself could make the difference for him and his clan branch."

"My lords!" Both her tone and her look was exasperated. "I am not of a mind to wed again. Friarsgate has three heiresses. It is safe from Uncle Henry and his brood, for I shall seek husbands for my lasses from afar. But if I were to wed again, I should make my own choice of a husband this time. I am weary of being instructed that because I am a woman I must do what I am told. Friarsgate has never been more prosperous than it is with me. Aye, Edmund and Owein aided me, but the decisions I have made have kept my manor flourishing. I am capable of making all decisions involving me and those in my charge."

"God's nightshirt!" Thomas swore lightly, and then he said, "Your pardon, prior. Rosamund, I advise you not to be so outspoken before the king and queen. The king does not like women who are forward, and the motto the queen has taken is something saintly and to do with serving and obeying. I can tell you the king was mightily pleased by it. This friendship you have formed can prove valuable to our family. Do not ruin it. No one, I am certain, will force you to wed again, and especially against your will. You will not be at court long enough for the queen to interfere in your life. Frankly, dear girl, you are not important enough. You may successfully hide yourself behind your mourning and your widowhood. Queen Katherine respects and understands such traditions. It is not necessary for you to become voluble regarding your feelings. If the king should wonder how your estate is managed, you will fall back on your uncle Edmund and Owein and Prior Richard. I beg you, dear cousin, to accept my advice to you."

"I think," the prior said smoothly, "that my niece merely needed to express her emotions this one time. She has lived since her earliest years beneath a great burden and strain. You have not met my brother Henry. He can be a most difficult man."

Rosamund burst out laughing, her humor restored. "Aye," she agreed, "Uncle Henry is *difficult*, and more so now that his wife is cuckolding him with every man who winks at her. But at least it has kept him home at Otterly more, and less prone to attempt to interfere at Friarsgate." Then she turned to Sir Thomas. "I promise to be a model of feminine decorum while I am at court, cousin. And I am grateful for your advice. It is good counsel, I know."

They set out in the morning, after bidding Richard Bolton farewell, and traveled south again. The nights were spent at monasteries or convents, and occasionally as they drew closer to London, at inns. She had never before overnighted at such establishments. After eight days the spires of London finally came into view, but Sir Thomas did not take her into the city. Instead they turned off the high road onto a smaller path that led to a village on the city's outskirts. It was here that Sir Thomas Bolton had a house on the river.

"This," he told Rosamund, "will be your home while you are in London, dear cousin."

"Am I not to be at court with the queen?" she asked him, a trifle confused.

"Indeed, in a day or two, after you have rested, you will present yourself to the queen. Indeed, you may remain with her, but it is advisable to have a place away from the court where you may come for your privacy. The court is very crowded, especially now. You are not important or wealthy enough to be given your own apartment or a small room. You know from your previous visit that you will sleep wherever you can and will have very little space for your belongings. It is my advice that you leave them, or most of them, here in your own rooms, especially your fine jewels."

"Is that your house?" Rosamund looked up at the mansion they were now approaching. It was built of weathered brick, some of which was covered in shiny green ivy, had a gray slate roof, and stood four stories high.

"Aye," he said. "That is Bolton House, and it is at your disposal, dear girl."

"I have never seen so fine a house," Rosamund told him honestly. "Even the Venerable Margaret's house was not as fine."

He chuckled. "And it is so easy to get into the city from here. I have my own dock and barge. I shall obtain another barge and hire a pair of bargemen so you will have your own personal transport. We will have the bench in the cabin upholstered in sky-blue velvet, and in the spring you shall have a blue and gold awning to sit beneath when you are outside on the deck. It shall be fine enough to take you all the way downriver to Greenwich."

"Oh, Tom, you spoil me!" Rosamund said, clapping her hands together. "I have never had my own barge, nor even the need for one. I shall feel quite grand."

He laughed. "We shall have such a fine time, you and I, now that you have come to court. And when you wish to return home, I shall gladly escort you. I am dying to meet your brazen Scot, my dear girl. You have not told me. Is he dark, or fair?"

"His hair is black and most unruly," she said. It did not discomfit her to speak on Logan Hepburn now that he was so far away. "And his eyes are a blue-blue. I have never seen any like them."

"I am already intrigued," Lord Cambridge said.

They rode through the iron gates that enclosed the park belonging to Bolton House, and down the gravel pathway to the dwelling. There they stopped, and stablemen hurried forth to take their horses from them, saying, "Welcome home, my lord. Welcome, my lady." The front door to the house was opened, and they entered. Lord Cambridge nodded at his majordomo as they passed beneath the threshold, and then Sir Thomas led his guest into his hall.

It was a wonderful room with a coffered ceiling and great leaded paned windows that looked out over the river. The room ran the entire length of the house. It was paneled, and at one end there was a large fireplace with a fire now burning in it. The firedogs were actually large iron mastiffs. The floor of the chamber was covered in carpets. Rosamund knew what they were for she had seen them before in the royal houses. They came from an eastern land. There were several tapestries decorating the wall. The furniture was of oak, beautifully wrought and obviously well kept. There were bowls of potpourri scenting the air, and on a sideboard there was a silver tray with several decanters and goblets.

"What a beautiful room!" Rosamund told her cousin. She went to the window and looked out. "I shall find it difficult to go to court now, Tom. I could live here in this house forever."

"You would miss your beloved Friarsgate," he teased her.

"Probably I would," she said, nodding, "but I think I shall love this house as much. It is comfortable."

He chuckled. "I fear that is my humble background showing, dear girl. I know all the right things to do and to say, but I must, I simply must, be comfortable in my own home. Let the others go for an over-abundance of elegance in their living quarters. I shall keep such graces for my wardrobe, which can be seen by all, and not just a favored few. What good is it to be wealthy if you cannot flaunt your riches before your friends?" he said with a grin.

"Are you liked?" she asked him mischievously.

He laughed. "Of course," he told her. "My wit and my generosity are legend, dear girl. Come now, and sit by the fire. I will pour you a dram of my excellent sherry."

"I shall not think you generous if you give me but a dram, Tom," she said dryly. "And dare I mention that I am ravenous? We have not eaten since morning, so determined you were to sleep in your own bed tonight. We did not even stop at midday."

"I could not abide another night of flea-infested mattresses and monastery fish, as it is Advent and a penitential season. I am sure I do not remember ever having denied myself in Advent. We shall eat shortly, I promise, and the meal will be a revelation, for my cook is a miracle in himself."

Now it was Rosamund who laughed. "You say such funny things, dearest Tom. I am not certain that I understand you half of the time you are chattering at me. You must remember that I am a simple country lass, cousin."

"Country perhaps," he said, "but simple? Nay, my dear Rosamund, no one who took the time to know you would say you were simple. If you are to get on at court, however, I would suggest that you practice your simpering a bit. Simpering, and a low neckline, always gets a lady far."

"I am who I am," Rosamund told him proudly. "The Venerable Margaret liked me. Once when he was a prince, young Henry sought to seduce me, but you will not repeat that, cousin. If the man who is now king liked me, then I have naught to fear. Besides, I have come because the queen wants to comfort me and give me pleasure in return for my aid to her when she was brought so low. I find it odd that those who scorned her, who never lifted a finger to help her in those desperate hours, should now be so high in her favor. And they are the same people who looked down on me when I was last at court and will no doubt look down on me once again."

He nodded. "You are wise to understand the lay of this land, cousin. And those very men and women who now stand in royal favor would as quickly fall away should the queen be out of the king's favor. True friends are not easy to find, Rosamund. Queen Katherine knows it."

"When shall I present myself to the queen?" Rosamund asked.

"I want you to take a day to rest from your travels. Perhaps even two days. Tomorrow I will go to court and tell the queen that we have arrived. We will follow her directive," Lord Cambridge said. "But it must be soon."

The servants began bringing in the meal now, and so they adjourned to the high board, which was placed facing the river. The meal was exquisite. Rosamund ate with her usual hearty appetite. There were prawns that had been steamed in white wine and were served with a mustard-dill sauce. There were wafer-thin slices of salmon braised in red wine and served with wedges of lemon. There was a fat duck stuffed with apple, pears, and raisins. It had been roasted golden brown and was served with a sweet sauce of intensely flavored dried plums. There was roasted beef, three ribs standing upon a platter, minced game birds in individual small pastries, and a ragout of rabbit. Artichokes in white wine and butter were served, and Lord Cambridge showed his cousin how to eat them with delicacy. There was a salad of braised lettuces. The bread was freshly baked and still warm as she tore off a piece. The butter was newly churned and sweet. There were two varieties of cheese. One was a hard yellow cheddar, and the other a soft runny Brie that came from France, Tom told her. Lastly came a pastry with a latticed crust filled with apples and pears that had been baked and was now served with a clotted cream.

Rosamund finally sat back, replete, a smile upon her face. "Cousin," she said, "if a man may indeed be called a miracle then your cook is certainly one. I have never eaten such a delicious meal away from Friarsgate. The meats were all fresh, and your cook did not overspice, for he had nothing to hide. I shall eat here as often as I dare while I am in London."

"I should not have it any other way," he told her, pleased at her compliments.

They sat for a time talking before the fire, and then Annie came, wide-eyed, to escort her mistress to her room.

"You have eaten, Annie?" Lord Cambridge asked the girl.

"Aye, sir, and 'twas delicious!"

"Then I will bid you both good night, but perhaps I will stop to see you settled later," he told them. "I will tell you before I go to court tomorrow, Rosamund." He waved a languorous hand at them, and directed his attention to his goblet and the fire.

"You should see the apartment, m'lady! 'Tis not just a room, but two for you, and another small one for me! And a separate place for your clothing and two fireplaces! And I've called for a bath for you. They have set this great tub before the dayroom fire, and are filling it with hot water now. This is a palace, m'lady!" Annie, who had never been off Friarsgate land in her entire seventeen years was in awe of just about everything she had seen since leaving her home. She hurried up the wide staircase that led from the entry hall to the upstairs of the house where the bedchambers were located.

Rosamund's apartment was spacious, with windows that looked out over Lord Cambridge's gardens and lawns that swept down to the river. The walls were paneled. The wood floors covered in more Turkey carpets. The drapes at the windows and about her bed were rose-colored velvet with gold rope pullbacks. The candlesticks were silver. Bowls of flowers were upon the sideboard in the dayroom and on a table in the bedchamber. Where had they found flowers in December? Fires burned in both fireplaces. As they entered, the last of the footmen departed carrying their empty buckets. Steam arose from the large oak tub that had been set up for Rosamund.

Annie hurried to add her mistress' scent to the water while Rosamund began to remove her boots and stockings. After the scent had been added to the water the young maidservant helped her mistress to undress and then assisted her into the tub. Rosamund sank down into the hot water with a sigh of deep pleasure.

"I am going to wash my hair," she said to Annie. "I have the dirt and dust of the roads between here and Friarsgate clogging my scalp. I would it be gone."

"Mistress Greenleaf, she is his lordship's housekeeper, has assigned one of her maids to aid me. All I have to do is pull at the bell cord, and she'll be here. Her name is Doll," Annie informed her mistress. "I've hung out your gowns, and Mistress Greenleaf says that Doll will help me prepare them, especially the one you'll first wear to court."

"I'll want my cousin's advice on that," Rosamund said.

"He's an odd gentleman, m'lady, but my, don't he have a good heart," Annie noted. "I know that life would have been far more uncertain for us if it hadn't been him that called to fetch us here. Let me help you with your hair."

An odd gentleman. Rosamund smiled to herself as Annie scrubbed her hair. She wasn't quite certain what to make of Thomas Bolton, but she knew that in their short acquaintance she had come to depend upon him, and she was deeply fond of him. For all of his flamboyant manners and his peacockish dress and his funny language, he was a kind man, *and* he had become a good friend. He was her blood. A Bolton. For the first time she was not afraid to be coming to court again because she had her cousin to ease her way and to be her bulwark.

Bathed, clothed in a clean smock, her hair dried by the fire, Rosamund sat comfortably in her bed. Doll had come and taken away the dirty laundry, bobbing a shy curtsy at Rosamund and then going off with Annie, the two girls chattering. She felt warm and relaxed, and when there was a knock upon her door, she called, "Come in."

"I've brought you a warm mulled wine," Lord Cambridge said. "You have found everything to your satisfaction, cousin?"

"Your hospitality is wonderful, Tom. I thank you." She took the goblet from him and sipped it. "Mmmm, 'tis good."

"It will help you sleep. Rosamund, I would speak to you if you are not too tired to listen," he said seriously.

"Why, Tom, what is it?" she replied.

"I would have no secrets between us, cousin. You may hear things about me at court that distress you. Perhaps you will not even understand them. Some of the courtiers enjoy being cruel, as they have little else but gossip in their lives. Dear country cousin, I am, I know, unlike any man you have ever encountered. Am I correct in that assumption, Rosamund?"

"Aye," she agreed, wondering what he was all about.

"I am a man who likes women, Rosamund, but I do not love them. Do you understand?" His warm amber eyes were cautious.

"Nay, Tom, I do not," she had to admit.

"I do not take women as lovers, Rosamund. On occasion, but not often, I will take another man or a boy for a lover. My behavior is condemned by the church. There are some at court who know of my predilections. If among them I have enemies, and everyone certainly has enemies, these people may seek to hurt you by revealing my habits because they believe you do not know them. I tell you this not to shock you, but so you will not be taken unawares."

"Oh, cousin," Rosamund replied candidly, "I do not really understand, yet I do. Still, you are my blood. You have been good to me. I love you as I love my uncles Edmund and Richard. I do not care what anyone will say about you. I know who you are, and we are not simply relations. We are friends, Tom. That is all I need, or want, to know. I will hear nothing wicked said against you."

"I see I shall have to watch over you very carefully, Rosamund," he answered her almost sadly. "Your heart is much too good. Now, dear girl, we must decide what you will wear to court on your first visit. Annie!" he called out, and Rosamund's young tiring woman hurried into the chamber. "Annie, bring me both of your mistress' black gowns. I must decide in which she will first dazzle the court on her arrival."

Annie brought the two black gowns from the wardrobe.

Lord Cambridge made an immediate decision. "The black with the gold," he said. "The brocade is of an excellent quality, and the embroidery quite fine. Annie, have Doll show you how to fix your lady's hair while she is at court. She cannot wear that charming plait. And, cousin, I shall arrange for you to have an English hood with your veils. It is particularly suited to one with such a charming and young face. The more elegant French hood and the gable hood are too old for you. No, the English hood for the first visit, and then perhaps later your cap back to reveal your hair worn with a veil. Now, jewelry. The pearls with the cross are perfect, but you will need something else." Reaching into his gown he brought forth an object and pressed it into her hand.

Rosamund looked down at a lovely broach. It was a large round creamy pearl set in gold and surrounded by tiny diamonds. "Oh, Tom!" she said, "I will be honored to wear it. You are so kind to lend it to me. Was it your mother's?"

"Nay, I purchased it for a friend, who, as it turned out, was not a friend. It is yours to keep, dear girl." He bent over and kissed her upon the forehead. "Good night, my dear cousin. I will see you before I go to court. Sleep well." He arose from the bed where he had been seated. "Annie, you and Doll will prepare the black brocade with the gold embroidery for the Lady Rosamund. And see that one of her lawn veils is ready." He exited the bedchamber, Annie in his wake, asking further questions about her mistress' garb for court.

Rosamund lay back now in her bed, the pearl broach in her hand. She had never heard of men who preferred men as lovers. She didn't really understand it at all, but her cousin Tom was a good man. It was all she needed to know about him. Her eyes grew heavy, and the broach fell from her hand to the coverlet where Annie found it shortly afterward. The young servant took the jewel and placed it in the velvet bag with the rest of her mistress' few pieces of jewelry.

The sun was long up when Rosamund awoke. "Gracious! How long have I been sleeping?" she asked Annie.

"You've been abed for fourteen hours," Annie answered.

"Lord Cambridge?"

"Not yet gone. These city folk keeps odd hours, m'lady," Annie observed. "Now his lordship says you are to stay in bed today. I will go and fetch you a bit of something to eat." She curtsied and hurried from the chamber.

Rosamund breakfasted upon lamb chops, bread, butter, cheese, and strawberry conserve. The tangy ale was of an excellent quality. She had just finished when her cousin arrived to bid her good morning. He was elegantly garbed in a calf-length velvet coat that was lined and trimmed in a rich dark fur. It was a deep claret in color. About his neck was a beautiful gold chain of small square links decorated in black enamel. She could see his gold-and-claret striped silk hose beneath his gown, and his heeled shoes were of black leather.

" 'Tis early, my darling, I know," he said, "but the best time to catch the queen's eye is after the mass. I shall be there just in time," he told her. "Then I must arrange with one of her secretaries to give me an audience so I may tell her that you are here." He sighed.

"Can you not just say that I am here when you catch her eye?" Rosamund asked him. "It seems like a lot of bother just to say the lady of Friarsgate has arrived, your highness."

"It is," he said, chuckling, "but we must

follow protocol. The queen is very particular about protocol. And that, dear cousin, is why you will remain snug in your bed, resting from your journey. I should return sometime before midnight, if I am fortunate, with news. If not, I shall see you tomorrow. I have instructed your Annie and young Doll exactly as to your gown. You are in good hands. Farewell, dear girl!" He blew her a kiss, and then turned and hurried from the bedchamber.

Annie came to remove her tray, and Rosamund found to her surprise that she was still quite tired. She slept until early afternoon when Annie woke her to say her meal was ready in the dayroom. She climbed from her bed and padded on bare feet into the next room where a little table had been set before the fire. Here her main meal of the day was laid out. There was cod in a dilled cream sauce and a dish of raw oysters, a capon stuffed with bread, celery, and apples and flavored with sage, a thick slice of ham, a pastry of minced rabbit, a bowl of tiny beets in butter, bread, and cheese. The sweet was a large baked apple dusted with sugar and cinnamon, sitting in a bowl of heavy cream.

"I am going to become quite plump if all I do is eat this heavenly food and sleep,"

Rosamund told Annie. "I must say, however, that this is a far more pleasant place for me than the last time I visited court."

"Maybel said there weren't no privacy," Annie volunteered.

"Nay, there isn't, except for the rich and the powerful," Rosamund told her. "You will come with me when I go, of course."

"Doll is jealous," Annie said, giggling.

"Perhaps we will take her with us after we have been received," Rosamund said, "but she will find that a familiarity with the court is likely to engender an aversion to it. Her own master is not like most. His heart is a generous one." Rosamund, having eaten her fill, finally stood up from the table. "I must dress," she told Annie, "but we will not use one of my fine court gowns since I am not going out other than to perhaps walk about my cousin's riverside garden. It is walled where his property touches his neighbor's, so it is unlikely that I shall be seen by any."

When she was dressed and her hair neatly plaited, Annie showed Rosamund downstairs to the door leading to Lord Cambridge's garden. She instructed her servant to remain behind so she might have a bit of privacy. In a few days' time there would be no privacy for either of them. The court was just too busy a place, and the well-meaning queen would keep Rosamund by her side, she knew. The day was neither chill nor warm. There was no wind. The sky was a pale blue, a smudge of thin white clouds showing, indicating a change in the weather to come. The sun was watery, but shone as brightly as it could under the circumstances. It would soon set, for it was December, and the days were very short now.

Thomas Bolton's garden was an orderly one, but she suspected that in the warm months it was a beautiful one. The beds were neat, the small flowering trees and bushes as well as the roses were pruned perfectly, awaiting the winter. There was a small green maze. Rosamund entered it and easily found her way through it. There was some rather interesting marble statuary, mostly of young men, which left nothing to the imagination. Rosamund had never seen such statues before. She found them rather beautiful, especially one of a tall youth with a hound lying at his feet. The boy was covered in graceful draperies and had exquisite ringlets, his head topped with a crown of leaves.

Rosamund walked the smoothly raked gravel paths, finally finding her way down to the riverside. The barge she had seen moored there the previous day was now gone from its dock. She stood on the little stone quay, wrapped in her blue cloak, and looked out at the river. It was beautiful to her eyes, and for a time she could not bring herself to leave its side. She was glad that her cousin did not live in the midst of the city of London. Having Bolton House to retreat to when the court became overwhelming was going to be a blessing.

She wished again as she had wished before that she wasn't here at all. The queen meant well, she understood, but Rosamund's previous experience at court had taught her that queens do not have time for real friendship. So what was she to do? She knew no one. Had no friends. Meg was long gone, and Queen of Scotland. The Venerable Margaret was dead and buried. What in the name of heaven was Rosamund Bolton doing here when her daughters, when Friarsgate, needed her? Rosamund felt a tear begin to slip down her cheek. She swallowed hard. She must not cry, but she couldn't help it. Leaving the dock she sat down upon a stone bench, watched the river more, and wept. She missed Friarsgate. She missed her lasses. She missed Owein! How could he have died in such a needless accident, dammit?

"I want to go home," she whispered

aloud. But she could not. She would go to court, embrace the queen, and thank her for her generosity in inviting her. She would be a diversion for Katherine for a few days, and then the queen's interests would turn in another direction. And Rosamund would remain, an outsider, alone, until she might beg leave to return home again, where, hopefully, she would be forgotten by the queen and could live the rest of her life in peace.

It was getting dark, and a slight wind had begun to come off the river. The tide was going out, and the visible mudflats stank of rot. Arising, she walked slowly back to the house and upstairs to her apartments again. The house was quiet, and she saw no one until she entered her own rooms. Annie hurried forward to take her cloak and her gloves.

"Gracious, m'lady, I was thinking I must go and fetch you," Annie said. "Come and sit by the fire."

"The garden is beautiful," Rosamund told Annie. "In summer with all its color, and I suspect that my cousin has lots of color, it must be quite striking." She looked toward the windows. " 'Tis dark already. I love all the feasts in December, but I hate the short days."

"Go and rest," Annie said. "I'll have a

bath set up. The hot water will take the chill of the afternoon from your bones. Then we'll toast a bit of bread and cheese on the fire. His lordship ain't back yet, but who knows what tomorrow will bring?"

Rosamund dozed, and the bath was brought again. While she soaked, her long hair pinned atop her head, Annie went down to the kitchens to fetch the food. The hot water felt marvelous, taking the deep chill from her body. She sighed, relaxed, even as the door to the dayroom flew open and Lord Cambridge strode into the room.

"Cousin!" he greeted her gaily.

Rosamund gave a small shriek of surprise, and wondered if any of her person was visible other than her neck and shoulders.

He waved her concern aside. "Nothing vital is showing, dear girl. Besides, the bumps and curves of womankind are of no interest to me at all. Fashionable women receive callers in their bath."

"I shall never be *that* fashionable," Rosamund told him, "and from the statues in your garden, cousin, I would suspect that female flesh is indeed not of interest to you, particularly in light of what you have told me about yourself. Still, I have never entertained a caller not my husband in my bath."

"So you and Sir Owein bathed together."

He chuckled. Then he grew serious. "I managed to get in to speak with her highness, the queen, late this afternoon. She will receive you tomorrow afternoon at two o'clock, dear girl. I have told her that you will make your home with me while you are here in London. She is anxious to see you, and happy that you will be here to spend the Christmas season with her. The court is moving to Richmond in a few days. Don't fret. It's nearby," he smiled. "We will have Doll to help your Annie. Doll is a marvel with hair, and you cannot go to court with that charming plait you wear each day. You must have a more elegant and sophisticated style, dear Rosamund, if you don't want to be laughed at. Well, I shall leave you to your bath. I am positively fatigued. The court is overflowing with people, for the king enjoys making most merry and is generous with his father's wealth. I wonder if the last Henry Tudor considered that his son would spend that which he so carefully hoarded." He chuckled, blew her a kiss, and was gone from the apartment as quickly as he had come.

"Was that his lordship?" Annie asked, shocked, as she returned with a tray.

"It was," Rosamund said, rising from her tub and reaching for the towel on the warming rack. "He says fashionable ladies receive gentlemen in their tubs." Rosamund laughed.

" 'Tis mad, he is," Annie said, a scandalized look on her pretty face.

"We're going to court tomorrow afternoon," Rosamund told her servant. She dried herself off thoroughly and slipped her smock back on as she sat down.

"Your gown is ready," Annie said. "Doll and me sewed the pearls on it today while you was asleep, m'lady."

"Pearls?" Rosamund looked confused. "What pearls?"

"His lordship gave me a beautiful length of ribbon, all decorated with little pearls, and said to sew 'em on the neckline of the gown. They do look lovely, m'lady, and Doll says they give the dress real style."

Rosamund laughed. Her cousin was determined that she make a good impression at court. "Remind me to thank his lordship tomorrow," she told Annie. "Now, let us have our bread and cheese. All that air out in the garden has given me a good appetite."

Annie had brought not only bread and cheese but sausage, as well, and another dish of the delicious baked apples that Rosamund had had earlier. They toasted the bread over the fire, melting the cheese atop it and adding the sausage. Mistress and servant ate together before the fire. Rosamund let Annie have some watered wine, for the girl was not used to wine. She, however, drank her wine unwatered. It was ruby in color, and sweet to her taste. She shared her apples with Annie, and when the servant took the tray back to the kitchens, Rosamund sat by the fire, thinking again. She felt better than she had this afternoon at the river. Her cousin Tom always seemed to cheer her with his presence. She considered that Owein had been a wee lad of six when he joined the Tudor household. He had survived. Indeed he had thrived. She knew she would, too. *What a stay-by-the-fire I am.* It was time she came out of herself, and there were so many opportunities for her at court. She might even find possible matches for her girls. She didn't want them having to choose between Uncle Henry's family or some wild Scots borderer like Logan Hepburn.

Now how had *he* slipped into her thoughts? Rosamund wondered. Yet for a minute she saw unruly black hair and those blue-blue eyes of his. What was he doing now? Was he snug in his hall at Claven's Carn? Or was he out beneath a border moon raiding some hapless neighbor. She shook her head impatiently. *Begone!* she shouted silently at the mocking smile in her head, the echo of his voice. She started suddenly. She could have sworn that she had heard his voice, and yet now as she strained to listen the house was very silent. *I must go to bed,* Rosamund told herself. The journey had indeed been too much for her. She should not have thought it, for she had always been a strong girl. Without even waiting for Annie to return she climbed into her bed and was quickly asleep.

She awoke to a sunny morning. Annie brought her breakfast, and then she bathed her hands and face and scrubbed her teeth with her little boar's bristle brush. Now she was ready to begin getting dressed, for it would take some time, and then there was the trip down the river to London. The Thames was a tidal river, and they must travel at a certain time in order to get there easily. It would not matter if they arrived at Westminster long prior to her audience with the queen. What was important was that she not keep her patroness waiting. She sat patiently as both Annie and Doll fitted her soft knit wool stockings over her foot and up her leg. Then to her surprise they rolled a second pair of stockings atop the first. These were black silk, embroidered with gold thread leaves and vines.

"His lordship?" she asked Annie.

"Aye. He says the wool are to keep you warm, for the river will be cold and so will the palace. The silk are for elegance. Even if no one can see them, you will know you are one of the most fashionable women with the queen," Annie explained, her explanation obviously a parrot of what Sir Thomas Bolton had told her when he gave her the silk stockings for her mistress.

"How kind of cousin Tom," Rosamund said, a small smile on her lips as the two servants affixed garters fashioned of golden ribbons with pearl-studded rosettes around her thighs to hold up her stockings. She had never owned anything so pretty, and she would enjoy them.

Rosamund stood up now, and her smock was removed to be replaced by a chemise of fine linen that would show just a scrap of ruffle above the gown's neckline.

"Sit down, my lady," Doll said. "The master has instructed me as to how he wants your hair fashioned today." She picked up the pearwood brush and began to undo the plait and brush it out. Rosamund's long hair was thick and straight. It shone with just the hint of golden lights. "You watch me, Annie," she said, "and you can learn how to do this style. It will be very flattering for our mistress." She parted Rosamund's hair in the middle, and then working quickly, she fashioned it into a chignon, pinning it securely at the nape of her neck. "There now," she said, "and doesn't that look grand!"

Rosamund looked at herself in the glass that Annie held up. A woman she just barely recognized looked back at her. "Oh, my," she said softly.

"It's real different, m'lady," Doll said. "French, in style, it is, and new to this country. Most of the queen's ladies wear their hair old-fashioned and long beneath their headdress, although I'm told some of the older women pin up their hair like washerwomen."

"It's beautiful, Doll, and I thank you," Rosamund told the girl. It was a pity, she thought, that the elegant style would scarce be seen through her veil. Still, she suddenly felt very confident.

Carefully the two servants helped Rosamund step into her skirts, and then they drew them up, tying them at the waist. Next came the bodice and sleeves. The black brocade was very beautiful with its delicate gold embroidery. The addition of the small pearls at the square neckline and on the wide cuff of the sleeves had turned a pretty gown into a splendid garment. Her cousin had a good eye for fashion. Finally everything was tied and laced and taped. The skirt on its narrow hoop took a bit of getting used to, but she quickly found it was manageable. She sat again, and Annie affixed her pearls with the gold and pearl cross about her neck. She then handed Rosamund the pearl broach that her cousin had given her. It was affixed to the center of her neckline. Her wedding band and her garnet ring were the two adornments she chose for her hands.

When Doll saw them she said, "Oh, his lordship said this is to go with the broach, my lady." She drew a small box from her gown and handed it to Rosamund.

"How wonderful!" Rosamund was delighted as the open box displayed a large baroque pearl ring. She slipped it on her finger, admiring it and realizing that it was suddenly very easy to accept beautiful gifts from her good-natured cousin. She knew little about Tom Bolton, but for his bloodline. "Does his lordship have any brothers or sisters?" she queried Doll.

"Aye," Doll answered. "He had a younger sister. Much younger. His lordship don't look it, but he is forty this year. He was fifteen when his sister was born. He adored her from the moment of her birth. She died five years ago in childbed, and her youngling with her. She was twenty. He never seemed to get over it until he brought you to London, my lady. We're all so glad to see his lordship happy again. He's an odd gentleman, but a kind and generous master."

"Aye," Rosamund agreed. "He is kind and generous." She slipped her feet into the shoes that Annie placed before her. "Doll, I cannot take you with me to court this time, but I promise I shall another day. And I thank you for your good service to me."

" 'Tis a pleasure to serve you, my lady," Doll answered her. Then she carefully set the sheer lawn veil and the little English cap on Rosamund's auburn head. "Annie has your cloak and gloves, and you're ready to go, my lady."

Rosamund stood up. "Do not cover me with the cloak until my cousin has seen our efforts," she said. Then she walked from her apartment with Annie carrying her outdoor garment and gloves in her wake.

Watching her descend the staircase Sir Thomas Bolton thought his cousin Rosamund most elegant. He kissed her hand as she reached the bottom, and said to her, "You are as fashionable as any lady at court will be today, my dear girl."

"I thank you for the ring, Tom. Was it your sister's?"

"Aye," he nodded, "I thought how well it would suit you."

"What was her name?" Rosamund asked him as Annie slipped her fur-lined and -trimmed cloak about her shoulders.

"Mary," he said. " 'Twas a simple name, but she was born on May Day, and my mother would have it no other way than her daughter be called for the Blessed Mother. But I called her May for she was the very essence of that month. Bright and warm and full of fun. Like you, dear girl, she accepted me for who I was. I shall always miss May. She was the light of my life, but you, now, dearest Rosamund, have made your own place in my heart."

"My birth date is April thirtieth," Rosamund said. "And my eldest daughter, Philippa, was born on the twenty-ninth of April."

"Ah, then you are Taurus," he told her. "As my sister was. I am a Scorpio, the opposite of Taurus."

"What on earth are you talking about?" Rosamund asked him as he escorted her down through his garden to the dock where his barge was awaiting them.

"You have never heard of astrology? The

science of the stars? My dearest darling girl, I have the most wonderful man! We shall have your chart drawn while you are at court. Many do nothing without the advice of their astrologer. I simply prefer a yearly overview." He helped her into the vessel. "I shall explain all to you as we go to Westminster." He settled himself next to her and drew a fur robe over their laps. Then he waved his hand at the bargemen, and they pulled away from the dock at Bolton House and headed down the river to London.

Chapter 15

The late morning was chilly, but the sun sparkled on the river.

"There is Richmond," Lord Cambridge said as they passed the great palace. "You see how near it is to Bolton House? I have a house near Greenwich as well. I purchased a charming little vessel for you while I was in London yesterday," he chattered on. "And I have hired two men to row you. What color should we make their livery, and do you have a motto that we may design on their badges?"

"Friarsgate blue and silver," Rosamund answered him promptly, "and the motto of the Friarsgate Boltons is *Tracez Votre Chemin.*"

"Oh, I do like your motto," her companion enthused. "I shall have a broach designed for you with those very words. Our Boltons chose *Service Tourjours.* It is so uninspired. Blue and silver, eh? Very stylish, my dear. Everyone is changing to Tudor green these days, which is really quite boring. It makes it impossible to see whose servants are at court, unless one can get close enough to peer at the badges. And, that, of course, is in the worst possible taste."

"I dislike putting you to such expense, cousin," Rosamund said. "Is it really necessary? You have already been too good to me."

"I have always meant to have a second little barge for guests, dearest girl. Your arrival has but caused me to act." He smiled and patted her hand. "Having your own wee vessel will allow you to escape the palace when you are not needed by the queen."

"I will admit to still being nervous about having been called to court," Rosamund told him. "I do not belong here."

"But here you are, Rosamund," he said. "Listen, darling girl, and while we skim our way downriver I will tell you why you will be a breath of fresh air for the queen. You know that she lost a child at the end of January past. However, it was worse than that. Those overprotective fools who surround her were afraid to tell the king that the queen had miscarried of a daughter. So they continued to allow the queen to believe she was with child. And she blew up like a sheep's bladder that is filled with air."

"But how could she not realize she was no longer with child?" Rosamund asked, shocked.

"Because, dear girl, she is a Spanish princess and has been sheltered from common sense, among other virtues. Well, it did not take the king long to realize what had happened, for the swelling disappeared as quickly as it had appeared. The queen was devastated and thought she had somehow failed her husband. It was he who convinced her that it was God's will. Then he quickly impregnated her once again."

"The queen is with child?" Rosamund was astounded.

"Why, yes, dear girl. You did not know?" He was equally surprised. "Why, the child is due at the beginning of the month of January. Yesterday was the last day the queen was receiving gentlemen in her chambers, which was why it was so important that I get to her. She will go into seclusion now until her child is born, and be served only by women. Her ladies take over all the positions normally held by men in order that the queen's household continue to run smoothly. How could you not know this happy news? But then with the confusion over the miscarriage, it is possible, and your Friarsgate is very isolated. But that is not all the gossip, dear girl.

"There was a most delicious scandal early this autumn. The queen learned that the king was having an affair with the sister of the Duke of Buckingham. But which of his sisters, for he has two, and both were serving the queen, no one is certain. Lady Anne Hastings is currently residing in a convent some sixty miles from London, contemplating her sins, whatever they may be. Her sister, Lady Elizabeth FitzWalter is also gone from the court, taken away in the black of night, it is said. And their husbands are banned as well. It seems the more chaste sister, whoever she was, spoke with her brother, the duke. She thought the other sister was involved with the king's boon companion, William Compton. Buckingham is a terrible snob, and the Comptons are hardly the social equals of the Stafford family. Compton, however, was acting as a shield for the king. The lovers were using his house for their illicit trysts! The Duke of Buckingham was furious that his sister should demean herself in such a manner with who he believed was a man of lesser status. A family conference was convened. Worse, the innocent sister tattled to the queen, who then berated the king for his behavior in a very loud argument, which, though it took place in her privy chamber, was heard by half the court, who then reported it to the other half.

"Well, dear girl, one does not take Henry Tudor to task for his behavior. He is the king. He will do as he pleases, as those of us who know him understand. Besides, all kings have mistresses. Why the queen's own father, King Ferdinand, had several, and was known to have sired a number of bastards. And King Henry was certainly being discreet. His little indiscretion would never have been known had not the duke's sister spilled the beans." Lord Cambridge chuckled wickedly. Rosamund sat in stunned fascination.

"The duke is a dreadful snob," her cousin went on. "Of course he did not think Will Compton socially acceptable as a lover for his sister. Or, if the truth be known, does not even think the House of Tudor is good enough. After he bearded Compton and raised riot with him, Compton, a longtime companion and confidant of the king's, went directly to him. The king called the duke into his presence and raised merry hell with him. The upshot was that the duke left the court in a temper. I suspect the king was angry at his secret being made public. He is genuinely fond of the queen and dislikes having her distressed. And, that, darling girl, is what has happened to date."

"Has the queen forgiven the king?" Rosamund asked him.

"There was nothing to forgive, for it is Henry Tudor's right to do as he pleases, Rosamund. The queen has been quite rightly scolded, by not just her husband, but by her father and by her confessor. She is, after all, Queen of England. Nothing can change that, but she cannot expect her husband to refrain from satisfying his manly appetites when she is with child and therefore forbidden to him. And he was discreet, but that she obviously suspected something of him, given his passionate nature. She set her women to spying on him. The king considered sending them all from court, but that it would have caused a dreadful scandal," Lord Cambridge explained.

"Poor Kate," Rosamund sympathized.

"She is a good woman, if naive in some ways," her companion replied. "No one who serves her dislikes her. They become quite fanatically loyal, but these ladies must remember that their first loyalty lies with the king, not the queen. I hope, dear cousin, that while you serve the queen you will remember that." He patted her gloved hand.

"But all is well between the king and his spouse?" Rosamund asked. "They are now reconciled?"

"Aye, but it will never again be the same between them. The queen has been forced to face the fact that the honeymoon is long over. She must accept what she cannot change, and she will never change the king. He, while annoyed yet, has forgiven her. He believes that she will never again remonstrate with him for his peccadilloes, especially as she is unlikely to know of them. The queen's women have learned their lesson, it is to be hoped, and will not impart gossip regarding the king's amorous nature to their mistress in the future."

"I think now more than before that I wish I was home," Rosamund said with a small smile. "I do not know if I am up to all this intrigue."

He chuckled. "I will be here for you, dear girl, and you can always escape to Bolton House."

About them the river traffic was busier than it had been earlier. They were approaching the city itself. Great flat-bottomed boats ferrying cargo from ships moored in the London pool downriver appeared. Smaller barges with farm produce passed them by. Fishing vessels and other passenger barges surrounded them. The spires and turrets of Westminster loomed to one side of the river as their barge began to nose itself shoreward. Annie's eyes were wide, and her ears were burning with all she had heard. Realizing it, Lord Cambridge cautioned her to keep her own council.

"Do not gossip with the other servant girls, but rather be pleasing in manner, helpful, devout, and keep your own ears open so you may report to your own mistress anything of interest. If you appear slightly stupid and countrified you will be considered unimportant and other servants will gossip in your hearing. Do you understand, Annie?"

"Aye, m'lord, I will be careful, for I *am* but a simple country girl just like my mistress," she replied, her eyes twinkling mischievously.

Lord Cambridge chuckled again. "Why, my girl, you are far more clever than I would have anticipated. You may prove very useful to your mistress." And he gave her a wink.

Their barge bumped against the stone quay as a palace servant swiftly made the vessel secure so that its occupants might disembark. Lord Cambridge was helped out first, then waited while Rosamund and Annie stepped upon the dock. Without a word he turned and hurried off into the palace, the two young women swiftly following behind him. Rosamund vaguely recalled landing here years back with Meg and Kate and the rest of the royal family. Some of the interior seemed familiar to her as she trailed behind her cousin. Then they came to a large double door with the royal crest upon it. On either side of the doors stood a young woman in red velvet skirts, a leather breastplate gilded in gold leaf, wearing a small helmet and carrying a pike. Their pikes crossed in defense as Lord Cambridge and his party approached.

"Lady Rosamund of Friarsgate, widow of Sir Owein Meredith, and her servant, at the queen's invitation," Sir Thomas said.

"She may pass, and her servant as well," one of the female guards said. They uncrossed their pikes, and one of them flung wide one of the doors.

"Farewell, cousin," Lord Cambridge said, kissing Rosamund upon her brow. "If you need me, you may send a page for me. If I am not here, I will be at Bolton House." He then turned and departed down the corridor.

Rosamund, Annie in her wake, slowly entered the queen's apartment. It was filled with women, and it would appear that she knew none of them. She wasn't even certain of the proper protocol to gaining the queen's attention. She stood confused, and then a sweet-faced woman approached her, smiling.

"Lady Rosamund, you may not remember me. I am Maria de Salinas. My mistress bids you welcome back to court. Will you come with me to greet her majesty?"

"Thank you," Rosamund replied, and followed the queen's favorite lady, and her best friend, who had come with her from Spain and who had remained with her devotedly through all the years of her difficulty.

They passed through the main receiving room of the queen's apartments and into the queen's privy chamber where Katherine lay sprawled gracefully upon an upholstered settee. Her belly was greatly distended. The queen's eyes lit up as Rosamund approached, and she held out her beringed hand in greeting, a smile on her lips.

Rosamund caught up the queen's hand and kissed it, curtsying as she did so. Behind her Annie curtsied as well.

"My friend," the queen said in her accented English. "How good it is to see you once again! I am happy to have you here. Especially now. I have assigned you a chore, Rosamund of Friarsgate. I do not forget how beautiful your hand was when you wrote me. You will write my correspondence for me while my secretaries are forbidden my presence. I allow no idleness among my women."

"I am honored to serve you, your majesty," Rosamund replied.

"You are making your home at Bolton House?" the queen asked.

Rosamund nodded. "My cousin Tom is a kind and generous fellow, your majesty. I cannot remember ever being treated so well."

"You will have a pallet here in my apartments while you are with me and on duty," the queen explained, "And you will take your turn sleeping in my chamber on the trundle. Your servant is permitted to go in and out of my apartments and the palace, to fetch whatever you may need. We are all removing to Richmond in another day, I am glad to say. I realize you know none of my ladies, so you may want to go into the dayroom and be introduced."

She was dismissed. Rosamund curtsied once again and backed from the room, Annie behind her, wide-eyed and practically speechless. The queen had eight ladies-in-waiting. There were seven countesses among them. The wives of the Earls of Suffolk,

Oxford, Surrey, Essex, Shrewsbury, Derby, and Salisbury, as well as Lady Guildford, the mother of two of the king's jousting partners. The queen had thirty maids-of-honor and among them some of the most illustrious names in England, but also Maria de Salinas and her sister Inez. It was Inez who introduced Rosamund to these women. The queen's ladies were pleasant, but there was no great warmth in their welcome, and Rosamund once again felt out of place.

"Do not pay any attention to them," Inez de Salinas said softly. Her brown eyes were understanding and sympathetic. "They are all much taken with themselves and spend their days, when they are not in the queen's presence, comparing their pedigrees. They enjoy being superior to one another."

"I am hardly superior to anyone," Rosamund said matter-of-factly.

Inez laughed. "Actually your presence acts to prick their consciences," she explained. "The queen has not been shy about telling them how you were her champion from your manor in faraway Cumbria. How your kindness often meant the difference between poverty and complete penury for her. They felt guilty because any of them might have helped her, but they were all so afraid of doing the wrong thing, of offending the old king, of embarrassing their families, that they ignored my poor mistress and left her to her tribulations.

"And then there was you, Rosamund Bolton. It did not matter to you what anyone might say or think. You did whatever you could do to help my mistress because it was the right thing and because you believed in her. You did what any good Christian woman would do. They, these superior English miladies, did not. They will avoid you and ignore you for the most part, though some might be kind; others will speak harshly to you when they think the queen is not about to hear. You must not be disheartened."

"I know that I do not belong here," Rosamund replied, "I came because the queen asked me. Thank God I have my cousin!"

"Sir Thomas Bolton?" Inez laughed again. "He is the most amusing fellow. Of course there are those who say scurrilous things about him."

"Much is said, I am certain," Rosamund answered, "but what has been proven against my cousin? Nothing. The court is so rife with gossip. I remember it well from my youth when the Princess Margaret knew everything said and the truth of it all. One cannot help but listen, but it is not necessary having listened, to believe."

"You are the most practical English-woman I have ever met," Inez told her.

"That is because I am a country woman, and not a great lady," Rosamund reminded her.

Inez presented Rosamund to the queen's other ladies. Most barely looked at her. One young woman said, "Oh, yes, the shepherdess from the north." Some of the younger girls laughed meanly, but then Lady Percy said, "Only someone very ignorant would insult the lady of Friarsgate, who is the queen's friend, Mistress Blount. Sir Owein Meredith's widow, and heiress in her own right, holds some of the finest and most beautiful lands in all of Cumbria. And if her wealth comes from sheep, why would you lay scorn on her for it? Much of this country's wealth comes from sheep, as any educated person could tell you. I also happen to know from my relation, Lady Neville, that Friarsgate raises some particularly fine warhorses." She turned to Rosamund, "You will forgive Mistress Blount, my lady?"

"Ignorance is best corrected, not forgiven," Rosamund replied.

Some of the ladies gasped, but Lady Percy laughed. "Well said, Rosamund Bolton!"

"You have made a good beginning," Inez whispered, "but I think you may have made an enemy of Gertrude Blount. Still, she is not that important in the scheme of things, and it is obvious that Lady Percy approves of you."

So Rosamund joined the queen's ladies, and two days later the court decamped Westminster, to everyone's relief, and moved back upriver from London to Richmond. As the ladies jostled against one another to find space in the various transports, Rosamund offered Inez de Salinas and her maid passage in her own little barge. Inez was delighted not to have to travel upriver in cramped quarters.

"You have your own barge?" She was surprised.

"A gift from my cousin Tom. He feels I should have my own transport while I am at court," Rosamund told her as the four women settled themselves in the little cabin.

It was a chilly day, and the skies were gray and threatening. The cabin of the barge, however, was warm, for beneath the bench seats were small flat braziers of hot coals. The two bargemen bent their backs as they rowed with the incoming tide, keeping pace with the rest of the royal travelers. When they reached Richmond, Rosamund saw the

536

king for the first time in over seven years. She was very surprised, for Henry Tudor was probably the handsomest man she had ever seen in all of her life.

He stood six feet four inches in height. His hair was a brilliant red-gold. She did not remember his hair being so bright before, but of course it must have been. She had not been interested in him because in those days he was but a lad. She was his senior by three years. Now, however, he was a man. And what a marvelous man he was! she thought, blushing at the boldness of her own thoughts. He swung about to look at the barges landing, and she would have sworn that for the briefest of moments his blue eyes met her amber ones. Bat then he turned away, laughing with his companions at something that had been said.

"We shall not be able to partake in the Twelve Days of Christmas festivities," Inez said sadly, "but once our mistress the queen has been delivered of her child there will be great celebrations."

"My husband is dead but a few months," Rosamund told her. "I am not of a mind to celebrate, though they will at Friarsgate for the sake of my daughters. Still it will be a sad celebration with their father dead and in his grave, and their mother away at court."

"I will go home to London on Christmas Day to be with my husband," Inez said. "He is a minor functionary for King Ferdinand. I know he misses Spain, but like me he feels we must remain loyal to Queen Katherine."

"Are you older than your sister?" Rosamund asked.

"By two years. My parents were able to dower one daughter, and they dowered me. Maria, it was believed, would be taken care of by her princess, and one day she will. Lord Willoughby would court her, or so the rumor goes. He has never spoken to the queen — or to Maria."

December was passing quickly. Christmas came, the queen and her ladies celebrating the first mass of the holiday in the queen's private chapel with the queen's confessor, Frey Diego. Rosamund had heard that the priest was a very carnal man, and more than one of the ladies was enamoured of him. It was also said that he used any woman who offered, and many did. Rosamund kept to the rear of the chapel, bowing her head low. She had no wish to attract the notorious priest's attention. St. Steven's and Holy Innocents' passed. And then on the thirty-first of December the queen went into labor. With the first realization of the event the queen's chambers erupted with excitement, women running to and fro chattering. The queen's physician and the midwives were sent for, and they came with all haste. The king was notified. He remained in the Great Hall of Richmond drinking with his companions as he awaited the birth of what would surely be his first son. He had prayed. He had made a pilgrimage to Our Lady of Walsingham, and would again. Everyone said that the way Katherine carried meant she was carrying a son. Despite that small distress she suffered because of the Duke of Buckingham's sisters, she had not lost the child. A girl, delicate and fine, she might have miscarried of, but she had not. Everyone assured Henry Tudor that it certainly meant that the queen would birth a son.

The requirements for a royal birth had been set down years prior by the Venerable Margaret herself. Rosamund was amazed by the complexity of it all. The chamber in which the queen would give birth was hung all over, walls, ceilings, and windows but for one, with the most beautiful tapestries depicting only the happiest scenes from the Bible, so that neither mother nor child would be distressed. The floors were covered with thick Turkey carpets. Only one window was left unfettered in the event the laboring woman might desire fresh air. When all of this had been accomplished prior to the birth, the great carved oak bed in which the queen would afterward receive her husband and guests was brought into the room and set up.

"I have never seen such a bed!" Rosamund whispered to Inez.

"Because, I suspect, there has never been such a bed," Inez whispered back. "The mattress is stuffed with wool, and atop it is the featherbed. The sheets are of the finest lawn, their hems embroidered by the nuns on the island of Madeira. The bolsters and the pillows are all stuffed with down. The coverlet is scarlet trimmed with ermine, embroidered with gold crowns and the queen's own coat of arms. It matches the tester and the curtains about the bed, although they are of scarlet satin, and not velvet. They are trimmed with blue, gold, and russet silk fringe. And see the scarlet tapestry on the sideboard and the baptismal font, in case the child is weak and needs immediate baptism?"

"God forbid!" Rosamund said, crossing herself, remembering her own little son.

Inez nodded and crossed herself as well. "And, of course," she said, "there is a small altar set up for the queen to pray."

"Where is the birthing chair?" Rosamund asked her friend.

Inez smiled. "Here at court we call it the groaning chair. There is one, of course, but I suspect the queen will not use it. It lacks dignity, and the queen is, above all things, dignified."

"There is nothing dignified about giving birth," Rosamund said, and she thought of her own birthing chair in the hall at Friarsgate. She thought of Maybel and of how Owein preferred to remain with her until Maybel would chase him out if she could. The dogs remained with her, and the cats would wander by, rubbing her bare legs with their bodies as if in sympathy. It was a far cry from this overstuffed crimson chamber where the Queen of England now labored to bring forth her own child.

She did not, as Inez had predicted, use the birthing chair. Instead, modestly garbed in a fine Holland linen smock and double petticoats, she lay upon a pallet bed next to her great bed, where surrounded by her ladies she might have a modicum of privacy. All night long she labored. There was no pain medication they could give her, and so the Girdle of Our Lady, a holy relic, was brought to her from Westminster Abbey. It was said to ease the pain of childbirth, and indeed Katherine said it did, and gave thanks even as she pushed the infant from her body.

At last, as the new day was about to begin, the child was born. It was the desperately sought after son and heir! The queen collapsed with relief, and the king was notified. The canons ranged along the wharf at the Tower of London were shot off in salute, and all the church bells in London began to peal in tribute to the new prince. The king was jubilant, and the court with him. Bonfires were lit in the streets. The lord mayor of the city ordered that free wine be served to all of London's citizens so they might drink a health to the new prince. The king rewarded the midwife generously, and accepted the congratulations of his friends for siring a male heir.

The new prince was to be named Henry after his father. Wrapped in tight swaddling bands, he lay beneath a crimson velvet coverlet that was trimmed in ermine, and fringed in gold. His painted wooden cradle was two feet wide by five feet long. It was decorated in silver gilt and had silver buckles to secure his swaddling bands so that he would not roll about the great cradle.

"The cradle in which he will be displayed

to important visitors is even bigger," Inez confided.

Rosamund just shook her head and considered her babies when they had been first born, placed in a simple hooded oak cradle with its little featherbed and lambskin. She wondered if the poor little prince could even breathe properly he was so tightly swaddled.

The queen was now moved into her great bed, clothed in a circular mantle of crimson velvet. She had been freshly bathed to remove all traces of her travail. Her beautiful hair was plaited and dressed with pearls. Frey Diego, the first man allowed into the queen's suite since the confinement, said a mass at the queen's private altar while she sat in her splendid bed.

"All over London, my queen, Te Deums are being sung in thanksgiving to God and his Blessed Mother in honor of you and the new prince," Frey Diego told her.

The king came now and congratulated his wife, beaming proudly over the son he had sired. "I will go again to Walsingham as I promised the lady," he told Katherine. "I will return in time for our son's christening on January fifth. I have chosen Archbishop Warham, the Earl of Surrey, and my aunt and uncle, the Earl and Countess of Devon, to be our son's godparents. His august sponsors will be King Louis of France and the Duchess of Savoy, Margaret of Austria, the emperor's daughter. This is as we have previously discussed, wife."

"It shall be as you wish, my dear lord," Katherine said obediently.

The king smiled, well-pleased. "You are such a dutiful wife, Kate. No king could have a better wife, or queen." He bent and kissed her on her forehead. "Keep well while I am gone." And then he departed his wife's chamber, barely nodding to her women with whom he was still very displeased. But he had noted the pretty lady of Friarsgate among the women. How long would she be with them? he wondered.

Rosamund was called to the queen's side, and Katherine dictated several letters of thanks to people she wanted to remember with her personal announcement of her son's birth.

"You may give your script to my secretary, along with the list of people to whom it will be sent. He will see the correspondence rewritten upon my own paper with its seal," the queen instructed Rosamund.

The queen would not nurse her own son, nor would she have a great deal to do with raising him, especially in his early years. He would be raised in his own household, under a set of rules laid down by the Venerable Margaret. The nursery staff was managed by Mistress Poyntz, who was styled the prince's lady mistress. There was a wet nurse and a dry nurse, there were maids and rockers and a physician for the prince's household. The nursery at Richmond was furnished richly, and it was here the little prince would reside, away from the dangers and bad air of the city.

After a month the queen was *churched*, and the court removed back to Westminster where the celebrations began in honor of the birth. There were magnificent tournaments. Rosamund had never seen a tournament. The king was titled as Sir Coeur Loyal, or Loyalheart. The armor was polished. The trappings of cloth-of-gold, cloth-of-silver, green satin, and crimson velvet were beautiful. The pageantry surrounding the tournaments was like nothing seen before. A huge cart made up to look like a forest with trees, hills, and dales was displayed with knights and ladies upon it. The men wore costumes and performed masques before and after the jousting. And in the evenings there were more pageants, and dancing, and music.

Sir Thomas surprised his cousin with four new gowns he had had made for her. While she had been at court serving the queen he had taken one of her gowns, and the seamstress who made his own garments had taken the gown apart, made measurements from it, and put it back together again. Then she proceeded to fashion the four dresses.

"Are you surprised, darling girl?" her cousin demanded of her. "The dark colors are elegant, I will grant you, but you are too young to keep to mourning for long. The colors I chose are not too garish, are they?" He looked at the four gowns upon her bed. One was a tawny orange, one a rich wine color, the third violet, and the last a true Tudor green, unlike her deep green velvet gown. They were the most fashionable gowns possible, embroidered and sewn with gold, small jewels, and pearls.

"Tom! I shall be the envy of the queen's ladies, I vow," she told him, laughing. "You should not have, for I shall not be here that long, but oh, my! How beautiful they all are! Thank you!" She threw her arms about his neck and kissed him soundly on the cheek.

He flushed with pleasure. "Of course I should spoil you, Rosamund," he insisted. "Your company has made me happy for the first time in a long while."

"But I shall go home as soon as I may," Rosamund said. "You will be lonely then, and I do not want that, dear cousin."

"Then I shall come to Friarsgate when the loneliness overcomes me. Then when I am bored with a surfeit of simple country living, I shall return to court again. It is the perfect solution, is it not?"

"What shall I wear tonight?" Rosamund asked him. "There is to be something titled *An Interlude of the Gentlemen of his Chapel Before His Grace,* followed by a pageant, *The Garden of Pleasure.* They say the king will wear purple satin."

"The king would do better to accept my fashion direction," Lord Cambridge sniffed. "Instead he will have his costume approved by those roughnecks with whom he is always jousting and drinking. He will have gold H's and K's sewn all over the garment, my dear girl. This fantasy of romantic love he persists in presenting to the world, when we all know he married the queen because she was available and he needed to sire an heir immediately, is ridiculous."

"Oh, Tom, she is really a good lady, and so brave," Rosamund defended her mistress.

"Aye, my dear Rosamund, she is, but I am a man of the world. Believe me that, contract or no, Henry Tudor would have married someone else had there been a proper princess of the right age available. This nonsense with little Eleanor of Austria was a farce, and we all knew it. King Ferdinand knew it, but like his daughter he hung on with great tenacity. Only at the end, when it became apparent that the old king was dying, did Spain have Katherine's dowry transferred to their Flemish bankers across the channel. Then the king died, and the prince became the new king, and suddenly he was most anxious to make Katherine his bride. And his counsel was so very reasonable about the dowry that had to be transferred back to England. No, dear girl, the king married his wife because he hoped, as his father hoped when he matched her to Prince Arthur, that she would prove to be the breeder that her mother was. Already the king's eye has wandered, and it will not be the last time, I promise you."

" 'Tis true his eye is quick," Rosamund admitted. "I see him in the chapel now and again casting his gaze among the women there."

"Hmmmm," Lord Cambridge said. Then his tone grew intimate. "Does his eye linger on any one lady longer than another, dear girl?"

She swatted at him and laughed. "Not that I have noticed. He certainly does not look at his wife's ladies, I assure you. I think the debacle with the Duke of Buckingham's sisters cured him of that. The queen's women all have their own opinion of who it was, with most of them favoring the Lady Anne." Then changing the subject she asked him, "What will you wear tonight, cousin?"

"Black," he said. "It is simple, and I suspect that simple should be the order of the evening if one is not to compete with the king and his purple. Besides, he is letting the general public in, which I never consider a wise thing."

Rosamund put on the tawny orange gown and preened happily about her chamber. Doll brought her a flat box, another gift from Tom. It contained a beautiful gold chain decorated with golden topaz, and a matching broach in the shape of a diamond and set in gold. Instead of her blue cloak Annie put a new cloak of rich brown velvet trimmed in marten over her shoulders and then drew up the fur-trimmed hood, for the February day was raw and windy.

"You spoil me outrageously, cousin," Rosamund told Lord Cambridge as they prepared to leave for Westminster, each in their own barge, "and I must admit that I love it!"

He smiled, pleased. "Having you with me is like having my sister back with me again, Rosamund. I know you are not May, but you are much like her in your youth and sweet-ness."

The palace was more crowded than Rosamund had ever seen it. The public had been allowed in to view the royal festivities. As Lord Cambridge had suspected, it was a bad idea. When the pageant was over and done with, the crowds surged forward, tearing at the players' costumes for souvenirs. The king found himself stripped down to his doublet and hose, and laughed uproariously, particularly when one of his gentlemen, Sir Thomas Knyvet, was stripped stark naked and had to climb a pillar for safety. When the crowd began to tear at the gowns of the ladies who had danced in the pageant, the king ordered the guard called in, and the public was ushered firmly from the palace. The court then went in to eat a large banquet that had been prepared for the occasion, despite the condition of their finery, although Sir Thomas Knyvet was forced to withdraw and find some garments to wear.

And then news arrived on February twenty-third that the little Prince of Wales had died suddenly that morning. Rosamund was in the queen's chamber when the king came to tell her. He took her into her privy chamber, and her sudden great cries of anguish alerted her women to the tragedy. And to everyone's surprise the king remained with his wife comforting her as best he could, forsaking his own grief in an effort to ease the queen's sorrow.

"It will begin again," Lord Cambridge murmured to his cousin as they spoke quietly together in a corridor of the palace. "He should have possessed his soul of patience and found another princess. She has lost two children now, God help England."

"She is in agony, poor lady," Rosamund told him, "but you are right. It does England little good. Still, her mother and her sisters have proven themselves good breeders and yet lost a few along the way. It will be different next time."

"I pray you are right, cousin," Lord Cambridge told her.

They walked together back toward the queen's apartments, and then the door to those rooms opened and the king exited. Sir Thomas Bolton bowed gracefully, and Rosamund curtsied. The king nodded brusquely in their direction, and then he stopped suddenly.

The blue eyes fixed Rosamund with a look, and he said, "You are the lady of Friarsgate, are you not, madame?"

"I am, your majesty," she answered him

softly, her heart pounding with excitement. He had not mattered when he was a boy, but now this was the king who spoke to her.

"Aye, I remember you," the king told her with a small smile. "My behavior toward you was churlish, and Sir Owein said so quite plainly. Yet you were not in the least abashed to learn a wager had been made involving your virtue. You gave poor Neville quite a setdown and he took it badly, but you did not scold me, as I recall."

"One does not reprimand a young man who will one day be your king," Rosamund said smoothly. "A king can do no wrong, and makes his own rules, I know. Besides, my lord, you held no grudge, for you witnessed my formal betrothal to Sir Owein and told me to remember it, for I should tell my children one day that you did."

"And my father reminded me that I was not yet England's king," Henry said, and laughed. "I am sorry about Sir Owein. Was he a good husband?"

"There was none better, my lord!" Rosamund said, and to her surprise she felt tears in her eyes.

"And you had children?" the king continued, seeing her tears.

"Three daughters, my lord, and a son lost at birth," Rosamund told him. "It was a foolish accident that took my husband from me."

"We are glad you are here with our queen, to whom you were so kind in her difficult years," the king said. Then he bowed and moved on down the corridor and out of their sight.

"God's nightshirt!" Thomas Bolton swore softly. "There is a story here, cousin, you have not told me. And may heaven help you, for I could see his interest as he looked at you. And you said all the right things to him! Never again tell me that you do not belong at court, Rosamund Bolton, for you are far wiser to the ways of the court than I previously believed."

"I know he is the king," she responded, "but you must remember I knew him as a boy. Of course I respect him as my king, but I still think of him as that mischievous lad, Prince Hal."

"God help us! He will surely seduce you this time, my dear cousin! And while you may not realize it, you are ripe for it! Oh lord help us, my dear! Go back to your mistress, the queen. I must consider this new state of affairs," he told her.

"You are making something of nothing," she told him, laughing. "The king was kind enough to remember me from a time long ago. I am indeed flattered that he did. That he remembered who I was is in itself wonderful, Tom. I am not numbered among his high-and-mighty friends, and yet he recalled my name and an incident from our brief shared past."

"He will get the queen with child again as quickly as he can, I assure you," Lord Cambridge said, "and then he will cast his eye about for a lady to amuse him in the coming summer months. And mark my words, cousin, you are very much on his mind now."

"You are mistaken, I am certain," Rosamund said. "The king was polite and gracious. Nothing more, nor can there be anything more."

Lord Cambridge shook his head in despair. His lovely cousin was innocent in many ways. And how he was to protect her, he did not know.

The little prince was buried in Westminster Abbey, following a period of mourning in which his frail little body was displayed in an elaborate coffin surrounded by hundreds of candles that burned day and night until his midnight burial. He was given a torch-lit ceremony attended by the entire court, all garbed in deepest black. His soul was now with God and among the innocents.

The penitential season of Lent was now upon them, made all the more somber by the recent royal death. The queen prayed incessantly day and night, wearing a hair shirt, eating little and but once a day. The meals served in the queen's chambers were spartan. Just brown bread and fish. At Easter the king received a Golden Rose from the pope, which the pontiff had blessed himself. It was a sign of great favor. And immediately after Easter, the court removed to Greenwich to celebrate the month of May.

Chapter 16

"It is exactly like Bolton House!" Rosamund said, very surprised, as the barge approached her cousin's house at Greenwich.

"Of course," Tom told her. "Bolton Greenwich is identical in every detail to Bolton House. I dislike confusion, dear girl, and I abhor the chaos of dislocation. When I bought the property at Greenwich I commissioned an architect and builders to replicate Bolton House. Even the decor is the same. The servants come with me as I do not like paying them to be idle at Bolton House while I am at Bolton Greenwich. It is a perfect solution, as you will discover."

Rosamund laughed. "Actually I believe I already like the idea, and I know Annie will. She has been so fretful of learning a new place when, as she says, 'I am finally just getting this house right.' Doll did not tell her, for Doll loves to play her tricks on my poor Annie." Rosamund's eye moved just past Bolton Greenwich. "Is that the palace beyond, Tom?"

He nodded.

"God's blood! You are next door to the king and his court, cousin. That was either most clever of you or most fortuitous."

"It was both," he replied loftily, "It is not a large property, which is why it was thought an undesirable acreage. Now, however, I am the envy of all. I have had any number of offers to purchase it from me, but for the time being I enjoy keeping it. It is not a property that will lose its value. Once again, I fear I display my less-than-noble roots by thinking like a merchant," he said with a chuckle.

The barge had reached its destination. It docked, and Lord Cambridge's servants were there to help their master and Rosamund from the comfortable vessel. She sniffed the air curiously.

"What is that smell?" she inquired of her cousin.

For a moment he appeared puzzled, and then he said, "Why it is the sea, dear girl. We are nearer the sea here, downriver. Of course! You have never smelled the sea before, or even seen it, have you? Landlocked in your Cumbrian hills you have not had the opportunity."

"But I have been to Greenwich before," Rosamund told him.

"It is the way the wind is blowing today," he explained.

"How interesting," she said, "but then, when the wind blows in a different direction at Friarsgate the scent is different. In the winter when it comes from the north I can smell the snow on it."

They entered the house, and again Rosamund was slightly taken aback. As Tom had told her, the interior of Bolton Greenwich was identical to that of Bolton House. It was a bit confusing because she knew she would expect the outside to be as it was upriver at first, but, she supposed, she would get used to it as she had gotten used to any number of things since her arrival at court five months ago. "I will not have to worry about sleeping at the palace unless I am needed," she said thoughtfully. "I like that, Tom."

"Aye, my dear, you have but to go through the wall door in my gardens into the king's park. You will be the envy of all."

Rosamund sighed. "I wish the queen would allow me to go home, but she has said naught, and I am afraid to ask lest I offend her. I would not imply that her company was dull, but I miss Friarsgate, and I miss my children, Tom."

"Do you miss your brazen Scot as well?" he teased her.

"*I do not!*" she cried indignantly. "Why are you so damned curious about Logan Hepburn, cousin?"

Tom Bolton shrugged. "Your characterization of him rather intrigues me, dear girl. Nothing more. I hope that I shall get to meet him when I return you home."

"But when will that be?" she wailed with a deep sigh.

"I hear a rumor that the king will make his summer progress in the midlands this year. That will take you in the direction of home, Rosamund, and probably at that point you may request your release from the queen. She will understand your concern about your daughters."

"It will be almost a year," Rosamund said. "Bessie and Banon will not know me at all. It is not as if my presence is necessary or vital to the queen."

"I know," he said sympathetically, placing an arm about her shoulders and giving her a little squeeze, "but poor Katherine believes that she is doing you a good turn. For her the court is the world but next to heaven itself. Be grateful at least that her concerns for an heir have kept her from matchmaking, dear girl."

"God forbid!" Rosamund responded.

The court prepared for May Day. A maypole was set up in the gardens of Greenwich, and ladies were chosen to dance about it as an entertainment. To her surprise Rosamund was one of those ladies. She was not usually included in such events as a participant. She had decided to wear her Tudor-green silk gown in honor of the queen. There would be a hunt in the morning, but she would not take part in it. She did not like hunting, which put her at odds with most of the court who seemed to find the blood sport so stimulating. Rosamund, however, did not consider chasing a hapless animal through the woodlands with dogs only to kill it when caught, entertainment.

The sun had not quite crept over the horizon when she, Annie, and Doll came from the house to go a-Maying. They would first gather the dew of the morning, which was said to be most beneficial for the complexion. Then they would gather greens and flowers with which to decorate the hall. The three young women were barefoot and wore simple skirts of linen, their chemises acting as blouses.

"Do you think they will serve green food in the king's hall tonight?" Annie wondered aloud.

"Of course!" Doll replied, "The master says the king loves May Day of all holidays, and keeps its traditions."

"The meat is sometimes green in the king's hall," Rosamund observed wryly, "which is why I eat there as infrequently as possible."

The two young servant women laughed.

A large patch of dew was found, and they gathered it in their hands and spread it liberally on their faces. Then they went about the task of gathering flowers, flowering branches, and other greens for the hall at Bolton Greenwich. Rosamund eventually became separated from her two companions as she wandered about her cousin's gardens. Suddenly she heard a voice singing softly, and she followed the sound. It led to the door in the brick wall between the garden in which she now stood and the king's park beyond. Still, the voice was so intriguing that she opened the portal and peeped through. There beneath a tree sat the king, strumming on his lute and singing quietly to himself.

"Now is the month of Maying, when merry lads do play

561

"Fa la la la la la la lala! Fa la la la la la lala!

"Each with his bonnie lass, a-dancing on the grass

"Fa la la la la! La la la la la la la la! Lala Lala!"

Rosamund laughed, and the king, seeing her, jumped up, leaving his lute on the grass. "My Lady Rosamund of Friarsgate. I bid you a good May morning." He came toward her. "Did you enjoy my song, madame?"

"I did, your majesty, very much," she told him.

"Once you called me Hal," he said, and his voice was suddenly low and very intimate. He was now standing directly before her.

"You were not my king then, your majesty," she said softly, almost breathlessly. This was a dangerous game she was suddenly playing, but she could not seem to back away from it.

Reaching out his big hand he caressed her cheek gently. "The queen says you have the perfect English complexion, fair Rosamund. It is still damp with the dew of this May morning, though I do not think you need to resort to any artifice. You are beautiful enough." Then his fingers caught her chin. He tipped her face up to his, and his lips brushed hers tenderly. "Beautiful, and gentle, and virtuous," he said, and one arm wrapped about her to pull her close. "Do you know how often I have thought of you over the years, fair Rosamund?"

"Your majesty flatters me," she managed to say, although where the words came from she was not certain. She could hardly breathe.

"Do you like flattery?" he questioned her, a small smile on his lips, his blue eyes locking onto her amber ones.

"Only if it is sincere, my lord," she responded.

"I should never approach a lady without sincerity, fair Rosamund," he murmured, his lips dangerously near hers again.

Was she going to faint? Her legs felt like jelly. His gaze was simply mesmerizing. His breath was scented with mint. Rosamund sighed, unable to stop herself.

The king's mouth met hers again, kissing her this time with the beginnings of passion. His arms were now wrapped tightly about her. She could feel the strength of his big body, and she felt absolutely petite in his embrace. She let herself float away. She hadn't felt this safe since Owein had died. *Owein!* His name slammed into her brain, and regaining her tenuous grip on reality, she pulled from Henry Tudor's grasp.

"Oh, your majesty!" she said, her eyes wide with the terrible realization of what they had been doing.

"Fair Rosamund —" he began.

She backed away toward the garden door. *"No, your majesty!* This is most unseemly, and you know it as well as I do. I beg your majesty's pardon for my shameless behavior. I certainly never meant to tease your majesty or lead him on into sin." Then she curtsied quickly, and turning, dashed back into her cousin's garden, pulling the door shut behind her as she went.

He heard the sound of other female voices calling to her. The king grinned, well-pleased. She was delicious. She was the most tempting confection he had come upon in a long time. Her sweetly submissive acquiescence had set his loins afire, but this time he would keep his lust to himself. He had no intention of letting those sharp-eyed harridans who served his wife catch him again, even if he was plucking the prettiest flower from their midst. Her show of modesty had delighted him, yet she had spirit. But no one, not even his closest companions should know of his interest in the lady of Friarsgate. How convenient that her cousin's house was his neighbor. He would have her in her own bed. There would be no palace servitors, or anyone else to catch them. No one would see him coming through the midnight gardens. Only her cousin would know, so that he might leave a side door open for the king. Lord Cambridge was known to be a bit eccentric, but he was also said to be an exceedingly sensible man.

The king began to hum as he headed back toward the palace. He picked a bunch of wildflowers just coming into bloom for his wife. Kate was trying so hard to conceive another child for him. He would surprise her with the May morn bouquet. Perhaps he might even spend a few private moments with her before the hunt. The heat in his loins was great, and his seed needed immediate release. His lust would have made it potent, too. Yes, a little futtering with the queen before the activities of the day began would be most pleasant indeed. And then tonight, or perhaps tomorrow night, he would seek out the fair Rosamund and have his way with her. Henry Tudor smiled, pleased with himself and pleased with the world in general.

As the queen enjoyed the hunt herself, Rosamund knew she would not have to put in an appearance until it was time for the maypole in midafternoon. She rejoined her two companions, and they returned to the house, arms filled with flowers and branches with which they decorated the hall of Bolton Greenwich. When Lord Cambridge joined them later he expressed his pleasure at their efforts.

"You are such a lay-abed," Rosamund teased her cousin. "The dew is all gone now, and you have got none of it."

He chuckled. "You mean you saved none for me, you selfish wench. I am offended, but I will forgive you, for the hall is lovely."

"Tom, I must speak privily with you," Rosamund said quietly.

He heard the serious tone in her voice, and said as quietly, "Let us walk in my gardens, cousin. The day is fair, and I have not yet taken the air. Nor am I apt to unless I am in your company."

On a stone bench overlooking the river she told him of her adventure earlier that morning. Thomas Bolton listened, not in the least shocked, for he had suspected that sooner rather than later the king would approach his cousin with seduction in mind. The tenor of her voice told him that she was both distressed by her behavior and yet tempted by Henry Tudor's handsome looks and power.

"What am I to do, Tom?" she said to him despairingly.

"He will not resort to rape," Lord Cambridge said slowly. "That has never been his style. Not only would it violate his personal code of chivalry, but his sense of self as well, for the king thinks most highly of himself and his honor. Yet despite his marriage vows he would not think his honor compromised by bedding a woman other than his wife. The queen is there to breed up heirs for England. That is her raison d'être, dear girl. That he is fond of her, that her pedigree is flawless, that she knows how to conduct herself as a queen of England, these things are all of benefit to him and to his realm. Queen Katherine serves her purpose. Other women, however, are another thing entirely, Rosamund. Other women are there to be pursued, to be courted, to be bedded. They are for the king's pleasure, but certainly nothing more. He will not force you, but he will seduce you, cousin."

"I remember the boy," she said. "I know much more about him than he would suspect, for Margaret Tudor spoke of him all the time. He is not a man to accept rejection gracefully, Tom. So what am I to do? I have my honor as well, and I serve the queen."

"You have two choices open to you. You could ask the queen this day for her permission to return home to Friarsgate, but if she refused you, what would you do? You risk offending her *and* the king without solving your dilemma. Or you can surrender yourself to the king should he require it, but if you do, you must confide in no one about your relationship, and you must be more discreet than a nun visiting the pope's bed in Lent. While a king is expected to take his mistresses, notoriety is not a good thing for those ladies, my dear. We are not, after all, French," he finished with a disdainful sniff.

"Do the French kings then brag on their mistresses?" Rosamund asked him, surprised. "What lady of decent moral character would want it known that she serviced her king like a ewe sheep services a ram?"

"My dear girl, the French consider it an honor to *service*, as you so quaintly put it, their king. Why, even sisters have been known to share a monarch's favor," Lord Cambridge replied. "And their allies, our neighbors to the north, are as bad. The Stuart kings are considered the most loving men in all of the known world. There is scarcely a family in Scotland that they have not mingled their blood with, I am told. Why, the current King James could not be brought to wed with our own Princess Margaret until someone in his court, with more sense than the king himself, poisoned his longtime mistress, Maggie Drummond. Only after Mistress Drummond and her sisters who were at breakfast together were murdered, did James Stuart honor his contract with England. But he is known to have several other ladies in his favor as well, although it was the Drummond girl who had his heart, they say. No. Kings have mistresses the world over, but here in England we attempt to keep it as circumspect as we possibly can."

"For a man who doesn't love women you have a great understanding of them and of human nature, cousin. Perhaps I should be better off going home to my brazen Scot," Rosamund said with a small smile.

He smiled back at her, then replied, "The die is now cast, cousin. Aye, you can refuse the king, but you will suffer the consequences if you do. You must try to see his advances in another light, dear girl. If you are very discreet and beg the king to be doubly so, it is unlikely anyone will find out about your naughtiness. Who would believe that the king would approach you, a widow of an unimportant family, and no connections? And given the debacle of last spring, the king will certainly be looking to be very, *very* discreet." Lord Cambridge chuckled. "So it is unlikely that anyone will learn of your misstep along the road of virtue. The king is young, and he is handsome. He is known to be both passionate and kind. He can be generous, and you have three daughters you will need respectable husbands for one day, my dear. You are a widow and will bring no shame on your husband or his family name, unlike the Duke of Buckingham's bawdy sisters. And in his whole life Henry Tudor has never been known to forget a favor done him."

"You reason like a whoremaster, cousin," Rosamund told him.

Thomas Bolton laughed. "You are not a virgin, Rosamund," he reminded her with a rather wicked grin.

"You are shameless, Tom!" she scolded, but she was smiling.

"And would you like to be?" he teased her back.

"Aye," she said, surprising him. "I think I would. My whole life I have done exactly what was expected of me, even when I didn't want to, cousin. Still, my conscience is troubled, for I love the queen."

"Your conscience will always trouble you in this matter, my dear girl," he said wisely, "but there is no help for it, I fear. Henry Tudor should not have married Katherine of Aragon. He should have taken a little more time, but she was convenient, she was there, and he has always been an impatient man. His father meant him for the church until poor Arthur died. Henry would have never made a good priest."

"Not with his passion for women," Rosamund observed. "Is it just Katherine, or would he have been unfaithful with another wife, Tom? I don't understand it."

"It is his nature to take whatever he desires, be it a sweetmeat or a woman," Lord Cambridge replied. "Now, dear girl, I have had enough of this subject. You know what you will do, must do. What I want to know is what you have chosen to wear today?"

"The Tudor-green silk," she responded. "Somehow it now seems even more appropriate now than when I first chose it."

He nodded. "Go along then and prepare yourself," he advised her, but Lord Cambridge remained seated upon the bench overlooking the river Thames considering all he had heard. He knew, if Rosamund didn't, that the king, having approached her this morning, would of course seek to have her as soon as possible. And wishing to be cautious he would probably visit her here at Bolton Greenwich. And soon. And the king's nature being what it was, the affair would last no longer than summer's end, if then. Aye, he would encourage Rosamund to beg the queen's leave to go home to Friarsgate in late summer, to leave the progress somewhere in the midlands and travel south to Cumbria. It would be better for all concerned.

I shall go with her, Lord Cambridge decided. While Friarsgate was primitive by his standards, it was nonetheless a comfortable house. He would remain through the autumn and return home to Bolton House for the Christmas festivities. Having settled his calendar for the remainder of the year, Tom Bolton got up and returned to the house where he prepared to escort his cousin back to the palace in the afternoon.

Several hours later, ready to depart, the cousins admired each other's costumes. Rosamund's gown was of Tudor-green silk with a split skirt showing an embroidered and quilted underskirt of a deeper green and white brocade. The low square neckline of her dress was embroidered with gold thread and tiny pearls. Her deep cuffs on the sleeves of the gown were also embroidered in gold and pearls. Her chemise was so sheer that it was almost invisible above her bodice but for its delicate round neckline which was sewn with small pearls. The banded cuffs of the chemise's full sleeves which showed beneath her gown sleeves were also decorated with pearls. A simple veil, held with a wreath of flowers, topped her auburn head.

"It is perfect," Lord Cambridge said, delighted with her costume.

"You also, cousin," Rosamund replied as she considered his dress this day. His white silk hose were decorated with embroidered gold leaves and vines. He wore a short, full, pleated coat of Tudor-green silk damask with full puffed embroidered and slashed sleeves. The high stand collar of his shirt was pleated and showed above his coat just enough to be admired. The exaggerated codpiece he wore was decorated with multi-colored jewels and pearls. His gloves were gold velvet with pearl embroidery on the cuffs. His square-toed shoes were of a fine soft black leather, and on his head he wore a hat with a silk taffeta crown and a stiff flat brim. It was green and sported a white ostrich plume.

Sir Thomas preened for Rosamund, posing and displaying his rather handsome legs. "Well?" he demanded.

"I am at a loss for words, Tom, for I have never seen you so decked out," she told him.

"It is May Day, and the king's favorite holiday," was his answer. Then he smiled. "Shall we go, dear cousin?"

Because it was more convenient, they decided to walk from Bolton Greenwich through its garden and into the king's park to the palace. The hunt was over. It had been successful, and several deer were now being butchered and hung for future meals. The king and his companions had decided to stage a small tournament with jousting for everyone's amusement. The winner of the tourney would choose the queen of the May. Rosamund and her cousin took their places in the stands with the rest of the court, Rosamund positioning herself among the queen's women while Lord Cambridge joined some friends.

The knights were brave and bold. One by one they found themselves unhorsed until only the king and Charles Brandon were remaining. Brandon was a worthy opponent for the king. Time and time again they clashed, their lances ringing loudly against their shields. But finally the king's horse stumbled slightly, and Brandon's lance sent Henry Tudor from his mount. A cry went up from the stands, and Brandon was immediately off his horse and running to the king's side.

The king struggled to his feet, laughing as he pulled off his helmet. "Well played, Charles," he said, graciously acknowledging his defeat. Then he looked around and said, "It would appear that my horse threw his shoe, but then that is the luck of the joust." He waved a groom forward and instructed him to see the horse was cared for, the shoe restored, and to make certain that the beast had not been injured in the accident. Turning again, he announced, "I declare Charles Brandon the winner of this May Day Tourney, and say it is his duty to choose the queen of the May for us now."

Charles Brandon stood before the royal box. "Your majesty," he said to Katherine, "it would not be seemly for me to ask you, already a queen, to be this festival's queen. I ask your royal permission to choose from among the ladies with you."

"You have my permission," the queen replied, smiling.

"Then I would choose the Princess Mary," Brandon answered without a moment's hesitation.

The king's fifteen-year-old sister stepped forward and received the delicate silver and gold wreath of the May Queen from Charles Brandon. "I am honored to be your queen, Charles Brandon," she said.

The king's eyes narrowed speculatively, Mary was young, and she was a romantic little fool. He had other plans for her, and he did not think he wanted Charles Brandon, for all their friendship, interfering with those plans or meddling with his sister. But the king looked benevolently on this scene as his sister smiled at his opponent. He must see that from now on they did not spend any time together. Then, as he looked briefly at the ladies surrounding his wife, he saw the fair Rosamund. How beautiful she looked, he thought. She was the perfect English rose. Then he smiled and bowed to his wife and her ladies. Aye, the fair Rosamund was a delicate treat, and he intended to have her.

She had felt his eyes lingering on her but the briefest moment. She had not looked at him, nor appeared to notice. Whatever happened she must never give hurt to the queen. And once again, as she had so often these past months, she wished that she were safe at home at Friarsgate. Edmund kept her informed on a regular basis with his letters. Everything was fine, he assured. Her daughters thrived, and other than Philippa, gave little indication that they missed her. The ewes had birthed an unusual number of lambs this season with more double births than he had seen in many a year, Edmund reported. The planting was done. Henry had not visited. All was exactly as it should be. It was somewhat unsettling to think that everything was all right at Friarsgate and she was not a part of it.

They had left the stands, and the ladies chosen to dance about the maypole now went to take their places. The music played, and the dance began. Each lady held a different-colored ribbon silk. The colors were red, deep blue, green, yellow, violet, pink, sky blue, lavender, gold, and silver. The ten women danced a seemingly simple step as they moved about the pole, weaving their ribbons into an intricate design as they sang about the month of May and all its beauties. Finally the dance came to an end. The pole was decorated, the ribbon ends fluttering in the gentle late-afternoon breeze.

A feast was now held. In keeping with the beautiful spring day, tables had been set up on the lawns of the palace, and as the guests found their seats the servants were already running back and forth from the kitchens with platters and bowls. Pits had been dug where sides of beef packed in rock salt were being roasted slowly on enormous iron spits. Each side had four young lads serving as turnspits. There were barrels of oysters that were cracked open and served raw. Platters of trout, salmon, and prawns were offered. There were any number of roasted birds, ducks, capons, and swans. There were meat pies filled with rabbit, small game birds, and venison. There were stuffed piglings, lamprey eels in a spicy sauce; black-manger, which was a chicken dish made with rice, almonds, and sugar; artichokes that had been steamed in white wine; braised lettuces; new peas; breads and butter and several varieties of cheeses.

By tradition all the food should have been green in honor of the day, but the queen had put her foot down though the king protested. Only the trenchers of bread that were used had been dyed green. Since the trenchers were hollowed out to serve as dishes it didn't make a great deal of difference as they simply looked like green pottery. To the delight of many, old-fashioned mead was served on this holiday, along with the wine and ale. The court ate, and it ate, yet when the subtleties were finally served they were as eagerly devoured as if the guests had eaten nothing before them.

Archery butts had been set up on the lawns. The men competed at shooting, the king winning the competition. They played at bowls until the twilight made it difficult to see the pins and the balls. Torches were set out. The musicians played as the court danced in line, or in a circle. Eventually the king danced for them all, leaping high, twirling his sister Mary about, as she laughed, both encouraging and taunting him to even greater jumps. No one, it was honestly said, could dance as well as King Henry Tudor. Finally the queen withdrew, taking her women with her. She was tired, and she knew that the king would visit her bed again tonight, for he had already made his intentions known to her earlier. She was not yet pregnant, and while the little prince was yet mourned, a live heir was desperately needed.

"Will you remain here tonight, Rosamund?" Inez asked.

"Nay, I am not required," Rosamund replied, "and one of the benefits of coming to Greenwich is that my cousin's house is next door to the palace. I have my chamber there. If you need a sleeping place, Inez, I could accommodate you."

"Nay," Inez replied, "but I thank you for the offer. Maria has a little room of her very own, and I sleep with my sister."

"Then I will bid you good night," Rosamund told her, and departed the queen's apartments. She saw Tom speaking with the king's friend, Will Compton, and he waved at her. She waved back, and continued on her way into the darkening park and through the trees to the brick garden wall that separated Tom's house from the king's palace. Finding the latch in the almost dark she hurried through into the gardens of Bolton Greenwich, thinking suddenly how convenient it was that this garden was identical to the one at Bolton House. She had no need of light for she knew exactly where she was going.

Within the house again, and upstairs, she found Annie, but the house had been deserted otherwise as Tom had given his servants the evening off. Annie, however, had declined to go with Doll.

"She's a bit fast, and I wouldn't want the men thinking I was like her," Annie explained to her mistress.

A bath had been set up in the dayroom before the fire at the very last before the servants had left. It was still warm, though not as hot as Rosamund liked it. Still, divested of her clothing and in the tub, she decided that the warm, scented water felt good. She did not linger, however, climbing out, drying herself, and putting on a clean smock. Annie undid her elegant hairdo and brushed the long auburn hair out.

"Leave it loose," Rosamund instructed her.

"You do have such lovely tresses," Annie admired, giving the hair a final swipe with the pearwood brush.

Rosamund climbed into her bed as Annie added a bit more fuel to the bedroom fire, saying as she did so, "Master says Doll and me is to sleep in the attics with the other servants for now, m'lady."

"It would be best," Rosamund agreed quietly.

"If I do, everyone will know you have taken a lover, m'lady," the servant told her mistress bluntly. "At least that is what Doll says, m'lady."

"Doll says too much," Rosamund responded sharply. She tied the pink ribbons on her nightcap with a snap. "And what do you say, Annie, in reply to Doll's slander?"

"I says you ain't hardly got time for yourself when you are in the queen's service, so how would you have time to lure a man and make him your lover? Doll laughs and says all women have time for a lover. That men will be like dogs, sniffing around, and that a bitch will always wag and then lift her tail for him."

Rosamund sighed. "Doll is too worldly for her own good," she said. "Where is she now? Do you know, Annie?"

"Aye," Annie said slowly. "She be celebrating the May with menservants from Greenwich Palace. She'll not be back till the sunrise. At least that's what she told me, m'lady."

Rosamund nodded. "I want you to wait up for Lord Cambridge, Annie. Then you are to tell him what you have told me."

"Oh, m'lady, I couldn't! I only told you because we are both Friarsgate folk. I would not have your reputation tarnished by the likes of Doll. Her heart is sometimes good, but her tongue is very bad. She would scratch out my eyes if she knew I told on her."

"Which is precisely why you must tell my cousin. Doll is one of his people from his home estate of Bolton Park. I'm sure the Bolton Park folk are like those at Friarsgate. Doll is young and has been in London with his lordship's household perhaps a bit too long. She needs to be back home where she will regain her values. I want you to tell his lordship that I told you to report her behavior to him, and suggest that she be sent home so she will not get into trouble over her behavior."

"Well," Annie hesitated nervously.

"My cousin is a good master, Annie. You know that. Perhaps it is even time for Doll to be married, and he can arrange that for her. If Doll's behavior is getting out of hand, it might be best for her that he did so before she disgraces herself and ruins her chances of a good marriage." Then she looked sharply at her servant. "What are you not telling me?"

"Oh, m'lady!" Annie began to cry.

There was a rapping on the apartment door at that moment, and Rosamund instructed her servant to answer it. Lord Cambridge entered.

"Excellent," he said. "You are still up. Annie, dear lass, bring us some wine, and you, cousin, shall exchange the gossip you have obtained this day with me." He plopped himself down on the edge of the bed with a grin. "You look as fresh as a daisy even at this hour."

Annie hurried to bring Lord Cambridge and her mistress small crystal goblets of sweet Madeira. As she handed the goblets to them, Rosamund spoke. "Annie has something to tell you, Tom. Annie."

"Oh, m'lady, do I have to?" Annie sobbed, her blue eyes overflowing with her tears. When Rosamund nodded solemnly, Annie said in a small voice, " 'Tis about Doll, m'lord," and she told him what she had previously reported to her mistress.

When she had finished her brief recitation Lord Cambridge said, "It is all right, Annie. I know you are no telltale and spoke only to protect your mistress. However, I have already prepared to send Doll back to Bolton Park in the morning. Other word of her behavior has been brought to my ears by Mistress Greenleaf, and tonight I had the misfortune to see Doll's misbehavior first-hand. Her fate was sealed then and there. Now run along, lass, and seek your own bed. You are not responsible for Doll's adversity. Mistress Greenleaf always thought her a bit young to be sent down from Bolton Park. It is possible it is time for her to be married and settled. Mistress Greenleaf has a nephew, my blacksmith. He is widowed, and strong enough to handle a spirited girl like Doll. She would have no time for mischief as his wife, I assure you. The man has seven children all under the age of ten, and expects a meal in his smithy each day at noon, plus a big supper at day's end. Aye, given what I saw tonight that might be the best solution," he chuckled.

"What did you see?" Rosamund asked him, now very curious.

"Do you know, Annie?" Lord Cambridge asked the girl.

"Aye, m'lord," Annie nodded.

"Well, tell us then," he pressed her.

"Doll lifts her skirts for the lads," Annie began. "She don't do it for naught, though.

'Tis a ha-pennie a peep to look at it, a whole penny if they wants to touch it and feel up her titties." And having said it, Annie blushed beet red with embarrassment.

Lord Cambridge roared with laughter at Annie's explanation. "Aye, that is what I saw. She's an enterprising lass, our Doll. Well, the smithy is a lusty fellow and should keep her more than busy both in and out of the bed. Run along, Annie. And if Doll should confide her woes to you in the morning before she is sent home, say I saw her and was simply shocked." He chuckled again.

Annie curtsied and went from the room. They heard the door to the dayroom close as she departed her mistress' apartment. Still, Lord Cambridge got up and looked outside to make certain the young servant was gone from their hearing. Then he came back in and sat down on the edge of the bed again.

"The king spoke briefly with me tonight," Lord Cambridge began. "He said I was to leave the garden door to the house open and a small lit lantern outside that door. Do you understand, Rosamund?"

She nodded. "Aye, I do. God's blood, Tom, he is visiting the queen tonight! And then he will come to me?"

"The king is a dutiful man, Rosamund,"

her cousin said dryly. "He will do his duty first, and then seek his pleasure afterward." He stood up. "Remember, dear girl, that you must be discreet for everyone's sake, but mostly for your own. You are not the first woman the king has futtered after having taken the solemn vows of matrimony. You will not be the last by any means. This king is a very sensual man. What a pity he is not of another persuasion as well. It should save him much difficulty," Lord Cambridge finished with a droll wink.

"Tom, I should laugh, but I do believe that you are serious," Rosamund said, surprising even herself with the observation.

"Good night, dear girl," he told her with a grin, and then he was gone from the bed-chamber.

Should I sleep? Rosamund wondered to herself. *Can I sleep?* She closed her eyes. Discretion. She must practice that very fine art. And she could remain awake all night waiting for the king to put in an appearance. What if something prevented his coming? Come the morning she would be exhausted with lack of sleep and her own nervousness. Yet she would still be required to get up and serve the queen. Katherine had gotten into the comfortable habit of dictating personal correspondence to Rosamund rather than to one of her official secretaries. Rosamund knew that the queen was becoming too easy with the arrangement, but she could not continue on with it. She needed to go home, and Tom's suggestion about leaving the progress in the summer was really a good one. She would seek Inez's advice on a replacement. Surely among the queen's many women there was one other who had a legible hand that would suit.

Aye, she had been ready to go home since she had come, and yet now she was willing to admit that it had been a most interesting time for simple Rosamund Bolton of Friarsgate. Far more exciting than when she had first been at court as a royal ward. She would have such stories to tell her girls! And the connections she had made here could prove valuable in the future. She did not intend to have her daughters marrying Bolton cousins, or the like. She wanted fresh blood brought into the line to keep the Friarsgate inheritance a strong one. And she should never have thought about life in such terms but for her exposure to the court. And to her cousin Tom Bolton. Tom had already hinted in the broadest terms possible that she and her daughters would be his heirs one day. What an amazing turn of events, she thought. A year ago she hadn't even known that Thomas Bolton existed. She had been content to be Sir Owein Meredith's wife and the mother of his bairns.

But Owein was gone. *Why?* she asked silently as she had asked a thousand times over these past months. But there had been no answer forthcoming. She knew there never would be. Her eyes finally closed, and Rosamund fell into sleep.

Chapter 17

The king had done his duty by his queen. He had joined Katherine in her bed for a second time that day. She was garbed as always in a plain long garment tied tightly at the neck, an embroidered nightcap on her lovely red-gold hair. Her hair, he thought, was her best feature. She lay dutifully upon her back, her blue eyes tightly shut. For all the time they had been wed, he could still not get her to open her eyes when he entered their bedchamber. He had always heard that the Spanish were hot-blooded, but while his Kate was sweet, and while she was dutiful, he could not ever in his wildest imagination call her hot-blooded.

He did what he always did with her, first untying the ribbons at her neckline and opening the all-enveloping garment to display her breasts and belly. She had pretty breasts. Small, but fuller since the birth of their son. He could see the marks on her stomach from where the skin had been stretched during her confinements. Kate did not have good skin. Not like an English-woman.

Not like Rosamund Bolton. And at the thought of *her*, he felt a tingling in his man-hood. Rosamund Bolton of the auburn hair and the clear amber eyes and the sweetly rounded breasts. His member began to harden and swell as he thought of the deli-cious little widow of Friarsgate, of how he would enjoy futtering her later on this evening. But for Sir Owein all those years back he believed he would have had her, and he did not think that she would have been merely dutiful and acquiescent.

"Draw up your gown, Kate," the king or-dered his wife as he pulled off his nightshirt. She complied immediately. He pushed her legs open and mounted her, sinking himself deep into the fecund flesh, pumping, pump-ing, pumping slowly until he could release his seed. "May God and His Blessed Mother grant us a son," he intoned as he withdrew from her.

"Amen!" the queen replied, pulling her night garment back down again, but never once opening her eyes to look at him.

Henry Tudor climbed from his wife's bed,

and bending down, kissed her forehead. "Good night, Kate. Sleep well."

"Good night, my lord," she responded as he departed her bedchamber through a small private door that permitted him to avoid being seen by her women.

The king hurried through the narrow privy hallway back into his own bedroom. He bathed his private parts with the water in the basin that had been left for just that purpose. His body servant brought him a fresh nightshirt, and when the king had put it on, the man silently wrapped his master in a green brocade robe and knelt to slip a pair of leather house shoes on his feet.

"I will be gone two to three hours, Walter," he told the man. "Where is the dark lantern?"

"By the outside door, your majesty," the servant said, and then he added, "My lord Henry, I understand your need for discretion given the incident of several months back, but if there is some sort of emergency in the night —" He stopped and looked questioningly at the king. "What am I to say?"

The king laughed softly. "You have always kept my secrets, Walter," he said. "I shall not be far. At Lord Cambridge's house next door to the palace. You will, of course, tell no one, but should an emergency arise in the next two to three hours, you will run through the park to fetch me, eh?"

Walter bowed, smiling, "Yes, my lord Henry," he said, and ushered the king out of his bedchamber through another small private corridor, down a flight of stairs, and to an outside door. Bending down, he picked up the dark lantern and handed it to the king with a bow, then closed the door behind his master.

Using the light of the dark lantern, which only fell on the path at his feet, the king hurried across his gardens and into the wooded park beyond. There was no moon this night, which made his passage through the trees a slow and cautious one, but finally the garden wall belonging to Lord Cambridge loomed up before him. He could see the little door in the wall, faintly shadowed, and putting his hand on the latch, he lifted it, opened it, and stepped through into Tom Bolton's garden. Within, even in the darkness, he could see that all was orderly. He made his way along the carefully raked garden paths until he reached the house. His blue eyes moved to find his landmark, and there it was. A small lantern burning brightly by another small door. He set down his own dark lamp, and taking up the small light, he entered the house. Following exactly the directions given him by Lord Cambridge, he made his way upstairs to Rosamund's apartment. He entered and went through the dayroom into the bedchamber. *There she lay!*

The king blew out the small lamp and set it down upon a table. He pulled off his brocaded robe and laid it aside. Then he moved to the bedside, and bending, he kissed her face with a half-dozen kisses until her eyes opened and she smiled at him.

"Hal," she said softly.

He thought it a sweet welcome. "Will you remove your smock for me?" he asked her. "I want to see all of you, fair Rosamund."

"If you will remove your nightshirt," she told him. My God! Rosamund thought. Was she a born whore that she was falling so easily into this shameful affair? But she didn't feel shameful. He wanted her. He had wanted her as a lad, and he still wanted her. He was the king of England, and it was damned flattering. What did it matter as long as the queen wasn't harmed by it? A brief liaison, and she would be gone back to Friarsgate never to see him again. Sitting up, she pulled off the white linen smock, tossing it aside, and undid her nightcap so that her hair flowed freely. Then she threw back the coverlet, displaying herself to him.

"Do I please you, my lord?"

"Aye, fair Rosamund, you please me mightily!" the king said. He reached out for her and drew her from the bed.

How very tall he was. She knew it, of course, but standing before him it seemed even more so. Reaching up, she undid the ties of his nightshirt, opening it wide, her small hands slipping beneath the fabric to smooth across his chest, which was furred with the same reddish gold of his hair. His chest was broader than any she had seen, even clothed. His shoulders were wider. "You are a giant, my lord," she told him softly. She pushed the nightshirt from him, and it fell to the floor at his feet. He stepped from it, and she saw that his feet, while big, were narrow and almost delicate.

"No woman but my nurse has ever seen me as God made me, fair Rosamund, until you," he told her.

"The queen?" How she had even dared to utter the word under these circumstances she did not know.

"Prefers my dutiful attentions in darkness and as clothed as possible — *and* I have never seen her as I have now seen you," he said.

"Oh," she replied, surprised and perhaps a little embarrassed to learn such an intimate fact about their marriage. She had not thought the queen would be so prudish with her husband. Particularly with such a handsome, young, and lusty mate.

His big hands clasped about her waist. He lifted her up in order to bury his face between her breasts. "Ummm, what is that delicious fragrance that seems to cling to your skin?" he asked her, nuzzling deeper in the shadowed valley of her bosom.

"White heather," she told him, steadying herself with her hands on his shoulders. God's nightshirt, she had missed a man's tender attentions. She could feel a wonderful warmth beginning to suffuse her body as he began to kiss her flesh.

"It suits you," he told her. "I shall always think of you, my fair Rosamund, when I smell the scent of white heather." He lowered her back to the floor, making certain that her ripe, soft body slid the length of him.

She felt his chest, his belly, his hairy thighs. He was hard all over, having the body of a warrior. When he wrapped his arms about her and kissed her, Rosamund thought that she would swoon with the pleasure his lips gave her. His tongue plunged deep into her mouth, seeking her tongue, finding it, demanding immediate homage from her. Her head was absolutely spinning, and she swayed in his embrace.

He held her close and murmured in her ear, "How sweet, how compliant you are with me, my fair Rosamund. You are the perfect female, my darling. You are experienced and passionate, and yet there is an innocence about you that I must possess!" He set her back from him and took one of her breasts into his hand, cupping it so that it rested in his palm like a small white dove. With the fingers of his other hand he delicately caressed the smooth firm flesh. He bent his head and teased the nipple with his hot tongue; then, his hungry mouth fastened over that sentient nub, and he sucked hard on it.

A small cry escaped her. He was the most damnably sensuous man! Owein had certainly loved her, but never like this! He lay her down now upon her bed, and she saw his male member for the first time. It was surely of a goodly size, and obviously most ready for pleasure. She held out her arms to him, and he smiled.

"Such a charming welcome, fair Rosamund. Are you as eager for me as I am for you, my darling?"

"Oh, yes, Hal!" she assured him. *"Yes!"*

"I must be careful not to crush you, my sweet," he said.

"I am stronger than I appear," she said.

"But have you ever taken such a weapon within you as the one now before you?" His hand wrapped itself about his manhood, and he displayed it for her proudly.

"I have known only my husband, Hal. He was surely not as well-endowed as your majesty is, but I am no virgin."

Carefully the king straddled her, but his eagerness overcame him, and he was unable to refrain from thrusting immediately into her. "God's nightshirt! Ah, what bliss!" he groaned. "Is there no end to your sweet welcome, my fair Rosamund?"

She had been ready for him, much to her astonishment. She was wet, and he slid easily and deeply into her love sheath. Rosamund wrapped her arms and legs about the king, her little mewling cries of delight spurring him on and increasing his passion. *"Oh! Ahhh!"* she cried as he stoked her fires with his skilled love lance. *"Oh, your majesty! Oh, yes!"* She was reeling out of control, but she did not care. She soared, and she flew higher than she ever had. His passion overcame her, and finally as the crisis peaked, she actually swooned away in his hungry embrace.

When Rosamund began to finally come to herself again she realized two things. She was lying atop the king, her cheek against his chest, and he was still deep and hard within her. "Oh, God!" she half-whispered. "Did I not please you, Hal?"

"Very much, and there is so much more to come," he promised her, and she heard laughter in his deep voice.

"You are . . . you are still . . ." She couldn't find the words.

"Aye," he said in a nonchalant manner, "I am." Then he laughed as he understood her confusion. He rolled her over again so that they were now face-to-face. His blue eyes met her amber eyes, and he said, "You have known only one man. An old man, your husband. I am not quite twenty, fair Rosamund. My appetite for female flesh is great. I can do this all night, and I am certainly not yet satisfied by you, my darling, but by the dawn we will be both well-pleasured." Then he began to move on her again, and she was almost weeping with the delights that he offered her.

His lust seemed to go on forever. To her surprise she was every bit as lustful as he was. She had never known anything like this, but she knew that she craved more of it. She didn't remember his leaving her, but when Annie came to awaken her just before sunrise she was alone amid a tangle of bedding, and she was still naked. That was careless of her, she realized at her servant's shocked look.

"Was Doll right, m'lady?" Annie whispered, handing her the goblet of Maybel's strengthening potion.

"You have seen nothing, Annie," Rosamund replied, taking the goblet and drinking it down. She would need to be strengthened if the king was as vigorous each time he visited her. "Hand me my smock."

Annie complied, "I don't understand," she told her mistress.

"It is better that you don't, but your silence is most necessary. If it will make you feel any better, Annie, and I tell you this because you are my loyal servant and I trust you, Lord Cambridge is aware of all that goes on beneath his roof. Even this."

"You will have to bathe before you can go to the palace," Annie said, her equilibrium slowly being restored as she began to consider the entire situation. "The scent of coupling is strong about you."

"Quickly then, for I must be at the palace in time for the mass. The queen is most unhappy with her ladies when they do not attend the mass, Annie," Rosamund explained.

Annie nodded, and exited the bedchamber.

Rosamund lay beneath the coverlet now and considered the night past. She had had no idea that a man could be so enthusiastic in his lovemaking, but the king certainly was. She had also not realized that young lovers were different than older ones. Owein had been almost forty when he died, twice the king's age, but she had been quite content with his attentions. Now, upon reflection, she even thought she liked them better than the king's. Her husband had shared himself with her. The king took all she would give and gave little in return, while demanding more. The night had been a time to satisfy his desires and his lusts, not hers, although she had certainly been satisfied herself. But he had been kind, she had to admit. However, she had learned more about the royal marriage than she really wanted to know. The queen truly believed that the only purpose of coupling with her husband was the getting of children. That was sad, but that the king believed it too was even sadder. She and Owein had enjoyed their coupling and yet had healthy children, but for their unfortunate little son. There would have been other sons had not Owein fallen from that damned tree, and they would have enjoyed making them. She had been tempted at the time Owein died to fell every murdering tree in the orchard, but that her uncle Edmund had prevailed upon her not to be so foolish in her grief.

Strangely, the king had touched Rosamund. She was astounded to realize that she felt sorry for him. He was a lonely man, and there had been little warmth or real kindness in his life. His mother had loved him, but she had had little to do with him until his elder brother had died. His father had been embittered by the loss of the beloved Arthur and at first, despite his wife's wise words, angry that Henry had survived instead. Then the queen had died in a futile effort to get another son. The king had told Rosamund that he always wondered if his father considered him not fit to rule England. If there had been another son, would Henry VII have made a will in his favor and not Henry VIII's? His grandmother, the Venerable Margaret, was the one person that the king had admired and respected, but she was a hard woman who expected the rules to be followed without exception. No, there had been little warmth or love in the king's life.

As for the queen — and here Rosamund again felt a twinge of deep guilt — she was incredibly grateful to Henry Tudor for marrying her and making her long years of neglect worthwhile. She idolized her husband, but she did not see him for who and what he really was. Her gratitude was like that of an abused puppy taken up from the kennel and spoiled. She was Katherine of Aragon, and she knew her duty. But she did not know how to really love, and the king needed love more than he needed anything else.

Annie's head popped around the bedchamber door. "I've set up the old-fashioned small tub for you, m'lady. 'Twill save time."

Rosamund got up and bathed quickly. The sky was already turning light as she finished dressing in her claret silk gown. With Annie by her side she hurried through the gardens and across the palace park. They entered Greenwich and managed to join the queen 's women as they filed into the chapel royal for the morning mass. And afterward, as they broke their fast in the queen's hall, Rosamund suddenly realized how absolutely exhausted she was. Yet she dared not show it publicly.

The king had been up early to hunt with his friends. One of them wryly remarked that he should visit the queen more often for he was in high good humor today. William Compton, the king's closest friend, said nothing, but he realized it was something other than a visit to the queen's bed that had set the king in such excellent spirits. Compton was nine years the king's senior, and had been in his service since his childhood. He came from a wealthy, but not noble, family, yet was accepted by everyone despite his less-than-stellar family connection.

"You choose not to confide in me over this latest liaison, eh, my lord?" he gently probed when they could not be heard.

"What liaison, Will?" The king smiled mischievously.

"Very well, my lord, I shall keep my own counsel and ask you no more questions. We want no repeats of last autumn's little fiasco. You do not want a reputation like the French monarchs', nor do you need be made an object of humorous scorn."

"Aye, Will, keep your own counsel," the king said, looking directly at his companion. It was something he rarely did. The king did not like to make eye contact with others, and when he did it was serious business. "My liaison, as you so carefully put it, is an extremely discreet one. It is unlikely to be discovered unless one of us behaves foolishly, and we are both too wise for that. Do you understand me, Will? I want no clever hints among the others, and certainly no prying by my wife's ladies this time. This is but the king's affair."

William Compton bowed servilely, saying, "It shall be exactly as your majesty wishes. Perhaps one day, however, you will tell me, for I will admit to being mightily curious."

The king chuckled but said nothing more. He was pleased with himself, and he was particularly pleased with Rosamund. He had never in his life known such a warm and loving woman. Why was it that kings could never marry such women! How much happier they and their children would all be if that were so. Kate, God bless her, was so dutiful. He could not fault her, but dammit, why was she so damned reticent in their lovemaking? Just once he would have liked to see her eyes glaze with passion and satisfaction, but he knew it would never happen. She was too intent on giving him a son. She had a religious fervor about it, murmuring prayer beneath her breath as he rode her. He could not fault her, but oh, the hours last night spent in the fair Rosamund's arms! He could scarce wait for this night to come.

Rosamund watched the king surreptitiously in the hall that night. If he noticed her he gave absolutely no indication of it. In a way it was a great relief. Mercifully, she was dismissed early from the queen's service, and together with Annie she hurried back to Bolton Greenwich. There she found her cousin in his hall.

"Come and watch the sunset sky with me," he called to her, and she joined him. "You look tired, my dear girl."

Rosamund curled herself into the window seat next to him. "I am," she admitted. "I have never known such a man, Tom."

"He is the king, dear girl. Kings are different, or so I am told by those who claim to be in the know. Be warned that once he has a new toy in his possession he plays with it quite relentlessly."

"You are telling me that I may expect him tonight," she said. "I must get some rest then before he comes. He is incredibly vigorous in his bedsport, and then I had to be at the palace in time for the early mass. You know how the queen feels about her ladies attending the mass each morning." She looked out over the river, now dappled with a glorious and colorful sunset, and sighed. "He is so sad, Tom. He is not truly happy."

"You must not judge him as you would an ordinary mortal, my dear girl. He is not an ordinary mortal. While he may possess a certain sadness in his character, he is not truly sad. He has what he has always wanted. He is king of England. If Arthur had not so conveniently died, Henry Tudor would have gone out and conquered another land for himself. He has always desired to be a king. And kings often marry princesses who may be very suitable, but are not particularly loving in nature."

"There is a vulnerability in him, Tom. I am but two years his senior, and yet I feel as if I am centuries older than him. Last night he stormed me like a man taking a castle, but when I had gotten past the shock of it, I realized that all he wanted from me was to love him."

"Be careful, my dearest girl," Lord Cambridge warned her. "You are beginning to sound like a woman who could fall in love. You are vulnerable, too, Rosamund. Your husband is not gone a year, and your whole life there has been a man to take care of you. This man, however, is a king. He cannot take care of you because he hasn't the faintest idea of how to take care of anyone, even himself. Give him your body, but do not give him your heart."

She sighed again, a deep sound of resignation. "I know you are right, Tom. I must keep my own emotions under firm control." She lay her head on his shoulder. "You are my shield and my buckler, cousin. You will defend me against the dragon."

"Dragons," he drawled, "absolutely terrify me, dearest girl, and especially the Tudor Pendragon of Wales. So he is vigorous, eh? I am not certain that I am jealous of you, cousin. Is he *big* all over?"

She raised her head from his shoulder, her amber eyes twinkling and filled with mischief. Then she nodded silently.

"Ah, me," he said. "Some of us are luckier than others!"

"You are terrible," she replied, rising from the window seat. "And I am going to bed while I may get some sleep." She kissed his smooth cheek. "Good night, dearest cousin," she told him, and left the hall. Upstairs in her apartment she undressed, bathed her face and hands, and brushed her teeth. She peed in the china pot Annie brought her, and then climbed into her bed naked. "I might as well," she told the surprised Annie.

"Who is he?" Annie whispered.

Rosamund shook her head, "I will tell you one day, but not today," she said. "You must be satisfied with that, Annie. It is better that you do not know for now. Will you trust me?"

"I always have," Annie said. Then she curtsied. "Good night, m'lady." The door closed behind her as she departed.

There was still a bit of twilight in the sky beyond her windows. Rosamund listened to the songs of some bird not quite ready to relinquish the day. Her eyes grew heavy, and she slipped into a deep sleep. It was past midnight when she awakened at the sound of her door clicking open. She lay silent until she felt his weight upon the bed, followed by his kiss on her lips.

"I could hardly bear to leave you this morning, fair Rosamund," the king told her. "I saw you in the hall tonight, and the mere sight of you set my loins aflame, my darling!" He yanked his nightshirt off and slipped beneath the coverlet she held open for him.

She enfolded him in her arms, and his leonine head lay on her breasts. "You must think of me as your refuge, my lord," she told him sweetly. "Did you hunt today? I did not see you until this evening."

"I visited my shipyards at Gravesend," he told her. "I want to build a fleet. England must be a strong sea power, fair Rosamund."

"Why?" she queried him. "Can we not use the ships of others to transport our goods? We do now."

"I don't mean a merchant fleet, sweetheart," he explained, "I mean a war fleet. We are isolated on our island, and susceptible to attack by our enemies. We need a strong fleet to protect our country."

"I am far enough from the sea in my Cumbria that I do not think of things like that, Hal." Her fingers caressed the back of his neck. "A king must be very wise and foresighted, I can see."

"You must be foresighted in order to keep your Friarsgate safe and profitable. I am told by your cousin that you are the guiding force on your manor. Is that so, fair Rosamund?" He nuzzled at her breast, his tongue slowly licking at a nipple.

She shivered with pleasure, and then said, "I have always relied on the advice of my uncles, but for one — and my husbands. But in the end the decisions are mine alone, Hal, for I am the lady of Friarsgate, and none can speak for me. I must seem forward to you, I know. But that is who I am." She kneaded his nape now.

"I like women who know their place in this world," he said. "But I do not like stupid women. While you are the voice of authority on your manor, sweet Rosamund, you are wise enough to listen to the good advice given you by your menfolk. Do you have a priest?"

"Father Mata," she said, wondering what that young man would think of her current situation. "He is a great comfort to me and to our people, my lord. We could not do without him."

"My grandmother was like you," he said. "The Venerable Margaret, but God's nightshirt, she frightened me to death!" And he laughed.

"She was a great woman, my lord, and I learned much from her while I was in her care."

Suddenly he raised his big head and looked at her. Rosamund blushed and lowered her eyes, knowing he did not like a direct stare, but the king said, "No, fair Rosamund. You may look at me, for I love to see your eyes filling with passion when I make love to you." He threw back the coverlet and let his eyes roam over her naked form. His big hand covered her mons, and he said, "You do not pluck?"

"Nay, my lord, it is not a country custom. If it displeases you, however, I shall do so," she told him.

His thick fingers entwined themselves in

her full auburn bush. "Nay, I quite like it. There is something tempting and seductive about it. Nay! I forbid you to pluck." He lowered his head and kissed her Venus mont, eliciting a fierce shudder from Rosamund who had never been approached in such a manner. When he rubbed his face against her there, she began to tremble. He could not help himself, for she was so alluring, the white heather she wore mixing with her natural female scent. His fingers began to tease at her nether lips, and finding them already pearled with her love dew, he taunted her further. "You are a very naughty lass, fair Rosamund." His head moved up so that he might whisper in her ear. He licked the sweetly curled flesh, pushing his tongue into its narrow passage even as his fingers pushed past her nether lips and found her love button.

Her senses were very acute. She could feel the fleshy ball of a single finger begin to graze and chafe the sentient kernel of flesh by means of both pressure and friction. Just one finger that fretted her until she thought she would die of the incredible sensations filling her. His lips touched hers. Then his tongue slid over her mouth, licking at it, licking at her face. She moaned, and the sound was one of pure delight to his ears.

Suddenly he ceased the wonderful torture and instead thrust two of his thick fingers into her love channel. *"No, no,"* she pleaded with him. "I want more! Please, more."

Laughing softly, he withdrew the fingers, and covering her slender body with his big one, he pushed himself slowly into her, stopping and looking down into her face. "Did you not get enough last night, my fair Rosamund? Will you drain me again and again and yet again this night as well?" He began to pump her with slow majestic strokes of his manhood. Soon they were both crying out with their shared pleasure. It was almost dawn when the king realized that if he did not return across the park to the palace he might be seen and his secret revealed.

Rising, he pulled on his nightshirt and his brocaded robe. He bent and placed a kiss upon her lips. "If you see me today, my fair Rosamund, you will think of this night past. I cannot come tonight, however, but soon, my darling. *Soon!*"

"Farewell, Hal," she replied softly. "I will miss you, but if I do not get a full night's sleep there are those among the women who will know I have taken a lover and wonder who. You know what your wife's women are like." And she laughed low.

"Vixen!" he said with a grin, and then he was gone.

When Annie came to wake her shortly afterward Rosamund could not get up. She simply couldn't. She was utterly exhausted by the delicious excesses of their passion. She had never imagined that such a lover as the king existed. He was unstoppable, and his energy was inexhaustible. And he needed her. He really needed her, and she was amazed by the realization that a man as powerful as Henry Tudor could need the love and caring of a simple woman as herself. But Rosamund did not fool herself. He would in time become bored with her. And she would move graciously away because he would need her to do that, too, for the king did not cope well with guilt.

"Go to the queen," she instructed Annie. "Tell her that I am ill with a flux that has afflicted my bowels. Say that I beg her indulgence, but I must keep to my bed this day."

Annie nodded, and then she said, "This mysterious man who visits you, m'lady, must be magical that he could reduce you to such a state. Are you certain that he is human and not some creature from the dark world? I have heard of demons taking human form and then choosing lovers. They saps the life from 'em, I'm told. Are you certain that this man is not one of them?" She looked very worried.

Rosamund swallowed back her laughter. "My lover, Annie, is the most human of gentlemen, I swear it. Now hurry to the queen. If you run you can catch her before the mass. Leave me to sleep until the afternoon, and then bring me something to eat, for I shall be ravenous by then. And tell my cousin that I have decided to remain in my bed." She turned over, pulling the coverlet over her shoulders as Annie went from the bedchamber.

Rosamund was awakened by her cousin who had himself brought her a tray with sweet wine, beef, bread, butter, and cheese. "Arise, you slug-abed!" he teased, smacking at her coverlet-covered rump. "It is almost four o'clock of the afternoon. Her majesty sends her best wishes for your recovery and hopes to see you on the morrow. His majesty gave me a rather broad wink, which I pray was not observed by any but myself. I have not seen him so jovial since his son was born. These little nighttime excursions of his obviously agree with him."

"He is inexhaustible," Rosamund muttered sleepily. "Turn your back, Tom, but hand me that smock at the foot of the bed first. We must talk." She took the garment from him and pulled it over her head and down her body. "Can you hand me my hairbrush, cousin?" She took it from him and began to brush the tangles from her tresses. "He remains practically the entire night, and I get no rest. I cannot serve the queen and service the king! What am I to do?"

He took the brush from her, for she was struggling with a knot. "There is little you can do but caution your lover to be more circumscribed in his enthusiasm. Is he coming tonight?"

"He said not, and I pray it is so!" Rosamund responded.

"Ah, yes, the Venetian ambassador and his wife have arrived at Greenwich today. The king and the queen will be entertaining them until the wee hours of the morning. There is to be a pageant of some sort involving Robin Hood and Moors in gold turbans, and God only knows what else. The king has a most fertile imagination. It is up to his friends to see that his ideas are put into reality, such as reality is at the court." He unsnarled the tangle in her hair and continued to brush her long locks. "If he told you he would not come, then he will not. Is that why you stole the day for yourself, dear cousin?"

"Aye! And tomorrow I shall request the

queen's permission to depart the progress somewhere in the north. Have you heard when we are to leave Greenwich yet?"

"Mid-June, or so the rumor goes, and usually the rumors about a progress are accurate, for those fortunate ones to be visited by the king's August presence need to depart for their homes to prepare. A visit, even a short visit, from the king can beggar a man. In another week you will see a small exodus begin," he chuckled. "There! Your hair is now like a swath of silk, dear girl." He lay the brush aside, and stood up. "I shall join my friends at court tonight so I may view this elaborate spectacle that has been planned to honor the Venetians. The Italians adore such elegant charades."

"I am sorry to miss it, but I dare not appear until the mass tomorrow, lest it be suspected that I have indulged in a bit of playacting myself," Rosamund told Lord Cambridge.

"Do you think, dear girl, that before you ask the queen for her permission to go home, you might ask the king?" he queried. "You are Henry's new toy. He will not relish the idea of giving you up and will be very annoyed if it comes as a surprise to him."

"He must give me up sooner rather than later," Rosamund said, "but perhaps, cousin, you are correct. I will tell Hal before I tell my mistress, the queen."

"I believe you have made a wise decision," Lord Cambridge said to his cousin, and then with a wave he was gone.

Rosamund appeared at court the following morning, mingling among the queen's women to take up her duties once again. The queen had several letters to write that day, and Rosamund was kept busy. Late that night the king arrived at Bolton Greenwich to be with his secret mistress. After they had made passionate love for the first time in two days, Rosamund told him what she was planning.

"I shall ask the queen's permission to leave the progress when it reaches its furthest northern point, Hal. I have been away from Friarsgate for many months now. My daughters need me. I am not the kind of mother who willingly leaves her bairns in the care of others. I want to go home. I need to go home."

"*I forbid it!*" he exploded angrily.

"My lord! While we are at Greenwich you and I may enjoy a sweet idyll and keep our liaison a secret from all. Even my dear Annie does not know it is you who visits me. She wonders if my *lover* is not some demon taking human form, for she believes that only someone like that could have lured the lady of Friarsgate from the path of virtue. Only my cousin Tom knows your identity. Perhaps we can keep our secret while we reside at Greenwich, but once we begin your summer progress it will be difficult for us to meet at all, let alone in secret. I will not willingly harm the queen, who has been my friend, who is my daughter's godmother. Nor should you hurt her, for she is devoted to you and is a good wife. If you have any tenderness of feeling for me, Hal, you will let me go. We both know I cannot really ever be a part of your life."

"Do you love me, fair Rosamund?" he asked her softly.

"Aye, I believe that I do," she answered as softly.

"Then how can you desert me when I need you so very much?" the king said plaintively.

He was her king. He was a man to be sure, she thought, and yet he was still a boy. "How can you jeopardize what we have, even knowing that it cannot be forever?" Rosamund countered. "How can you consider hurting your queen yet again when she loves you with all the devotion that is in her heart and soul? I adore you, Hal! But I am ashamed of my behavior, for it does disservice to a woman who has been kind and generous to me, and is completely loyal to you."

"You reason like that city lawyer, Thomas More," he grumbled at her. "Dammit, fair Rosamund, I am your king!"

"It is because you are my king, and because I love you, that I speak frankly to you, Hal. If you refuse to allow the queen to let me go home, what excuse can you make for it that will not arouse suspicions? Even if Kate does not consider it, there are those among her women who will consider it. And then they will begin their spying and seeking out in order to protect the queen. If it becomes public knowledge that you took a northern lady of no great family to be your mistress, you will become the butt of mockery not only in England, but in France and Spain and in the Holy Roman Empire, in the Low Countries. You are young, my lord, but you will be a great king one day. I know it!"

"You are a far wiser and more clever wench than I had anticipated," he said, tumbling her back among the bedclothes.

"Did you learn nothing from our first encounter those years ago, Hal? I told you then that you should not seduce me until I chose to be seduced. I was but fourteen then, and a virgin. I had my good name to protect, and that of my betrothed husband's to consider. This time I chose to allow your seduction, for my obligations have changed and I found I could not resist you." She reached up and stroked his cheek. "You know I am right."

He bent and slowly kissed her lips. "Aye," he admitted. "You are, my fair Rosamund. Ask the queen for your release tomorrow, and I will not stand in your way. Indeed I will approve my good wife's request, but you, in turn, must promise me something."

"What?" she asked him.

"That we will remain lovers until you leave the progress for your beloved Friarsgate, fair Rosamund. That is the price that I will exact from you for my cooperation," the young king said.

"I will gladly agree," Rosamund told him, opening herself to his male member, which was now seeking to gain entry to her warm and loving sheath, "but you must swear you will do nothing that will allow the queen to learn this secret we harbor — *Ahhhh, God, you fill me full, my lord king!*" Her lithe body arched against him, and she felt herself beginning to lose control.

"*Agreed,*" he growled into her ear, grinding himself as deep into her sweetness as he could. "God's nightshirt, fair Rosamund, I shall never get enough of you! You will forever be a sickness in my soul, and when you leave, you will take a part of my heart with you."

Her legs wrapped about him, and her carefully pared nails dug into his broad shoulders. "I think my Annie is right, Hal. You are a demon, for only a demon could steal my heart and my soul as you have done!" Then she kissed him passionately, and together they pleasured each other until the moon had set and the morning star began to rise in the gray false dawn of the eastern skies.

Chapter 18

The king's royal summer progress was similar to the journey Rosamund had taken north when she had first left the court as a girl, going home to be wed with Owein. That journey had had a purpose however, to bring Margaret Tudor to Scotland. The annual summer progress was simply a means of entertaining the king and his court, and keeping them from the city's summer. It was an enormously expensive undertaking for those who were to be honored with a royal visit. And it could be extremely uncomfortable for the men and women who served the king and his company. It could be equally difficult for the courtiers who accompanied their majesties, because housing was not always guaranteed, and had to be foraged for by one's servants or the courtier him or herself. Still, to not be invited on a progress, or to not go, was considered social disaster or a serious faux pas.

Lord Cambridge's informant had been correct. The progress would go north into the Midlands of England. And Tom Bolton, a man who did not like being without his comforts, immediately learned the itinerary from the royal chamberlain. He then proceeded to arrange accommodations in the best inns along the route for himself and for Rosamund. And the lady of Friarsgate had now begged the queen's permission to leave her service and return home from Nottingham.

"Are you not happy with us?" Katherine inquired solicitously.

"It is a joy to be in your majesty's presence, and especially in her service," Rosamund said diplomatically, "but I miss my children, madame. I have been away almost a full year now. I need to go home."

"Are your daughters not well cared for?" the queen asked, for she was reluctant to let Rosamund go. While she certainly had closer friends, she enjoyed Rosamund's gentle company, and she particularly liked having a woman write her correspondence. It was a great convenience.

"My daughters are in good hands, your majesty, but I am their mother. Great ladies must, of necessity, leave their children to the care of others. I am not a great lady. My uncle Edmund and his wife are no longer young, and my uncle Henry will try to force my eldest into a marriage with his odious son if I am not back soon. Mistress Blount would be so honored to take my place by your side, I vow. She would gladly, if asked, take over the responsibilities of your correspondence."

"You do not like Gertrude Blount," the queen said with a little smile. "Yet you would recommend her to me?"

"What I want, or who I like, is of no importance, your majesty. You need, and must have, the best person to replace me. That lady is Mistress Blount, on my honor."

"We shall ask the king's advice in this matter," Katherine said, and she turned to her husband. "Henry, the lady of Friarsgate would leave the court at Nottingham for her own home. She does not want to come back. She recommends Mistress Blount to me in her stead. What think you, my dear lord?" She put a hand on his green velvet–covered sleeve, looking up into his face with a smile.

"Dearest Kate, what you decide for your household always has my approval," the king said smoothly. "If the lady of Friarsgate wishes to go home, then release her from

624

your service." His head abruptly snapped up. He looked directly at Rosamund, "You have children, madame, as I recall, do you not?" he asked her casually.

She blushed, curtsied, and replied, "Aye, your majesty, I do."

"Then you are released, with our grateful thanks, for the many services that you have rendered our dear consort and wife," the king responded. Dismissing her as suddenly as he had approached her, he turned and began speaking with Will Compton, who was seated on his left.

"My lord and husband has spoken for us both," the queen said mildly.

Rosamund curtsied again, saying, "I shall be happy to continue my duties until we reach Nottingham, your majesty."

"Excellent," the queen answered, "and you will show Mistress Blount what she is to do for me after you are gone."

"I will, your majesty," Rosamund replied. God's nightshirt! Had anyone wondered why she had blushed when the king had spoken to her? She hoped that they would just think she was overcome by briefly having the royal attention, being an unimportant lady of no great family and not used to being addressed by Henry Tudor.

Gertrude Blount sidled up next to her.

"Why would you do me a favor?" she demanded of Rosamund. "We are not friends, and we certainly do not like each other. I am not certain I like being in the debt of someone like you."

"You are not in my debt, Mistress Blount," Rosamund replied evenly. "When I leave the court I shall not return. I but spoke the truth to the queen."

"Writing the queen's most personal correspondence is a great honor," Gertrude Blount said. "Whether you wish it, or not, I am now in your debt, for I cannot refuse the queen's appointment."

"Nay, you cannot," Rosamund murmured, "nor can you impart anything that you write to anyone else. You are a girl who loves to gossip, but you will not be able to do so now lest you bring dishonor upon your family, Mistress Blount." And Rosamund smiled sweetly.

"*Ohhh!*" Gertrude Blount's blue eyes widened with the realization of what the lady of Friarsgate had done to her. "This is your revenge on me because I do not like you! How mean you are.!"

"Mistress Blount, it matters little to me whether you like me or not," Rosamund told her frankly. "Your family name is greater than mine, but my pride in who I am is far greater than yours is in who you are. I will not be spoken down to by the daughter of Lord Montjoy. I am the lady of Friarsgate, not by marriage, but in my own right. I have recommended you to the queen because you write a fine hand and you are already one of her ladies. It is an honor to serve Queen Katherine. You owe me nothing for this appointment. Now, on the days that the queen requires my services you will come with me and learn how the queen's most personal correspondence is done, and how it is kept."

Gertrude Blount nodded, temporarily cowed, but was soon bragging about the queen's chambers that it was she who would now be taking the queen's most intimate dictation, that she had been recommended for the position, but she did not say by whom, and no one bothered to ask her, because they did not care.

The progress departed Greenwich, moving to Richmond briefly while last-minute preparations were finalized. Then the travels began in earnest. The king had continued to visit Rosamund at night while they were still at Greenwich. He came to her one night at Bolton House from Richmond, but he had to travel via the river to reach her, which meant his bargemen knew he had left the palace and where he had gone. It was not a good situation, for Henry did not choose to be caught with a mistress again at this point in his life. While he would not be denied his pleasures, he wanted everything to appear circumspect to his world.

The progress moved to Warwickshire, that county which was divided into two parts by the beautiful river Avon. To the south lay the Feldon, a beautiful swath of green meadows and pastures dotted with wildflowers. To the north lay the Forest of Arden, and in the far north, which was not tillable, were sandstone quarries and coal and iron mines. While the castles and churches were built of sandstone, the towns were mostly black-and-white timber framing and subject to fire.

The progress visited two great castles in Warwickshire. First Warwick, which stood on a great bluff above the Avon, and then Kenilworth, which was nearer to Coventry. Warwick had originally been a Saxon fort, but two years after the Norman conquest a castle had been begun. In the fourteenth century the Beauchamp family had turned the castle into the magnificent edifice that Rosamund now saw. It was a great and proud fortress that had been lived in by great and proud families.

Kenilworth on the other hand was the

most romantic place that Rosamund had ever seen in her entire life. It was neither massive nor imposing like Warwick. Begun in the twelfth century it owed its elegance and its beauty to John of Gaunt, a son of King Edward III, who spent a fortune on the castle that had once belonged to Simon de Montfort, the notorious kingmaker — and troublemaker. The Great Hall of Kenilworth had the most beautiful windows anyone would ever see. Oriel, they were called, Tom had told Rosamund.

In Coventry they attended a high mass at the cathedral. But the highlight of the visit to that great market town was a performance of one of the famed cycle of mystery plays, executed by the local guildsmen. These plays had been enacted for centuries in Coventry and were known far and wide, even in France and Spain. The queen had wept at the beauty of what she saw, and it was whispered among her women that her strong emotions indicated that she was with child again. Hearing the news the king strutted about among his friends very pleased.

The progress now moved north again, making for Nottingham where the king and his court would spend time at Nottingham Castle. It was virtually impossible for Henry to find a secret moment alone with

Rosamund, and strangely, she felt relieved. She had fallen half in love with him, but she was not a foolish woman, and she knew that what they had shared was almost over, and must be.

At Nottingham the king indulged himself in sports and in gambling. Some of the younger courtiers introduced the monarch to acquaintances from France and Lombardy. It was not long before the king's longtime friends noticed that he was losing a great deal of money on dog races, bear baiting, cards, and tennis matches. Will Compton noted that the young English courtiers would entice and taunt the king into foolish wagers. Henry's pride would not allow him to cry off, and he would invariably lose. When Compton saw one of the courtiers later splitting the winnings with a French friend, he tipped the king as to what was happening. The king quietly sent both the young courtiers and their bad companions from court, informing their families of their misbehavior as well. Then his behavior became genial and jovial once more as befitted the monarch.

Now the time had come for Rosamund to leave court. She asked her cousin to discreetly inform the monarch of their going, for she did want to say a private farewell if it was at all possible. Lord Cambridge managed to engage the king in a quick conversation, catching him alone for a minute as he came from the tennis courts. Stepping into the king's path, Tom Bolton bowed with an elegant flourish.

"You must teach me how to do that some time," the king said with a grin.

"Gladly, your majesty," Lord Cambridge replied. "I thought you might want to know that Rosamund and I will be leaving Nottingham shortly. She is most anxious to get home. She would render her good-byes privily, if that is your majesty's desire."

Henry Tudor shook his head. "She is the most loving woman I have ever known, Tom Bolton. I cannot let her stay, but I do regret her going. Aye, I would say our good-byes privily. My body servant, Walter, will tell you when and where." The king passed on into the castle keep.

The meeting was set for midnight the following night, in a small room in the east tower of the castle. Walter came to lead Rosamund to the place of the assignation, opening the door to allow the lady in, then remaining outside. It was a tiny chamber with but two chairs and a table upon which were two goblets of wine. The king embraced Rosamund, his lips taking hers in a passionate kiss.

"I wish you did not have to leave me," he said to her.

She smiled, curling into his lap. "You are flattering me when you say it, but we both know I must go. Kate is more than likely with child again. She must not be distressed by anything. She needs your love now more than she has ever needed it, Hal."

"Pray God she is indeed ripening again," he said, slipping his hand into her bodice to fondle her plump breast. "Damn! I want to fuck you, Rosamund! I must have you one more time before we part!"

"My lord, but how?" she asked, but she wanted him, too. She had missed his passion and his vigor these past weeks.

He yanked his hand from her breast, and reaching around her, undid the laces of her bodice and pulled it away. He unlaced her chemise and pushed it from her shoulders. Then his hand moved beneath her skirts, and he began to play with her, his fingers twining amid the auburn curls of her Venus mont, rubbing against her slit, pressing and glazing over her love button, even as he buried his face in her bosom, groaning with his longing.

Oh, she wanted him! She could be his whore forever if he would but let her, she considered, shocked by her own thoughts. It was madness, but her juices flowed as she imagined him deep inside her, his manhood where his fingers now plunged. Suddenly he was lifting her up to straddle him, commanding her to raise her skirts, fumbling with his codpiece. He lowered her onto his thick, engorged love lance, and she screamed softly with the pleasure his entry gave her. The walls of her love sheath closed around him, holding him, teasing him.

"Oh, Hal!" she moaned. "Make me soar, my dear lord!"

And he did. When it was over, and she had collapsed on his neck with a deep sigh, he said, "I will never forget you, my fair Rosamund, my beloved lady of Friarsgate." He held her in his arms for what seemed a long time, and then finally he said, "We must leave our hideaway, my love. It is time our tryst was ended."

She slid reluctantly from his lap, lacing up her chemise and slipping on her bodice, which he neatly did up for her. He straightened his own garments into a semblance of order. Then together they toasted each other with the goblets of wine, and when the goblets were empty the king said, "It is time, fair Rosamund. I will take you from the tower, but Walter will escort you from the castle to your inn."

She nodded as they exited the little room. "We leave in the morning," she told him.

When they had descended the tower and reentered the wider hallway, the king pulled Rosamund into his arms a final time and kissed her hungrily. Then he turned quickly, without another word, and was gone into the darkness. Rosamund turned to follow the king's body servant, but he was no longer anywhere in sight. It was Inez de Salinas who stepped from the shadows of the hallway.

"I saw you!" she hissed furiously at Rosamund.

Oh, God, that this should happen now, Rosamund thought, but then she said to Inez, *"You saw nothing."*

"I saw you in the king's arms playing the whore," Inez accused.

"You saw nothing," Rosamund repeated.

"Will you deny that you were kissing the king? When I tell the queen of your perfidy! Even I was fooled by you, the meek and gentle lady of Friarsgate, but you are no better than the rest of these English *putas*. You all seek to advance yourselves on your backs like French bitches!"

"You are insulting, Inez, and you have no

right to be," Rosamund defended herself. "If you run to the queen you will upset her needlessly. She could lose the child she is carrying. Do you want to have that sin on your conscience?"

"How dare you!" Inez cried, "It is not I who was in the king's arms this night, and you, *you would not upset the queen?* You are as bold a creature as I have ever met!"

"It was not the king," Rosamund said. She had to say something.

"Then who was it?" Inez demanded suspiciously. "It certainly looked like the king."

"I don't know how you could tell in this dim hallway," Rosamund replied blandly.

"If it wasn't that satyr my mistress is married to, then name me your lover, Rosamund Bolton," Inez said.

"Before I tell you, you must swear not to repeat what I say, Inez. He is not my lover, at least not in *that* sense. It has been a harmless little flirtation on progress. We were saying farewell, for my cousin and I depart tomorrow for my home in Cumbria."

"Who?" Inez said a third time.

"Charles Brandon," Rosamund said.

"I would have sworn it was the king," Inez persisted.

"You know how alike they are, Inez. Everyone says so. They are both big men, and in the dark it is certainly possible for you to mistake Charles for the king. Please don't tell on me, Inez! It was little more than a few stolen kisses and cuddles. Thank the Blessed Mother that I am leaving court tomorrow else I be led into serious sin. I could not help myself. I miss my Owein so much." She dabbed at her eye with her handkerchief, which she had pulled from the pocket of her skirt. *I am surely going to hell,* she thought. She could not believe that she would tell such lies, but she would not harm the queen further.

Inez de Salinas sighed. "I have never known you to lie, Rosamund Bolton, but I am still certain it was the king you kissed."

"It was Charles Brandon, Inez, I swear it! I know that you and the queen's other women have never gotten over his bad behavior with the Duke of Buckingham's sister, but I am not she. Why would the king be bothered with a woman like me? The king, who could have anyone, would hardly choose me. If you tell the queen this story, based on such evidence, you will embarrass me, and you will embarrass Charles Brandon. The king will be very angry, particularly if your vile gossip does injury to the queen. Now, if you will excuse me, I am going to leave the castle and return to the inn. Tom and I want to make an early start, for we have a long way to travel over the next days." She turned to go.

"It was the king," Inez said implacably.

Rosamund whirled about. *"It most certainly was not!"* she snapped, and hurried off, away from the Spanish woman. Dear God, she prayed silently, don't let her tell the queen. Why should it matter to her so very much? I am gone on the morrow, no matter who it was. She ran down a large flight of stairs and into the courtyard. There at the castle gates she found the king's servant awaiting her. Torch in hand he escorted her into the dark streets of the town toward her accommodations.

"I will warn the king," Walter told her.

Rosamund nodded, but said nothing.

"I will tell him how well you protected him by swearing it was milord Brandon. That was cleverly done, m'lady, if you do not mind my saying so." And Walter chuckled. "I think you have confused her enough that she will be silent."

Rosamund finally spoke. "I would not hurt the queen."

"I know that, m'lady. She is generally harmed by those closest to her who always claim that they are doing her a good turn," Walter observed.

They finally reached the Crown and Swan Inn. Walter left Rosamund at its entrance, and she hurried inside and up to her own chamber where Annie awaited her.

"I just want to go to bed," Rosamund said. "I will bathe in the morning before we leave."

Annie nodded, seeing that her mistress seemed angry.

Rosamund was subdued the next morning, and for the next week as they traveled north through Darby and York into Lancaster and finally Rosamund's home county of Cumbria. They stayed a night at Carlisle at St. Cuthbert's where Rosamund greeted her uncle Richard happily. Then they continued north and east toward Friarsgate. Now that she was so close to home Rosamund did not want to stop. Lord Cambridge was becoming exhausted, but, she told him, he could rest at Friarsgate.

"It will take me days to recover from this pace you have set," he complained to her.

She could smell it. The fragrance peculiar to her lands. She thought she might have forgotten, but no. She could smell it! The hills were familiar, and suddenly there were landmarks that she recognized all about her. The road topped a hill. Rosamund stopped.

Her heart soared! She felt the tears slipping unbidden down her cheeks. Below lay her lake, sparkling in the September sunlight. There was her home! Her village! Friarsgate lay before her. She kicked her mount and galloped down the road toward it.

"Will she ever love anyone the way she loves Friarsgate?" Lord Cambridge said to the serving man, Sims.

"Probably not," said the pragmatic servant.

Lord Cambridge's party continued down the hill road toward the manor. Thomas Bolton had hired two dozen men-at-arms to escort them from Nottingham. Tomorrow he would pay them their wages and they would depart back the way they had come. By the time they reached the house Rosamund was already there, embracing Edmund and Maybel, hugging her three daughters, tears tracing down her cheeks.

Maybel comforted Rosamund, "They have been such good girls. Philippa reminds me of you at that age. She is most helpful and obedient."

Lord Cambridge was welcomed back. They went into the hall for the meal, which was simple, for they had not been expected. Afterward, the children gone to their beds, they sat about the fire, talking and drinking newly pressed cider.

"You wrote that the ewes had produced a greater number of lambs this year," Rosamund said to Edmund, "but I did not see evidence of it as I rode in. Were they diseased?"

Edmund Bolton sighed, and then he said, "Let us discuss this matter in the morning, niece. You are surely tired from your travels, and poor cousin Thomas is falling asleep in his chair. On the morrow I will give you a full report of all that has happened in your absence."

It was the tone of his voice that alerted her to the possibility that something was not right. "Tom is already asleep," Rosamund noted. "I would know what it is you are keeping from me."

"Tomorrow, Rosamund," he responded.

"Now!" she said sharply. Her first visit to court had taught her the value of good connections. Her second visit had taught her how to wield her authority.

Edmund Bolton had never before heard his niece speak with such command. She has finally grown up, he thought to himself, and then he said, "The Scots have been raiding the flocks, I fear."

"How is this possible?" she demanded to

know. "Our steep hills have always protected us from raiders. What have you done to combat this thievery? Do you know who it is?"

"They have taken to coming in the night," Edmund began, "and only when there is a border moon to light their way. They steal from the meadows closest to the hilltop. They have killed two of our shepherds and strangled their dogs to keep them from barking."

"How many sheep have we lost?" she queried him.

"Over a hundred head, Rosamund," he told her.

She looked at him astounded, and then she shouted, "Uncle, that is intolerable! How many times have they come to help themselves to my flocks? And you have done naught to prevent it?"

Lord Cambridge was now fully awake again.

"What can I do?" Edmund said helplessly.

"You know that they strike when the moon is full," she said.

"But we do not know where they will strike," he countered. "The flocks are spread over several hills and in many meadows."

"Then we must gather the sheep together and separate them into two or three large flocks, that we may have better control of the situation. Then we will post guards with the shepherds and arrange a signal so that when the raiders come the manor may be alerted. We will have a better chance of catching thieves if we do. Friarsgate has been thought impregnable forever. If it is known that the Scots are raiding our flocks, Edmund, heaven only knows what they will raid next!"

"It will take several days to gather the sheep in and realign the flocks. Where will you put them?"

"I must think on it," Rosamund told him. Then she asked, "When is the next border moon? I do not intend losing another single sheep to these borderers. Damn the Scots! I wonder if Logan Hepburn is involved."

"I do not know," Edmund answered her honestly.

"It would be like him to do something like this just to show me that he is cleverer than clever," Rosamund muttered. "Where is this Claven's Carn of his anyway, Edmund?"

"Why?" asked her uncle.

"What is a border moon?" Lord Cambridge asked.

"Because I think it is time I paid the Hepburns a visit," Rosamund answered Edmund, and then she said to her cousin,

"It's a bright full moon, Tom, when traditionally the borderers on both sides of the hills go raiding, because they can see their way about then."

"I am not certain that it is a good idea that you go to Claven's Carn," Edmund said.

"Why not?" she demanded of him. "You say the Scots are raiding my flocks, but that you do not know if they are Hepburns. Well, whether or not they are, I think I should pay Logan Hepburn a visit, uncle. If it is indeed he or his clansmen raiding us, he will know we are aware of it. Perhaps he will even cease, having made some point or other with his behavior. If, however, it isn't Logan Hepburn raiding my flocks, then perhaps he will know who it is."

"And you think he will tell you?" Edmund asked.

"Yes," she answered.

"Why?" Edmund wanted to know, but Thomas Bolton was already chuckling with his understanding of her tactic.

"My dear girl," he said, "what a clever puss you are! Of course he will tell you whatever you want to know. How naughty of you to use the man against himself."

Rosamund grinned at her cousin, then said to her uncle, "Logan Hepburn claims to be in love with me. Well, if he is indeed, then he will want to help me, won't he?"

"I don't like it," Edmund said. "It is somehow dishonest for you to behave like that, Rosamund."

Maybel spoke up. "You will have to show her the way, Edmund, or she is likely to get herself lost, for you know whatever you may say Rosamund will go to Claven's Carn." Rosamund threw her a grateful look, "You had best go tomorrow, my lass, if you are rested by then."

"Nay, tomorrow we must prepare for the raiders. Then the day after I will go to Claven's Carn. Tom, will you come with us?"

"Dearest girl, I thought you would never ask! Of course I will come with you. I cannot miss meeting your brazen Scot."

"Mata will take her," Edmund said, glancing curiously from Tom to Rosamund. "One of us must remain here to oversee the preparations."

"Agreed!" Rosamund decided. Then she stood up. "I am tired, and am glad to sleep in my own bed after these many months. Good night." She walked slowly from the hall.

"Will you not go with her, old woman?" Edmund asked his wife.

"Nay," Maybel responded. "She is Annie's responsibility now."

"You are surprised that she has changed," Lord Cambridge noted.

Edmund nodded slowly, "It is time," he said, "but I am still surprised by it. I think you may have eased her way at court."

"We Boltons are not a great or influential name," Tom replied. "I had a younger sister who died in childhood. Rosamund reminds me of Mary, and I have come to love her as I would my sister. It was her friendship with the queen that smoothed the path before her. She will tell you all, but the queen was so fond of her that she asked Rosamund to write her most personal correspondence. Not official documents but letters to her father, her family, her close friends. She thought Rosamund had a fine hand."

"Oh, I cannot wait to tell Henry Bolton that!" Maybel exulted.

"He has been to Friarsgate?" Lord Cambridge said.

"Nay," Edmund replied. "He knew she was gone, and he wrote to ask that we notify him when she returned."

"Do not, at least not yet," Lord Cambridge said. "Give Rosamund time to straighten this business out with the Hepburns. Rosamund does not need another annoyance, and surely Henry Bolton is a great irritation to her," he finished with a smile. He stood up. "I shall follow my cousin's good advice and go to my bed now. Good night, cousins." And he departed the hall.

"I wonder if he would make a good mate for our niece," Maybel said thoughtfully. "Rosamund tells me he intends to remain a while."

"I do not think so, wife," Edmund told her. "It is as he has said. He harbors brotherly feelings for her. And, she, I believe, treats him the way she would have treated her brother had he lived. Nay, put those thoughts from your head, woman. Thomas Bolton is not the marrying kind. Of that I am firmly convinced."

Rosamund was up early. She ate scantily after the mass, and then hurried to the little privy chamber where she had her manor records. Everything was, she was pleased to see, in perfect order. Her uncle came and told her he had already given the order for the flocks to be gathered into three large groupings instead of the smaller clusters.

"Put them in the three meadows bordering the lake," Rosamund said. "They cannot be driven off easily from there. And I want bonfires prepared at each site, and armed men with the shepherds, and more dogs.

Whoever finds themselves under attack will light their fire to alert the rest of us. There will be no more sheep stolen from Friarsgate by those damned Scots!"

It took the entire day to bring the various flocks of sheep in from their pastures and re-settle them in the meadows that Rosamund had designated. It was four days until the full moon, but the lady of Friarsgate ordered that all be ready by the following day. Lord Cambridge, who put in an appearance in early afternoon, was amazed by the activity and surprised by his cousin's air of author-ity. This was the same woman who had lain swooning in the king's embrace. His respect for her grew mightily, and he suddenly realized that only a woman of such strong character could have survived Henry Tudor and not been destroyed by him. It was she who had wisely broken off the liaison and kept the king's friendship in the bargain.

On the following day they departed for Claven's Carn, Father Mata their guide and strangely their protector, for no one would attack a priest. Particularly a priest related by blood to the Hepburn himself. Rosamund had never been over the border, and she was surprised that the landscape was similar to that of Friarsgate. They rode for several hours beneath a bright blue sky,

647

the sun at first in their faces, and then finally overhead, warming their shoulders. They spoke little, although the priest had assured Rosamund that it could not possibly be his half-brother who was stealing her sheep.

"Claven's Carn," Father Mata finally said, pointing.

Ahead of them, atop a heather-covered hill, they saw it. A stone keep, dark and very old in appearance. There were two towers. They approached the edifice slowly. Its gates were open, and they rode through into the courtyard. To Rosamund's surprise Logan Hepburn was there, obviously awaiting her.

"You sent to him that we were coming?" she asked the priest.

"Aye," he answered. "You could hardly appear unannounced, my lady. We do not do that here in the borders. The Hepburn would want to be here for your visit, and he does have other business to attend to, so I sent to him."

The blue-blue eyes looked up at her. She stared haughtily down on him from her horse. "I have come to say one thing, Logan Hepburn. If you raid my flocks again I will see you hanged for it!"

"Welcome to Claven's Carn," he replied, smiling at her. He reached up, his fingers fastening tightly about her waist, to lift her from her mount. "You are more beautiful than ever, if such a thing is possible. And I am not raiding your flocks."

"You lie!" she spat at him.

He took her chin between his thumb and his forefinger, forcing her head up so she had to look directly at him. *"I do not lie, madame!* Now, tell me who this overdressed fop is who accompanies you. If he is a new husband be warned I shall be forced to kill him on the spot."

Lord Cambridge slid lazily from the saddle. "I am her cousin, my lord," he told Logan Hepburn. Then he said to Rosamund, "You are right, dear girl. His eyes are blue-blue and really quite marvelous."

"Tom!"

Logan Hepburn burst out laughing. He clapped Lord Cambridge on the back, staggering him, and said, "Come into the hall. I've some fine whiskey I keep for friends."

"I am not coming into your house, damn you! I have said what I came to say, and now I will go home," Rosamund told him.

Logan Hepburn shook his head. "You will not be an easy woman to live with," he told her. Then he picked her up and strode into his hall with the struggling, swearing woman in his grasp.

"Put me down, you damned Scots bastard!" she yelled at him. "I don't want to go into your house! I want to go home! *Put me down!*"

He put her on her feet and then stopped her mouth with a hard kiss. Rosamund reared back and hit him a blow that caused him to see stars. He kissed her again, this time his arms wrapping themselves tightly about her, pulling her hard against his long, lean body. She tried to draw away, but he held her fast. For a moment she couldn't breathe, but then she was able to yank her head away from his. Still he had her arms pinioned firmly, and she could not hit him.

"*Let me go!*" she said through gritted teeth. Her eyes spit sparks at him.

"Never!" he growled back. "You and I have played this game long enough, Rosamund Bolton. I love you, though why I do not know, for you are the most difficult woman I have ever met. I want you for my wife. I have driven my clansmen to distraction by refusing to wed because I would have none but you. Now the time has come for us to marry, and for you to give me an heir, for I know you are capable of it. God only knows I am capable of it as the number of my bastards will attest. I have not been stealing your sheep. The only thing I want from Friarsgate is its mistress."

"Well," she said, gasping. "Dammit, Logan Hepburn, I cannot breathe if you will hold me so tightly; if you are not stealing my sheep, then who is? There are any number of Scots, I suppose, from which to choose."

He loosened his grip on her. "I will help you find the culprits, Rosamund," he said calmly to her, "and then you will pick a wedding day, my fine auburn-haired lass."

"I can find the guilty myself. I've already set a trap for them. *And I'll not marry you.* I'll not marry ever again. How dare you, Logan Hepburn! I am not some ewe sheep to be bred by the Scots ram. If you want heirs, then get them on some simpleminded lass who will think you are wonderful. *I do not!*"

"You'll spend the night," he said calmly.

"I'll not!" she shouted, pulling away from him and hitting him a blow that he barely avoided, seeing it coming. Her fist glanced off his shoulder, and it stung him.

"Why would I want some milk-and-water lass when I could have you?" he asked her. "I like a woman with spirit. She breeds up fierce sons and fiery daughters," he said with a wicked grin.

"You will not get Friarsgate," she said stonily.

"I don't want it. It belongs to your lasses

651

by Owein Meredith. Our bairns will be of Claven's Carn, not Friarsgate."

"I am going home now," she said, and turned away from him.

"Very well," he said. "My men and I will ride with you, for you cannot travel the borders so close to the full moon without a proper escort. We'll remain and help you catch the thieves."

"*No!*"

"*Aye!* Mata, for God's sake reason with her."

"My lady," the young priest began, but Rosamund walked from the hall without another word.

"Have some whiskey," the Hepburn said to Lord Cambridge. "Are you really her cousin?"

"Aye, I am, but aren't you going to stop her?" Thomas Bolton looked a bit nervous.

"She can't go anywhere until she has her horse back, and she'll not get it until I give the word. Mata, find my brothers and tell them to gather the men and be ready to leave immediately." He went to a sideboard and poured out two dram cups of whiskey, handing one to Lord Cambridge. "What the hell is your name?" he asked.

"Thomas Bolton, Lord Cambridge, at your service, my lord."

"Are you in love with her?" Logan Hepburn demanded.

Lord Cambridge laughed. "Nay, though I do love her. She reminds me of the sister I lost. Do you mind?"

"Nay," Logan Hepburn said, and downed his whiskey in a gulp.

"And you actually intend to marry her?" Lord Cambridge asked. "You do understand that she is not an easy woman?" He quaffed down the dram cup of whiskey, gasping, his eyes watering at its potency.

"Aye," Logan Hepburn said, and added, "I make the whiskey in my own still. Do you like it?"

"Oh, it's grand," Lord Cambridge said, wondering if all the flesh had just been stripped off the insides of his throat, or just the top layer.

The young priest came back. "The men are ready, Logan, and Rosamund is walking because they would not give her her mare."

Thomas Bolton laughed aloud. "Oh, 'tis going to be a grand match between you two," he said.

They went into the courtyard and after mounting their horses followed after Rosamund, whom they found half a mile down the road, grim and determined. The clansmen surrounded her, and Logan said, his voice filled with laughter, "Get on your horse, madame. We'll get back to Friarsgate a lot faster if you do." Then he slid from his stallion and boosted her into her saddle. They reached the manor just after sunset when the twilight was still lighting the skies above them. Edmund came to greet them.

"He says he isn't our thief, though I am not certain I believe him," Rosamund said as she dismounted her horse.

"We've come to help," Logan Hepburn said.

"Thank you, my lord," Edmund Bolton replied gratefully.

"You surely don't believe him?" Rosamund snapped. "Wait. The full moon will come, and there will be no raid upon our flocks."

"I do believe him," Edmund said. "The Hepburn of Claven's Carn is known to be an honorable man, niece."

"Billet his men in the stables. They may come into the hall to eat," she said, and hurried into the house.

"He says he is going to wed her," Lord Cambridge said as he dismounted his gelding. "They already spar with words like an old married couple."

"I *am* going to marry her," Logan

Hepburn said implacably.

For the next two days Logan Hepburn's men kept well out of sight, remaining in the stables or in the hall, sleeping, eating, and dicing among themselves. The night of the full moon was clear. The planet rose and cast a bright light over the landscape. In the meadows where the flocks now grazed, the sheep were easily visible. The lake bordering the pastures reflected silver as the moon reached midheaven. Rosamund and Logan Hepburn stood peering through the window of her privy chamber on the second floor of the house.

"There!" he said suddenly to her. "Look to the hillside left. See the shadows moving down? I believe our friends have arrived. Let's go, my lass, and see who it is."

She did not argue, but followed him downstairs and outside where their horses were already waiting with the Hepburn's clansmen. "Tom," she said to her cousin, "if anything happens to me, the lasses are yours to mother. Promise me."

Maybel began to weep softly.

"Cease your greeting, old woman," Rosamund told her. "I do not intend anything to happen, but if it does, he is younger than you, and can gain the king's ear against uncle Henry. Father Mata, bless us, and confirm my wishes should it be necessary."

"Aye, my lady," the young cleric said, and he blessed the group.

They rode off slowly, carefully, so as not to alert the raiders that they had been discovered. Halfway to their destination the bonfire in one meadow sprang to life. This meant the raiders were now enclosed within the circle of sheep. Logan Hepburn raised his hand, and they spurred their horses into a gallop. Within the circle the Friarsgate shepherds and their companions were already engaged in hand-to-hand combat with the raiders. The dogs were barking and attacking where directed. Before their unwelcome guests might escape, the Hepburn clansmen reinforced the circle, and the battle was quickly over; the enemy was disarmed and forced to kneel before the mistress of Friarsgate.

Rosamund dismounted and moved around the kneeling raiders. She suddenly saw a face she recognized. Reaching out, she fastened her fingers in a head of thick hair and yanked it up. *"Mavis Bolton!"* she exclaimed, very surprised.

"You're hurting me," Mavis snarled.

"Let my mother go!" came a young voice next to Mavis.

"Why cousin Henry, how you have

grown," Rosamund drawled to the lad next to Mavis.

The boy looked up at her, eyes filled with hatred.

Rosamund laughed. "Does your father know what you are about, young Henry? Or is my uncle here among you, too?"

"Him?" Mavis said scornfully. "Not bloody likely."

"Why have you been stealing my sheep, you false bitch?" Rosamund demanded.

"Because they was there," Mavis snapped. "Because all I ever hear from that useless old man who calls himself my husband is how Friarsgate should be his, not yours. Well, he wasn't man enough to get it from you, so I decided that we would take it from you piece by piece. Otterly is a poor place, and not likely to grow any richer with Henry Bolton's heavy hand guiding it. I'm tired of being poor! My lads and my daughters deserve better. Why should you have it all? Are we not as worthy?" She glared at Rosamund.

"You have killed two of my shepherds in previous raids," Rosamund said coldly. "I could hang you for it, but I will not. You will instead pay an indemnity, or rather my uncle will, to the families of the men whose lives you stole. And you will pay for the dogs, too." She turned to Logan Hepburn. "My lord, will you transport this bitch, her son, and the others back to Otterly Court, and relate to my uncle what has happened? Tell him my people will come for my sheep tomorrow. We will expect him to pay the penalty at that time as well. He and his family are forbidden from ever coming on my land again. I'll kill any who do."

"I will be happy to be of service to you, madame," Logan Hepburn said with a small bow. Then he sent her a wicked look, "I have always fancied being married during the Twelve Days of Christmas, Rosamund Bolton. While I am Logan for my mother's family, my Christian name is Stephen. I shall come for you on his day, and we will be married."

"*I will not marry you,*" she said, turning her horse and riding off.

"*Oh, yes, you will,*" he called after her. "You have three months in which to prepare, Rosamund Bolton." Then the Hepburn of Claven's Carn signaled to his men, and gathering up their prisoners, they began to drive them up and over the hills to Otterly.

Epilogue

St. Stephen's Day

FRIARSGATE,
DECEMBER 26, 1511

Epilogue

"She is not here, my lord," Edmund Bolton said apologetically.

Logan Hepburn stood in the hall at Friarsgate, his clansmen behind him, his brothers at his side, his piper at the ready. He sighed deeply, but then he had known marrying her wouldn't be easy. "Where has she gone?" he asked, noting that her three daughters were in evidence in the hall.

"She has gone to Edinburgh with Sir Thomas," Edmund replied. "An invitation came for them from Queen Margaret just a few weeks ago. She said that having seen King Henry's court, she thought she might also see the court of King James, for where else would she be able to wear her fine gowns again? Certainly not in the hall of your lordship's stone tower."

Logan Hepburn laughed. "She's a clever vixen, Edmund. Once again she has slipped my net, but while she may know the Queen of Scotland, I know Jamie Stuart himself. In Edinburgh I will have the advantage. The wily wench will not slip from my grasp again, I promise you." He turned to his men. "Let's go, laddies. We're off to Edinburgh on the morrow. And with a wave of his hand he turned.

"Good hunting, my lord," Edmund Bolton called after him, and Maybel smacked her husband on the arm.

Logan Hepburn laughed again, his blue-blue eyes dancing. She was a wife worth having, and as God was his witness, he would wed his fair Rosamund one day. *One day very soon.*

Bertrice Small has written thirty novels of historical romance and three erotic novellas. She is a *New York Times* best-selling author and the recipient of numerous awards. In keeping with her profession, Bertrice Small lives in the oldest English-speaking town in the state of New York, founded in 1640. Her light-filled studio includes the paintings of her favorite cover artist, Elaine Duillo, and a large library — but no computer as she works on an IBM Quietwriter 7. Her long-time assistant, Judy Walker, types the final draft. Because she believes in happy endings, Bertrice Small has been married to the same man, her hero, George, for thirty-nine years. They have a son, Thomas, a daughter-in-law, Megan, and two adorable grand-children, Chandler David and Cora Alexandra. Longtime readers will be happy to know that Nicki the Cockatiel flourishes along with his fellow housemates, Pookie, the long-haired greige and white, Honey-bun, the petite orange lady cat with the cream-colored paws, and Finnegan, the black long-haired baby of the family, who is now three.